A NOVEL ABOUT HEALING

P·L·A·G·U·E

BY TOBY JOHNSON

BOSTON • ALYSON PUBLICATIONS

Quotes from *Beyond Illness: Discovering the Experience of Health*, by
Larry Dossey, M.D., used with permission of the publisher.

Published as a trade paperback original
by Alyson Publications, 40 Plympton St., Boston, Mass. 02118.
Distributed in the U.K. by GMP Publishers,
PO Box 247, London, N15 6RW, England.

First U.S. edition: November, 1987

ISBN 1-55583-125-7

For a significant segment of the American population, the 1980s has been dominated by a health crisis of proportions rivaling the plagues of old. Politicians, public officials, medical personnel, and health activists have recognized that education represents the major bulwark against the spread of the disease.

While the lessons about risk reduction are relatively simple, the public has sometimes seemed resistant to hearing them. Health educators have suggested that a variety of teaching methods are called for — from scholarly lectures, slide shows, pamphlets, and made-for-TV movies to street theater, protest demonstrations, and "safe sex" pornography and videos.

The following is a work of fiction. The plot and the characters are imaginary. The names of medical treatments and drugs have frequently been altered. The social problems created by this disease and the plight of people with HIV infection, however, as well as the instructions about risk reduction and the teachings about attitudinal healing are accurate. The projections for the resolution of the plague that haunts us in 1987 are reasonable extrapolations of current medical fact.

For Kip Dollar
— the real Rif Koestenbaum in my life

•Prolog•

The Recent Past

"You've got to bomb the whole area . . . it's the only chance . . . only chance, I tell you!" The distraught voice boomed out of the speakers, echoing in the Central Communications Control Room.

"Get those two old men out of here," muttered Major O'Hara, the Communications Chief, to the young man from the public relations office who'd just escorted two visitors into the room. O'Hara reached out and pushed a button on the console and the raving voice went silent.

"Both Mr. Wilson and myself have top security clearance," Edward Buchanan announced. "You will not 'get us out of here' without a good explanation."

"Mr. Buchanan, sir," spoke up the P.R. officer, "I'm sure the Major didn't mean any offense. It's just . . . it's just that this doesn't have anything to do with your audit of the agency."

"Let me be the judge of that, let me be the judge," Buchanan declared.

George Wilson, standing behind Buchanan, felt sorry for the P.R. officer who'd been assigned to guide them through the facility. Now, by sheer coincidence, while the young man was explaining to them the extensive network which coordinated the various projects of Alternative Weapons Research Corporation, they walked right in on that unexpected and disturbing communication. That was a message outsiders weren't supposed to hear.

But Buchanan and Wilson had heard it.

"We've been contracted to oversee this agency. Frankly, Mister, I'm not sure there's anything around here that isn't our business," said Buchanan, a tall heavy-set man with broad shoulders and an impressively oversized head crowned with snow-white hair. In his career as a weapons consultant and agency auditor he'd learned to use his size and his presence to intimidate those around him.

"Edward, perhaps we should allow them to submit a report on this through regular channels." This suggestion came from Wilson, Buchanan's sidekick and business associate. Wilson, a small man with thinning brown hair greying at the temples and a small, well-trimmed mustache, looked dwarfed beside Buchanan's towering bulk. As Buchanan's partner he'd learned to seem polite and meek to coax cooperation from the programs they were auditing.

"Where is this communication coming from?" Buchanan asked, appearing to ignore Wilson's comment.

"I guess you'd better tell them," the P.R. officer spoke up. "He's right that this is part of his job."

"A research station near Ilebo," O'Hara replied. His tone did not sound cooperative.

"Where's that?" Buchanan asked. And, half to George, he added, "Is that one of the projects we're supposed to be auditing?"

"A couple of hundred miles east of Kinshasa," O'Hara answered.

"Zaire." George announced. "Central Africa." He was paging through the thick contract document he carried.

"And I don't know what projects you're supposed to be auditing," came back O'Hara's surly answer.

"Stop fighting us, Mister, and play the damn message," Buchanan said. "Or else..." he added with a tone that meant business.

"Here it is on my list," Wilson said. "Ilebo Station."

"Okay." O'Hara sighed and turned to the technician sitting at the console. "Start that tape over from the beginning."

"(static) ... the thing got out of control..." a strained voice blared into the room a moment later. "... can't stop it. I'm about done for ... only one left here ... the animals broke out ... Oh God, a whole wall of 'em came at me ... (sobs) ... attacked us ... everybody exposed ... went rabid ... Oh God, all dead now, all dead ... except me ... Animals escaped...

"...You've got to bomb the whole area ... it's the only chance ... only chance, I tell you!" the voice began to scream.

Then suddenly the speaker composed himself, "Believe me,

I've been thinking about this. This thing could destroy the world. I don't think there's any other way. And there isn't much time. I mean it. It'd be worth it. An atom bomb — like the one we dropped on Hiroshima — that's about the only thing that can stop this .. this ... (silence)"

"What is that man talking about?" Buchanan demanded.

"Look, sir," the communications chief answered, apparently struggling to be polite, "I don't know what your security clearance actually is. I do know this particular project is about as secret as they come. Maybe you're supposed to go over there and audit them. I don't know. You can do that, if you still want to," he added. "But I'll be damned if I'll explain to you what any of this is about."

"He's probably correct, Edward," spoke up Wilson. "It's not his place to explain."

Seeming to reverse his position, Buchanan answered, "Yes, well, I suppose so ... I suppose so." He turned to the P.R. officer who'd been acting as guide, "I think it's time you took us to somebody who *can* tell us what this is about. I want to know what kind of money this country's sending over there. And I want to know what's happened and why that damn fool wants us to drop atomic weapons on Africa. This is the 1970s, not the 40s. The world's a powder keg. What that guy's talking about could trigger a nuclear war."

•One•

Early Autumn
in the Possible Near Future

1

Jon quietly closed the hospital room door behind him. He leaned against the door jamb and — after self-consciously checking to see that this end of the hall was deserted — buried his face in his hands and let out the sobs he'd been holding back during his visit with Ted.

It only took him a moment to pull himself together. In fact, it surprised him that he was so emotional. Jonathan Stiers had visited a great many dying people in his career as Education Director for the AIDS Action Project of the San Francisco Department of Health. He'd learned to maintain what he thought of as therapeutic objectivity.

But, of course, visiting Ted was a different case entirely. As much as Jon struggled to maintain his clinical distance, the fact was that in this instance he was much more a member of the patient's grieving family than he was a therapist or professional AIDS activist.

A few minutes ago, while he had been struggling to make hospital small talk with the withered, almost comatose body that was all that was left now of Ted Warmboldt, he'd been swept with a memory of Ted sleeping peacefully in a very different bed. Jon had awakened early and sat in a rattan chair by the side of that bed to admire the soft evening light slanting down through venetian blinds onto Ted's tanned body sleeping under the crisp white sheet. That day they had both been glowing with life after several hours in the bright Caribbean winter sun, a warm shower, and a nap before cocktails and dinner. Ted had seemed so vital, so beautiful, so eternal. Jon remembered believing then that their relationship would go on forever.

He struggled to hold on to the warmth of that moment as sobs began to well up in him again.

🐾

"Are you okay, Jon?" a voice interrupted his disturbed reverie. Jon looked up to find a young man hovering near him; it was one of the volunteer buddies from the Castro Village AIDS Support team.

"Oh, I guess so," Jon answered, composing himself again. "He looks so awful with all those tubes sticking in him. It's hard to believe it's even the same man."

"Yeah, it can be pretty upsetting," the young man answered gently. Then added, "I was just down the hall visiting my PWA. He fell asleep after the nurse gave him some pain meds. I was gonna get a cup of coffee before heading home. Wanna come with me?"

"Sure," Jon answered, coming out of his daze.

"You're pretty involved emotionally," the young man observed as he steered Jon toward the elevators.

"I'm sorry," Jon deflected the comment, "I have to admit I've forgotten your name."

"Mark. Mark Hartman. And I don't think we've ever really met. Tho' I've seen you at meetings and stuff."

"Well, I try to keep up with the volunteers. Good for morale, I think. I do recognize you. And I recognize your name. But I'm not sure I'd have put the two together. Though to be very honest," Jon added with characteristic candor, "I *have* noticed you."

"I know," Mark answered, smiling cryptically, as the automatic door slid open and he stepped back to allow Jon to precede him into the already packed elevator.

🐾

"I was surprised to see you so emotional," Mark said, reiterating his observation after the two of them had made their way through the food service line and taken a table in the basement cafeteria with their coffee and piece of chocolate meringue pie they'd agreed to split. "I remember you telling the buddies how important it is to keep from getting too involved with the PWA's."

"You're right, of course," Jon answered. "But the guy I was visiting, Ted, used to be my lover."

"Oh . . ." Mark seemed a bit chagrined.

"He was so beautiful. It's hard to believe he could have turned into that emaciated cadaver up there, with all those tubes and respirators." Jon's voice faltered.

Mark gently laid his hand on Jon's wrist. "It's rough."

"You know, I've seen an awful lot of people with AIDS by now. Some of them have been good friends. But it's never affected me like this before. Somehow all the others were just, well, other people. But Ted's like a part of me. I mean, I knew his body so well and, uh, when he got sick and started losing weight . . . it was like I didn't know him anymore. And I hadn't meant to lose him like that . . .

"I'm sorry," Jon recovered, "I'm rambling, aren't I?"

"It's okay. You wanna talk about it?"

"Good boy," Jon smiled. "You did that well."

Mark blushed, then added with therapeutic aplomb, "You have a hard time being the grieving client."

"It's a hellava lot easier being the therapist," Jon shot back.

"Maybe for you," Mark smiled. "But right now you're not. And you don't have to be. It's okay right now to feel sad and scared and angry."

Jon relaxed. "When you came up to me in the hall there I was remembering a trip Ted and I took together. We'd gone to Jamaica for New Year's, sort of a second honeymoon. It was such a great trip. That's how I've wanted to remember him."

"Was that before he got sick?"

"Oh, that was really a long time ago. Nearly ten years, I guess . . . hadn't realized it was that long . . ."

"Have you and Ted been lovers all that time?"

"No. Ironically our relationship broke up fairly soon after that trip. That was our fourth anniversary. Just after we got back, Ted's boss asked him to take over the New York office of their firm. Ted was in advertising. It was a real promotion for him. He just couldn't turn it down. And I didn't want him to.

"But I didn't want to leave San Francisco. I was working in a job I really liked in a community mental health clinic. I didn't want to move to New York. I didn't think I could find anything comparable. And besides, Ted and I thought carrying on a long-distance relationship would be very modern of us.

"His job brought him back here about once a month anyway. And the raise in salary was enough to pay for one or the other of us to come for occasional weekends in between. He was hoping I'd like New York enough to move up there eventually."

"You never did?" Mark asked.

"I didn't like New York at all. And I didn't like what it was doing to Ted. He started changing. I mean, you know, there's a lot of
difference between New Yorkers and Californians. I'd been a
flower-child back in the sixties and all Ted's success and money in
New York seemed to violate my values . . . or something like that."

"So you broke up?"

"Well, it was very friendly, at first. We recognized we were
drifting apart emotionally. And we both thought we were drying
up romantically in the long-distance relationship. So we agreed to
open up the relationship and see other people. Then I fell in love
with somebody else. That didn't last very long. But I asked Ted to
cancel a visit he had scheduled out here. That made him angry.
And then he said he wasn't sure he wanted to make love anymore
. . . and, well, things just fell apart."

"When did he come back to San Francisco?" Mark inquired
softly.

"He got sick several years ago. His boss was real supportive at
first. They had a big contract with the company that makes those
Nouvelle Cuisine dietetic frozen dinners. He didn't want them to
know why Ted was sick. But after his second bout with pneumocystis, Ted just looked like an AIDS victim. That was around the
time Rock Hudson died and the public got to see what AIDS did to
you. So Ted went on indefinite sick leave and came back here.

"He's been in and out of the hospital since then. Now it looks
like the last time. . ."

"He's dying?"

"Oh, I hope so," Jon said emphatically. "He's just a shell. His
mind is almost gone. He only recognizes me a fraction of the time.
I think the virus has destroyed his brain. Though the doctors don't
think so. And they keep him alive because they say the disease still
responds to the medication. But, you know, it's like Ted's gone and
they're just treating the body now. . ."

Jon began to sob again. "I wish I could do something to help
him."

2

The red and blue neon sign of Louie's Pizzeria, in Washington,
D.C.'s Foggy Bottom area, blinked off soon after the last customers
of the evening ordered: a young couple seeming enraptured with
one another. She was a thin, almost wispy blonde only recently
moved to the District from western Wisconsin; he was a short,

tightly muscled dark Italian also recently relocated, in his case from the heartland of the Midwest. It was getting late and the café was starting to close down. As other patrons finished their meals, they were leaving the place — which now seemed that much more romantic — to Lynn and Billy.

After toasting with their glasses of red table wine, and for a moment gazing deeply into one another's eyes, they both looked away shyly.

"I hope the manicotti's good," Billy said self-consciously. "It was always my favorite dish when I was growing up."

"It'll be new to me," Lynn answered.

After a moment of silence, Billy remarked, "Well, the pizza looks good," and he called Lynn's attention to the "chef," a teenager in an outsized chef's hat, who was twirling dough into a large flat disk.

"Wonder who that one's for?" she asked. "Looks like we're the only people in here."

"Probably for a take-out order. But let's come back here soon and try the pizza."

"Yeah, it's sure convenient," Lynn answered. Her new apartment, which she shared with her best friend from high school, was just down the street.

After another silence, Lynn toasted her new-found boyfriend once again and then remarked, "Well, I didn't tell you about the job I applied for today." Lynn Graves and Billy DePalma had met one another a month ago at a job-hunting seminar at George Washington University.

"Does it look good?"

"Oh, I don't know. I'm a little afraid of the place, but I think it'll pay pretty well. The temp agency sent me out there today to do filing for them. It's a consulting firm on the Beltway that does some sort of research for the government. They had a pile of questionnaires three feet thick that had to be sorted. Anyway, Mr. Buchanan, the boss I think, came in while I was taking a coffee break and got to chatting with me. And he sort of offered me a job. He gave me an employment application and told me he thought if I answered the questions right, I'd have a good chance of getting it."

"Doing what?"

"Oh, I guess typing and filing, that's probably all."

"Do you want the job?" Billy asked solicitously.

"Oh, you know, I'm desperate for a job. Though I do think this place might be a little funny."

"What do you mean?"

"Well, the employment application asked awfully personal questions. I kinda lied on one of them," Lynn tittered.

"What was that?"

"Oh," she said embarrassed, "the questionnaire asked if you were a virgin. And, you know, well, thanks to you," she smiled, looking down at the red-checked tablecloth, and whispered, "technically, as of two days ago, the answer is no. But I had been for so long . . . and it didn't seem like any of their business anyway, so I answered yes."

"Oh," Billy said, with a slight look of hurt in his eyes. "That's a funny question for a job application."

"Well, the research they do has to do with teenage chastity. At least that's what the questionnaire I was alphabetizing was about. And, Billy, don't take my answer personally. I just thought it was what they wanted. I really need this job."

"Oh, I know. I didn't expect you to hang my bedsheets out as a flag or anything," Billy laughed. "But I wonder what you're getting yourself into."

"Well, maybe it's a job."

"What else was on the application?"

"Oh, you know, the usual stuff: job history, training, skills. Then these funny sexual questions, like I told you."

"Were there others besides being a virgin?"

"Well, there were a series of questions about what you thought of certain, uh, sex practices. It asked you to rank these, uh, sex things according to their degree of perversion."

"Oh?"

"Yeah, like fetishism and homosexuality and bestiality and, let's see, bondage and domination, crazy stuff, you know?"

"On a job application?"

"Oh, and then there were some questions about V.D. Whether you'd ever had gonorrhea or syphilis or herpes. And whether you'd been exposed to AIDS. Oh my God, what a question that was. And whether you were HVI positive . . ."

"You mean HIV?" Billy corrected her.

"Oh yeah, that's it. That's the AIDS virus, isn't it? I thought so. It asked if you'd been tested for it. 'Course I answered no to all of those."

Billy was looking down at the table. He was twisting a paper napkin in his fingers.

"Hey, something wrong?" Lynn asked.

"Oh no, I . . . uh . . . I guess . . . I was just sort of worried about what kind of job this is."

"Well, then there were some questions about patriotism and willingness to take a loyalty oath. Then some questions about religious attitudes and church attendance."

"Lynn, I think you oughta be careful," Billy said, now sounding more assertive. "That sounds like some kind of right-wing nuthouse."

"Oh, Billy, don't be so paranoid. I think they were just including me in whatever kind of research they do around there. The place has got this real American governmental sounding name: 'Liberty Bell Foundation.'"

"Well, do you think they'll hire you?"

"I answered apple pie and motherhood on every question." She wagged her head sort of proudly. "And, you know," she added a little hesitantly, "that's really how I am..."

"Oh, that's just why I love you," Billy smiled at her. He leaned across the table to give her a peck on the lips.

Just then the waiter arrived. "Manicotti Supreme," he announced, "for two."

3

Pat Stratford had a coughing fit. After too many minutes of convulsive coughs, he began to fear he'd suffocate. He started tearing at the covers of the bed, trying to get free so he could stand up. He hoped that would help him regain control.

Managing to sit up on the edge of the bed, he clutched at the cloudied and finger-stained water glass on the bedside table. He barely had the strength to hold the glass and get it to his lips. He was proud when he succeeded at that.

Then just as he started to swallow the sip of water, a paroxysm passed through him and he convulsively coughed out most of the water and spilled the glass onto his emaciated thighs. In a fit of anger, he hurled the glass across the room. With his meager strength, it only sailed a couple of feet and bounced on the rug.

But the coughing subsided with that last paroxysm and Pat caught his breath. He sucked in as much air as he could. His chest burned with pleurisy when he inhaled too deeply. His struggles at deep breathing soon turned to sobs.

Why don't I just die? he thought.

Pat sat up, afraid that lying down would start the coughing again. Finally he let himself sink back into the pillows. The linen cases were yellowed and greasy, like the sheets, soaked from Pat's nightly sweats. Still the soft coolness of the pillows felt good.

A cramping pain clenched at his back as the muscles resisted his change in posture. There was so little muscle mass left on his skeleton that practically every move was met with such resistance and deep muscle pain. His lower torso still ached from the workout the coughing fit had given the tired muscles of his abdomen.

Pat Stratford was fighting an inevitably losing battle with pneumocystis pneumonia, called familiarly in knowledgeable AIDS circles by its acronym PCP, the C standing for "carinii," the somehow poignantly euphonic word in the name that was almost always omitted. Pat now understood why. There was nothing even faintly pretty about this disease. It was just pure hell.

❧

Pat's life had not always been hell. Up until just a few years ago his life had been an almost perfect success story of the gay yuppie.

Pat was a tall and lanky blond with high cheekbones and deep-set dark blue eyes. As an adolescent in Natchez, Mississippi, he'd been scrawny and gawky with a long neck and a pronounced Adam's apple. The kids at school nicknamed him Ichabod Crane. He wore his hair long and shaggy, as was the style, till he got drafted during the closing years of the Vietnam War. He came out of the army still shy and reclusive, but well-muscled and broad-chested. After finishing a B.A. at Tulane, he was accepted into an M.B.A. program at Stanford.

By the mid-seventies, with his C.P.A., a well-paying job, and a fancy apartment in a high rise on Market Street just behind San Francisco's civic center, he was enjoying a life of urbane affluence.

But not anymore.

Peering over the sheet that he clutched with both hands up around his neck, he surveyed the room he'd ended up in. *Is this what my life has become?* he asked himself morosely.

Besides the bed, the room's furnishings consisted only of a cheap card table with matching metal folding chair, a bedside stand with a fifties gooseneck reading lamp, and a dilapidated chest of drawers with the bottom drawer missing. Atop the chest was Pat's last possession from the old days, a brightly modern Sony Trinitron TV with remote control. Across from the bed was the door into the hall. On the left wall near the door was the small bathroom and next to that was an arched alcove that contained a tiny kitchenette.

The walls were covered with a beige and lavender flowered

paper that was now badly discolored and peeling along the ceiling. In the blue-white glare of the streetlights and the colors of the neon signs outside, the lavender flowers looked mawkish. A bare light bulb hung suspended in the middle of the room in a deco-imitation double-stemmed candelabra. The cardboard tube of one "candle" was gone and the other was snapped off entirely at the base.

I wish I were dead.

He switched on the gooseneck lamp and hunted around to find the Sony's remote control. After a frustrating search he found it wadded up the bed linens. He turned on the TV. There wasn't much to watch, and he really wasn't paying attention.

Maybe fifteen minutes passed — he wasn't watching the time either. There was a faint and tentative knock at the door. Pat wasn't sure he'd heard right. *Who'd be coming at this time of night?* He stretched back behind him and located the makeshift buzzer his friend Blum had wired up for him so he could let visitors in without having to get up and still keep the door locked — a necessary precaution if he were going to keep the Sony.

He shut off the TV. The knock was louder, firmer. "It's Blum," a muffled voice announced.

Pat pressed the buzzer. Blum Blumgarten let himself into the room. "Well, how're ya doin'?" he asked with affected good humor. "I was out for a cup of coffee over on the strip and walked back by here and saw your light on."

"I'm glad you came, Blum. I guess I'm not doing so good. I've been coughing all night and can't get to sleep."

"Gee. I'm sorry, Pat. You look pretty worn-out."

"Well, how are you?" Pat asked.

"Couldn't be better," Blum chirped, "...I guess." (Pat sometimes got annoyed at Blum's eternal cheerfulness.) "To be honest with you, I think I'd be a whole lot better if my friends were better. I hate seeing you like this."

"Yet you keep coming around."

"Sure. If I didn't, well, who would?"

"Maybe I'd just go off someplace and crawl in a hole and die."

"Hey, now don't talk like that. Gotta stay positive."

"About what?" Pat answered irritably. Then he softened. "I'm sorry, Blum. Nice to see you. You're right. I gotta stay positive."

"I heard some news this afternoon. I was gonna come by in the morning to tell you. Your doctor's got that new experimental drug he wants to try. He thinks it might clear up not only the PCP, but maybe even the underlying immune system damage."

"Are you serious?" Pat asked, perking up. He'd been through this before. And been disappointed. But this was what he was keeping himself alive for — the promise of a cure.

"Sure I'm serious. I talked to Jon this afternoon. It's definite they're gonna try the stuff out on you."

"I'm gonna call Jon," Pat announced precipitously.

"It's pretty late, ain't it?"

"He said it was okay to call anytime," Pat answered as he started dialing. A moment later he heard Jon's laconic answering machine: "After the beep you may leave a message for Jonathan Stiers . . . (beep)"

"Jon, sorry to call so late. This is Pat, Pat Stratford. Blum just told me you got me into a new experimental program. I wanted to find out about it. I'm excited. Thanks. Call me tomorrow."

Pat's death wishes were gone. Again. For another few weeks anyway.

4

Even though it was after three a.m. in Washington, Lynn Graves was still half-awake. She was lying in bed in the dark, unable to sleep: partly because of the street noises outside to which she was unaccustomed, never having lived in a major city before, and partly because she was thrilled by the events of the last few days. *Finally, I'm getting to really live,* she thought.

Lynn and her best friend Lee Ann had moved to Washington nearly six weeks ago from LaCrosse. Lynn was homesick for the first week or two. She missed her mother and called home almost every day at first. Now she only called with news. So far she hadn't told her mother about meeting Billy DePalma. *How am I ever going to do that?* she wondered.

Oh, but I'll call her tomorrow and tell her about this job. I mean, if I get it. That'd be wonderful. A job. Thank God.

In the restless darkness of her room, Lynn remembered how desperate she'd felt about finding work. It seemed like this whole plan of hers to get away from home and start her own life was going to fail miserably if she couldn't find work. Lynn had spent the first two weeks diligently looking for a job. She applied everywhere. She'd felt especially desperate and ill-prepared when Lee Ann found a very good secretarial job within only a week of their arrival.

Then one morning on her way down to the Metro Stop at

Foggy Bottom she'd seen a flyer on a bulletin board at G.W.U. for a two day seminar on resume preparation and job-finding. Right then she had decided to take the seminar.

Lynn hadn't gotten a full time job out of it yet, but she did find out about temporary work and was getting assignments from Kelly Temporaries about three days a week. And she met Billy.

He'd shyly asked Lynn if she'd like to see the new Mel Gibson movie with him. "I don't like going to movies by myself," he admitted. "It makes me feel like some sort of outcast. But I just don't know many people in Washington yet."

Lynn remembered that moment with affection.

She had been more than happy to accept. She was in a similar situation. The only other person in Washington she'd managed to befriend was Charley Johnston, an older gay man who lived in the apartment across the hall. Charley had brought over a bottle of wine the evening Lynn and Lee Ann moved into their 1930s fourplex a few blocks from G.W.U.

Lynn liked Charley. She'd never met anybody like that before, she'd thought. It made her feel like she'd really arrived in "The Big City." But Charley was pushing forty, Lynn barely twenty. Not much of a match there And Lynn was almost as afraid of "the strange people" in the city as she was fascinated by them.

She was a small town girl. She didn't think she'd known any homosexuals before — except, of course, maybe those kids in high school that the others used to shout "queer" and "faggot" at. She used to feel sorry for them, but she hadn't befriended any of them. What if the other kids had been right!

But Charley seemed so nice. Nothing wrong with him.

That first night he'd brought the wine over, she'd gotten to worrying about AIDS. She'd heard a lot about the disease on the newscasts, of course. She knew you could only catch it from having sex or sharing needles, and she wasn't going to do either with Charley Johnston. But, just in case, after he left she carefully scoured the wine glass he drank out of with lots of soap and the hottest water her hands could take.

Tonight she cringed as she remembered that. But she was still reluctant to go over to Charley's apartment and every time he stopped by for coffee in the afternoon, she still washed the cup he used more thoroughly than necessary.

Oh, I don't want to think about Charley. I want to think about Billy. Lynn relished the recollection.

Two days ago, after seeing another movie — they'd seen a lot of movies during the past month — they'd stopped at Billy's apartment so he could show off to her the portable computer terminal he'd been given after only two weeks on his new job as a programmer specialist.

"I could probably have gotten this job even without taking that job seminar," he'd said, proudly acknowledging that he'd become a real computer whiz in high school. "I even once got a visit from these two guys from the F.B.I. warning me to quit hacking or they'd turn me over to the D.A.'s office. I was scared, but I was sure proud. I musta broken into some kinda really secret files or something."

Lynn was impressed.

"But I'm sure glad I took the seminar anyway," he continued, " 'Cause otherwise I wouldn't have met you." His voice had become real soft and Lynn had felt herself melting.

"Me too," she said as he embraced her and then pressed his lips against hers. She was nervous. But she'd been waiting for this. Wondering when it was going to happen. And now, when he kissed her, it looked like it was going to be now. And so she gradually allowed her mouth to open, and she could feel his warmth surge into her.

They'd kissed each other before, but very primly. Neither had exactly acknowledged sexual interest in the other, though they'd talked innocently about sex, usually over coffee after the movies. They had both acknowledged how inexperienced they were.

But now that was going to change. Now.

In the passion generated over the month of going to movies and sightseeing together in the nation's capital, Lynn easily let Billy take her all the way. And he did it so smoothly and lovingly, she'd been surprised. And he even had the good sense — though it broke the mood for a moment — to run fish a condom out of his bureau. Lynn was pleased to see he was conscientious and responsible about that.

Lynn thought how glad she was Billy hadn't pushed her any faster. She liked the slow game of their courtship. It made her much more comfortable with the whole idea. She'd been scared badly before; back in high school in LaCrosse, on one of her first dates, a boy named Joe Avalon had tried to force her into sex in the back of his dad's pick-up. She'd fled in terror and spent several hours wandering around in a half-built, deserted subdivision on the edge of town till she found the highway and made it to a phone in a filling station and called her father to come get her. After that, she hadn't let any boy come any nearer than a polite kiss on the cheek. But then she met Billy.

🐾

Thinking how wonderful it felt when he held her and when she held him, she wished he'd stayed the night again tonight. But, after the delicious dinner of manicotti, he'd said he hadn't come prepared to do that. And he said he really wanted to, and suggested they make a date for tomorrow night.

Thinking about tomorrow night, Lynn finally fell fast asleep.

5

Jon Stiers was up till early morning talking with Mark Hartman. After they left the hospital, they went for a drink at the Café San Marco at the upper end of Market Street and then, when last call was announced, they walked around the corner to Andy's for coffee and doughnuts. Jon was surprised at the intensity of his feelings for Mark. Between periods of bleariness from lack of sleep, Jon realized he was feeling smitten.

"I'm from LaCrosse, Wisconsin," Mark said. "Ever heard of it?"

"As a matter of fact, I have," Jon answered. "Years ago, after high school, I joined the religious order that taught at my school. They had their novitiate just outside LaCrosse. I lived there my first year away from home."

"You were like a monk?"

"Well, sort of. At least my year up there was really like being a monk."

"You look sort of monkish," Mark grinned.

"Oh, I know," Jon answered. "That's because of the way I'm balding, I guess."

"I didn't mean that to sound like 'old' or 'unattractive,'" Mark spoke up. "Sometimes I think you look like a little boy. I guess maybe you look innocent or something . . . Anyway, I like how you look."

"I'm glad," Jon answered, blushing. Then he changed the subject. "How long have you been out here in San Francisco?"

"Almost six months now."

"And what do you do besides volunteer for the buddy project?"

"I'm a graphic artist. I've been working on a degree in architecture. Still have a year to go. But I wanted to get away from the midwest. So I came out here. I'm freelancing, doing artist's renderings of proposed buildings or renovations. I've been lucky. I've gotten contracts with several big architecture firms. I even got a couple of drawings published in the *Chronicle*."

"Congratulations."

"And I've had a couple of drawings published in the gay papers..."

"Sexy men?" Jon asked in a provocative tone.

"Yes, but tasteful," Mark answered a little defensively. "And under a pseudonym."

"Oh?"

Mark grinned sheepishly. "The name's a little silly. On the spur of the moment, I switched the first syllables of my names. 'Hart Marksman.'"

"I like it. Sounds sexy." After a pause he added, "Have you got a string of men after your heart, Hart?"

"That's what I came out here for . . . oh, not a string of men, but the opportunity to meet somebody heart-to-heart. Back in LaCrosse, at the urging of my wise and surprisingly accepting grandmother, I went to see a therapist a couple of times. He warned me that, as rule, homosexuals suffer from 'internalized homophobia' and experience unrealistic doubts about their self-worth. 'Take more risks' was his advice."

"That sounds like good advice."

"Well, that's why I came here. But if I really acknowledge the truth, my six months in San Francisco have contained more blows to my self-esteem than encouragement. I discovered a city full of beautiful and attractive men. But too many of them, I've also discovered, seem either self-obsessed and attitude-ridden or shell-shocked and demoralized from the effects of AIDS — or both."

"I know," Jon answered softly.

"I've dated several guys I liked. We had safe-sex without much romance or affection — which seems to me the reverse of what it's supposed to be: safe sex ought to mean lots of affection and foreplay with less emphasis on ejaculation, since it's the semen that poses the threat."

"I appreciate the irony..."

"A couple of the guys called me back and suggested second dates. Only one followed through. In fact, I dated him about a month till we both acknowledged that something was missing. I've been realizing lately that I can't blame the other men for my failures at relationships: it's at least a fifty-fifty proposition.

"I know I'm desperately afraid of rejection. In spite of what everybody tells me about my looks, I don't see myself that way. I'm afraid people won't like me, at least once they discovered the 'truth' about me."

"What's that?"

"I don't know. That's the problem. It haunts me."

"I think that truth is that down inside you're a sweet warm little kid that wants lots of love."

Now Mark blushed.

❧

It was almost three a.m. when Jon arrived home at his apartment on Liberty Street, on the city side of Dolores Heights. He peeled off his clothes, brushed his teeth, and fell into bed without taking care of any of the chores of his usual bedtime ritual: he left the cat outside, the mail in the foyer box, and the five messages on his answering machine unheard.

It had been a long day. Jon was wonderfully tired. Thankful for the soft comfort of his bed and thankful for the heartening excitement of his meeting a new friend, he fell asleep.

6

"Q ... R ... S ... T," Lynn muttered under her breath as she sorted the second pile of questionnaires into alphabetical order. *I've been sorting through these things for so long now I'm getting punchy. I'm not sure if I can remember the alphabet.*

Yesterday there was one pile. Today there's another. How many of these damn things have they collected? Well, it's a job. A job. Oh God, I need this job.

"Oh, Miss Graves, why don't you take a break?" said Mrs. Hodgsdon, the heavy-set matron who was Lynn's immediate supervisor. "You've been at this a long time."

Lynn looked up to see the prim and formal Mrs. Hodgsdon come into the windowless little room in which she was working. "Oh, it's almost lunchtime. Why don't I keep at this till noon?"

"Well, I believe Mr. Buchanan would like to see you before lunch. This'll wait, dear. You have a cup of coffee or something and comb your hair and then go down to Mr. Buchanan's office," the older lady said, nuturingly but authoritatively.

"Is this about the job?" Lynn asked excitedly.

"Well, now, that's not my place to say, dear. Mr. Buchanan will explain everything. Run along now."

Lynn picked herself up off the floor where she'd been sitting amid the stacks of thick questionnaires. She dusted herself off, nodded to Mrs. Hodgsdon, and headed down the hall toward the employee's lounge area just inside the front door of the Liberty Bell Foundation's suite of offices.

Lynn took one look at herself in the mirror and realized she needed to clean up a little before daring to approach Mr. Buchanan. Her hair was astray and she had black smudges on her hands and face from the ink of the questionnaires.

She found the full-length locker assigned to her, and after two tries got the lock open. Thinking how this reminded her of high school, she rummaged through her purse to find a comb and compact.

Lynn washed up in the little lavatory off the lounge marked "Ladies." She decided to be sparing with the make-up. While most of the women at Liberty Bell dressed professionally, none of them wore more than a hint of rouge and a little eyeliner.

She skipped the coffee Mrs. Hodgsdon had suggested; she didn't want to be perspiring. She caught herself on that thought. *Sweating,* she corrected herself. *I am not the sort of person who says perspiring, even if I am in a prim and proper office. Though I guess I'd better make sure I don't say "sweat" out loud around here. I need this job.*

🕊

"Come in, come in, Miss Graves," Buchanan said, standing up as Lynn knocked on the partly-open door. "Please sit down."

Edward Buchanan struck Lynn as an imposing man. He stood six-foot-two or -three, with a barrel chest, wavy white hair, and bushy eyebrows. He wore a well-tailored charcoal grey pin-stripe suit that camouflaged his girth.

"You wanted to see me, sir?"

"Yes, yes," he answered.

There was an uncomfortably long silence as Buchanan sat looking across his desk at Lynn. She got no feeling at all of being ogled or even of being sized up. But the silence unnerved her and she wondered: *is that precisely why he does it — as a ploy to put opponents off balance?*

"Yes, sir?" she finally asked timidly.

"Well, well, I've been looking over your employment application. Emily, Mrs. Hodgsdon that is, tells me you've done a good job with the work she's given you. Your answers to the personnel questionnaire all seem in order. I think you might make a very good employee for the Foundation."

Lynn felt herself relax. "Well, thank you, I certainly hope so."

"Now, now. It's not just hope that makes a good employee. It's determination and discipline."

"Yes sir."

"And, of course, belief in what we're about here. I think you may not be fully aware of what the Liberty Bell Foundation does. Is that correct, young lady?"

"Well, Mr. Buchanan, sir, I know that you do research. I don't know much about what kind of research, though I have looked briefly at those questionnaires I've been filing. But, sir," Lynn hastened to add to make sure she'd sound diligent and respectful, "I haven't looked past the first page. I didn't think it any of my business."

"Well, good for you, young lady. Good for you. Some of the projects we work on around here are classified, you know."

Another pause.

"You know, I like the name very much," Lynn spoke up, not wanting to have to sit through more silence. "I came to Washington, sir, because I want to work for America. My dad raised me to be patriotic. He was a Vietnam War vet."

"Yes, I noted that fact in your questionnaire. In your favor, young lady. In your favor. I served in Vietnam myself. And I'm pretty proud of it — even though those peaceniks at home spoiled that campaign. In a way this firm got its start over there. George Wilson and I — we're the founding partners — well, we met in Danang. We were with one of the first groups of military advisors this country sent to help stabilize the South." Buchanan gazed off into space with a mixed look of sadness and pride in his eyes. "America's been good to us. The Foundation still does a lot of work for the Pentagon. Why, George has just completed a major project developing a computer program to assess ratios of target combatants versus nontarget casualties. Very interesting. . ."

"Sir, you mentioned classified information. May I ask if the reason for the very personal questions in the employment application were for a government security clearance or something?"

"Not exactly. I mean, not a government security clearance. But certainly one for the office here. We want to know just what kind of people we have working for us."

"Oh, yes sir."

"Do you think there'd be any problem with your getting a security clearance?" Buchanan inquired, leaning forward and placing his arms on the top of his broad desk.

"Oh, no sir, not at all. I asked because, well, I was sort of excited about the idea of getting top secret clearance."

"Ho, ho," Buchanan made a sound like a department store Santa. "Well, not yet, young lady, not yet. No, for the time being, we'll just be having you do simple secretarial work. I think you'll find the work fulfilling though. As you get to know us, you'll discover that we're involved in some very interesting things around here. All of them for the good of America. Things I think you'll believe in yourself." Buchanan reached down and pressed a button under his desk. "Emily will show you around the office."

Lynn was surprised the interview was over. Buchanan never did explain what kind of research the Liberty Bell Foundation was doing. And they'd never talked about salary or benefits.

"Mr. Buchanan, please sir, before we finish let me ask you about my, uh, salary."

"Oh, you take that up with Mrs. Hodgsdon. She knows all about that. But we pay well here. We pay well. Don't you worry about that."

"Aren't you just pleased as punch with our new girl?" Mrs. Hodgsdon said sparklingly to Mr. Buchanan from the door as she opened it and then stepped back, obviously holding it for Lynn to exit.

"Give her the grand tour, Emily. Though, of course, I've already explained to her about security and all that. . ."

Outside with Mrs. Hodgsdon, Lynn let out a deep breath and smiled. "Thank you for the recommendation, ma'am."

"Well, you're very welcome. I think you'll enjoy working here. Now, it's lunchtime. You go down to the cafeteria and treat yourself to something nice as a celebration. When you get back, I'll show you around the office."

7

While Lynn Graves was preparing to go to lunch in Washington, across the continent — and, on the clock, three hours earlier — Jon Stiers was just getting out of bed.

Though he knew he hadn't had enough sleep, after the third snooze period allowed by his radio-alarm he forced himself to get up. While coffee was brewing in the kitchen, he threw himself into the shower. The stinging needles of hot water revived him, and with full consciousness came back his recollections of his feelings of last night. As he luxuriated in the warmth of the shower, he realized how delighted he'd been by the animated and laughing conversation with Mark. As he soaped his body he felt arise the physical urges he intentionally suppressed last night lest he rush into something precipitously. He was glad for his caution. If something was going to develop with Mark, he wanted it to be serious. But he was also glad for those feelings. It had been so long since he'd felt them.

Still dripping wet from the shower, he rushed into the kitchen and poured himself a cup of coffee. He resolved to take Mark up on his offer to stay in touch. *Indeed,* he decided, *I'll invite him to dinner tonight.*

Trying to dry himself with the towel in one hand while balancing the steaming cup in the other, on his way into the bedroom he noticed the number of calls on his answering machine, proclaimed by bright L.E.D. characters on the face of the device. *Too many to listen to now. I'll call in from the office and get them later.*

In spite of his late night, Jon arrived at his office by nine-thirty. With the intention to call Mark a little later in the morning still on his mind, Jon perfunctorily sorted through the pile of mail he pulled out of his box in the receptionist's office. *Nothing personal,* he noticed in his first sorting. In his second run-through his eye was caught by a C.D.C. document that one of the officials in the Department of Health had xeroxed for him. It was a summary of public monies already spent on treatment and care of AIDS patients with projections for future costs to society. The predictions were truly staggering: upwards of fourteen billion dollars a year.

Such predictions, Jon thought, are unrealistically provocative. They simply ignore the possibility that, like with so many other new diseases, people will begin developing natural immunity, spread will level off, and effective treatments will be found. What they really reflect is the enormous dependence Americans have on the medical profession and the profession's capacity for eating up more and more money for tests and treatments that only give patients time but no real cure.

Of course that's the horror of this disease, Jon reminded himself. *It doesn't kill; it just leaves its victims open to the next infection. Maybe, because AIDS is a disease of the immune system itself, it's unique. And the new drugs, like Atripvir, are successful in stopping the virus from growing but don't cure it; they just create another set of medical disorders that require treatment. So maybe these predictions are going to be right. A pretty scary proposition.*

As he leafed through the document, Jon remembered to call home for his telephone messages. He punched in his phone number, waited a moment for his short message, then punched in his identifying code. In a moment the electronically-generated voice answered that there were six new messages. (*Somebody must've called already this morning,* Jon thought.) "Playback new messages?" the totally inhuman but oddly familiar voice inquired. Jon punched a button to answer affirmatively.

The first two messages were dial tones. *Why do people do that?* he
wondered. The third message announced efficiently: "This
is Richard Hawkins' office calling. Mr. Stiers, please call Dr. Hawkins as soon as possible. The number is 796-4521. Thank you." Jon
grabbed a pencil to write down Hawkins' phone number.

The fourth message was more personal: "Jon, this is Dick
Hawkins. I'm home now. Call me anytime before, say, midnight.
My home phone number is 869-4222. Oh, and keep that number
to yourself please. It's unlisted." Well, Hawkins must have something important to talk about if he's willing to reveal that secret
home number.

The fifth message: "Jon, sorry to call so late. This is Pat, Pat
Stratford. Blum just told me you got me into a new experimental
program. I wanted to find out about it. I'm excited. Thanks. Call
me tomorrow."

I'd better talk to Hawkins before I call Stratford, Jon realized. *What
if Hawkins has bad news? Damn, I wish Blumgarten hadn't been so helpful
. . . not yet, anyway. Though maybe Hawkins is calling to say he's ready to
take Pat.*

"Playback next message?"

"(beep)," Jon answered.

"Jon, this is Mark Hartman." Jon's heart fluttered. "Maybe
you're still asleep. My alarm woke me up regular time. Just called
to say thanks. I'm gonna go back to bed for awhile. I got a job to
work on this afternoon so I'll definitely be around the house.
Gimme a call. 669-8001. 669-8001," he repeated.

"That is all your messages. Repeat? Change announcement?"
the answering machine rattled on as Jon hung up the receiver.

That's sweet, Jon thought. *And efficient.* He pulled the card
from the Café San Marco out of his breast pocket and confirmed
the phone number: 669-8001. He replaced the card in his pocket
and patted his chest.

Looking back at the AIDS expense projections, he punched in
Dr. Hawkins' office number.

"Hi, Jon, sorry to keep you waiting," Hawkins said after a
hold-time of several minutes. "I wanted to talk to you about that
patient of yours, Patrick Stratford. We were going to start him on
that new protocol for PL-17. I called up his old records and I see he
was treated with Atripvir when he was hospitalized last year. That
means I can't put him in this study."

"How come?" Jon quizzed, struggling not to sound argumentative.

"Well, the protocol requires that no other experimental drugs have been used. They'd possibly contaminate the results, you know."

"How about starting him back on Atripvir again then?"

"Didn't work last time. Why bother?"

"How about using Atripvir along with Septra? His PCP's responded well to the Septra all along."

"Well, you can't use 'em together and the fact is he isn't responding to the Septra now. That's why the pneumocystis is flaring up again. But anyway, the study I'm doing is on PL-17. If he doesn't fit the protocol I can't include him in the study."

"But what if PL-17 would stop the HIV from growing? That'd help, wouldn't it?"

"Sure, it'd help," Hawkins answered, an edge of annoyance in his voice. "But he doesn't fit the protocol."

"Are you gonna just let him die?"

"Look, Jon, *I'm* not gonna 'just let him die.' The PCP is. These patients die right and left. You can't try to save them all."

"I know that, Dr. Hawkins. I didn't mean to argue with you. It's just, well, one of the buddies has already told Stratford he was getting in the study. And, well..."

"I told you not to tell any of them yet."

"I know. The buddy just got over-zealous. I made a mistake letting him in on the news."

"Well, anyway," Hawkins continued, changing the subject, "The second guy you referred, uh, Charles Thomas. He looks good. We'll be ready for him tomorrow."

"Will you call and arrange that with him?" Jon asked.

"Yes, I think it would be best if we let my office handle that," Hawkins answered a little high-handedly.

"And what about Buz Kramer?"

"Let's see, Kramer ... Kramer ... Oh, we're still waiting to get his chart from the hospital in Newark. But he looked good on preliminaries."

"You'll let me know?"

"Sure. Oh, and Jon, I'm sorry about Stratford. And sorry to leave you in a bind," Hawkins' voice softened. "Look, you know, Hernandez over at U.C.S.F. is doing Atripvir studies. If you think it'd do Stratford any good, well, why don't you try there?"

"Oh, frankly, Dick," Jon dared to use his first name (after all, that's what he'd called himself in his message), "I wasn't so hot on the Atripvir in particular. I just wanted to try to do something for Pat."

"You can't do everything," Hawkins consoled. "Most of these

guys are just gonna die. And there's not a damn thing we can do about it. Stratford in particular looks pretty bad. But, look, I've still got him on my service. Get him to come into the hospital first thing Saturday morning. I've got some time then. I'll stop by and see him and try upping the Septra dose. He's handled it pretty well in the past, never got toxic. Maybe we can burn out this infection right away. Wouldn't hurt him to be in the hospital for a few days."

"Okay, thanks, Doctor," Jon answered and hung up. *Yeah, it wouldn't hurt him. It's gonna just cost more money to the taxpayers and it's probably not gonna do any good. And what just might have done good — who knows? — is X'ed out by bureaucratic restrictions.*

Damn, I hate calling Pat with news like this, Jon thought. *I better call Blum first and find out how much he told him.*

Jon hunted up Blumgarten's phone number. While it was ringing, his attention was caught by a paragraph at the end of the expense predictions. He let the phone keep ringing while he reread the section.

Political Implications

It is the opinion of this analyst that growing costs of care for AIDS patients will increase social intolerance against the victims of this disease. As expenses for ineffective treatment that only delays inevitable death begin to take more and more out of the national economy, it can be expected that politicians will respond to public pressure by moving to restrict anti-discrimination measures both for AIDS sufferers and for members of high risk groups in general.

Already, this analyst has observed, opinion is turning against homosexuals not only because of conservative moral objections but also because of the financial burden AIDS places on the medical industry. While not yet representative of general opinion, a Southern state legislator has perhaps articulated the trend by presenting a bill to his legislature which prescribed the death penalty for "sexual promiscuity" and "reckless fornication." The legislation in question (to avoid judicial objection, in the opinion of this analyst) applied to both homosexual and heterosexual activity. But, in spite of public concern in the past year about heterosexual spread, it would have been virtually impossible to enforce this measure among the general public. While the bill was voted down in committee, the trend is perhaps apparent.

"Hello," a sleepy voice answered, "is something wrong?"

"Oh, Blum, this is Jon Stiers. No, nothing's wrong."

"How come you rang so long?"

"I'm sorry. You still asleep? I just wanted to find out what you'd told Pat Stratford about that research project."

8

"I'd like to train you on the word-processing machines," Mrs. Hodgsdon said as she gave Lynn the promised tour of the office after lunch. "We have several different systems in the office."

"Oh, I'm pretty good at WordStar already and the standard IBM-PC program. We used to have an IBM in the office I worked in in LaCrosse."

"I don't know what WordStar is," the older lady said rather formally. "Our machines here are Burroughs though we have one Xerox PC. Do you have any experience with either of those?"

"No, ma'am. But I'm sure I can learn."

"Yes, I'm sure you will. Now, as you can see, this is the secretarial room." Mrs. Hodgsdon showed Lynn into the largest room in the firm's suite. It was divided by shoulder-high partitions, some of them glass and others upholstered in a tasteful grey fabric.

"Now I'll want you to finish the filing that you've been doing. We'll keep you on the chastity project for a while." (Lynn smiled to herself when Emily Hodgsdon referred to the study with the same anachronistic name Lynn had used jokingly with Billy the night before.) "There'll be some follow-up letters to type and then, of course, the final report. I'm sure you'll be quite competent with the machines by then..."

Lynn was only half-listening. She was excited about the possibility of learning new skills. She recalled that, at least back home, good word-processors were making over fifteen dollars an hour.

"Oh, look," she exclaimed, interrupting her superior. "There's an IBM just like the one we had at home." She pointed at a computer sitting idly in a small partitioned area next to the windows.

"That is Mr. Wilson's machine. You're not to use that one," came the authoritarian reply.

"Oh..." Lynn felt surprisingly rebuffed. "I'd only meant..."

"Mr. Buchanan explained about classified information, didn't he?"

"Why yes. Do you mean that machine's got classified information stored in it?"

"I mean, Miss Graves, you're to do as you're told. That machine is for Mr. Wilson."

"I'm sorry. I just meant to say I recognized..."

"Come down to my office and let us complete the discussion of your salary. I'm sure you'll be pleased." The older lady turned and walked back toward the central hall.

"Oh, yes, certainly." Lynn hastened to catch up with her, forgetting all about the PC sitting unused by the window.

9

The morning sun gave the lavender flowers in the wallpaper their best color of the day, though Pat sometimes wished the curtains were heavier so they'd keep out the daylight. About the only good sleep he got was in the early mornings. On those frequent days when overcast and low-lying clouds delayed the appearance of the sun till after noon, Pat slept well. But in these October days that in San Francisco's idiosyncratic climate were the warmest and brightest of the year, Pat Stratford usually missed his sleepy mornings.

So Pat had been awake for at least an hour, feeling rising expectation for a reprieve from certain death, when Jon Stiers returned his phone call of late last night.

"I'm sorry I didn't get back to you last night. I didn't get in till really late."

"I called pretty late, but that's okay," Pat said, suppressing his anticipation of the good news he knew Jon had for him. "Hot date?"

"Well, no sex," Jon said jokingly. "But it was a very good date if I can call it that. I met somebody at the hospital last night and we went out afterwards to talk."

"At the hospital?" Pat asked morosely. *Who could you meet interesting at a hospital?* He didn't have *any* good associations with such places. "Blum told me you had some good news for me," he continued, fishing.

Jon paused for a moment. "I don't know about 'good news,' Pat. But I do have news. I talked to that doctor I had you go see last week, Richard Hawkins. He said he'd like to get you back in St. Francis Hospital and he'd readjust your medication dose. He thinks he can get the pneumocystis back under control."

"I thought he had some new experimental drug..." Pat felt crestfallen. "Blum said..."

"Yes, I know. I've spoken with Blum this morning. I think he probably got your hopes a little higher than he should've."

"Goddamn," Pat muttered and then began to sob softly. "I thought something good was going to happen to me for once."

"Pat, pull yourself together. Lots of good things have happened to you in your life. And, right now, things aren't so good."

"Yeah, right now I'd be better off dead."

"Well, maybe so. I don't know about that. What I know is that Dr. Hawkins would like to get you into St. Francis first thing tomorrow."

"What about this new drug Blum was talking about?" Pat ignored Stiers' statement about going into the hospital.

"To be honest with you, Pat, Dr. Hawkins had considered trying a new medication on you, but when he looked into your medical history he saw you didn't fit the requirements for the study."

"Requirements for the study?" The tone of voice revealed a helpless anger.

Jon wasn't sure what to say. He was angry himself at this turn of events.

"Maybe I should just die," Pat said morosely.

"You sound pretty depressed."

"I'd gotten my hopes up. I didn't realize it was ... Jon, are you gonna bring me to the hospital?" he asked, changing the subject.

"Believe it or not, Pat, my job here at the Education Project demands I do some work," Stiers said jokingly. "Blum Blumgarten said he could borrow his roommate's car and drive you over."

"Blum's a nice guy," Pat replied sullenly but honestly.

"I'll come visit tomorrow afternoon once you're settled in your room," Stiers said in a tone that was obviously intended to end the conversation.

"Bye, Jon. Thanks."

"Bye, Pat. And good luck."

Pat replaced the phone on the bedside table. Then rolled over on his side and cried quietly. What was the use of having any hope? The whole disease seemed like just one long, slow process of giving up hope.

❧

Pat Stratford knew all about losing hope. This was his third bout with PCP. The first time landed him in the V.A. hospital in Lubbock, Texas for almost three months. He had been out there on a business trip, auditing a small oil company for the nationwide CPA firm he worked for. That was when it all started.

Pat had been conscious of being sick before leaving for the trip. The lymph glands were swollen under his arms and in his neck and those nightsweats had started. But he told himself it was just psychosomatic. He was having sympathetic symptoms with his friends who were really suffering from AIDS.

Pat was sure he didn't have the disease. He had dramatically cut down on the frequency of his sexual behavior when the first news stories appeared in 1982 about the strange diseases plaguing gay men in New York and San Francisco. Those stories made it patently clear that the people who got sick were the people having too much sex. Even the homophobes Pat wouldn't ordinarily have paid any attention to at all caught on to the meaning of the statistics. They attributed it to God's wrath. Pat knew better. But he knew what he thought was obvious: too many anonymous sex partners wears out your immune system.

Then during what was supposed to be his brief sojourn in Lubbock, he caught cold. He went to work the first couple of days, but he was obviously feeling so bad that a co-worker insisted he take a couple of days sick leave to recuperate. By the end of those two days his chest was burning with pleurisy and he was gasping for air. The co-worker stopped in at his hotel room after work, took one look at Pat, and called an ambulance.

He was rushed to County Emergency and then, once he detailed his hospitalization coverage and medical history, he was transferred by another ambulance to the V.A. Hospital. Pat's tour of duty as a supply clerk on the fringes of the Vietnam conflict guaranteed him access to the Veteran's Administration hospital system. But even his honorable discharge and purple heart from when he'd been struck in the leg by shrapnel didn't guarantee him respect or dignity in the hospital once his pulmonary disease was diagnosed.

The first day there, his bed was in an open ward. Early the next morning, when his sputum samples were analyzed and suspicions aroused, he was moved to a private room. There he was subjected to one of the most painful examinations he'd ever experienced. The doctors, all gowned, masked, and gloved — *like creatures out of some cheap science-fiction flick,* he thought in his delirium — inserted a hard rubber funnel into his mouth and snaked a long tube they called a bronchoscope down his throat so they could examine his lungs and scour out a sample of tissue. The examination seemed to last for hours, and for days afterwards his jaws ached from the rigid hyperextension.

Within hours he was moved again, this time to a room within a room. "For infection control," he was told. *For solitary confinement,* he realized, finally recognizing the nature of his illness. In spite of his well-meaning sexual abstemiousness, he had come down with the gay plague. His closet was burst asunder. And his death sentence was proclaimed.

A couple of young medical residents visited him regularly. They seemed genuinely interested in his case. One of them, Pat thought, was probably gay and had more than just professional interest in this disease. The other seemed to have megalomaniacal delusions of discovering the cure for what was then still a "mystery disease."

Practically none of the other hospital personnel entered his sealed-off isolation room. The food service crew left his meal trays outside in the antechamber. If he was lucky one of the friendly residents would bring the tray in before the dry and tasteless food dessicated and hardened beyond eating. Pat didn't care so much about that anyway; he had no appetite. The only thing he craved were ice-chips to cool his parched lips. Once in a while a nurse would respond to his frequent ringing of the call button and, draped in layer upon layer of gauze and latex, bring him a cup of ice.

The medication they gave him worked. And it worked pretty fast. In a week he was up and around. The hospital wanted him to stay for further tests and, he suspected, to be their guinea pig. Apparently he was one of their first AIDS patients.

Pat called his boss. "I think I can come home to San Francisco and maybe resume work in about a week."

"That's great news," the boss replied. "But don't rush it. We don't want you getting sick again. Just take it easy, Pat. Go ahead and use up your sick time — there's still some left. And then we'll arrange a disability leave. You're one of our best men. We won't desert you."

"Thanks for the support," Pat managed to reply. "I'm sorry this had to happen."

"Stay in Lubbock till you're really well," the boss had said. "Stay away from here" was how Pat understood the subtext of the communication.

There wasn't much to do in the hospital. He was kept in the isolation room, though he was assured by most of his doctors that nothing he had was contagious. They kept assuring him that the isolation was to protect him from diseases the *other* patients might have. He didn't altogether mind the privacy. Most of the other men in the rambling facility seemed to be old alcoholic rednecks — not the kind of men he'd select for friends. But then, he had to admit to himself, he was probably stereotyping them unfairly.

Although the pneumocystis pneumonia was being held in check by the medication, he was still losing weight and he felt generally pretty punk — "general malaise," the doctors called it. A lot of it was just boredom: *My God, I'm so sick of soap-operas*, he complained silently.

One afternoon toward the end of his third week in the hospital he watched a local TV news program that featured a spokesperson from the Lubbock AIDS Foundation. *How come nobody in the hospital told me about them?* he wondered. He listened carefully as the guest explained the symptoms of the disease and then described the services offered by the Foundation.

"We provide counseling and support groups both for People with AIDS and for what we call 'the worried well,' people who have no symptoms but are anxious and worried about developing AIDS." (*I used to be one of those*, Pat thought wistfully. *Some good it did me!*) "Our most important service is probably the buddy program."

"Explain how that works," the interviewer broke in.

"Each PWA is assigned a 'buddy,' a volunteer who's trained to provide companionship and basic assistance in living..."

"Excuse me a minute," the interviewer interrupted again. "You used the acronym 'PWA'; would you explain what that means?"

"Oh, certainly," the earnest young man from the AIDS Foundation answered. (Pat was surprised to see how attractive the guy was. *I always thought gay activists were toads and losers*, Pat thought to himself.) " 'PWA' stands for 'People with AIDS.' The men and women who've got this disease realize that the strongest thing they've got going for them is their own willpower. Doctors can't do much for them. Some alternative healing methods work. But what seems to work best is their own intention to get better. That's at least partly why, right now, we think AIDS is psychologically modulated.

"At any rate," the young man continued, seeming to realize he'd gotten off the track, "calling them AIDS *victims* only takes their power away from them. It classifies them as powerless. And they aren't *patients* except when they're in a hospital. You know, 'patient' is almost like 'victim,' it means somebody passive who something is done to. So rather than call them AIDS victims or AIDS patients, we just want to call them People with AIDS."

"And these 'People with AIDS' " — the interviewer said it like it was in a foreign language — "can get a buddy from your Foundation?"

"Right. Just call us on the hotline and we'll arrange to come visit. That number is ... uh, you know, I can't remember," he laughed self-consciously.

"That's okay. The engineers will run the number on the screen at the end of the program ... oh, the director says it's on right now."

(*Dumb ass*, Pat thought bitchily, *you'd think he could remember a simple phone number*. But he carefully repeated the number to himself several times while he hunted in the deskside table for pen and paper.)

"Thank you, Larry Farrington from the Lubbock AIDS Foundation, for being on our show this morning. Tomorrow, my guest will...." Pat switched off the TV sound and picked up the phone.

Two days later, Larry Farrington himself showed up in Pat's room along with another surprisingly handsome young man whom he introduced as Pat's new buddy, Clark. They were the first people Pat had seen in weeks who weren't dressed in isolation suits.

"If it's okay with you," Larry said right off, "we're not gonna bother with all those gowns and masks and stuff. AIDS can't be transmitted casually." Pat was surprised to discover these were nice guys who didn't treat him like some kind of pariah.

"We ordinarily don't assign buddies to people while they're in the hospital," Larry explained. "There usually isn't much for the buddy to do. But since you're from out of town and don't have any friends to visit, we're gonna make an exception."

"Well, thanks," Pat answered. "I sure could use some company. I feel like I'm in solitary confinement." He realized he was mellowing out. *God, what a bitch I've become!* he thought with chagrin. He hadn't felt so relaxed and comfortable with anybody since he'd first gotten sick. He was feeling hopeful for the first time since he'd heard the fateful diagnosis.

"I'll see about arranging a pass to get you out of here," Clark offered enthusiastically. "Lubbock's not like 'Frisco, but at least it'd be better than staying inside all day."

"I'd love to see Lubbock," Pat answered. And then added, like any good San Franciscan, "You know, the city is called San Francisco, not 'Frisco. No self-respecting gay man should ever call The City 'Frisco."

Clark and Larry both laughed.

&.

Now, four years and three bouts with PCP later, Pat wondered if he were any kind of self-respecting gay man. And he wondered what he'd ever seen in San Francisco. He wished to God he'd stayed at home in Natchez. He'd come to hate The City and what it had done to him. He wondered why he ever let himself feel any hope at all.

10

"Well, so, I got me a job, Mama. Oh, this man that interviewed me was so funny," Lynn was saying over the phone. "He kept repeating everything he said — like saying 'no, no' or, uh, 'good for you, good for you.'"

"I guess I know what you mean. Anyway, do you like the job? And are they paying you well?"

"Oh, Mama, I'll be making practically ten dollars an hour and they said there's an automatic raise after six months if I haven't messed up on anything."

"Well, I'm proud of you. That's almost what I'm making and I've been at this for years."

Lynn thought about her mother's job. In a way she felt sorry for her. A few years ago Alice Graves had been an emergency room nurse, making very good money and feeling respected and important. Then she had a mild heart attack and retired. Now she worked part-time with the Visiting Nurse Association. Her patients were homebound invalids; she helped them with their baths, changed the linens, made sure they were taking their medication properly, checked their vital signs, or just quietly kept them company. Lynn thought it sounded boring.

"How's your job, Mom?"

"Well, we're having an early winter. Already got snow. Lynn, you know, it's gonna be a bitter year, I said to myself just this afternoon, gonna be hard on the old people. Maybe give me some extra work.

"Do you still like the job?" Lynn asked tentatively. She felt a twinge of guilt about leaving home.

"Right now, I love the job. I'm over at Alma DeGutis's. Got the phone forwarded over here. It's cozy and warm inside. Not a thing for me to do but put my feet up. Alma's sitting up in bed watching 'Wheel of Fortune' and I'm on the phone with my darling, wandering daughter."

Lynn blushed. She didn't know what to say. She felt a veiled rebuke in her mother's last attempt at affection.

"Well, I've got an interesting new job myself," Alice ended the awkward slence. "Last week the agency got called to visit a young man with AIDS. Most of the nurses on the staff were reluctant to take the case. I didn't see any problems. In fact, it seemed kind of exciting."

"Are you sure it's safe, Mama?"

"Of course, I'm sure. I know how to take infection precautions. And, you know, Lynn, frankly, this business sometimes gets real dull. I mean, after my fifteen years in the Emergency Room, sitting with senile old ladies just doesn't cut it."

"I guess not, but I'd be really worried about AIDS. You know they don't really know all about it yet."

"Well, they know a lot more than the press, or the fanatics, would let you think. I've been reading up on the studies about contagiousness."

"Is the patient a, uh, a ... ?"

"Homosexual?" Alice completed her daughter's sentence. "Yes, I think so. I didn't ask him, but, well, you know..."

"Do you mind?"

"Lynn, I raised you to be open-minded. I guess back then we weren't thinking about strange things like homosexuality. But I think the principle's the same. It's not like I haven't been around." Alice laughed knowingly.

"Now, Mama. I didn't mean that. In fact, I've sort of made friends with one of them myself."

"Oh?"

"There's this nice man down the hall named Charley."

"Well, you be careful."

"Mama," Lynn scolded affectionately, "I thought you said to be open-minded."

"Well, I guess you're right. I just worry about you being in a big city like Washington. Oh, by the way, have you seen the president yet or anybody famous? Oh, ... Lynn, I better let you go. I see Mrs. DeGutis trying to get out of bed. Last time she tried that she fell on her face and had to get stitches. Hang on just a minute..."

"Mrs. DeGutis ... Alma ... I'll be right there, you stay where you are," Alice shouted down the hall.

"I gotta go too, Mama, need to get ready. I got a, uh, uh, a dinner engagement tonight," Lynn's voice revealed her nervousness.

"Well, you have a nice time," Alice answered, not really paying attention to what her daughter had said. "Thanks for calling, honey. Gotta go. Alma's still struggling to get her legs over the side of the bed. I love you, Lynn. Bye-bye."

11

Oh my God, Jon thought, *it's mid-afternoon already. I was going to call Mark right after lunch.*

He looked up from the keyboard of the personal computer on which he'd been working non-stop since he'd talked with Pat Stratford. He was preparing an outline for a course on AIDS prevention measures and risk reduction.

Jon Stiers was a health educator. His work with PWAs was volunteer, and was supposed to be outside work hours. As it turned out, however, it was almost impossible to distinguish between work and volunteer time and even (he sometimes feared) play.

"This AIDS business is getting to me," Jon was finding himself saying in casual conversation more frequently than he liked. "It's been going on too long!" *But what am I going to do?* he answered himself. *The damn thing won't go away just 'cause I'm tired of it. And, my God, I'm not the only one who's tired of it.*

🕱

Jon looked over the work he'd done so far. He was pleased with it: an up-to-date summary of evidence about sexual transmission and some suggestions for relationship development. *Funny,* he thought, *here I am working away at figuring out how other people can get relationships going and hold them together, and I'm forgetting about my own hopes for a relationship. Maybe I'm just timid about calling him . . . but he called me this morning,* Jon reminded himself.

Pulling the card from Café San Marco out of his breast pocket, Jon reached for the phone. He punched the number in.

"Hi, this is Mark—"

"Well hi, this is—" Jon said, then stopped, realizing the voice that answered was still talking.

". . . I can't come to the phone now. Please leave a message after the beep."

Damn, I missed him, he thought. "Hi, Mark. Sorry I'm so late calling. I got busy," Jon said after the beep. "This is Jon Stiers. We met last night at the hospital," he added, reintroducing himself in an effort to appear as proper and unpresumptuous as possible.

(click-click)

"Now I know perfectly well who you are," Mark's laughing voice broke in.

"Oh, hi."

"Hi, Jon. Sorry it took me so long. Sometimes I let the machine answer to avoid salesmen and wrong numbers. But then when I heard it was you, I couldn't find the handset. I've got one of those cordless dealies, and sometimes I set that thing down and don't remember where."

"I'm glad you found it," Jon answered amiably.

"Well, it isn't like I've got that big a house. Just two rooms and a bath plus this really great sunporch with a truly FAB-ulous view," Mark spoofed one of the popular gay exaggerated and overused words. "You'll see." (Jon was pleased by that comment.) "But it's a great house, three-storey Victorian with lots of gingerbread. Reminds me of my grandmother's house. It's all broken up into little apartments, kinda ruined. I'd love to buy this place and restore it . . . But I'm rattling on. How are you and what's on your mind?"

"I'm fine and I was calling to invite you to dinner."

"I accept," Mark said easily. "When do you want me and where?" he added seductively.

"Oh, how'd you like to come by my place for a drink? About seven. Then I thought we'd go out. I know this Cajun place on Valencia around the corner from me. A bit of a dive, but good food."

"Sounds great. I've got your address. I think I can find it easy."

"Good. And Mark, thanks for the call this morning. I guess I'd already left for work. You know, I really enjoyed myself last night too. I like you," Jon said softly, realizing he was daring a little by acknowledging his feelings.

"Me too," Mark answered, the gentleness of his voice belying the ambiguity of the words. "See you at seven."

Jon hung up, feeling a mixture of excitement and anxiety. "Me too," Mark had said. What did that mean? Was what Jon hoped for really happening? Or was he just letting himself get set up for a serious disappointment?

Jon sat, slightly numbed, for a few minutes. He had come to doubt the kind of love he hoped for was ever going to happen to him again. One of the social symptoms of AIDS seemed to be that while many individuals — gay and straight — were deciding to seek stability in their relationships and to adopt a policy of monogamy, others were beginning to fear coupling altogether and adopting virtual celibacy. At the same time that relationships were being prized more, they were also becoming harder to find.

Jon looked at a photo he'd recently pulled out of an old album and framed to sit on his desk: Ted Warmboldt and he in bathing suits, sitting side by side on the wooden railing of the guest house terrace with the deep blue Caribbean stretching out behind them.

"Well, honey, I've honestly doubted there'd be any more relationships," Jon's voice broke as he spoke out loud to the photograph. "I'm getting old, you know." He smiled at the photo and then felt a shiver of guilt for feeling sorry for himself for aging when Ted was dying.

He looked longingly at the photograph of Ted's lanky body. How good he'd looked on that trip! The sun had bleached golden highlights in his dark blond hair. The tan and the pose had given his muscles such fine definition.

Jon studied his own body in the photo. He too looked good. He was thinner then, more boyish, but actually not as fit as now; he'd recently been working out more in an effort to stave off the passage of time. He had more hair then. Jon looked up at the pane of glass in the side wall of his office. It had once been a window; the other side was now painted over dark blue, making it a kind of mirror. He saw that he still looked monkishly innocent, boyish — *the way gay men do*, he thought — but obviously older. The blue backing gave the reflection a sickly cast: "as through a glass darkly," in the words of St. Paul, made so familiar as the title of the Bergman movie. "I'm getting old, Ted. A fate you're escaping.

"I don't mind getting old, but I'm scared of getting lonely. I had too many years of that as a kid. Gay liberation was such a relief. It meant we didn't have to be lonely anymore. But now AIDS has spoiled the dreams of a future with easy relationships. Relationships just aren't easy anymore.

"You know," he continued his monologue with the photograph, "the re-evaluation of sex and love that the health crisis caused has been good. The sexual revolution has matured. Ted, I was just writing that in those notes this morning," he said, pointing at his computer as though somehow the smiling, wind-blown Ted would appreciate the significance, "but now the liberation's gonna be lost if we don't stop this thing.

"We've all been trying to create a world that the next generation of gay kids could grow up in without feeling the terror and the loneliness, now we've got to create a world they can grow up into without disease.

"*I've* got to," he corrected himself. "And if I don't do my share then your death will just be a waste.

"Wish me well tonight," he grinned to the smiling face forever locked in time. "I've got a date." He turned away to start the computer's print routine.

12

Hearing the shower go off in the bathroom, Lynn hurriedly re-tucked the towel she had wrapped around her chest. "Which towel can I use?" came a young man's voice from the bathroom.

"The pink one by the door's clean," Lynn answered as she pulled a comb through her long wet hair, struggling to get her looks in shape.

"Hey, honey, you look beautiful," Billy DePalma said, sneak-ing up behind Lynn. She was still combing her hair in front of the mirror of the deco style vanity that came with the furnished apart-ment. Billy closed his arms around her, hugging her from behind. His bare chest felt warm and solid against the back of her shoul-ders. She blushed with his compliment.

Lynn turned her head as far around as she could and kissed Billy lightly on the lips, then turned back and gazed at their reflec-tion in the mirror. *How handsome he is.* Putting the comb back on the vanity, she reached up with both hands and caressed his forearms. She loved the thick dark hair that curled across the tops of his arms and across his chest.

They both happened to look at each other's reflection simul-tanously and caught each other's eye. *Oh, he's got such a sweet face,* Lynn thought gazing deep into his dark brown eyes.

"I'm so lucky," she said aloud. Billy squeezed her tighter and then relaxed his hold as she squirmed against him to turn around to face him. As she did, the towel she'd so carefully wrapped about her came loose and fell from her breasts.

"Oooh," she exclaimed and then felt embarrassed by the silly girlishness of the sound she'd made.

"It's okay," Billy said, pulling the towel away altogether and then pulling off the towel he'd likewise wrapped around his waist. "I don't think we have to be prudish with one another anymore."

"Well, I know..." Lynn answered and hugged him tighter, laying her cheek against his chest. "It's just, well ... you know..."

"I know," he answered gently.

"I love you," Lynn murmured into Billy's chest, half-afraid he'd hear and half-afraid he wouldn't.

Billy took her head gently in his hands and turned her face toward his. She pulled away from him a little, though their lower bodies remained pressed together. "I'm so glad," he said, " 'cause I love you too, Lynn. You're the first girl that I've ever felt this way about. And I just feel it so deep. It's wonderful."

They held one another's gaze. Lynn was surprised to realize, even though they'd just finished making love a short time ago, that she could sense Billy's body beginning to stir again against her. And she could feel herself responding with a flush of warmth in the bottom of her abdomen.

Lynn turned them around so her back was toward the bed and pulled Billy backward with her, trying to keep him still pressed up hard against her. But she reached the bed sooner than she expected and tripped on the spread they had earlier thrown off onto the floor. She lost her balance. As she fell, giggling, she pulled Billy down with her.

"Wanna do it again?" she asked, realizing that her subtle seduction had been spoiled by her misstep.

"Oh, I'd love to," Billy answered hesitantly. "But aren't you hungry? What about the pizza we were gonna get?" Earlier, when they made their plans to spend the evening making love, they'd decided to eat again at Louie's — to try the pizza.

"I'm hungry for you," Lynn said, surprising herself with the raw sexuality of the comment. "Wouldn't you rather make love than eat?"

"Uh, well, uh ... I guess I'm pretty hungry."

Lynn realized Billy's arousal was gone completely.

"Was something wrong?" she asked timidly.

"Oh no, not at all. It's just, well, I only brought one rubber and we used it."

"Well, you know, I'm in a safe time in my period," Lynn answered with a sophistication she barely realized she possessed.

"Oh, I don't know about that. I mean, I don't want to take any chances. That could just ruin everything for us."

Lynn's years of abstinence were showing themselves in her hunger for the experience she'd passed up. "C'mon, Billy, it'll be okay."

"Oh, Lynn, don't push. Anyway, now I'm not sure I could get it up again."

"Well, snuggle with me a minute and let's see."

Lynn soon realized Billy's heart — or at least his sexual apparatus — wasn't really in it. They held each other close and the closeness felt good. Some of the romance they'd been feeling earlier returned, but not the sexual arousal.

"I'm sorry," Billy said.

"It's okay," Lynn answered. "Let's not let this spoil our wonderful evening. And, hey, what about that pizza. I think I just got a craving for cheese and Italian sausage..."

"How about pepperoni and green peppers and mushrooms?"

"...and black olives?"

"...and anchovies?" Billy rejoined, laughing now with the light-heartedness of the game.

"Ugh," Lynn answered. "You Italians are all alike."

"Well, honey, if you're gonna stay with me, you better start learning to like the olive oil and the anchovies," he came back with his mock accent. "Or maybe you finda youself takin' a swim in da Potomac with concrete galoshes...

"Oh my!" Billy stopped his jest, "I didn't mean to sound so violent."

"That's okay. I can take a hint. I know how you Italian guys are. All sauve on the outside, but full of fire down below," Lynn joked as she grabbed at Billy.

"Well, the fire'll be back, Lynn, I promise you. I just want to be safe."

13

"Well, Louisiana Oyster Loaf sure is a lot of bread," Mark laughed as he washed down the last of his meal with a swallow of wine.

"More?" Jon proffered the carafe of white wine.

"I'll split the rest with you. I don't need much more to drink. In fact, I'd like coffee."

"Me too," Jon answered, remembering his young friend's ambiguous play with words earlier today. *The evening has come off well so far*, he thought, *he's been perfectly open and forthcoming.* Jon gazed across the table admiring what he saw as Mark's radiant beauty. The waiter happened by with a pot of coffee just then and poured for them both. As Mark was adding cream to his, he looked up and caught Jon's eyes.

"Hi," he whispered.

Jon's heart stopped for a moment. That was such a surprise getting caught in his moment of admiration.

"You know, when I first came to San Francisco I heard sex was easy to find — even in spite of AIDS," Mark said.

"And?" Jon fished.

"Well, I don't know. I guess I haven't found it so. At least not the way I wanted."

"I'm surprised you haven't had men falling all over you," Jon said jokingly, letting the humor relieve his tension momentarily.

"Well, thank you. But if they have been, I haven't seen it."

"That's a common complaint," Jon answered, switching into

his role as therapist and gay cultural analyst. "Even the most beautiful men in the world sometimes don't see the attention they get because they've been conditioned out of it. Many of them even take the looks they get as put-downs or rejections. Most of us are just so afraid of getting rejected that — unless we're just out blatantly cruising — we usually avoid letting anybody else know we're looking at them. And that implies that all the people who're looking at us aren't letting us notice it either. So none of us realize how many men really do find us attractive."

"That's a great insight, Jon," Mark answered. "You know, I'm glad I just caught you looking." He giggled shyly.

"Too many gay men mistake just giving other men attention or looking for love with hunting for sex."

"I disagree," Mark answered. "I think most of them really are looking for love, but settle for sex because it's less threatening. Besides, having sex can make you terribly vulnerable emotionally unless you're consciously steeling yourself against it."

"Are you?" Jon asked, turning the tables for a moment. Up to now Mark had been the one to say things like that.

"Steeling myself?"

Jon nodded in assent.

"Yeah, probably," Mark answered. (And Jon felt a chill of fear run through him.) "I mean, I've had sex with a couple of men I thought were real attractive, but afterwards they didn't seem to pay much attention to me and I didn't seem to mind."

"I guess I know what you mean. Did you feel they weren't attractive enough for you?" Jon asked, changing the subject a little — to protect himself, he realized.

"No, I meant that having sex right away got in the way of developing a relationship. And now, Jon, don't go categorizing me as some sort of narcissistic pretty boy. And—" he dropped his eyes to the table "—don't pretend *we* aren't working on developing a relationship right now."

"Oh." Jon felt at a loss for words. Mark's directness surprised him, even as it thrilled him.

"You don't think the reason I didn't invite myself home with you last night was 'cause I thought myself too pretty for you, did you?"

"Well, frankly, I thought it was because it was too late," Jon answered laughing. "But, Mark, I mean, I know we were really, uh, clicking with one another last night. But you know I'm forty-three. I guess I thought that, well, I'm a little old for you."

"Do you mean you're too old for me? Or I'm too young for

you?" Mark asked. And for the first time Jon was aware of Mark's timidity.

"You're as afraid of getting rejected as I am, aren't you?" Jon said softly.

"Well, of course I am," Mark answered, sitting up and squaring his shoulders. "I haven't wanted to ruin things by rushing too fast." He reached across the table to touch Jon's hand. "I think you're the neatest guy I've met in this whole city—"

"Coffee?" The waiter interrupted them and Mark quickly pulled his hand away.

The second cups of coffee changed the mood for a moment. They chatted lightly about the decor of the place. Then, as Mark drank down the last of his coffee, he announced matter-of-factly, "Well, I got to see your apartment. I'd love for you to see mine. I'm really quite proud of it. But I can only let you stay for a few minutes. Even though it's Saturday, I have work to do tomorrow morning and you kept me up too late last night as it is," he scolded smiling.

Jon understood the meaning of Mark's limited invitation. "You're a remarkably mature young man for being only twenty-four."

"Well, I'm glad you noticed," Mark answered cockily. And they both laughed.

14

It was after two a.m. and Pat Stratford still couldn't get to sleep. He kept reminding himself that Blum was coming by to take him to the hospital early in the morning. *I need to get some sleep.*

A little while ago Pat had heard noises percolating up from the street below: human voices chattering, people laughing, car horns honking. That meant the bars had just closed. It was a Friday night. Crowds of party-goers had been turned out onto the pavement. He remembered how he used to roam those same streets at this same time of night. That was a long time ago.

Pat was staying in a rent-by-the-week apartment on lower Larkin Street just on the edge of San Francisco's Tenderloin District. When he sat at the window in the late afternoon, he could see the young hustlers who lived in Tenderloin hotels straggling down the street on their way over to Polk to ply their trade among the after-work crowd. *Don't they know what they're risking?* Pat thought.

"Maybe they're using rubbers and safe sex now," he allowed

during a conversation a couple of days before with his old friend —
and maybe now only friend — Blum.

"Well, you know, AIDS is just a virus and we know how to
stop the transmission," Blum answered. "I hope somebody's teaching the hustlers or, at least, the johns."

"Yeah, back in my day," Pat replied sadly and sourly, "who
knew about viruses?"

Tonight Pat was wishing one of those sexy young hustlers
would just happen to come knocking at his door. He'd be happy to
practice safe sex. He hadn't been held, really held, in years. His
body ached from lack of touch as much as from the ravages of his
illness.

But no hustler was going to come up. No boyfriend was going
to come visit and make love to him. He looked down at his emaciated frame and felt revulsion. *Who'd want to touch a body like this?*

Pat tried to feel sexual, not just needy. He remembered how
he used to recall sexual memories when he couldn't sleep and they'd
always act as a lulling and comforting soporific. He touched himself, but his shriveled penis barely responded. Pat longed for sleep,
if only to allow him a few hours' escape.

He couldn't lie for long on his side because the pressure on his
shoulder would give him shooting pains down his arm, but for now
he curled up in fetal position and pulled the sheet up over his head
and huddled inside himself and his memories. They were all he had
left.

Pat's mind ran quickly through what he'd come to think of as
his "index" of erotic memories: those associated with anonymous
hot sex, those with romantic loving sex, those with strangers, those
with regular fuck buddies, those at the baths, in the park, at home,
at tricks' houses. He quickly came upon his favorite — it was one
that defied placement in any of the categories.

He had been at the baths (one of those, now closed, just off
Polk Street, only a few blocks from Pat's present abode). He was
with a man he'd been deeply and satisfyingly in love with. They
had lived together over a year, then the man had been transferred
to L.A. for six months. When he returned he and Pat started dat-
ing again. Pat was really glad to have him back and had hopes that
relationship would flower into a lifetime love. The sex was better
than ever. And then suddenly the man announced, "I don't want to
have sex with you anymore." Pat was crushed. He tried to stay
friends, but felt overwhelming pangs of frustration and longing
whenever he was in the man's presence. Still, he kept hoping. They

had dinner together now and then and talked on the phone.

And then one night Pat ran into him at the baths. He looked so good. He had let his beard grow and (at least in Pat's recollection) his chest and torso had developed both more bulk and definition. At first they seemed shy of one another. Pat didn't dare express interest for fear of another rejection. Then suddenly his friend kissed him. And then held the kiss. And then reached out and grabbed his shoulders and pressed Pat against his chest. The ecstasy of the skin contact surged through him. He'd wanted that feeling again so much he burned with desire. Now the sensation filled him and he melted into those longed-for arms.

In the past Pat was usually the top man in their sex play. This time the roles were reversed. He was thrilled to be taken by this man who tonight looked so strong and manly. And he let himself be swept along by the passions that roused between them.

The image that had become most firmly fixed in Pat's memory was of this newly-returned lover rising up on his knees between Pat's legs, driving himself deep one last time, as spasms of sexual ecstasy tightened the firm muscles in his chest and rushed into his face. He turned his head to the side, Pat recalled, and let out a deep and long cry of pleasure, just as Pat's own pleasure started. Perfect timing.

But now tonight that erotic fantasy was ruined by the gruesome thought that that very act of love-making might have been the vector of transmission by which this cursed virus entered Pat's bloodstream. He felt more cheated than ever. Not only was the disease stealing his life away, it was souring his most precious memories. And all he had left were those memories.

                                           𝕾𝕽

"Back in Natchez I'd felt so alone," Pat had remarked only a few weeks ago to the PWA group that Jon Stiers facilitated as a volunteer for Castro Village AIDS Support. He'd been attending regularly. Above all he enjoyed reminiscing with the group about his memories of San Francisco "in the ol' days."

"Coming here was one of the greatest things in my life," he remembered he'd said. "I mean, for the first time I didn't feel like a freak. And I stopped acting like one, too," he joked.

"That's a common phenomenon," Jon agreed. "For so many gay men, those experiences of being chosen sexually or romantically by another man — whether it was in a dingy bathhouse or a noisy disco or a romantic candle-lit café overlooking the bay — were a source of enormous self-esteem."

"Yeah," spoke up Greg Bens, a 26-year-old with Kaposi's Sarcoma lesions mottling his face and neck. "I'd really hated what I look like till I came out and discovered there were other gay men. And that they found me attractive."

"You *are* attractive, Greg," Jon answered.

"Well, thanks," was Greg's reply, Pat remembered poignantly. "But maybe not anymore," he added touching a finger to the raised purplish blotch that marred his right cheek.

I used to be attractive too, Pat thought. *But in spite of my looks, I was frustrated and lonely. Jon was right that all the attention bolstered my self-esteem, but I still needed something more. I needed to feel loved.* Pat was feeling that hunger when he met Blum.

Still hoping to lull himself into sleep, he thought about the young man who'd now become his only friend, who'd be coming in the morning to drive him to the hospital.

🐾

Blum Blumgarten had fallen madly in love with Pat Stratford more than eight years ago when Blum had just arrived in the city, a teen-ager from Bakersfield looking like a clumsy farm-hand with a pro-nounced jaw that spoiled his otherwise boy-next-door good looks. Pat had seemed everything Blum wanted himself to be.

Pat had befriended the boy and bedded him, but hadn't quite fallen in love. Both of them had been disappointed by that. But Pat did take Blum under his wing and provided him a place to stay (usually in the spare bedroom), a little spending money, and assist-ance in finding a job. They'd ended up "old friends." Pat hadn't seen much of Blum for a few years. They talked on the phone occa-sionally and ran into one another along Castro Street.

Then one day soon after Pat's return from Lubbock, Blum showed up at his door.

"I heard you were sick," he asked innocently.

"You heard right," Pat answered, showing him in.

"You still look pretty good to me," Blum said as he took a seat on the sofa of Pat's ninth-floor apartment.

"Thanks, but maybe your eyes need checking."

"No, I mean it. I mean, I guess you've lost some weight and you look tired—"

"You know what it is, don't you?" Pat challenged him.

Blum looked down at the oriental rug on the floor. "I heard the rumors—"

"Well, they're true."

"Look, Pat, I'm sorry. Real sorry. And I came up here today because I think I owe you one. You helped me when I was down. I wanna help you."

"That's sweet, Blum. But I'm running out of money . . . And you sure don't want to end up supporting me."

"Well, I guess I couldn't. But, Pat, I didn't come here expecting any money from you. I came here because I think you're a great guy . . . because I used to be in love with . . . because I think you need somebody."

❧

Pat started crying as he remembered the emotions of that moment. "Thanks, Blum," he had managed to say. Then, "Oh, please, hold me."

Blum had been glad to that day. He'd even taken his holding and stroking of Pat further than Pat expected — though safely. But they stopped what little sexual contact they had once Pat took sick the second time and turned skeletal. Yet Blum stayed around. He was still Pat's best old friend.

Still crying, feeling the warmth of Blum's devotion — he was almost afraid to call it love — Pat curled up and fell asleep at last. Another day was over.

15

Lynn and Billy spent Saturday morning at the National Gallery of Art, looking at the Impressionist exhibit that was on its second tour from France. In early afternoon, after leaving the gallery, they went over to Billy's. He lived alone in a modern highrise close in to government center. They'd have more privacy.

No sooner than Billy turned the latch on the door, Lynn had him in her arms. "I've been waiting a long time to get you alone," she joked.

"Well, I'm all yours," he answered. "And, look," he dug into his jacket pocket and pulled out a whole handful of foil-wrapped square packages.

"What are those?"

"Hey, dummy," Billy switched into his mafioso accent, "don't ya recognize da merchandise? Genuine, one hundred percent latex condoms."

"Whoopie," Lynn answered laughing.

"Oh, and I got something else. . ." Billy said hesitantly, then he defensively switched back to his mock accent, "Ever tried reefer, leettle girl?"

"Oh, are you serious?"

"Well, I could be. It depends on your answer," he said innocently. Then he switched back to the accent, "leettle girl."

"Oh, well, honestly. Yes, I have. Not a lot. Back in high school there was pot around. I didn't run with those kids, but Lee Ann and another friend of ours, Doris, got stoned a couple of times up at this vacation house Doris's folks had up the river aways."

"And?"

"Oh, I guess I liked it. We giggled a lot. You know how teenage girls can be. But I sort of avoided it; I guess I was scared my parents would find out or something and I'd get thrown in jail. What about you?"

"Well, I can't say I've had that much more experience. This, uh, friend of mine back in high school turned me on to grass. I did it with him, uh, off and on."

"Did you hang around with the potheads in school?"

"Oh, no, I was sort of a nerd in high school."

"You a nerd? I don't believe it," Lynn announced with mock authority. "You're beautiful."

"Well, maybe you think so, but my mom used to dress me in high water plaid pants and white shirts buttoned up to the neck. I think she was afraid the hair on my chest would show. She used to warn me about looking too sexually attractive 'cause girls could get pregnant," he laughed. "I think for a long time I really believed it could happen just from a girl looking at you too much."

"You were real naive . . ."

"Oh, you wouldn't believe. It really wasn't till this, uh, friend of mine sort of taught me the ropes that I understood much about sex and all. Anyway, he wasn't from school. He was a little older."

"Oh?"

"Well, you know, he showed me a lot about computers and stuff. I guess that's why I didn't mind being a nerd. I was practically having a love affair with my PC.

"Well, c'mon," he said, changing the subject, "take off your coat and sit down. Want something to drink?"

"I'd love a coke," Lynn answered, tossing her jacket over the modern sofa in the living room. "Diet, if you've got it."

"Don't think I can help you with the diet drink," Billy answered. "But you don't need to watch your weight anyway. In fact," he continued, "we needa to fatten you up some."

"No you don't," Lynn answered with a tone that rang both of humor and alarm. "Hey, now what were you saying about marijuana?" she called to Billy who had his head stuck in the refrigerator.

"Well, this guy at work yesterday turned me on to this," he said walking back into the room balancing a tray with two glasses in one hand and holding up a tightly rolled joint in the other. "I hear it really makes sex great."

"Oh, Billy, you know I don't want to start down the Big City road to perdition."

"Well, I wasn't talking about perdition and I wasn't proposing we ruin our job performance or get hooked on drugs. Just one Saturday afternoon. A little talk and a little love. Help us get a little closer, be more open."

Lynn laughed. "I'd just love to have that kind of experience with you. And I trust you," she said, getting up from her chair and kissing Billy on the mouth.

🕮

"How're ya feelin'?" Billy asked a little while later after the two of them, the joint smoked, had fallen into bed and were slowly peeling off one another's clothes.

"I'm feelin' no pain," Lynn answered and then burst out laughing. "Oh, I'm so embarrassed. That's such a stupid thing to say. I sound like some kind of lush."

"You're nothing of the sort, my lady. You are the most beautiful woman in the world . . . at least to me, right now," he added.

"Oh yeah?" she replied in mock offense.

"Oh yeah," Billy said in earnest, kissing her ardently.

Lynn was pulling at the jeans he was wearing, struggling to get them off him. Suddenly something in his back pocket slipped out. "Hey, what's this," she said as she grabbed his billfold and held it so she could see. "I bet you got this full of pictures of the most beautiful women in the world."

"No sir," Billy said sharply. "Ain't no picture of my darlin' in there yet." They both laughed heartily.

Pulling away, Lynn opened up the billfold. "Can I see your driver's license picture?"

"Not very good," he said, "please don't laugh."

She giggled a little, obviously trying to suppress her euphoric laughter, "You look like Clark Kent."

The I.D. photo of Billy did, in fact, show him wearing heavy black eyeglasses.

"I got contact lenses before coming to Washington," he confessed, grinning. "You think I look like Superman without my glasses? Just you wait till I show you my super powers..."

"Oooh, I can't wait," Lynn said, still examining the I.D. "William Danisi DePalma," she read. "What a middle name!"

"My mother's maiden name," Billy answered.

"Well, I don't find any pictures of girls in here," she announced proudly.

"See I told you so."

"Who's this?" she asked, holding out a tattered newspaper photo. It showed a male who looked somewhat older than Billy, but probably not old enough to be his father. "Your brother?"

"That's, uh, this friend of mine I told you about," Billy answered shyly. "Jeff."

"What'd he get his picture in the paper for?" Lynn continued her idle quiz. "Bank robbery?" she tittered.

"For dying," Billy answered soberly.

"Oh, Billy," Lynn sobered quickly too. "I'm sorry. I didn't mean—"

"I know you didn't."

"Hey, what's your middle name?" Billy asked, changing the subject abruptly. "I saw a letter on your desk addressed to Lynn R. Graves. What's the R for?

"Hey, you some kind of detective?" she asked, allowing the conversation to shift. She felt awkward making a bad joke about something that might have been tragic. "The R stands for Redfield."

"That's a pretty name. Was that your mother's maiden name?"

"Well, not exactly," Lynn answered. "Oh, Billy, I love you," she said suddenly, again changing the subject. "And I feel all tingly all over." She giggled just a little.

Billy pulled his jeans off quickly and helped Lynn get hers off. Then they clutched each other tightly, and let the euphoria pass beyond the verbal stage into a rolling delirium of romance and union of their bodies and souls.

🦋

"Hey, I know what. I'll tell you a secret, if you'll tell me one," Lynn suggested, as she later lay quietly with her head on Billy's chest.

"How come?" Billy asked, a little defensively.

"Well, that's a way to get more intimate," she responded. "You know, trust each other."

"I do trust you."

"Look, I'll tell you one and then you can decide."

"Okay, it's a deal."

"Oh, here's an easy one. I got an F in home economics."

"Well, that's not much of a secret," Billy said, "I got a D in P.E."

"Okay, okay, I'll tell you one I've never admitted to anybody.

When I was little I had this stuffed doll — I think it was supposed to be a rabbit. I carried it with me everywhere. Then when I started school my mom said I had to grow up and stop carrying the doll. She stuck it in the linen closet outside my bedroom. For years, I'd sneak out after they thought I'd gone to bed and get my doll to sleep with. And then in the morning I'd sneak it back into the linen closet, unless, well, unless I had a test or something at school. Then I'd wad it up in the bottom of my book satchel. For good luck, I guess."

"I had a doll like that. My dad used to actually beat on me when I'd carry it around with me. I mean, after I got too old. He'd shout at me and tell me boys didn't do things like that."

"Billy," Lynn said very seriously, "I'll tell you a real big secret about me. But don't laugh please."

"I promise."

"I lied a while ago when I told you my middle name. It isn't Redfield. It's just Red."

"I'm not laughing," Billy said. "But why's that a big secret?"

"Oh, I think it's just humiliating. See, say my whole name."

"Lynn Red Graves," Billy said. Then, with a tone of recognition, "I get it, Lynn Redgraves, like the actress."

Lynn buried her face in the pillow and hugged Billy. "My mother made this awful pun on my name. And I just hated it. All through grade school I was always getting kidded."

"Why? Lynn Redgrave is a really good actress."

"Yeah, but back then, you know what she was famous for? She'd been in that movie 'Georgie Girl' where she played this fat girl who everybody rejected. My mother had been fat as a young woman and, I guess, she really identified with this movie character and named me after her."

"Well, be thankful, they didn't name you George."

"Oh, don't you know I am," Lynn answered emphatically. Then she continued more seriously. "You know, this name business and my mother's concern about keeping me from getting fat, I guess like she'd been, well, it really screwed me up for a long time. I mean, for a while I was really anorexic. They ended up sending me to a psychiatrist." Her voice faltered.

"Oh, honey, I'm sorry," Billy said pulling her close.

"And I still worry about gaining weight. Would you believe I stay on a diet all the time?"

"Would you believe I think you're beautiful just the way you are? And I think you could stand to put on a few pounds. I really mean it. You're just skin and bones. You could use a little more meat."

"Oh, I'm so afraid of losing control. But, hey, now it's your turn."

"Oh, Lynn, oh my God," Billy said nervously. "I guess I'm glad we're stoned 'cause it makes this easier. I've been really needing to tell you about this and ... oh God, I just don't know how."

"It's okay, Billy. I promise I won't laugh. And I promise I'll still love you, no matter what."

"Oh, you don't know."

"Well, maybe you shouldn't tell me."

"No, I better. I've been worrying about this and I keep feeling it getting in the way."

"Okay," Lynn said, "Take your time."

"Well, I guess the place to start is to admit that I've told you a lie, sort of. I mean when I said I was a virgin."

"That's okay. No big deal."

"But it's more than that. I mean technically it's true. Before we made love last week, I'd never had sex with a woman, but ... oh God, here goes ... but I had with another man."

"I don't think that's so unusual for boys, is it?" Lynn said, again surprising herself with her apparent sophistication. She wasn't shocked by Billy's news.

"But I wasn't exactly a boy. I mean, I was. But he wasn't. You know, I told you about my friend Jeff. Well, he wasn't just a friend. He was my, uh, lover for most of my last two years of high school."

"You mean he was a child molester, a — what's the word? — a 'pedophile'?" Lynn asked indignantly. "I mean, an 'older man'?"

"Oh no, he wasn't that much older. He was in his mid-twenties. And, Lynn, he was really a wonderful guy. He did so much for me. I mean, it wasn't like he was taking advantage of me or anything. I'm the one who went after him. I met him at this computer fair. And I kept going by his house and, I guess, really making passes at him — at least, that's what he told me later. I don't really remember what I was doing. I just know I was fascinated with him. And I knew I wanted him to touch me and hold me."

"Billy," Lynn said very seriously, "are you telling me you're gay?"

"No, honey, no. I don't think so. I mean, maybe I was then," Billy shrugged his shoulders resignedly. "But we didn't have sex that much. Jeff was more like an older brother. He helped me find myself. I was so mixed up and lonely then. I didn't have any friends and my dad was an alcoholic and . . . well, you know.

"Jeff insisted I go away to college, said it'd make me grow up. In the four years since then I've never felt that way about any other man and never even been attracted to any other man. I think my sexual attraction is for women, though I've been real shy. I mean, I just haven't known where I stood sexually. Until I met you."

"Oh, I'm so glad," Lynn said. "I wouldn't have wanted to lose you, you know. Well," she said with a sound of finality, "I guess we've both been a little screwed up in the head."

"But, Lynn, I've got to tell you some more. Maybe this is the really hard part." Billy chewed on the nail of the middle finger of his left hand and stared down at the sheets without saying a word.

"Go on, Billy. Say it, you'll feel better."

"Okay, I told you Jeff died. That was two years ago. Lynn, Jeff died of AIDS."

"Oh," Lynn answered. Then asked, "Why is that significant?"

"Why?" Billy exclaimed, frightening Lynn with the intensity. "It means I might have been exposed to the virus. We split when I went to college. I mean, he could have had it while we were still together."

"Oh my God," the meaning dawned on Lynn, "You mean you might have it and have passed it on to me?"

"No. Oh, no. I've been careful about that. The only way it's passed is through semen, and I've been very careful about using a rubber. Every time."

"That's why you were so reluctant last time, wasn't it?" Lynn realized.

"Exactly. Lynn, I really love you. I guess we still don't know each other all that well, but you're the best thing that's happened to me in a long time. I wouldn't do anything to hurt you."

"Why haven't you taken the test to find out?" Lynn asked.

"I have. I mean, I did this week. After we made love that first time, well, I knew I had to. I'd sort of decided before that to just be celibate the rest of my life. Or at least until enough time had passed so I'd know I wasn't going to get sick. I wasn't looking to fall in love. Not even with you. I really just wanted somebody to go to the movies with so I wouldn't feel so lonely. And, to be very honest, even though I don't think I wanted that, I kinda thought if I fell in love again, like I did with Jeff, it would be with another man. So you seemed real safe. But that wasn't the way it turned out.

"And so after we did it, I knew it was just wonderful and that this was what I was waiting for. Well, I went out the next day to take the blood test."

"And what did it show?" Lynn asked eagerly, but fearfully.

"It takes them almost three weeks to come back with an answer," Billy replied. "I'm still in limbo. I just don't know."

"Is there any more you need to tell me, Billy?" she asked hesitantly.

"No, I don't think so. But I just want to say I'm sorry for not telling you sooner. I'm so sorry I didn't get this test months, years ago. But I just couldn't bear finding out. I couldn't bear going to some clinic and telling them that I'd been screwed for two years by this, this homosexual." His voice sounded strained.

"Calm down, Billy." Then: "What was it like the other day?"

"Well, surprisingly, it was pretty easy. I mean, there was a gay guy doing the interview for the test and he put me at ease real quick and somehow I didn't mind talking about it at all. In fact, I showed him Jeff's picture. He complimented us both. In fact, he made me feel proud of that relationship."

"I don't want you to feel any other way," Lynn answered, again aware of how much more sophisticated and understanding she was than she'd thought. "But I want you to be even more proud of our relationship." She kissed him innocently on the lips.

"Oh, Lynn, I am. I am."

·Two·

November

1

"But I don't want to die."

"Well, *I* don't want to *live* like this," Greg Bens answered Pat Stratford's angry outburst.

"Pat, I don't think you have much choice about dying," said Chuck Thomas, another member of Jon Stiers's PWA support group.

"What about the PL-17 or Atripvir?" Pat said.

"PL-17 isn't a cure," Greg answered. "It just keeps the virus from growing."

"Well, what if a real cure is found?" Pat answered plaintively. "What if there's a new drug just around the corner that'll make this whole thing go away . . . and bring back the old days, like the way it was. I liked things like that," he whimpered.

"Pat, I know you're angry and hurt," Jon observed calmly. "But the fact is that there is no magical cure. Even if a treatment for the virus is found, it may not restore your immune system. And if an immune restorative is found, it may not reverse the organ damage that's already been done."

"And nothing's going to bring the old days back," Greg shouted.

"Keep your voice down," Jon instructed. "One of our agreements here has to be to respect each other's concerns."

"I'm sorry," Greg replied, chastened. "I didn't mean to belittle Pat's worries. I'm pretty upset myself today."

"Greg," Jon asked patiently, "I understand you've been in the PL-17 study for a couple of weeks now. Would you like to tell us about that?"

"Maybe that's why I'm upset. When I started that program, I thought I was going to get well right away. But I really haven't. Dr. Hawkins says he thinks my tests look better. He says I'm showing some improvement. But I still feel bad. I don't sleep well. And I've lost another three pounds."

"Are you afraid the PL-17 isn't doing anything?"

"Damn right. When I started this a couple of weeks ago, my lover promised he'd move back in as soon as I started getting better and stopped losing weight."

"So maybe the reason you're upset is because you're afraid your lover isn't coming back."

"Well, Jon," Greg answered snidely, "that's very insightful of you."

"Okay, okay," Jon answered.

"I was going to get into that study," Pat Stratford spoke up. "But I was given Atripvir a year ago and so they wouldn't take me. I thought the PL-17 was going to be the real cure. I guess I'm glad to hear it doesn't work so well. At least I don't have to feel like they kept me from getting the cure."

"Well, piss on you, buddy," Greg answered angrily. "It was gonna be my lifeline."

"Hey, how come everybody's so angry today?" said Luis Garza, a despondent young Hispanic who hadn't uttered a word so far today. "I come here for support, you guys, and instead you all just fight with each other."

"Luis has a point," Jon responded. "But we all need support in handling anger. One of the roughest things about facing this is that there's no appropriate object for anger. We end up just fighting with each other, when what we really want to do is get angry at the disease."

"Goddamn it, I want somebody to blame. I'm mad at the doctors who haven't got medicine to give me. And I'm mad at the people who aren't sick. And I'm mad about all the false hope I keep getting. And, fuck it, Jon, I'm mad at you for being so goddamn calm. My God, we're dying horrible deaths and you sit there calmly making psychological observations."

Jon started to answer Pat, though for a moment he was at a loss for words. Anything he said was bound to sound like just another calm psychological observation.

"And I'm so fucking mad at myself for staying alive. Why can't I just die and get it over with it? This is a living hell. I'd be better off dead."

"Excuse me for sounding calm and professional, Pat. I guess I understand how annoying that might be sometimes. And, you know, the choice to stay alive or to die is really up to you. I mean, you could decide to terminate treatment and you might die.

"Dying isn't the ultimate evil, you know, not nearly as bad as living a lousy life. Remember when we were kids? Most of us were saying we wanted to live full and fast and die young." Jon noticed a couple of the guys nodding agreement. "It's your own desire to live that keeps you trying. And I want to commend you for that desire to live."

"Well, I think maybe I'm just scared," Pat answered.

"Oh, fuck it, Jon. You know perfectly well we're not the ones making these decisions about treatment," Greg shouted irritably.

"I think the reason you're all so angry today," Luis interjected in a quiet and timid voice, "is 'cause of that headline in today's *Chronicle*."

"What headline?" Jon asked. "I haven't seen the paper."

Chuck broke in, "That damn Senator Wanamaker from Orange County gave a speech last night calling for all PWAs to be rounded up and moved out to one of those camps they built for the Japanese in World War II."

"He said the cost of keeping the perverts alive in hospitals is exceeding the tax revenues from all homosexuals combined," Greg Bens added. "He also called for a special surtax on homosexuals to fund the concentration camps he wants to set up."

"I can see why you all would be upset by that kind of story," Jon observed.

"Upset?" responded Pat, once more attacking Jon. "The goddamn Nazi asshole wants the death penalty for homosexual sex. He said it would save society money to just gas 'em while they're well, rather than have to keep 'em in hospitals after they get AIDS."

"Oh, come on," said Blum Blumgarten, who'd been sitting quietly just outside the circle of chairs. "This is America. We have rights as citizens."

"The Supreme Court ruled that homosexuals are not covered under the Constitutional guarantees of citizenship," Chuck Thomas pronounced solemnly.

"Whadda you mean?" Blum asked disbelieving.

"I mean that the Court ruled that it's okay to outlaw homosexual relations. That means no life, liberty, and pursuit of happiness for us."

"That's not entirely true..." Jon spoke up.

"The goddamn judges thought that they could stop AIDS by passing laws against homosexuals," Greg retorted.

"Well, the Supreme Court justices weren't passing laws themselves," Jon tried to sound soothing. "But, Greg, I think you're right that all along the government has had a rather seriously mistaken notion of what homosexuality is. Treating it as though it were a deliberated act, like deciding to rob a bank, entirely misses the point of how homosexuals experience the need for love and affection and sex."

"If they wanted to make laws to prohibit promiscuity, why not create gay marriages? Everybody knows the best way to stop somebody from having sex is to get them married." The whole group laughed at Greg's remark. Realizing the double meaning of what he'd said, Greg himself laughed, then added: "I wish to God Bobby had married me. Maybe he wouldn't have left me like that." Greg's eyes filled with tears.

"Look, everybody," Blum spoke up. "It's not so bad. None of you are in the hospital now. You're all alive. It's a beautiful day."

"Maybe for you," Pat answered his friend sullenly. "You don't have AIDS."

2

After three weeks with Liberty Bell Foundation, Lynn still didn't know much about her employers. She was enjoying the job, but often she felt in the dark about just what kind of a job she had. A couple of times she'd been asked to type material in which the words just didn't make any sense. She joked with one of the other typists that government agencies communicate in a foreign language. "Consultantese, we call it," the other typist laughed. But Lynn was sure this wasn't just consultant jargon, but was actually some kind of encrypted message. She realized that sounded a little paranoid, but the idea of secret information passing through her typewriter made an otherwise boring job seem exciting.

This afternoon Lynn was in the windowless little room off Emily Hodgsdon's office sorting the last of the adolescent sex questionnaires when she heard Mrs. Hodgsdon's voice.

"Well, George, how nice to see you."

"Thank you, Emily, I came in early today because I need to talk with Edward. This is very important."

"You should've called for an appointment, George. In fact, we were going to close the office early today. I have a doctor's appointment."

"You can go to your appointment, Emily. I came to talk with Edward." Lynn heard the stern reply.

"But, George, Edward was—"

"Goddamn it, Emily, I said I came to talk with Edward. This has nothing to do with your doctor's appointment. And I'm a partner in this firm. I don't need an appointment."

Lynn realized that this was the mysterious George Wilson whom Mr. Buchanan had spoken of as his partner but who never seemed to be in the office. She could hear Mrs. Hodgsdon loudly slamming the drawers of her desk. *Must be getting her things,* Lynn thought. She quietly slid back against the wall of the little room hoping Mrs. Hogsdon would have forgotten she was in there. This was exciting. Lynn wanted to hear more.

"I'm sorry, George," Mrs. Hodgsdon answered coldly. "Of course, you're right. I'll just be on my way then. I'm sure you know how to lock up."

"Emily, I lock up every night. You don't have to remind me."

Lynn heard the connecting door into Buchanan's office close. For a moment she thought she heard Buchanan's voice, then silence. A moment later she heard Mrs. Hodgsdon pull the door closed to the hallway. She suddenly felt very alone and a little frightened. Her excitement seemed to have been baseless: She couldn't hear anything anyway. Lynn just kept sorting through the questionnaires, putting them into several smaller piles.

About thirty questionnaires later, Lynn jumped as she heard the door open from Buchanan's office. She could barely hear Wilson's voice.

"But, Edward, I'm not finished."

"Look, George, I don't want to listen to you whine." Buchanan's voice boomed from inside Mrs. Hodgsdon's office. "When we started this we all knew we were dealing with some very weighty issues, very weighty issues indeed."

"But, Edward, I think we're wrong. We've let this go on far enough. People are getting hurt." Lynn again felt the rush of excitement. This all seemed to reek of secrecy and intrigue. At the same time, she felt afraid. *What if they find me back here? I'm not supposed to be listening. But I can't very well come out now, can I?*

"George, people get hurt all the time," Buchanan continued.

"That's the consequence of original sin. Don't you tell me about human suffering. I know whereof I speak."

"I know all about your experience of human suffering, Edward." Wilson's voice grew louder as he apparently walked out into the outer office. "I've seen enough of your souvenir collection." Wilson sounded exasperated. Then his tone of voice changed to one of obvious concern. "Seriously," he asked, "haven't you ever wondered if that obsession of yours somehow affects your mind? Could it be like pornography; you've always talked about how damaging pornography is. Maybe exposure to all that stuff of yours does something damaging, maybe weakening your reason. Don't you see?"

"Look, George, I'm not crazy. My studies of human nature have only strengthened my soul. You're the one who sounds weak. My obsession, as you call it, has convinced me we have to do something about the state of the world before it's too late, before we all end up in hell, suffering like that for all eternity. But that's not the point. That's not the point. Let's go over this again," Buchanan said, lapsing into a pedantic tone of voice. "Was President Truman wrong in dropping the atomic bombs in Japan?"

"I don't know anymore," Wilson whimpered. "That's a different issue. Don't pull this on me again. Don't you see you're causing suffering in the name of ending suffering?"

"Of course I see that. That's what I'm talking about. And the atom bomb is the perfect example. Now answer me. Was Truman wrong in dropping the bombs on Japan?"

Lynn couldn't hear George's reply.

"Has every president since Truman been wrong in developing nuclear weapons?"

"I don't know." George answered softly this time.

"Answer me, damn it. Answer me. Has the United States been wrong to develop nuclear weapons?"

"I told you I don't know."

"Of course you know. You were one of the experts who helped make those decisions."

Nuclear weapons, Lynn thought. *Wow! I didn't know the Foundation was involved with anything like that. Hey, this is really neat.*

"Well, okay," Wilson finally answered. "Yes, we were right in going ahead and building the weapons. If we hadn't, the Russians would have, and they'd have destroyed us."

"Are we facing that same threat of destruction today?"

"We're certainly facing destruction from the Russian missiles."

"And do we have to keep our defenses up?"

"Apparently both our defenses and our offenses."

"And will innocent civilians be hurt if we have to explode those bombs to protect ourselves and our country?"

"Yes. That's the nature of modern warfare."

"And aren't we facing a moral warfare within our own country?"

"That's enough, Edward. Don't badger me."

"Okay, George. Look, you said you have figures to prove your point. Do you, in fact, have projections on the targets versus collateral casualties?"

"That's the problem, Edward, that's the problem," George said, perhaps intentionally mocking Buchanan's rhetorical habit. He sounded annoyed and angry. "I've been trying to tell you."

"What's the problem? What *is* the problem — if it's not you, George?"

"Look, when I put the parameters you gave me into the program, it comes out with totally unrealistic proportions of targets to collaterals. In fact, Edward, if you look at the latest sets of projections I've run you can see that graphed over time the percentages of casualties among the target populations drops while the casualties among the collaterals starts to soar. You're going to kill off far too many collaterals and maybe never succeed at neutralizing the targets."

"I'm not stupid. I'm not stupid, George. I see what's happening. But how can the target populations avoid the, uh, weapon?"

"Well, there are several possible explanations: One, the weapon has been totally misguided from the first and doesn't behave the way we expected; two, the target populations don't behave the way we expected; three, the targets are protecting themselves against the weapon; four, they are developing natural resistance.

"And, besides," Wilson announced authoritatively, "the fallout from this whole plan is just having too much effect. We never counted on the political outcry. It's changed everything."

Lynn felt lost. Again, for all the sense it made they might just as well have been talking in a foreign language.

"I understand that that was beyond our projections," Buchanan said humbly.

"Yes sir, indeed."

"Well, we're expecting that last point to turn to our advantage. But okay, George, okay. I accept your report. I'll take this up with the Board as soon as we can schedule a meeting."

"I want to be there, Edward."

"Yes, of course," Buchanan assented. "Now let me change the focus of this discussion a bit. I understand that in this computer of yours you've got information about AIDS research projects."

Lynn's ears perked up. All of a sudden they were talking about something that vitally interested her.

"I want to know about those. And I want to know about the amounts of money Congress is allocating to research on anti-AIDS drugs. And do you have information about the effectiveness of any of these drugs?"

"Of course I have all that information. What do you want to do with it?"

"Besides just knowing for myself, I want to reformat the information and insert it into the teenage sex prevention report."

"You want to do what? I thought it was agreed from the very start that my projects were absolutely secret and that none of the information was going to be used any other way."

"Right. But the information I'm asking you about doesn't have anything to do with the actual project you're on. It's filler we need for other reports of the firm."

"It was still supposed to be my data alone."

"George, where do you think your salary comes from? Listen, I want printouts of that information on my desk when you leave here tonight." Lynn heard what must have been Buchanan opening the door out to the hall. "Now, good night," he said sternly.

Lynn was both more excited and more scared. She waited in the little back room till Buchanan closed the door to his office and Wilson had time to go down the hall. Then quickly she rushed to the door. The hall was empty. She dashed to the employees' lounge, then paused to breathe and to look at her watch. It was time to go home.

As jauntily and innocently as possible, Lynn got her belongings from her locker and then walked down to the big typing room to check her desk. As she did, she noticed a strange man — obviously George Wilson — sitting at the IBM-PC by the window. *Odd,* she thought, *he's smaller than he sounded . . . and just a little queer-looking with that thin little moustache he's got.* The word 'queer' suddenly sent a chill through her, and she thought about Billy.

3

By the end of the group meeting, Jon was exhausted. "Look, you guys," he announced, "before we go for today I want to remind you all not to get so negative. We're supposed to be supporting each other, remember?

"Here, I xeroxed some pages out of a book by a doctor named Larry Dossey. You can take these home and read them more carefully—"

"Is this about a new treatment?" Chuck asked.

"Well, it's about how your psychological feelings affect your health," Jon answered.

"Yeah, but I want something to get me well," Greg answered testily.

"Okay, okay. Well, how about reading this over and see what you think?" There was no reply. Jon continued. "The book is called *Beyond Illness: Discovering the Experience of Health.* This section describes a 65-year-old woman who was brought to the hospital by her son because she had severe abdominal pain that she'd been basically ignoring. It turned out to be cancer.

"What I want you guys to pay attention to is her attitude." Jon read, " 'Her attitude to the diagnostic tests and to the surgical procedure was unusual. There was none of the expected dread, nor did she want to get on with the studies. There was no despair in her attitude, nor was there any feisty aggressiveness that many cancer patients show. There was, instead, a kind of dispassionate perspective. She seemed to be someone — as strange as it may sound — who both had, and did not have, an illness. She was not brought down by the disease, nor did she seem oblivious to it. Somehow, it just "was." At no time did she give any hint that she saw it as either good or bad.'

"A little further he says, 'Her cancer had been widespread — from ovary to liver, spleen, peritoneum, and lymph nodes — and it was impossible to remove it all at the time of surgery. But she recovered from her operation without a hitch, and proved to be a magnificent "responder" to the chemotherapy drugs which she and her oncologist eventually chose.' "

"She was pretty sick," Blum spoke up. "But she didn't die?"

"Here," Jon said searching through the text a little further. " 'Martha is still alive as of this writing. She is not disease-free, for evidence of her tumor remains. But she is pain-free, and feeling energetic and vital. She still putters in her garden. And she still manifests her enigmatic, inscrutable attitude toward health and illness.' "

"And what caused that?" Chuck asked, sounding skeptical.

Jon continued reading, " 'I do not wish to say that her course following the diagnosis of cancer was profoundly influenced by her transcendent approach to the fact of illness, although I believe it to be so. I do not want to imply a causal link between her marvelous clinical course and her mental state, because I have no sure way to prove it. In fact, I do not even believe it is important in any ultimate sense whether she "did well" or "did poorly" following diagnosis — for she herself was beyond such concerns. She had begun to employ a way of viewing life and death that had nothing to do with the presence or absence of disease. She had gone beyond, I feel, the "conditionalities" of health and illness to some ground distal to both. This posture she adopted not out of resignation or a sense of giving up, but from a sure awareness of "how things are." '

"Look a little further down," Jon said continuing, " 'I emphatically believe that Martha did not arrive at her transcendent perspective by asking herself the question, "Now what is the psychological strategy I should adopt if I want to 'beat' my cancer?" In this case she would have arrived at some outlook that would have been strictly utilitarian, having a fixed goal in mind, that of effecting a cure of her disease. This was patently not her objective. Indeed, she did not have an objective. She was "merely" dwelling in the unconditioned "suchness" ... She had entered the domain of Highest Health, the realm of no-health, the health-beyond-health. The payoff? Not being healthier in any ordinary sense, but the certainty of living in the One, the "invisible," "inaudible," and "untouchable" state which medicine does not describe.' "

Jon realized his usually argumentative group had become very quiet and attentive. " 'There are, of course, many forms of cancer treatment which have emerged in recent years,' " he continued, " 'which rightly recognize the relationship between the psyche and the immune process. The handwriting is on the wall in medicine today: not only cancer, but all the major diseases of our day have intimate connections with the psyche. Attitude, emotion, and feelings enter in vital ways into the process of disease. We can say of the techniques which employ this new understanding in the treatment of disease that they are consistent with our best knowledge. But we can say, too, that they stop short.

" 'Persons who enter programs which seek to maximize the positive use of mental states in treating illness may indeed experience a better result than if ordinary, non-psychologically oriented forms of treatment are employed. Pain may be diminished, extent of disease may be attenuated, and longevity may be increased. A sense of "being in control" of the disease itself can be developed, a goal which should be applauded. But these results are not to be confused with the "ploy" of Martha G. in the above case, for the plain fact is that she did not have a ploy. She did not intentionally invoke a mental state of a particular type out of a desire to improve her physical status. Even though the disease proved to remit in a striking way, she would have been, I feel, relatively unmoved had it not responded. Her goals were beyond "remission," "response rate," and "cure." She was not trying to "become" anything, not attempting to "gain" something. Such concepts imply time; they are anchored in a durational, flowing past, present, and future. Martha was beyond durational time in her perspective. There was nothing to be gained, nothing to become. In the "isness" and "suchness" which she experienced, there was only the present moment.

"'Future forms of therapy that emphasize the potency of the mind in the origin and course of human illness will recognize this fact. They will utilize psychological interventions to more effectively and humanely treat illness, but with the added understanding that there is something yet more important for the patient to learn. They will rightly acknowledge a state of health that transcends the problem at hand or any illness that might develop in the future. They will proclaim that the highest use of the psyche in the course of human illness is not for cure, but for transcendence of the conditional events we call health and disease, birth and death.'"

"Wow," said Chuck, "do you really believe that?"

"But I want to be cured," answered Pat, "not just learn to put up with disease."

"I know," Jon answered softly. He realized these kinds of quasi-religious ideas were hard for people to comprehend. They all sounded so paradoxical. "Well, maybe you'll read this whole section I copied for you. We can talk about it next week."

4

Mark had the dining table set with white linen tablecloth, a tall vase full of pink roses, and rose-colored wax candles flickering atop silver candlesticks. The lights in the room were dimmed so that most of the illumination came through the bay window that opened onto the view of Twin Peaks.

"Why do I need a reason to celebrate?" Mark answered Jon's question as he let him in. "You're home. Isn't that enough of a reason?"

Jon laughed with him.

"Well, I'm sure glad to be home."

"Rough day?"

"Late afternoon, I had my PWA group. They were all on edge today. We ended up doing more fighting than therapy. Though maybe that's good therapy for them too."

"How about for you?"

"One of the things the guys were talking about today was just giving up and letting themselves die. I don't know how to answer that. I think if I had AIDS and were getting toward the advanced stage of the disease, well, I wouldn't want to keep trying. It seems like clutching after straws. You know, for some of these guys, even if there is some sort of treatment developed, it's really too late. Short of a miracle restorative, their bodies are just shot."

"I understand that's hard."

"What do you tell them? I feel like I have a responsibility to keep them hopeful — if only because when they're hopeful they are less depressed and emotionally suffering. But is the hope realistic?"

"Jon, I told you my parents were killed in a car wreck a couple of years ago. I mentioned that I had to make some decisions about life and death, but I never explained that. You wanna hear?" Mark took Jon's leather jacket, hung it on the rack in the little entry hall that led into the main room of his apartment, then motioned to Jon to sit down on the sofa. "Like a glass of wine?"

"Sure," Jon answered. "To both questions."

Mark pulled a bottle of wine out of the little refrigerator in the small kitchen that opened into the living room. He ritually held up the bottle for Jon to see the label, a kind of mock stained glass effect, and then pulled out the cork. "I opened it this afternoon when I finished work. I'm done with that job."

"Oh well, congratulations. We do have something to celebrate!"

"Finishing the job gave me time to cook," Mark said, handing Jon one of the crystal goblets from the table. "What we're celebrating is that we're together." He poured the wine.

As Mark was putting the bottle back in the refrigerator, Jon asked, "You were going to tell me about your parents' death?"

Coming back into the room and settling down in the chair across the glass coffee table from Jon, and leaning forward to wordlessly toast, Marked started in on his story. "My dad was killed instantly. They were driving on an icy freeway and, I guess, hit a frozen patch and skidded into the side of a tractor-trailer. The car went under the truck and tore the roof off the car. . ." Mark paused for a moment in a rush of emotion.

"I get the picture," Jon answered.

"The police called me immediately. Our house was right near

the hospital. I was waiting at the emergency room when they brought them in. They told me right away that Dad was dead. The ambulance driver said Mom was alive. They rushed her into a room and left me waiting outside.

"After about twenty minutes — during which time I prayed as hard as I could that she'd be okay — a doctor came out. He took me aside into one of the other rooms and explained that Mom's skull had been crushed, but that she was still alive. They had her hooked up to a respirator and were checking for the extent of brain damage.

"I asked if he thought she had any chance of pulling through. He said there's always a chance, though he couldn't promise anything. He took me in to see her, but there was really very little to see. Her head was all bandaged. I could see her eyes and nose, but that was about all. It could have been anybody.

"After a while they left me alone with her for a few minutes. I tried talking to her. You know how they say sometimes a person can hear even when they're in a coma..."

"I know," Jon whispered.

"Well, I asked her what I should do, you know, if there were serious brain damage." His voice faltered, "And after a little bit, I sort of heard her answer me — I mean in my own head, of course."

Jon nodded.

"And she seemed to say to me, 'If I can't really be with you, Mark, don't keep me away from Jim.' And I understood what she meant.

"I was going to stay at the hospital all night, but one of the nurses urged me to go home to get some sleep. She said she was sure the few hours wouldn't make any difference. She said, 'The machines are keeping your mother alive. Nothing can happen to her while we've got her hooked up.' And I went home and cried for a while and thought about what that nurse had said and then thought about what I think my mother would have said if she could have talked. And I knew I didn't want to keep her soul imprisoned if there weren't any real hope.

"The next morning our family doctor started telling me about advances in neurosurgery. He said he thought there might be a chance of correcting the damage that was done to Mom's brain. He talked all about this study that was going on at the University of Minnesota Medical School.

"And so later when the resident at the hospital asked me what I wanted done, I told him all about the research in Minneapolis. I even got him to call the Medical School to ask about it. He came back and said that there was a study going on with restoring animal brains that had suffered trauma, but that it would be at least a year before they'd be accepting human subjects. He did say that they were interested in my mom's case. He said that she certainly could be kept on the respirator, maybe indefinitely. He asked if I remembered Karen Ann Quinlan...

"I walked around for a while, remembering what I'd thought Mom had said to me. I kept thinking about how all alone I was going to be. There was just my grandmother left. And she was already getting kind of senile — 'dotty' my mother always called it. And, you know, I thought about the family money.

"Well, I felt real guilty. I knew there was lots of money to keep Mom alive artificially for years, but that would use up all the money — maybe for nothing.

"Anyway, after walking around in the snow a while, I made the decision to tell them to turn off the respirator and let her go be with Dad. I started back to the hospital to tell them. When I walked in the door, this teenage candy-striper who'd been around during the morning came running up to me. 'Dr. So-and-so's been looking for you all day, hurry up,' she shouted at me.

"Well, I got excited and thought maybe Mom had come out of the coma. So I ran up to the ward following the girl. The resident was very grave. He asked me to step into a private office. I realized I'd got my hopes up for nothing. Then he said that the hospital in Minneapolis had called back. They were looking for a heart for a transplant and my Mom fit the requirements perfectly.

"I started crying. But I told him that that was fine. That that was what they should do. And not to keep her on the machines."

Jon's eyes were tearing in sympathy with Mark's.

"Oh, it was like this wonderful sign that I'd made the right decision. I mean, I knew I had to tell them not to keep her alive waiting for some experimental technique that might never materialize. But there hadn't seemed any way to know that was the right decision. But to keep somebody else alive..." Mark was sobbing.

Jon reached out to comfort him.

"Oh, I'm not upset," he said through his tears. "I think I've just gotten excited all over again about how wonderful that was." He started laughing even as the tears rolled down his cheeks.

"That's a beautiful story," Jon answered.

Mark wiped his face with his hands, looking embarrassed about the display of emotions. He jumped up out of his chair and announced, "C'mon, let's eat. My dinner's gonna be all dried out if we don't stop this yakking."

Jon stood up and grabbed Mark as he headed toward the kitchen. They hugged tight.

5

After leaving the Liberty Bell Foundation, Lynn remembered she and Lee Ann were supposed to go furniture shopping tonight. She wasn't sure she was up to that. But she wasn't sure she wanted to do anything else either.

Riding home on the bus, Lynn pondered the strange conversation she'd overheard between George Wilson and Edward Buchanan. She wondered what was in that "collection" of Buchanan's Wilson seemed worried about; she was especially intrigued by the remarks about studies of anti-AIDS drugs. *What if the firm is doing research on AIDS? Maybe I can find a cure for Billy.*

That thought sent her into an emotional tailspin. She'd been consciously avoiding thinking about this subject all day. Now, on the bus of all places, it suddenly surfaced with a rush of tears.

It seems like this is the guy I've been waiting for all my life, but now I'm scared to make love with him. He keeps showing me all these articles about how safe "safe sex" is and how this damn AIDS virus doesn't get passed on by kissing. But I don't know whether to believe this stuff. I'm too young to get this disease . . . and what if Billy gets sick and dies on me . . . and what about a family? Even if the virus can't be transmitted to me so long as we use a rubber, how am I ever gonna have a baby?

Tears poured down Lynn's cheeks as she huddled against the window, hoping nobody would notice her. She felt so embarrassed. It'd been almost three weeks ago that Billy acknowledged to her his possible exposure to the AIDS virus. At first she was shocked. Then she calmly denied the problem. For one thing, she didn't want to know about Jeff and that sordid-sounding period in Billy's past. She wasn't sure the information would have meant anything to her anyway. In spite of all the media coverage, she just didn't know much about AIDS — and hadn't wanted to. At least up till now.

Besides, I can just look at Billy, she told herself, *and see that he's healthy. He's strong. He's handsome. He's clean. He's so innocent and kind. People like that don't get these awful diseases. But . . .*

She went along with Billy's insistence on using condoms for sex. She did not want to get pregnant right now. And she was afraid of going to a doctor to get on the pill. She kept remembering the terrible things her mother had said about what birth control pills can do to a woman's body. And her mother was a nurse, after all.

Mama doesn't seemed scared of AIDS. I mean, she's doing nursing care for an AIDS victim, Lynn reminded herself. *Of course she's not sleeping with him . . .*

Last night all of Lynn's denial had broken down. Billy came over to her apartment late in the evening to report on his return visit to the Health Department Clinic. His test for the HIV antibody had come out positive.

"They are going to run a backup test," Billy told her. "And there's a new test they said that's available from private labs now that tests for the actual presence of the virus. They gave me names of doctors. I'll make an appointment tomorrow."

Last night she'd felt so strange. She hated the news. She kept hoping it would be wrong. At first she was sure they'd made a mistake. But Billy kept trying to calm her down and make her accept that it was true. She wanted to hold him and nurture him and tell him everything was going to be okay. And she wanted him to hold her in his strong arms and be the perfect lover she'd dreamed of.

But then she started worrying about herself. "You mean I could have it now?" she shouted at him.

"No, Lynn. We've been careful. You haven't been exposed."

She didn't know how to feel. When he hugged her she felt all mixed up inside. His chest felt so strong, his body so warm. But she tensed up realizing she was afraid of him now. It was like he was dirty or something.

He took her out for a pizza at Louie's. *Maybe he wants to stir up romantic feelings*, she thought lovingly. *Isn't he wonderful!* Then later, after a first glass of wine and she'd begun to mellow a little, she experienced a rush of paranoia. *What if he's trying to get me drunk so he can take me home and fuck me and contaminate me with this horrible disease! Maybe he's trying to get even by giving it to other people! What if he's been fucking around all over behind my back! Don't they say the homosexuals are spreading this virus on purpose!*

She tried to calm herself. She let Billy take her hand on the tabletop. And she felt his warmth and affection wash over her, stilling some of those anxieties. *That's all just crazy thinking*, she told herself.

After getting some food in her stomach — they devoured a large pan pizza with everything (except anchovies) — and a second glass of wine, she felt much better. *Billy isn't going to hurt me. I know he loves me. I really do. And I love him . . .*

When they got home, she let him hold her and kiss her. She

even participated in their undressing and falling into bed. But she wouldn't let him get fully aroused. "Not tonight," she said. "I'm afraid I'll just get crazy and ruin things."

℘

He was so understanding, she thought this afternoon as she was bounced around in the crowded bus. She just hated getting emotional in public like this. She was afraid people were staring at her. She was afraid they knew something was wrong. She was afraid they might somehow see that she'd gotten too close to this virus. *Maybe there's AIDS all over my clothes*, she worried irrationally.

6

Several hours after his aborted confrontation with Edward Buchanan, George Wilson was ready to go home. He was frustrated and tired. He was still smarting from Buchanan's reaction to his growing moral qualms about the project he was working on. And he didn't like the idea that Buchanan thought he could change the terms of their agreements so easily.

George's PC had fouled on him several times tonight. *Even it doesn't like giving away classified information*, he told himself. And the Xerox machine got away from him and made five copies of every page of the report he prepared for Buchanan. Even the paper shredding machine clogged up on him. There was so much paper in the bin that it wouldn't take any more.

I don't care, George said to himself. *If Buchanan doesn't think this stuff is classified anymore, then neither do I. And I'll be damned if they think I'm going to play garbage man for them. They have given me enough shit already.*

7

Billy De Palma wandered nervously around his apartment. *Officially*, he said to himself, *I'm working on my computer.* But every time he sat down at the keyboard, he'd find himself so restless that after a moment or two he'd get up to fix himself something to eat or drink or go to bathroom or something...

He was still shaken from the news yesterday that his HIV antibody test was positive, even though he'd honestly expected just that result. He repeated to himself what the counselor at the Health Department Clinic had told him: most of those who are positive for the antibody to the virus associated with AIDS, so far at least, have not developed any significant health problems whatsoever. It was partly the indefiniteness that was bothering him, and partly the ominous sound of the words "so far."

🎵

"The medical fact is," the counselor stated clearly and truthfully, "we just don't know what will happen in the future. This virus has not been around long enough for a definite profile of its natural history to appear. We still do not understand what causes the virus to begin proliferating. It apparently can remain dormant for years, probably throughout an entire lifetime. It may be that something has to happen to trigger it to begin growing. And it may be that some people simply have a natural resistance to it. Reseachers are looking into how that might work.

"We do know," she'd continued, "that the virus begins to replicate itself in an immune system that has been activated. That is, the AIDS-related virus only starts growing when your body is fighting off some other infection, or perhaps a re-exposure to HIV, or when your immunity gets stimulated by the absorption of semen into your bloodstream."

"What does that mean?" Billy asked.

"Well, it means three things: avoid re-exposure to HIV, avoid getting sick, and avoid taking semen into your body — especially rectally where it can be absorbed into the blood. Do you understand?"

"Yes. But telling me to avoid getting sick is pretty vague advice."

"Well, that's true. There are some diseases we can help you with. I'm going to refer you for a tuberculin test, for instance, so we can see if by chance you're incubating the TB germ. Some ten million Americans are infected without knowing it. And we're especially urging people to be careful about sexual exposures. Intercourse with a variety of partners can expose you to a lot of viruses like mononucleosis, hepatitis, CMV, and herpes, as well as re-exposing you to HIV."

"Well, I've got a steady relationship going now."

"Good for you. That's a real step in preventing the spread of this virus and in protecting your own health. You know, you must be careful that you and your partner not keep reinfecting one another. Has he been tested?"

"She," Billy answered, calmly he hoped, but, he knew, defensively.

"Oh, sorry." The counselor appeared flustered and, for a moment, looked down at the papers she had on her desk. "Excuse me, let me make sure I've got the right material here." (Billy's heart suddenly started pounding. Maybe they'd made a mistake and he really wasn't positive after all.) "You gave us the name 'Rudolf Valentino'?"

"Well, the first counselor I spoke to suggested that name," he acknowledged, crestfallen. *No mistake.* "I thought it was a little silly myself. But, yeah, I guess you got the right person."

"And you're in a heterosexual relationship?"

"Yes, that's right." Billy realized he'd acknowledged homosexual exposure previously. He must have confused the counselor.

"I see. You know, that adds a new concern. If you pass the virus on to your partner and she were to become pregnant, the chances are pretty high your baby would be born with the virus."

"I know that," Billy answered, a little angry that the counselor seemed to be giving him so little credit for understanding about the illness and suddenly embarrassed about the whole thing. For a moment he'd wondered if he shouldn't just end the relationship with Lynn now.

◣

He was still thinking that same thing this evening. And he was worried that she'd already made that decision. Here it was nearly ten p.m. and she still wasn't here. He'd talked with her on the phone just before she left work. She'd said she and Lee Ann were going to go look for a sofa for their apartment. She'd promised to come by when they were done. What if she didn't show up at all?

Billy began to wonder if this whole thing with Lynn were some terrible mistake. Maybe, now anyway, he really was doomed to stay in the gay world. *But I've never thought of myself as a homosexual,* he said to himself. *I mean I knew that relationship with Jeff Conant was homosexual and all, but that was something special and unique — just with Jeff. . .*

Billy threw himself down on his bed and let his fear and anxiety turn into tears. He cried for Jeff, for what was wonderful and for what was over — *a long time ago,* he thought. And he cried for Jeff's death, and for his guilt at never having gone to see him when he was sick. And he cried for fear that now the straight world would never accept him back in, that he'd always be tainted, that only the gay world would accept him, and that he didn't want into that world anymore. That had all ended when he said goodbye to Jeff.

He thought about Jeff and he thought about Lynn. *How different those two relationships are! They aren't opposites. They aren't in competi-*

tion with each other. Loving Jeff doesn't mean I can't love Lynn now. It's so different with her. What I feel is so different. Billy felt wrenching sobs pouring up through him.

The doorbell rang.

Billy jumped up and hurriedly wiped his eyes on a t-shirt he'd left lying across the back of the chair by his bed. Getting to the door, he tossed the t-shirt into a pile of clothes on the floor of the front closet. He peeked through the little magnifying tube in the middle of the door. There was Lynn outside, looking all distorted and swollen up in the lens like a blow-fish. Billy unlatched the door.

"Oh, you won't believe the wonderful deal we got on this sofa," Lynn breezed in. "And it is just *so* beautiful. All covered with tiny flowers and . . . Oh, Billy, you've been crying," she said as she turned back to give him a hug.

"Yeah," he answered, his eyes downcast.

"What's wrong?" she asked with obvious alarm in her voice.

"I guess I was afraid you weren't coming. . ."

"Oh, Billy," her eyes teared. "So was I. I mean, I thought about it. But, well," she proclaimed, "I'm here. That's what matters."

"Oh, I'm so glad." Billy hugged her tight.

After an extended moment, she said, "I hate to sound callous. And I'm not." She giggled. "But can I have something to eat? I'm just famished. Lee Ann is on a diet and wouldn't allow me to eat anything in her presence. And I've been looking forward to eating something the whole way over here on the bus."

Billy laughed. "Sure. I've got lunch meat, frozen dinners I can put in the microwave. Wanna see?" He was glad for the diversion. He realized he could use some food too. Maybe he'd become so emotional because he hadn't eaten anything either.

🐾

While two *Nouvelle Cuisine* dinners were heating in the little oven built into the cabinets in Billy's kitchen, Lynn turned to him and said, "I love you."

"I love you too, Lynn."

"And so . . . what are we gonna do?"

"Can we just go on like this? At least for a while? I mean, maybe there'll be some way to kill this virus in a few years."

"Do you know if you actually have the virus?" Lynn asked rationally.

"Not yet. I guess that's another chance we've got. It may be that I'm positive for the antibody but not for the virus. Wouldn't that be good news!"

"Oh, yes."

"I've been afraid to get my hopes up too much about that."

"Yeah."

"But I did call the doctor today and made an appointment to come in right after work tomorrow to get the test done. The nurse said it would only take a day."

"Well, that's better than three weeks. Anything else?"

"Yeah. I called the AIDS Project D.C. and found out they have a seropositive support group that meets on Monday nights. I got the address. I'm gonna go next week."

"That sounds good, Billy. The more we can learn the better off we are." Lynn pulled the plates out of the oven and carried them over to the little table in the living room that served as storage area for Billy as well as dining table. "Can you clear off some of that stuff?" She headed back into the kitchen to get silver.

"By the way," she said as she came out, her hands filled with utensils, paper napkins, and glasses, "I heard something interesting at work today. Mr. Buchanan asked his partner, this Mr. Wilson who seems to work only at night, to give him a list showing the effectiveness of anti-AIDS drugs.

"I wonder if that means the firm is doing research on cures for AIDS. I think most of what they do is about teenagers and sex. And then there's some, apparently real secret, stuff about nuclear weapons. I typed a memo about that today. The memo was all in so much code I couldn't make any sense of it at all. But if they're so involved with teenage sex, they must be interested in ways of preventing, or curing, AIDS."

"Can you find out?"

"As I was leaving I asked Lisa, the other typist, if she knew about any AIDS research. She didn't. But, like me, she thought it was the kind of stuff we do. She suggested I ask Mrs. Hodgsdon. But I'm afraid of that old lady. I think she might be offended if I mentioned these kinda words."

"Even if the firm is working on it?"

"Oh, especially if the firm is working on it. Everything's so hush-hush around that place. Mr. Wilson was real upset that Buchanan wanted to use his data in some other report. I don't think it's because anything is really so secret. But just that the big-wigs have all worked at the Pentagon, and they like to treat things as though it's all classified and top-secret. You'd think the location of the bathrooms around there was classified," Lynn joked.

"Strange bunch of people you work for." Billy felt a little worried about Lynn.

"Well, Billy, I was sort of thinking. If they do have some secret information about AIDS, maybe they know about ways to cure it."

"Oh, anything like that would have been announced in the news," Billy countered.

"Well, what if this were some kind of new drug or something that they didn't want to get everybody excited about yet. You remember a few years ago those French doctors announced a cure, then got laughed at when it turned out not to work. Well, Liberty Bell's always doing audits of one research project or another. Maybe they'd know about new drugs."

"Maybe."

"So, what I was thinking is that, well, it sure would be nice if we could clear up this virus in you. And, uh, you know a lot about computers and all that. Maybe you could, uh, sneak a look into the computer files of the Liberty Bell Foundation."

8

After their romantic candlelight dinner, Jon suggested to Mark that they run over to catch a lecture at the C.G. Jung Institute.

"A friend of mine is in charge of their public programs," Jon explained as he and Mark were finishing up the dishes. "She's been running a series of monthly lectures this year to commemorate the fortieth anniversary of publication of Joseph Campbell's marvelous book *The Hero With a Thousand Faces*. Campbell was a major influence on me. I met him — through my friend at the Jung Institute — back in the seventies when he was real big on the California lecture circuit. I've attended most of the talks in the series. And tonight's was one I really wanted to hear. The subject's going to be 'The Spirituality of the Suffering Bodhisattva in the Mahayana Tradition.'"

Mark giggled. "I don't think I understood half the words in the title. But if you want to go, I'll be happy to keep you company."

"You know, this may be about some of the same ideas we were talking about earlier. The big issue in Buddhism is the meaning of suffering." Seeing that all the dishes were dried, Jon hung up the towel he'd been using.

"I'll try to understand it. If it's important to you, I'd like it to be important to me. And, I guess, suffering *is* the big issue." Mark rinsed the sink. "Can we take my bike? It'll be faster and it's a beautiful night." At Jon's nod of affirmation, Mark pulled his leather motorcycle jacket from the coat rack. "Now what was the word you used after suffering?"

" 'Bodhisattva.' You ready for a lecture before the lecture?"

"Sure, but let's keep moving. It's almost eight now."

🎇

"Early Buddhism was all about getting out of the cycle of suffering by renouncing the world and sitting in meditation being detached and monkish," Jon explained as Mark pulled his little Kawasaki scooter out of the narrow passageway alongside the house. The night was cold, but brisk and clear: a nice night for a ride on the little motorbike.

"Later on, another tradition developed, called Mahayana, which was much less other-worldly. It wasn't restricted to the monks and it wasn't world-renouncing. In fact, it was pretty incarnational, sort of like Christianity."

"Hop on," Mark said. "But keep talking. I can drive and still listen."

"Okay. Well, the central figure of Mahayana is this character called a 'Bodhisattva.' His name was Avalokitesvara."

"That's a mouthful," Mark shouted over his shoulder as he revved the motor and started down the hill toward Castro Street. "Tell me where we're going."

"Oh, near Gough and California. Turn left here and then stay on Divisadero. I'll show you when to turn."

"Go on about Avalo-be-walla-walla."

"Avalokitesvara," Jon laughingly corrected. "The bodhisattva is sort of a parallel to Jesus Christ. The two myths come from about the same period in history. The Buddhist guy, Alavo-be-walla-walla..."

"See, I gotcha," Mark shouted as he turned left onto Castro and the bike labored to get up the hill.

"...Avalokitesvara felt such compassion for the sufferings of the world that he vowed to renounce his own entry into nirvana — you know, the total escape from suffering — until all other beings could follow. It was like giving up his own salvation for the sake of others.

"But by this vow Avalokitesvara virtually became a god. So it seems like compassion transforms the experience of suffering so that suffering isn't the same anymore. Through it you can enter into a totally different consciousness. The Mahayana Buddhist philosopher Nagarjuna said: 'Between samsara — that is, the everyday world of change and suffering — and nirvana there is not the least ascertainable bit of difference.' I think that sort of means you escape from suffering by accepting it, 'going with the flow' in the old sixties idiom.

"A variation on the myth is that the bodhisattva replaced all the other reincarnating beings, so that Avalokitesvara is the only being left. I mean, then, all of us are manifestations of that One Enlightened Consciousness, pretending we don't know who we are in order to fulfill that vow of compassion. That's like the Christian notion that we're all the Mystical Body of Christ and we should recognize Jesus in everybody else and treat everyone accordingly.

"Now you're gonna turn right on California Street."

🐾

After paying the donation at the entrance, Jon led Mark into the Jung Institute's big meeting room. The talk had already begun. Jon noticed his friend Barbara in the front corner, apparently counting up the attendance in the well-packed room. As Jon pointed her out to Mark, she recognized him and waved.

There were a couple of folding chairs leaning against the back wall which Mark opened up. As they sat, the speaker was saying, "...story in the *Panchatantra* which Campbell associates with the story of the suffering savior in Buddhism, Christianity, and the Grail legends.

"Joe Campbell is a great story teller," he said as a kind of aside, "and so in his honor, I'm embellishing the story a little beyond the text which, by the way, appears in Volume Four of *The Masks of God*.

"Four friends, stricken with poverty and seeking to get rich, meet a magician named Bhairavananda, i.e., "Terror-Joy," who gives them each a magic quill and instructs them to proceed north until the quill drops. There they will find treasure, he promises.

"They set out together, each with quill in hand. After a short journey, one quill suddenly drops out of its bearer's hand — working sort of like a dowsing rod — and sticks in the earth. The four men dig and find a rich vein of copper just under the topsoil. "Why go further?" says the man whose quill dropped. "Surely there is enough ore here for all of us and our wives and families to be comfortable the rest of our lives." But the other three leave him with the copper and go in search of more treasures.

"After a longer interval, another quill drops. Again they dig and find silver several feet beneath the surface. "Ah," says the new owner of a silver mine, "stay with me and the three of us shall be rich men indeed." But the other two depart.

"A yet longer interval passes and after a more strenuous journey, the third quill drops. The two men dig and, as expected, after much effort come upon a deposit of rich, purest gold. "We can be kings, the two of us; stay with me," says the one. But the other looks at the quill still in his hand and thinks to himself that the next mine must hold diamonds or emeralds or rubies large as hens' eggs: *I must go on.*

"And so the last seeker, the one whom incarnations hence would become the Buddha, sets out on the final leg of his journey. For many weeks he walks, through forests, over mountains, and finally into a vast desert. He begins to despair, thinking his avarice will be the destruction of him, thinking that he should have remained behind, satisfied with the copper or silver or gold. But the vision of precious gems sparkles before him and he walks on doggedly.

"After many days in the desert, his food and water all gone, his belongings strewn behind him as he lightened his load with each step, he was praying that the quill would drop, drop to show him a well of clear, cold water. For, by now, no treasure could be greater.

"Suddenly he looks up from the endless sand and rock over which he'd been plodding and beholds a strange sight. Before him in the desert on a whirling platform like the world-disk stands a man, arms outstretched as though embracing the whole world; and about his head spins a crown of bright shining razors that slice deep into his forehead. All down his body flow streams of blood."

The lecturer paused, looked out at his audience, and then in a dramatic stage whisper, said, "The quill drops.

"'What does this mean? Why is this wheel on your head?' asks the treasure-seeker. And immediately he finds himself beneath the blades of the spinning wheel.

"'Thank you,' says the other man who now stands freed. 'I have been waiting for countless eons for someone to come and ask what is the meaning of all this suffering, as you shall now wait, free of hunger and thirst, until someone else comes along to ask such a question.' And he departed."

The lecturer paused again and then commented familiarly, "Well, that's quite a story, isn't it?

"Now the purely worldly explanation is that the wheel of suffering was a device to guard the great treasure. But Campbell explains that originally this tale really was not about getting rich but about pursuing the path to Buddhahood. The implication then is certainly that 'the greatest treasure of all' is the full weight of the world's suffering. Perhaps this is because suffering forces us to change our attitudes and because it can teach us compassion. As we feel empathy with other beings we begin to see that ego-separation is an illusion and we're really all one. Campbell cites Viktor Frankl's experience of the Nazi concentration camp as a modern version of that same path to Enlightenment through suffering.

"Let us look at the origins of the bodhisattva myth to see..."

Mark tugged at Jon's sleeve. He mouthed the word "AIDS," and smiled knowingly.

Jon felt a shiver of awe, both at the young man's perspicacity and at the implication of meaning Mark recognized.

9

"Blum, don't you think there's anything you can do to get me into that PL-17 program?"

"Pat, we've been over this several times already. Jon has looked into Hawkins' program and another one at UCSF and another one in Berkeley. Your case just doesn't fit the research requirements."

"Well, how about getting it from Mexico?"

"You've asked about that before too. PL-17 isn't available in Mexico. It's a research drug here in the U.S. And that's all."

"Then you're just gonna let me die." Pat Stratford pitifully pulled the covers on his bed up to his neck. "I'm cold," he added.

"There's nothing we can do. It's not like it's my fault, damn it."

"You're right, Blum." Pat answered, feeling appropriately scolded. "Maybe I *should* just die."

"Well, you heard what Jon said this afternoon. You could stop taking the medication. You might die. On the other hand, you know, you might get better. The medication sure isn't making you feel any better, is it?"

"I don't know. I think it's keeping me alive. But it also makes me nauseous and dizzy. And I think it's part of why I can't sleep. I saw all these terrible side-effects listed in the P.D.R. up in the doctor's office. You know I don't like taking drugs."

"You mean medicines?" Blum said tongue-in-cheek.

"Oh God, Blum, I wish I were in a state for some good old drugs. At least some grass. I miss the ol' days."

"Yeah, but with your lungs in such bad shape, smoking grass wouldn't be good for you."

"Maybe not for my lungs, but it sure would be for my head. But I can't afford it."

"Neither can I," answered Blum despondently. "Marijuana's

getting real scarce. Government crackdown and all. Not much left now but the hard stuff, more money in it. And, of course, alcohol — the worst drug of all."

"Just goes to show you how reformers end up causing worse problems than they set out to cure."

"This country never learned how to use drugs."

"I guess we've got to take some of the blame for that," Pat answered with surprising rationality. "I mean, I think we sure overdid it. I bet that's a big part of why I got sick."

"Well, if you'd learned the right way to use drugs. . ."

"Yeah, maybe."

"I sure don't think all these medical drugs you're taking are that much better for you."

"Maybe Jon's right. I mean about stopping the medication altogether. But Blum, I'm scared of dying. A lot of the time I think being dead could not possibly be any worse than what I am now. I read that stuff Jon gave us about being in the suchness of life and all that shit. I just don't know. I grew up believing in heaven and hell. And it's scary."

"Don't you look forward to heaven then?"

"I'm not sure I think heaven makes any sense. Who'd want to be an angel floating around playing a harp? Besides, it's hell that's worrying me."

"You'd reject belief in heaven, but keep it about hell?" Blum asked incredulously.

"Isn't that what Jerry Falwell and his friends are always saying? I mean I must hear several times a week on the TV that I'm going to go to hell for getting this disease — and, of course, for being queer."

"You're listening to the wrong preachers, honey," Blum chided affectionately. "Jesus didn't say things like that. Jesus talked about being good and kind. And, Pat, I mean this real serious — at least before you got sick, you were a hell of a nice guy—"

"See!" Pat interrupted. "Even you've got me going to hell!"

"Bad choice of words. Funny, how we use words. But you know perfectly well what I meant. You were generous. You were sweet. Everybody liked you."

"Then how come God gave me the plague?"

"God didn't give you the plague. You got sick on account of a virus that mutated over in Africa. And that's all. If there is a God — I mean like the Christians say who loves everybody and even worries about the sparrows flying around — I bet the first thing

He'll do when you show up at the Pearly Gates is apologize."

"For what?" Pat asked.

"For not doing something about AIDS."

"You think even God can't do anything about AIDS? How come I'm waiting for the doctors?" Pat smiled.

"Well, if He could, you'd think He would have. And maybe you're right about the doctors. They aren't doing much better."

"Blum, I know we're joking about this now . . ."

". . . but I am sort of serious too."

"Yeah, I know. But I mean, so maybe you're right. Maybe I oughta leave this up to God, instead of taking all those meds." He pointed at the rows of amber plastic medicine bottles lined up on the top of his bureau.

"You know, Pat, maybe this is God's way of telling you He's ready for you to come home. That you served your purpose. Did what He wanted you to do. Maybe you ought to be running right back there . . . 'through dem Pearly Gates.'" Blum mimicked a Black Baptist accent.

Pat laughed. Then, suddenly, he twisted himself up in a knot, writhing in pain. "Oh, oh, my lung's burning. Blum, get me one of those pain pills, will you?"

"You sure?" Blum asked tentatively.

"Of course, I'm sure," Pat grunted through clenched teeth. "This hurts."

10

Lynn arrived early for work. She stood in the hall by the elevator for Emily Hodgsdon to get there to open up.

"Let me in, dear. I'll turn off the alarm," Mrs. Hodgsdon said as she motioned for Lynn to step away from the door. "You know, this thing picks up any kind of motion in the room. I've only got about a minute to turn it off. Now don't you get in my way or we'll both have to answer to the police."

"Yes, Mrs. Hodgsdon." Lynn wondered when she'd get to feel comfortable calling her Emily. She'd been at this job almost a month now. *Maybe never.*

"On the way out it gives you about seven minutes to leave the office after you punch in the code. Edward had it delayed on purpose because he walks kind of slow and they put that alarm box so far down the hall," Hodgsdon was saying as she unlocked the door.

"But on the way in — for me — it only allows a few seconds. I should probably talk to Edward about that. You know, dear, it almost gives me a fright every morning."

"I'll run in and enter the code for you," Lynn offered energetically.

"Oh, now, that's sweet of you, dear. But I can't give away the code, you know. Not that we don't trust you, of course—"

"Of course," Lynn replied obediently while the older woman swiftly padded down the corridor of the suite to the alarm keypad.

"Come in, come in. Time for work." Mrs. Hodgsdon always reminded Lynn of a schoolteacher.

ॐ

Lynn put her coat and purse in her locker. She carefully closed the locker and then, out of force of habit, pulled on the handle. It swung open. She tried again. *Something's wrong with the latch. That's okay, I trust everybody around here, even if they don't trust me*, she thought innocently. *But what's wrong with this thing?*

The latch closed, but the combination-operated locking mechanism wasn't catching.

Lynn looked in at the lock on the inside and then saw that her scarf had gotten caught on the latching device and was holding back a little spring from closing. *Well, that's handy to know*, she registered. *I guess I could save myself some time if I just twisted that spring back out of the way; I wouldn't have to keep doing the combination.*

For now, she simply tugged at the scarf and freed the spring mechanism so that it properly secured the locker.

She hurried down the hall to her desk. Seeing there was nothing in her IN box yet, she turned to another chore she'd taken on: straightening up the printer room. Each morning she'd throw away yesterday's messed up xeroxes, perforation strips from the printers, and nests of shredded papers from the secrecy machine (as she thought of the shredding device).

Today her eyes wandered over the piles of paper she was routinely dumping. She was surprised. One of the pages was titled "Anti-viral Drugs in Combat with AIDS Virus" and subtitled "Efficacy Comparisons."

That's what Buchanan and Wilson had been talking about last night. Lynn looked at the list of drugs and drug companies and research projects. *Oh dear*, she thought, *I can't memorize all this. It's practically Greek. I wonder if it would mean anything to Billy.*

One set of statistics caught her eye: a long list of what she assumed were drugs, with names like HP-25, ribavirin, interferon (she recognized that one from the news), AZT (Retrovir), ST,

D-penicillamine, Atripvir, and others. At the bottom was something called "Vir. Anti." Across the columns in the rows following that last name were 100%, 100%, 100%, 100%. In the columns above, the figures were always much lower: 47%, 16%, 76%, 53%. What was this?

A thrill ran through her. *Whatever this Vir. Anti. is, it looks like this says it's a cure for the virus!*

A moment later the thought struck her that Vir. Anti. was just some sort of totals row or experimental control figure — not anything like the new breakthrough she was hoping for. She noticed there were several copies of this page lying around. *Obviously this isn't something anybody had thought top-secret,* Lynn told herself. *I know it's sort of against the rules, but what the hell. I'll take one of these home to show Billy. Maybe it'll mean something to him!*

11

Jon decided to take the day off. He had some errands to run in the afternoon. He needed to visit Ted Warmboldt. And he just wanted to rest. When Mark's alarm woke them at seven-fifteen, Jon rolled over and announced, "You know, I need a 'mental health day.' I'm calling in sick. Can I talk you into a leisurely breakfast, my love?" he said with a joking hint of upper-class accent.

"You certainly can," Mark answered sleepily. "I don't have anything I have to do today. I'd love to spend the time with you."

Jon rolled around the rest of the way to face Mark and took him in his arms.

"What a wonderful way to wake up," Mark purred.

A little later, as they were drying off from the shower, Jon remarked, "You know, I really need to relax more. I had a restless night. I dreamed about being in the support group and having all the PWAs gang up on me and threaten to infect me with the virus by rubbing a teaspoon on my chest."

"I didn't know you could get AIDS that way," Mark said flippantly.

"Well, in the dream it was pretty scary, even though it sounds silly now. I woke up and worried a long time about those guys, especially Pat. He's really having a hard time. And another one has had his lover desert him. If the disease weren't bad enough, these guys have all sorts of social and relationship problems. It's partly because the future's so indefinite."

"I wonder if people wouldn't be better off," Mark rejoined, "if AIDS were like these cancers or something where the doctors tell you just how many months you have to live."

"Well, of course, the doctors are often pretty wrong about those estimates. But you've got a point. Part of the problem with AIDS is that you just might get well — or at least better — before you get sick again. There's no routine course of the disease. And that makes it hard on everybody." A draft of cold air struck Jon as he opened the door of the steamy warm bathroom and stepped out into the main room of Mark's apartment.

"I think this guy Pat would be fairly happy to die," Jon continued, shivering, as he pulled on a pair of Levis, "if he thought that was what was happening to him. But he keeps thinking that maybe some miracle is going to come along and cure him."

"Maybe it will," Mark shouted.

"Well, I truly wish it would. But I'm skeptical."

"Wouldn't it be wonderful if AIDS just disappeared?" Mark remarked off-handedly as he combed his hair into place and followed Jon out of the bathroom. "If we could just sprinkle fairy dust on our heads and turn around three times—"

"Get me the fairy dust," Jon laughed. "But, seriously, if people were all just responsible and stopped actually fucking or started using condoms and clean needles and took the necessary precautions, AIDS *would* just disappear."

Mark was standing in a shaft of warm morning light that poured into the little sun porch he'd set up as combination bedroom and studio. He was staring off into space, framed in the window next to his drawing table with its high stool. *He looks so beautiful,* Jon thought and felt a rush of sexual excitement: *it's enough just to touch and hold him.*

Mark was absent-mindedly stroking his trim stomach, not really quite listening. "I think I dreamed last night — different from you — that that had happened. I can't quite remember the dream, but what you said just now sort of sparked a memory.

"When I was a kid," he continued, "I used to have wonderful dreams. And I'd wake up in the morning and wish and wish that the dream would have become true. I don't think it ever did. But then maybe I wouldn't have known anyway."

"There is a wonderful novel about just that," Jon answered. "*The Lathe of Heaven* by Ursula LeGuin."

"I've heard of her, haven't I? Science-fiction writer?"

"Right, though this story's more spiritual fable than science-fiction."

🕷

Later, sitting at a table in the window of the Scandanavian deli on Castro Street, Jon wrote a brief inscription in the copy of Ursula LeGuin's novel he'd just bought for Mark. Jon had gotten so enthusiastic about the book, he'd insisted Mark should have his own copy.

> Mark,
> that all your dreams
> (especially with me in them)
> come true.
> Love,
> Jon

"Thanks, Jonathan." Mark smiled as he read the inscription. He held the paperback up in his hands, turning it from side to side.

"It's a really neat story," Jon said. "I promise I won't give away the ending, but let me give you some clues—"

"To whet my appetite?" Mark joked.

"Well, you know how I love to tell stories."

"I know," Mark answered. "I think by now you've told me the stories of most of your favorite movies."

"Oh no," Jon answered laughing. "You haven't even heard half of them yet."

"Go ahead. I enjoy listening to you. But wait a minute, lemme get us some more coffee." Mark popped up to get one of the self-serve pots from the coffeemaker at the back of the café.

Jon's perusal of the paperback was interrupted by a tap on the shoulder. He looked up to see his friend Barbara from the Jung Institute and Jeff Kettner, the speaker at last night's lecture.

"What a surprise!" Jon remarked. "Please join us."

When Mark returned with the coffee, introductions were made all around.

"You two seemed to be wrapped in an intense conversation when we walked in," Barbara commented. "You want to continue?"

"I was telling Mark about this book," Jon answered, holding it up.

"Go on," Kettner commented. "I've read that. I'd be interested in hearing what you have to say."

Jon started his retelling. "Well, the main character, George Orr, discovers that incidental items in his dreams turn out to come true the next day. The story is set sometime in the future and there's a constant rainfall in George's hometown — Portland, I think — as a result of the greenhouse effect from air pollution. Anyway, he has a dream in which he takes an umbrella from President Kennedy and says something like 'You won't be needing this anymore, Mr. President.' When he wakes up in the morning, the sun is shining and there's no more rain. The ecological problems have disappeared. *He* realizes that the whole world has changed, but nobody else does. For everyone else the world he dreamed is their reality."

"Wow, wouldn't that be something!" Mark commented appreciatively.

"Well, yes. But, in fact, the responsibility makes him so nervous he starts taking pills to stay awake to avoid dreaming and ends up getting sent to a psychiatrist. The shrink believes the story and tries hypnotizing George to test it out. And, lo and behold, he, the psychiatrist, can also recognize the changes in the world since he knew what he programmed into George's dreams.

"The shrink gets megalomanical. He hooks George up to a machine that controls his dreams and the doctor tries to fix the world to suit his idea of how things ought to be. But the dreams never happen the way he expects. I don't want to give away too much. Some of the twists are neat. One thing he tells George to dream is that there are no longer any racial problems on earth. So, in the morning, everybody's turned to a uniform shade of grey. The solution satisfied the suggestion, but not the way the doctor expected ... well, I'll let you read the rest. But, as you might imagine, the psychiatrist ends up practically destroying the world by trying to fix things up according to his own opinions."

"You can't blame him. Wouldn't it be great to be able to change reality like that?"

"I don't know. Maybe we do all the time," Kettner answered.

"You mean, by how we live our lives?"

"Sure. Maybe also by our — what would you call it? — our 'consciousness states.'"

"I'm not sure I understand..."

"Let's see," Kettner started, beginning to sound a little like his lecture of the previous night. "Intricately and inextricably bound up with how people's behavior changes the course of history are things like luck and coincidence or, if nothing else, absence of bad luck."

"Give me a for-instance," Mark asked.

"Okay. Adolf Hitler's behavior dramatically influenced the history of the world. But what if Hitler had been unlucky? Say he'd been accident-prone as a young man and had been blinded. He would never have become the *Führer*. For somebody to become influential — Gandhi or Martin Luther King, to use opposite examples — things must have worked out for them along the way. They were in the right place at the right time."

"Okay, so I'll accept that luck has something to do with success. What does that have to do with people's 'consciousness states'?" Mark queried.

"You know how you have good days and bad days?"

"Uh-huh. I guess I experience that. And I suppose I've always kind of known that my mood — the way I was feeling — had something to do with it. Is that the point you wanted to make?"

"Exactly. And haven't you been influenced by other people's moods? I mean by *their* consciousness states?"

"Okay..."

"Well, what if our consciousnesses are all sort of synchronized in some way, what if consciousness creates some kind of field around itself that influences other consciousnesses? The obvious example is what is called 'mob-behavior.'"

"Are you proposing something like ESP?" Jon asked.

"Or pheromones?" Barbara added.

"I'm not so much concerned with how the influence occurs. Just that it occurs," Kettner answered.

"Okay, I'll agree to that," Mark commented.

"If so, then our whole world is influenced by other people's consciousness fields. But because we aren't aware of its happening we explain it as luck, i.e., some influence that seems to happen uncontrollably and unpredictably."

"Okay," Mark agreed again, leading Kettner on.

"But the fact is luck isn't randomly distributed throughout the universe. Some people are very lucky and have everything going for them — including, but not limited to, being born rich — while others have nothing going for them."

"So what is this 'consciousness state' you're talking about that has such influence?" Jon asked.

"I think it's good will, the intention for success and prosperity for others. Or for their failure — in which case, it's ill will, the intention that other people have bad things happen to them. And isn't this obviously so? We all see that people whom the masses don't like have bad things happen to them. Racism, for instance. The majority of whites in society, even if unwittingly, feel superior to blacks and intend to keep them down. So even though there are all sorts of 'equal opportunities' regulated for them, the fact is that most black people find things just don't work out for them, they don't 'get the breaks' and most of them stay socially inferior. Many different things bring this about, of course. But maybe what underlies it all is the general opinions and intentions prevalent in society."

"What about gay people?" Mark asked, gesturing toward the patrons of the predominantly gay establishment. "We're certainly disliked by the masses."

Jon answered Mark's question, spreading his hands in a gesture of resignation. "AIDS."

"So what's the right consciousness state?"

"Let me answer that," Jon said, picking up the paperback on the table. "The best thing in this book is the character of George Orr. He's just a wonderful example of a saint — sort of Buddhist style." Jon nodded to Jeff Kettner. "Here, here's the passage I was looking for . . . this is describing George: 'He never spoke any bitterness at all, no matter how awful the things he said. Are there really people without resentment, without hate . . . People who never go cross-grained to the universe? Who recognize evil, and resist evil, and yet are utterly unaffected by it?

" 'Of course there are. Countless, the living and the dead. Those who have returned in pure compassion to the wheel, those who follow the way that cannot be followed without knowing they follow it . . . There is not one of us who has not known them. There are enough of them, enough to keep us going. Perhaps.' " Jon closed the book.

"That's beautiful," Kettner commented.

"I wish I could be like that," Jon replied, speaking very personally.

"I think you are," Mark answered.

"You're just saying that," Jon joked. "But seriously, those are the values I believe in. But when push comes to shove . . . well, I don't know if I've got the strength. But I really wish I could manage that kind of easy acceptance of life. It sure would make dealing with AIDS easier."

"And I think it would really change things," Kettner asserted, "if everybody in the world — or maybe only a few — were like that. Those people who never go cross-grained to the universe are the real world saviors, not just Jesus and the ones who got the press, but all the people who've lived well and done whatever it takes to keep the world going, those who returned in pure compassion to the wheel."

"I'm not sure I understand about returning to the wheel," Mark said.

"More of the Taoism/Buddhism," Kettner answered, "It's the bodhisattva story I was telling last night: the same wheel that was on the head of that man in the desert. And, of course, it's the wheel of reincarnation, of time. 'Returning to the wheel' is choosing to accept incarnation in spite of, or maybe on account of, the suffering and death that's inherent in being alive.

"Maybe the people who don't have any bitterness at all are the ones that really change things in the world, not directly, but indirectly because they've discovered the bodhisattva or Christ in everybody and aren't afraid of life anymore and that does something 'mystical' to change the way fate works."

"I don't know about mystical, but wouldn't that change the way people treat the PWAs?" Jon exclaimed. "I mean if all those Christian people who were damning them and calling for them to be put in concentration camps recognized them as manifestations of Christ."

"You know," Kettner answered, now really seeming to get into the religious conversation, "that is how Jesus himself said the world would be judged: 'Whatsoever you do to the least of my brethren—'"

"And sistren, of course," Jon interjected.

"'...you do to me.' According to Jesus, judgement wasn't based on obeying laws or being holy and churchy, but feeding the hungry, and clothing the naked, and renting rooms to people, and giving them jobs when they needed help, being good to people even when they didn't deserve it. Because whether you knew it or not, when you did it for them you did it for Jesus." Kettner suddenly seemed to realize he'd let his voice get loud and that people were looking at him. He smiled around the room sheepishly. "End of sermon," he whispered.

"You know your novel here reminds me of the notion in modern physics that all possible variations on events exist somehow in 'parallel time tracks,'" Barbara broke her silence. "Wouldn't it be great if there were some way to switch over from one universe into another? Maybe into a universe in which, say, AIDS had never come into existence?"

"I'm not sure," answered Jon. "You don't know what you'd lose. I mean, there have been a lot of positive changes within gay life as a result of AIDS. I guess what I'd like, since we're now dreaming about perfect realities, is to find one of those parallel universes in which the AIDS virus mutates out of existence and just disappears or in which people all become immune."

"Do you really think there are such things as 'parallel time tracks'?" Mark asked.

"I don't know," Barbara answered. "Maybe it depends on what you mean. I'm not sure that this is what the physicists are talking about, but I certainly do think it's obvious that people live in very different universes. I mean, what about all those people who've experienced being abducted by aliens in flying saucers, or who got cured of cancer at Lourdes or have Madonnas that weep real tears? Those things don't happen in my reality. Are those people nuts? Or how about all the people who experience Commie spies lurking everywhere, infiltrating society? And look how different the world New Yorkers live in is from the one we live in out here in California. They think *we're* nuts!" She laughed.

"I guess the trick is to find a universe that makes you happy and gives your life meaning," Jon answered.

"Well now, how do you switch universes? Is this book going to tell me how?" Mark held up Ursula LeGuin's novel.

"That's what prayer and love and good intentions are all about," Kettner commented. "There's a wonderful little book called *The Lazy Man's Guide to Enlightenment* that talks about changing reality. It begins with the premise that the only thing that needs to be changed is the amount of love in the world and that that would make everything better. If enough people — or maybe the 'right people' — put out that love, maybe the world would change for the better."

"I remember that book from the early seventies," Jon answered.

"Look at it again," Kettner said. "You'll be surprised how wise it is, even when it sounds real hippie."

"I've got a copy," Jon said. "I'll check it out."

Kettner continued, "*The Lazy Man's Guide* suggests little epigrams to say to yourself: 'Love it the way it is. When you learn to love hell, you will be in heaven. What did you think it *was* that needed to be loved?'"

"Well, so if good intentions get realized, do you think evil ones do too?" Mark asked. "Do you think something like AIDS happened because a lot of people were wishing evil on homosexuals?"

"Isn't that a scary notion?" Barbara asked.

"I think there's some truth to that," Kettner answered. "But it probably isn't so much evil intentions as good intentions that turn out to have evil consequences: like that for some people to be rich other people have to be poor, or that for one person to be right somebody else has to be wrong."

"That's what you said the psychiatrist in this book did, when his plans got twisted around," Mark commented to Jon.

"Right. A particularly disturbing implication of these ideas is that it was 'the good Christians,' the self-righteous ones — who are the most actively anti-gay — that are really responsible for AIDS. The message to get from that, I suppose, is that people really ought to be wishing good for one another, forgiving one another, instead of deciding who's committing the worst sins."

"So maybe love is the key to changing realities in the right direction," Mark summarized. "That'd be truly Christian."

12

"If I really loved you, I wonder if I wouldn't just pull out all these tubes and let you go," Jon whispered, mostly to himself, as he stood beside Ted Warmboldt's hospital bed feeling helpless.

Ted was barely conscious today. He acknowledged Jon but didn't seem to recognize him. Now as Jon tried to talk to him, Ted seemed to be slipping in and out of sleep. Ted's answers to questions about medical treatments and the like didn't make much sense.

Jon gave up trying to talk. He took Ted's hand and held it warmly, hoping the gesture would communicate something deeper than words. Indeed, Ted's labored breathing did slow down some.

Ted was barely recognizable. Practically emaciated, he had tubes running into his nose and out of his chest. A plastic mask over his nose and mouth fed him oxygen. An I.V. tube ran into the back of his hand. More tubes ran into an alternating-pressure flotation mattress that Jon knew was meant to slow development of bedsores.

"I wish I could carry you into one of those alternate universes Mark was talking about where you would be healthy and beautiful again. Maybe that's what heaven will be for you," Jon whispered. "I wonder why we're keeping you here..." his whisper trailed off.

Jon thought about the practical matters of Ted's hospital care. It was costing somebody — the taxpayers — probably hundreds of dollars a day to keep him like this. All that expense was hardly doing Ted any good. Even if one of the research projects discovered some promising news about an anti-AIDS drug today, it wouldn't help Ted. *What are we keeping him alive for? I wonder why he just doesn't pull off the oxygen mask in the middle of the night,* Jon thought. *That's probably what I'd do.*

Maybe he's scared of dying, Jon answered himself.

If that's so then it really shows what a bad job we're doing assisting the PWAs in handling their disease. I mean, they've got to know — at least once they're at this stage — that they're dying.

I guess the bad job of teaching about death isn't just on PWAs. We're all indoctrinated with the idea that death is something terrible, to be avoided at all costs.

Ironic, isn't it, that America keeps getting called a Christian nation. If we really believed in the Christian worldview, wouldn't we be happy to let go and speed our entry into heaven?

Jon felt a surge of memory from his youthful days in the seminary. The scent of incense. Monks carrying candles through a spring twilight to the shrine of the Blessed Mary out in the apple orchard. Sibilant tones of Gregorian chant on the evening air *Salve Regina, mater misericordiae...*

"Maybe this is my purgatory," Jon imagined Ted to say. And the Gregorian melody in his memory shifted to a solemn *Requiem aeternam.*

"Oh baby, it looks like hell," Jon answered the imaginary voice in his mind. "And you don't belong there. And if this *is* purgatory, I'll bet you've got a glorious heaven awaiting you. You'll have earned it."

Jon's Catholic memories brought back his grade school catechism. *Wasn't one of the spiritual acts of mercy to help your loved ones out of purgatory? Wouldn't turning off the oxygen be just such an act of mercy?*

Jon looked at the valve attached to the wall. It would be so easy. But he couldn't do that. It wasn't in his authority. Maybe it was in nobody's.

And that was the problem: nobody was responsible for making these decisions. Ted should have seen to that several weeks ago before he got to this stage. *His brain's probably so clouded now with drugs that, even if he wanted to make the decision to die, he couldn't hold it in mind long enough to do anything about it.*

That scene of Ted standing on the beach filled Jon's inner vision. *He was so strong then: tall, broad shouldered, ruggedly handsome with dark blond hair blowing in the wind off the ocean. How could anybody even guess this is the same person?*

✨

"Well, hello Dr. Stiers. Nice to see you on such a pretty day," one of the nurses beamed as she entered the room. "And how's he doing?"

"What's going to happen to him?" Jon asked, ignoring the small talk about the weather.

"Seriously?" the nurse responded, perhaps interpreting the tone of Jon's voice.

"Seriously."

"Right now, he's stabilized on the medication, though showing no improvement. As you've probably seen he's fairly delirious most of the time. What usually happens in these cases, I'll be real honest with you, is that they stay about like this till either a new infection sets in, the existing infection becomes resistant to the medication, or more likely a blood clot gets into the heart or brain and causes a fatal infarction. In some cases, it seems like the HIV virus does direct damage to the brain — it crosses the blood/brain barrier, you know—"

"I know," Jon answered.

"Then maybe the brain tissue itself breaks down and they either have a stroke or the nervous system just shuts down. In most cases, though, they die of the pneumonia."

"And suffocate?"

"Probably without any pain. I mean, Ted here is so doped up, he's not suffering any physical pain."

"I guess not."

"Probably not as much as you are," she continued. "I mean in emotional pain. Most of the real suffering I see around here is in the survivors. We can't very well medicate all of them." She smiled again.

"Thank you for your honesty," Jon answered.

"You know, though, they don't all come in here just to die. Just this morning we released this really sweet young boy, I think about nineteen years old. He's in really good shape now. I hope it was okay that I told him about you and the support group you run. We always give the patients that list of services and I mentioned to him specifically that I knew you were a really caring man."

Jon blushed. "Thank you. I appreciate that."

"If he calls you, his name is McCullough. First name: Robyn — just like mine. Only he spells it funny, with a 'Y.' Now, Dr. Stiers, can I ask you to excuse me? I'm going to give Ted a bath. Would you wait outside?"

"Oh, I'm going to go on for today. Thanks, Robin."

13

"Lite beer," Blum Blumgarten shouted over the loud music.

A moment later the bartender handed him an icy cold aluminum can. "This one was down at the bottom. Real cold. Is that okay?"

"Sure," Blum answered. "Beer's always better real cold." But even as he said it he realized he was already chilly. Though the sun was out, it was cold outside. And inside Savages, the Castro Street bar Blum had wandered into to while away a few minutes of the afternoon, it was pretty chilly as well. *Without a lot of people, the air conditioners get these places too cold*, he thought, realizing how dismal the bar looked this time of day, especially with all the flashing lights back over the dance floor.

Blum walked up to the front of the room and sat by the big plateglass window that faced the corner of Castro and Eighteenth, the center of San Francisco's gay mecca. Though the glass was tinted, Blum's eyes quickly adjusted to the brightness so he could no longer really see the back of the room or the long bar where maybe five or six other men were standing or sitting on tall stools.

Just as well, Blum thought to himself. *I didn't come in here to cruise ... though ... I guess it would be nice to meet somebody*, he corrected himself.

Five, six years ago Blum had been a real habitue of these bars. Gay life had seemed in its prime. Lots of wonderful sex was available, lots of beautiful men just asking to be laid. No cares in the world.

Now it's all changed.

In retrospect, Blum observed to himself, those good ol' days looked pretty good. *You sorta forget all the bad times. All the nights you stood around till closing time and then went home alone and lonely, feeling more rejected than ever.*

Blum still went out to the bars occasionally. He usually ran into people he knew and had a good time. He believed it was possible to still live out some of those sexual freedoms, as long as you played safe. Blum had developed an incentive for protecting himself. "I always consider *myself* negative for the virus," he'd say. "And *everybody else* positive. That gives me lots of reason to protect myself — I don't have to ever get AIDS. Besides, I think the least useful thought is that you're already infected and it's just a matter of time. What kind of incentive is that?"

Blum understood the mechanisms by which the AIDS virus was spread. He knew how to make love and play sexually without letting any semen into his body. He'd become a great frotteur, an aficionado of innocent sex, boyish sex— when all that mattered was feeling another body against yours, without any need to penetrate or perform.

Still, the whole scene sobered him. He worried about the people who were out in the bars. Were they all practicing safe sex? He worried about the possibility that there were men who'd gotten kind of crazy from the knowledge they'd been exposed or were getting sick and were actually trying to spread the disease. Blum didn't exactly believe those people existed or, at least, that there were many of them. But the media had played up that idea so much that it bothered him.

Most of all, he worried he'd get himself so worked up over some really gorgeous number he'd forget his pledge to play safe.

Blum surveyed the street outside the window. There was still a lot of activity in the Castro. *Like any other neighborhood, I guess. People still go to the grocery and the hardware store and the cleaners.* That reminded Blum he needed to stop by Cala on his way home and pick up some milk.

He noticed a familiar face crossing the street. *Isn't he pretty!* he thought to himself. He enjoyed a lascivious thought about the young man who'd turned at the corner and was coming up his way. Blum thought he recognized him from the Buddy Project. *Mark ... somebody. A graphic artist, I think. He did some pictures for the B.A.R. or one of those papers. Very attractive.*

The young man passed by the window, and Blum wondered if he could see in. Probably not. He started to rap on the windowpane, but decided not to. What if the guy didn't recognize him? Besides, if he's out there he's probably not cruising for sex.

There I go, Blum caught himself. *I hadn't thought that's what I was doing in here...*

Just then a bright light flashed as somebody pushed open the swinging door from the street and walked in. He stood near Blum for a moment, probably to let his eyes adjust, and then walked on back.

He's pretty too. Wonder what he's up to?

A moment later, the newcomer, beer in hand, came up toward Blum. "Mind if I join you? It's so dark back there," he pointed over his shoulder with the thumb of his free hand.

"Of course not," Blum answered, thinking, *how lucky can I get?* He felt his fears of the anonymous men in the bar dissolving. *This boy's gorgeous. Curly blond hair, big blue eyes, tight body.* "My name's Blum."

"Huh?"

"Blum rhymes with plum ... nickname ... short for my last name Blumgarten."

"How do you do?" the young man replied formally. "My name is Robert. But they call me Robyn — with a Y."

14

"There were several copies of this lying all over the xerox room."

"What is it?" Billy answered.

"I don't know. But it looks to me like a chart comparing various anti-viral drugs that are being studied to fight AIDS. And look, down here at the bottom, there's a comparison with this 'Vir. Anti.' It's rated one hundred percent in every column."

"Maybe that's the totals or something."

"I thought about that too. But none of the columns add up to a hundred. It could be some sort of control group. But it's listed just like the other drugs..."

"Hey, you guys gonna want to eat?" Lee Ann stuck her head through the kitchen door.

"Whatcha got?" Billy asked joking.

"How about spaghetti? And sauce with..." she held up a jar and then turned it so she could read the label, "Italian sausage and green peppers?"

"Sounds fine," Lynn answered.

"And I just made some coffee, if you want any," Lee Ann shouted over her shoulder as she headed back into the kitchen.

"Thanks. Just a minute," Lynn called, turning back to the table where she was sitting with Billy who was carefully reading the list she'd brought home.

"Honey, you may have struck it rich here. Thank you," he said happily. "Now we gotta get some more info. Like what this Vir. Anti. is and where we get it. Think you can find that out?"

"Oh, Billy, I doubt it. I looked through the files today and there's nothing under AIDS or any title I could think of. I don't see why this would be a secret project, unless they're auditing some project and don't want it known. I don't know. I've only been at the firm for a month, you know They haven't let me in on the family secrets," she snapped.

"Lynn, honey, calm down. I didn't mean to blame you."

"I'm so unhappy," Lynn suddenly announced, dropping her gaze, pulling her shoulders in, and slumping into the chair.

"What's wrong?" Billy reached out to touch her arm.

She pulled away from his touch. "I got so excited today that this was gonna be our salvation or something. And then I realized we don't know what to do with it. And, Billy, I just don't know about us anymore. I mean, well . . . I guess . . . I mean I really do want to marry you. I love you," she said in a louder voice. "But what future have we got? And . . . and, well, I'd just got used to having sex and then we get this news, and now I don't know if I want to do it anymore. And I'm getting kinda frustrated. And," she hastened to say, "I know it's not your fault. I don't want to blame you. But . . . but."

"Lynn, I miss making love with you, too. But we could. I mean, just because I've been exposed to this virus doesn't mean we can't make love anymore. It just means using a rubber or me not coming inside you. That's all."

"That's all — you think."

"No, I mean it," he said angrily. "You read too much of that garbage in the *National Enquirer* and stuff. This isn't still some big mystery."

"What about saliva? I like to kiss you, you know. They found the virus in saliva. That's what got all the dentists upset."

"No, what got the dentists concerned is that people bleed when they get their teeth worked on. The amount of virus in saliva was very, very small. And there is no evidence at all that the virus can be transmitted that way. If it could, it ought to have spread in families. And it hasn't."

"Whadda you mean 'families'? Homosexuals don't have families."

"Well, that probably isn't true. But Lynn, lots of people besides homosexuals carry the virus. The family studies were all done on families that have children with AIDS, you know, like kids that got it from transfusions or injections awhile back. Lynn, I think what you're really upset about is the fact that I've had those homosexual experiences."

"You expect me not to be upset?" Lynn retorted.

"How about a salad? What kinda dressing you want?" Lee Ann shouted from the kitchen. Then walked into the room. "Uh-oh, you guys fighting?" she asked timidly.

"How about Italian?" Billy answered. "And we'll be okay, we just have to talk this out."

"Well, that's real good. I mean, talking it out, not Italian." Lee Ann answered. "But Italian it is. And you just keep talking."

Lynn looked up at Billy and smiled. "I guess I'm a silly duck."

"Where'd you ever get that expression?" Billy laughed. Then he continued. "Lynn, I expect you to accept me for who I am. Now. Not who I used to be or what I used to do. And who I am now is a man who really loves you, and desires you. And I'm a man who may be carrying a virus that neither of us want you to get."

"Do you know about the test for the virus?" Lynn asked, skirting the emotional issue.

"I went by the office today and they drew blood. The doctor said the results would probably be in tomorrow afternoon."

"What did he think?"

"Well, he said not to get my hopes up too much. Most of the people who have the antibody also show positive for the virus. He said that still didn't prove they were contagious. There's still no way to do that. And he said it didn't mean I was gonna get sick. Then he repeated the same things I've said to you about risk reduction and safe sex and all that."

"Did you tell him about me?"

"Of course. I told him I was in love with a wonderful gal and we wanted to get married and have a houseful of babies."

"I never said anything about a houseful," Lynn retorted through her tears.

"The doctor said not to rush into children right away, unless we wanted to adopt. He said there might be vaccines in a few years which would protect you and consequently protect the baby. So everything could work out," Billy sounded kind of proud.

"Billy, I'll try to accept you just the way you are. You really are the best thing that's ever happened to me." She leaned across the table and kissed him on the cheek and then whispered in his ear, "And I do want to make love with you. Tonight. I hope you brought, uh, protection."

"Of course I did," Billy grinned. "Have every time I've seen you, even when you said you weren't gonna let me touch you."

"I never said any such thing," Lynn argued, laughing a little. "But, here, maybe this Vir. Anti. stuff is already available. We wouldn't have to wait for anything."

"I don't know if I'm ready for kids yet," Billy answered seriously.

"I didn't mean kids. I mean, you know, just getting this done with. I'd really like that," she said plaintively.

"Well, me too. What do you propose?"

"Now here's my plan ... I asked you about maybe taking a look into the Liberty Bell computer?"

"Umm. I could try. But Lynn, it may not be so easy. If this thing is as secret as you think, there'll be some kind of password to get into the files. I'll just have to try random combinations. There're lots of those. Chances are the guy who's running the program has some code that's personally meaningful to him. So the more I know about him the easier it'll be to figure out the password."

"I'm one step ahead of you," Lynn answered proudly. "We know the guy doing this study is this mystery partner George Wilson." She smiled as she pulled a piece of paper out of her purse and unfolded it. "And Wilson, or somebody, put this flyer up on the bulletin board yesterday."

Billy looked at the flyer, "Tonight??" Then at Lynn. "I'd rather spend the time with you."

"Billy, I'd feel a lot better about the time we spent together, if we knew something about this 'Vir. Anti.,'" Lynn responded firmly.

"I thought you wanted to make love tonight."

"I'll wait up," she answered quickly.

"Well, I hope you two had a good talk, 'cause my spaghetti's getting mushy and it's time to eat." Lee Ann plopped a big bowl right into the middle of the table.

"Oh," exclaimed Lynn, "Don't get sauce on this." Smiling knowingly at Billy, she snatched up the list of tables from the Liberty Bell Foundation.

15

"Nuclear weapons are simply too destructive. They have too many uncontrollable effects." George Wilson was answering a question posed to him by one of the students attending the panel discussion at Catholic University.

"Fallout blows all around the world. The explosions can't be pinpointed all that accurately. They are too big and kill too many innocent people. The firestorms that follow destroy too much property. Radiation contaminates farmland and food supplies.

"What we really need are more specific weapons: weapons that can be focused specifically on enemy soldiers or military installations. This idea of killing civilian populations in war is a very new idea, only conceived since World War II and the development of nuclear weapons and ICBMs. And it's barbaric. It makes war impossible. And that weakens the military strength of the nation."

"What does that mean?" the student who'd asked the question shouted angrily.

"It means that the business of the military is to fight wars. But wars have to be winnable. And they have to accomplish something. We'd all agree that the war in Vietnam was a tragedy. We weren't fighting to win and I still don't know that anybody knows what we were trying to accomplish. War isn't the problem, young man. Bad war is."

Wilson stepped away from the podium and sat down. He surveyed the room. Most of those in attendance were college students. There were some older faces and some priests and nuns in various degrees of religious dress.

Wilson looked down the row of seats behind the front table: Two military officers in uniform; a nun, in what he thought were really civilian clothes and no substitute for a habit, who'd become famous in the past year as an anti-nuke activist; a nuclear physicist, dressed in a white lab smock that George thought was just grandstanding, who proclaimed the safety of nuclear energy; and himself, the Pentagon arms consultant, dressed properly, he thought, in a dark pin-striped suit, who agreed that nuclear weapons were unwieldy, inefficient, and outdated. George began to think proudly what an elegant objection that was. Not at all messy and emotional like that nun who had talked all about radioactive babies.

The physicist was tugging at his arm. "Mr. Wilson, Wilson, that question was for you."

Wilson stood up. "I'm sorry, please repeat the question."

"What would you suggest as a substitute for nuclear weapons that *would* be more 'efficient'?" asked another of the ill-dressed and impolite students.

"As I said in my opening remarks, a weapon should be specific and controllable. A rifle is a good example. It only shoots one bullet and you can aim it at exactly what you want to hit."

"You mean *kill* don't you?" the student interrupted.

"Don't be snide," George said. "Of course I mean kill. At least when we're talking about fighting armies. Another example, something that is still science-fiction I suppose — perhaps our colleague here could enlighten us," he said, turning to the besmocked physicist, perhaps realizing he was now being snide himself, "would be a field-effect device that would detonate the charges in a foot-soldier's rifle. With such a hypothetical weapon only combatants would be affected. Or perhaps some sort of transducer that could be focused on an army to directly stimulate soldiers' pain centers. That might even turn out to be very humane, I suppose, if the pain didn't actually kill."

"Do any such weapons exist?" the nun on the panel asked.

"Well, the rifle, of course. Electronic weapons are certainly in development, but what I know about them is strictly classified, and I can't say any more. Gas, of course, was such a weapon, though as you know that's been considered inhumane. But other biological and chemical weapons could probably fit my requirements for efficiency."

"Please say more," the nun said when George started to step back from the podium.

"About what?" he asked.

"About biological weapons and the like," she answered.

"Well, this is not exactly my field," George said. "I'm not sure that I should be talking about this. But let me hypothesize a biological weapon that could be delivered, say by aerosol spray from an airplane or a missile, which would cause a fast-developing strain of rabies to spread through an army. The personnel would likely attack one another, disobey commands, and ultimately die."

"Wouldn't that spread rabies wildly — at least as nonspecifically as you objected to previously with nuclear weapons?" the physicist asked.

"That, of course, would be the trick. Could a strain of rabies, say, be developed which could later be immobilized by another aerosol spray? Or which one's own army could be vaccinated against? The trick would be to create your bacterium or virus so that it would spread only among a specific population. For the sake of example, let me suggest that a virus could be engineered that required certain proteins that occurred only in Russian vodka, or maybe beet soup. That would make Russians far more susceptible than Americans who drank Bourbon..."

"Or Israelis who ate chicken soup," one of the military men joked.

"That's enough," Wilson snapped. He didn't like being made light of. And he'd certainly said enough already to this audience. They just weren't sympathetic to the elegant logic he'd trained into himself.

"But what can we do about the existing nuclear threat..." the nun on the panel had stepped up to the podium. Wilson sat down for a moment, not bothering to listen anymore. Then he stood up and gingerly stepped away from the head table, bowing to the moderator to excuse himself, and slipped out the back door of the meeting room.

Wilson hurried outside and looked around for a taxi to take him home. As he stood on the sidewalk, he noticed an attractive young man with dark curly hair come out the same door he'd just exited. He thought he recognized him from the audience. Catholic U. student, George thought. Looks Italian, probably Catholic.

"Young man," he hailed, "know where I can catch a cab?"

"No sir," the young man answered nervously. "I'm not from around here. I parked in that lot right over there," he pointed. "It's pretty late. Might have to call one."

"Say, you were in that discussion upstairs, weren't you?"

"Yes sir, I was."

"Maybe you agreed enough with some of the things I said to consider giving me a ride — at least some place where I can catch a cab."

"Well, I don't know about agreeing with you, I mean, whether that makes any difference. I guess, well, sure, I can give you a ride."

16

Billy was nervous. He figured in some ways this was a lucky break, though what if he were to run into this guy Wilson again — maybe with Lynn? That would give them away.

Billy had gotten George Wilson talking about himself almost as soon as they got into Billy's little Honda Civic. *He's been talking all evening,* Billy thought to himself, *his adrenaline's high enough for him to keep on at least till he gets home.*

"I'll take you all the way," Billy had volunteered when Wilson offered to get a cab once they were off campus and could see regular traffic.

"That might be out of your way. Which way do you go?"

"Where do you live, sir?" Billy sidestepped the question. He'd come out here tonight determined to find out as much about George Wilson as he could. Since he'd got this far, he might as well play this thing through. After all, whatever damage was done — making himself recognizable — was already done.

"Up in Georgetown."

"Me, too," Billy fibbed.

"I live right behind the University. I can see the playing fields from my den. Sometimes I stand for hours watching the young men and, uh, women, playing ball or jogging."

Wilson was really talking. Now Billy's worry was that he'd get *too much* information from him. Can I remember all these names and things? he wondered.

During his talk Wilson had dropped a vast number of code names of missions during World War II and Korea and Vietnam. Billy had tried to write them down lest he forget. That list was probably the most fruitful place to look for the password he'd need. Now he was getting even more information. And this he couldn't write down.

Wilson was obviously Catholic. He made several religious allusions. During his talk he'd mentioned Moses and the plagues on ancient Egypt as an example of a well-applied weapon. He talked about the Blessed Mother's predictions of war during the Marian apparitions in the last century. And he talked about knighthood and chivalry. He used St. George fighting the dragon as an example of the warrior-saint who used just the right weapon to destroy his enemy.

"I go to mass daily ... over at the student chapel. But the Church isn't like it used to be, young man. Why, you know, you can't even go to confession in private anymore."

"Huh?"

"I mean, the priest sits there looking right at you. It's hard to, well, to tell the truth." All of a sudden Wilson's voice faltered. Billy wondered what that was about. Maybe he'd had a bad experience with confession?

"Turn right here, son. My place is the fourth house there on the left," Wilson instructed him.

"Where?" Billy asked, hoping Wilson would tell him the street number. Once before when he was trying to break into a file, he'd discovered that the programmer had used his home address as a password. But it was dark and he couldn't make out numbers on any of the houses.

"The house with the stained glass."

"Oh yeah, I see it."

"I brought that window back with me from my last trip to London. I'm quite proud of it. Came out of an old cathedral, survived the bombings in World War II. You see, it's set there in the landing between first and second floor. Gets pretty good sun."

"Well, Mr. Wilson, it was real nice meeting you. I'm glad I could be of assistance in getting you home," Billy answered as innocently as possible to cover over his nervousness.

"If you wait just a moment before driving off, I'll switch on the lights behind the window," Wilson said, obviously intent on showing off his collector's item. "Then you can get a good look."

"Well, uh, thank you, sir."

"Think nothing of it. And thank you for the ride." He got out of the car.

Billy made a point of turning around slowly. He pulled into the driveway in front of the house to make a turn, hoping also to get a look at Wilson's address. Maybe Wilson would turn on the porch light.

Indeed, as the man stepped up to his front door, the light switched on. *Maybe his wife*, Billy thought. *Or maybe some sort of automatic switch*, he corrected his theory as he noticed a tiny red flash from a box mounted at the front of Wilson's porch. *Probably got lasers all around the house attached to a burglar alarm or something.*

"Number eight," he said aloud to fix in memory the address in small bronze figures beside the door.

It was almost a second thought that caused him to look at the stained glass window that now glowed brightly from within. *That's where Wilson had gotten the business about St. George and the dragon,* Billy realized. There, shining above him, was a six-foot-tall depiction of a medieval knight, seated on horseback, driving a lance into the mouth of a snarling snake-like dragon that was coiled on the ground only a few feet from the legs of the knight's white charger.

Billy backed the car out of the driveway. His mind was racing. What had he learned? How could he use it? He was feeling excited about the job of breaking into Liberty Bell's computers. It wasn't just the possibility of finding a treatment for this virus that might be in his blood; he wasn't really very expectant of that working out. But he remembered the thrill of his old days as a hacker.

Driving back toward Lynn's apartment, he began to plot how he'd break in. He was so excited he'd almost forgotten about sex. He decided to report in sick tomorrow and spend the day in front of his console.

17

"Well, I'll be damned if I'm going to let them tie me down to some hospital bed and keep me alive against my will or experiment on me like a guinea pig. I'm not sick enough yet, but I'm sure going to take matters into my own hands when the time comes," Greg Bens said determinedly.

"Has my time come?" Pat Stratford asked from his bed.

"I don't know about that," Greg answered, suddenly changing the tone of his voice from vitriolic to timid. "You'd have to make that decision yourself, Pat."

"That's why I asked you over here. I need some help thinking about that. It's scary. When they had me in the hospital last month stuck full of I.V.'s and shit, I kept wishing I could die. What good did any of that do? Maybe I'm a little stronger now, not coughing as much, but why am I going through this? I want to get well. But if not, wouldn't it be better to just die?"

"Yeah, I guess so. To tell you the truth, I talk about suicide a lot, but I'm not sure I've got the guts to do it."

"Maybe we could all do it together," Pat suggested. "I mean, make a party of it. We could take some kind of drug that would get us all high and we could die laughing." He giggled nervously.

"I'm not sure that's so funny, Pat," Greg answered.

"Well, maybe not the party. But how about the idea of helping each other in making this kind of decision?"

"You ought to talk to Jon about that. Or maybe your doctor. Not me."

"But, Greg, you understand. What if you got sick and they came and took you away tomorrow and after a couple of days in the hospital you discovered you were dying? But then it'd be too late. They'd hook you up to those machines. You saw what they did to Tommy Hanson." A vision flashed through Pat's mind of the slow and protracted death of a member of their support group who didn't come to a meeting one day: he was in the hospital with an allergic reaction to medication. "He stayed in there for six weeks, practically a vegetable. There was no way he could have helped himself."

"He could have taken off the oxygen mask," Greg answered.

"I think it's too late to make the decision then. I know when I was in the hospital and all doped up, I couldn't have 'just pulled off the mask.' I think I thought about it, but it was too scary."

"Yeah," Greg answered. "Well, maybe you're right."

They both fell silent for a moment. The phone rang.

"Hello," Pat muttered, picking up the receiver from his bed-side table. "Oh, Blum, whatcha doin' calling so late? Isn't it after midnight?"

"You're still up, aren't you?"

"Sure, Greg's over here. You know, from the group."

"Let me say hello."

Pat handed Greg the phone. "What mischief have you been getting into?" Greg asked playfully.

"Oh, you did? . . . At Savages? . . . and what did you do with this young man?"

Pat was annoyed that Greg was keeping the phone. Blum was his friend. And it sounded juicy.

"Here, Pat, Blum's got quite a story for you." Greg handed him the receiver. "Look, I'm gonna run."

"Thanks, Greg. Think about what I said . . . I mean about doing something together." Pat buzzed the door latch and then put the receiver back to his ear. "So. . ." he said knowingly.

"So," answered Blum. "I met this beautiful young man this afternoon. I spent the whole afternoon with him talking."

"Is that all you did — talk?" Pat asked leadingly.

"Well, not exactly. But let me tell you what we talked about."

"I want to hear about the 'not exactly,'" Pat said, realizing at the same time that he really didn't want to hear what Blum did with this guy he met at Savages. It was only going to make him jealous.

"What was important was that this guy — his name's Robyn — has really cured himself by the way he thinks. I mean, he told me about this group he belongs to that does 'Attitudinal Healing' based on something called *A Course in Miracles*. Robyn says he's healed himself of AIDS using these visualization exercises. He was just in the hospital today for tests and they said he was practically cured."

"I thought you were calling with some sleazy story of sex in an alley," Pat chided, both a little relieved and a little annoyed that Blum didn't have that kind of story, and surprisingly disinterested in hearing about somebody else's miracle cure.

"Well, let me tell you about the 'not exactly' then," Blum changed the subject for Pat. "After we got over to my place, Robyn explained about his diagnosis and said he wouldn't do anything that would endanger me. He asked if I knew about safe sex. And, of course, I said yes. And we hugged and touched each other — he's got a real hot little body — and well, you know . . . Safe as a pin."

"Really!" Pat said unbelieving.

"Yes, really. And then we talked for hours. I fixed us dinner. He told me all about the importance of positive thinking and these exercises. . ."

"I know about the exercises," Pat interrupted.

"You do?"

"Oh, yeah, Jon talked about that stuff in group several times. Weren't you there?"

"I don't think so."

"I just don't believe in miracles."

"You were hoping for one last week," Blum answered insistently.

"Well, maybe so."

"Pat, you know, even if you don't get over your . . . uh, illness, maybe it would help you to feel better if you did some of these exercises. Robyn said he'd come to group next week. In fact, it was a sort of coincidence. He already knew about the group and was planning to come."

"Blum, look, I'm gonna go to sleep now. I'll come meet your young man sometime. Sorry to sound so down tonight. Guess it was that visit with Greg. Anyway, glad you had fun." Pat hung up the phone without waiting for Blum to answer. What he'd said was true, he thought — about being glad for Blum — but he didn't want to hear any more of that tonight.

Then he realized, in fact, he was angry.

It just isn't fair that other guys are out there still meeting each other and . . . and I'm cooped up in this ugly room, too weak even to walk down to the street. And nobody's gonna ever hold me again . . . or hug me and touch me and tell me what a hot body I've got.

Goddamn Blumgarten, what right does he have to call me up and gloat over his little trick . . . and all in the name of telling me about some fuckin' miracle this kid's had.

Pat's anger gave him surprising strength. He got out of bed and went over to the window and peered down at the street below.

"Goddamn fuckers!" he shouted. "Goddamn you all. It's not fair. It's just not fair." Pat could see people walking along the street, some of them together. His eyesight wasn't good enough anymore for him to tell, but he assumed they were gay couples. "It'll serve you right, giving each other the goddamn plague," he shouted.

Then stopping himself, he realized he had to warn them, stop them. "No, no," he shouted. "Don't let this happen to you." But, of course, nobody could hear him.

He pounded on the windowpane as though the noise would attract attention. The window rattled. Then suddenly Pat's open palm went right through the glass. Pain shot up his arm. The window shattered and a gust of cold air blew hard against his sunken chest. Pat looked at his hand. A sliver of glass had cut right across his palm. Half dazed and half burning with the pain, he stared at the cut and at the deep creases in the withered flesh of his hand.

One of those is the life line, isn't it? Looks like the glass has cut me a brand new one. All full of blood.

The sight of the blood pooling in his open palm fascinated and appalled him. *That's the virus there, right there . . . That's what's killing you*, his interior voice screamed inside his head. He looked and saw smudges of blood on the broken fragments of the glass still sticking out crookedly from the wooden frame. He thought about reaching out through the window and then slowly turning his hand to allow the blood to pour out — onto the sidewalk, onto the walkers below, onto the couples going home to hug and touch each other and . . . and . . .

But he pulled away from the window and clutched his wounded hand with the other and then limped toward the bathroom. He washed his hand in the hottest water he could stand, then worried about washing the virus down the drain into the city's water supply. And while a rational part of his mind assured him that the virus would die quickly in the filtration process, he shivered with guilt for exposing the whole population to his disease.

Pat wrapped a white towel around his bleeding hand. Maybe he was shivering not so much from guilt as from the cold wind blowing through the broken window. He pulled on the old robe that was hanging on the bathroom door. Looking down at the faded robe, he remembered how beautiful it had once been. A Christmas present from a boyfriend. Deep blue velour with grey trim. And a hood. Like a monk. With his good hand, he pulled the hood up over his head, and grasped the lapels tight around his neck. The robe was faded now and the elbows threadbare, just beginning to tear.

Like my life, he thought.

Pat limped back to the window. He pushed the frame up, being careful not to let the broken fragments fall out onto him or onto the street. With his towel-wrapped hand he brushed the slivers from the window sill onto the floor. And then, pulling the robe even tighter around himself, he sat down in the open window and painfully drew his legs up so he was balanced on the inside of the sill. He remembered how, as a child, he sat in the window of his room like this and watched planes fly overhead and wished he were somewhere else.

Pat wasn't sure how long he sat there, calmly looking down at the passersby below. He wondered if any of them saw him up there on his precarious perch. After a while he stopped noticing the cold. He kept thinking that he had a decision to make. Soon. Tonight, maybe. A life and death decision.

18

Mark and Jon were enjoying the bright November morning together. Mark rode down on the Metro with Jon since he was planning to visit one of his architecture design clients in the Embarcadero 5 building. As they walked through the plaza beside the Hyatt Regency, Jon's eye was caught by a headline in a newspaper box. He stopped, stuck in a coin, and yanked out a paper. Spread across the front page were headlines that shocked Mark as well as Jon.

AIDS PATIENT PLUNGES TO DEATH
ON DOWNTOWN STREET
Streetworkers won't clean blood

"Oh my God," Jon exclaimed, "it was Pat Stratford."

"Who's that?" Mark inquired.

"I was talking about him the other day. He got real mad at me at group. C'mon, let's get over to the office. I ought to call some people about this. Find out what happened.

"Look, Mark," Jon added, "you don't have to come along, if you want to go to your interview."

"Oh, I'm in no rush. And Jon, I'd like to stay with you. You look pretty flustered. Maybe I can help."

&

"Jon, I don't think you have any reason to blame yourself," Mark was saying an hour later as he sat Jon down at a booth in the back of the self-service cafeteria in the renovated pier where Jon's office was located. "I'll get you some coffee. Want a roll?"

"Oh, Mark, it's okay. I can serve myself. I guess I'm not all that upset. It was just sort of a surprise. Especially to learn it that way."

"Let me wait on you. I like doing that," Mark answered truthfully.

"Well, you know, I'm really much less upset about Pat's death than I am about all the publicity," Jon said as Mark returned to the table with two cups of coffee and a couple of bearclaws.

"I thought these looked good," he said as he sat down.

"They do. Thanks. Well, from talking to Pat's friend Blum and the policeman I reached, I gather that Pat had gotten pretty despondent last night. He was talking about suicide with one of the other PWAs. Apparently, in the middle of the night, about the time the bars let out, he climbed out his window onto the ledge and started shouting to people on the street. That brought the crowd. I wish somebody had had the sense to call me. Anyway, according to the police report, it isn't clear whether he actually jumped or just slipped and fell, but he'd left a note saying goodbye and — here's the clincher — he thanked me for helping him make his decision."

"Oh, Jon, I'm sorry. I don't suppose you needed to hear that."

"It was partly true. I mean at group last week I reminded him that if he didn't want to keep living — and suffering — he could do something about it. I meant terminating his medication, not jumping out the window. I can think of a lot better ways to die than that."

"It was probably pretty quick," Mark answered, hoping to console Jon with what he thought was a positive interpretation.

"You're right about that. Seems like it would be scary though. But probably no more so than suffocating with pneumonia. That's what I was thinking about as a way for Ted to die."

"Is Ted thinking about suicide too?"

"Oh no, he was virtually in a coma yesterday. I didn't tell you about that visit, did I?"

"No, and I didn't press. I thought that was probably pretty private."

"I guess so. Ted was barely responding to me at all. I was kind of thinking that he'd be so much better off if he'd just take off the oxygen mask and let himself go. Maybe I feel so funny about Pat now because I'd been thinking about the same thing with Ted yesterday."

"Pat's not suffering anymore."

"That's true. I guess. He was sort of nutty religious at times. I wonder if he reconciled with God."

"Who knows? At least he's not suffering from the doctors. Maybe there's something heroic about that."

"I can just imagine some public health official now declaring how heroic it was to save the city so many thousands of dollars in health care and welfare costs. It could sure look ugly. Especially with that Senator Wanamaker carrying on."

"Well, look at it positively. Maybe that was a heroic thing to do — I mean even if that wasn't what Pat was up to."

"Mark, I'll be okay. You wanna run your errand now? I ought to call the other guys in the group and see how they're reacting."

As they walked back out into the sunshine, Mark patted Jon on the shoulder as a polite farewell and headed off toward the towering Embarcadero Center. Jon turned and strolled along the front of the piers toward his office. *The City is so beautiful from here*, he thought. *I sure wouldn't want to die. But I guess maybe if I felt sick all the time and couldn't appreciate the beauty anymore, I'd be real glad to get out of here.*

19

"You want *me* on the Donahue Show?" Jon asked surprised. "How come?"

"We're doing a program on AIDS and we just saw the news today about the patient who killed himself last night," answered the assistant producer who'd called Jon in mid-afternoon. "We'd like you to come on and talk about that."

"Oh, now I think this thing is getting too much publicity as it is. I don't want to contribute to that."

"I appreciate your concern, Doctor. But, you know, by the time this show airs the story will have died down."

"When do you want to do this?"

"We will do the show next week, the Tuesday before Thanksgiving. We'll pay your way, of course. You'll be getting a free Thanksgiving vacation on us out of this."

"Well, thank you. What if I already had plans?"

"Have you?"

"No."

"Well, then we're glad you'll be on the show."

"I didn't say that."

"You mean you don't want to be on the Phil Donahue Show?"

"I didn't say that either. Who else are you asking?"

"A Person with AIDS from here in New York who'll speak about his belief that suicide is wrong. And State Senator Charles Wanamaker from Orange County."

"That bigot?"

"Well, I guess he's been described that way. In fact, his office called and started us on this whole program. Wanamaker seems to think all PWAs ought to kill themselves to save society — or society ought to kill them, *he* said."

"Hmmm, there's a big difference there," Jon replied.

"Come on the show and explain."

"Okay." Jon said decisively. "Now give me some information about topic and about arrangements."

❧

Me. On the Phil Donahue Show. Wow! Jon's head was racing with excitement. He called Mark but there was nobody home. He left a message on the answering machine about good news, but didn't give it away. He wanted to see Mark's face when he made the announcement.

What am I getting myself in for? he asked himself a little later as the excitement wore off and he realized that every time he made a public appearance he usually alienated somebody. Last time he was on a local talk show, he almost got himself canned from the AIDS support team because he commented that since male-to-male transmission of the virus seems more direct in unprotected anal intercourse than male-to-female — let alone female-to-male — transmission in vaginal intercourse, AIDS is likely always to be primarily a disease of homosexual men. Other activists accused him of calling AIDS a gay disease.

You never know what you're going to say wrong, he thought. *And this is going to be national. And, of all things, it's gonna be about the suicide issue. Oh my God!*

He laughed to himself, even as as quaked with anticipation.

20

"I've spent the day trying to find that file you had," Billy announced wearily. "I got into Liberty Bell pretty easily. The password into the main directory menu was 'freedom.' That was so obvious it only took a couple of tries. I just can't find any other sub-directories. You know," Billy continued, "at one time today I got into a letter you were typing."

"Me?" Lynn answered.

"Sure, you were correcting a file that had the initials 'EB-lg' down at the bottom. I take it 'lg' is you."

"Yup," Lynn grinned proudly. And 'EB' is Edward Buchanan, the big boss. He'd dictated a thank-you letter to some group that invited him to observe an underground nuclear test. Right?"

"That's it. In Nevada, next month?"

"Right." Lynn was thrilled with Billy's success. She'd known his claims to be a great computer hacker, but she'd never seen those skills demonstrated. Besides, the success today just might mean their dreams of a life together could come true. "But nothing about the AIDS research studies?"

"Not a thing. Are you sure it would be on the mainframe? Could there be more than one computer at Liberty Bell?"

"Well, of course!" Lynn exclaimed. "I hadn't thought about that. Wilson has his own little IBM. It's probably not connected up at all. Though it's bound to be connected to the printers."

"Well, that's not enough," Billy said annoyed. "If the machine hasn't got a modem, I can't get into it. Can you check tomorrow? Besides, if Wilson only works at night, the machine's probably only turned on then. We'll have to try at that time."

"I'm sorry, Billy," Lynn suddenly said very affectionately. She'd just realized how tired and disappointed he was. She felt guilty that she hadn't told him this simple piece of information that now in retrospect seemed so obvious. "I'll look tomorrow. We've still got lots of time."

She'd been standing behind him, looking down over his shoulder while he faced the computer monitor. She leaned over and kissed him on the cheek. He smiled, and the tension in his face relaxed. He turned his head slightly and brought his lips to hers.

A wave of anxiety passed through her. She remembered her panic earlier in the day when he'd called to tell her his test for the virus had come back reactive — it *was* in his blood. But the research at Liberty Bell gave her a new reason for hope. *I trust Billy. He won't hurt me.* She let her mouth open gently and felt his warmth.

He tastes of stale coffee, she thought. She realized she was more aware of the coffee taste than of her fear of the virus.

"I could use a drink," Billy said, standing up and taking Lynn in his arms. "How about you?"

"Sure thing." She pressed her cheek against his strong chest, feeling the black wiry hair where her face touched his bare skin inside the open collar of his shirt. *I love this man*, she thought to herself realizing what a predicament she'd got herself into.

"Then I want to sit you down and explain to you how we have to set up that IBM so we can get into it through the phone lines."

21

"I just don't think death is something to be afraid of. It's okay to die."

"Maybe for you, but not for me. And I think you're a damn

fool for thinking that way. And I think you're liable to do a lot of harm to people preaching that kind of shit."

"Wait a minute," Jon broke into the gradually escalating debate that had been going on between Greg Bens and newcomer Robyn McCullough. "One of the agreements of this group is that we won't insult or attack one another for having a different opinion."

"Okay," Greg answered. "I'm sorry. It's just that I'm still pretty shaken up by what Pat did last night. And I think it's pretty, uh, cavalier for this guy who didn't even know him to come in here and say it was all okay."

"I didn't mean to say that your friend's death wasn't tragic," Robyn answered calmly. "What I meant was that, in general, death is okay. It's just a part of living. Being afraid of it doesn't help us to cope with it."

"Are you saying we should all just give up and die? Isn't that kind of despair just gonna kill us?" interrupted Luis.

"I think just the opposite," Robyn answered. "My health has gotten much better as a result of the attitudinal healing work I've been doing—"

"Tell them about your case," Blum broke in.

"Are you a PWA?" Chuck Thomas asked, sounding rather cynical.

"I was," Robyn answered enigmatically.

"What does that mean?"

"Well, I got sick last year with what seemed like flu. Over about a week it got much worse and I went out to S.F. General to get some antibiotics. The doctor in the emergency room put me in the hospital and the next day they came in and said I had pneumocystis and they wanted to do a whole work-up for AIDS."

"Sounds familiar," Luis commented.

"Let him finish," Chuck said, annoyed.

"So I was positive for HIV and I fit the criteria for diagnosis with AIDS. Though, to be honest, I have to say I never really had any of those ARC symptoms. Other than feeling like I had flu, I hadn't been sick at all before any of this happened."

"Had you been exposed much?" Greg asked, now sounding more friendly.

"I moved here to San Francisco about a year ago. I was living at home in Kansas City before that. I'd been having a little bit of sex back home. After I got out here I heard about AIDS and safe sex. I was pretty much protecting myself. I guess I was exposed originally back home. You know, except for some scare stuff on

TV, I hadn't really paid much attention to AIDS. It seemed like something older men got from having too much sex. I didn't think I was like that. I mean, I was in high school."

"So what happened after you got diagnosed?"

"I got treated with Septra and got over the pneumonia in about a week and a half. I was real depressed when I got out of the hospital. I talked to some people at the AIDS Foundation, but didn't ask for a buddy or anything. But somebody there mentioned this woman Louise Hay who was doing healing workshops and a book called *A Course in Miracles* and the Center for Attitudinal Healing in Tiburon. But I didn't do much about it.

"About a month later my mom came out to visit me. And she took one look at me and got real upset. I'd lost a lot of weight and was looking pretty crummy, I guess. Well, she'd recently joined a Mind-Science church in Kansas City and had read a book by this guy Jerry Jampolsky called *Teach Only Love*. He was the founder of the Center in Tiburon. So my mom got me a copy of the book and then called the Center and found out about a group in the City..."

"Jon, did you know about this?" Greg asked.

"I've mentioned the *Course in Miracles* in here a few times. And one day I handed out some flyers about Attitudinal Healing. None of you guys seemed particularly interested. Remember last week I gave you that piece about attitude? But I didn't know about a group in the City. What I knew was that over in Marin, Jampolsky was working with children with cancer."

"So what happened?" Chuck pursued Robyn's story.

"I started going to these groups, thinking that I had AIDS and was going to die. And I got to feeling better and better. My mom had gone home, of course, but we talked on the phone a lot. She was real supportive—"

"Of your being gay?" Luis asked.

"Once I told her, yes. That was a big relief for me. And I think that had a lot to do with getting better. Anyway, last week she sent me some money to go get a complete physical, CAT Scan and everything, to find out how I was doing. And, believe it or not, I passed with flying colors. This new test they can do for the virus came back negative. It's like I got over it."

"Maybe you never really had AIDS to start with," Greg offered.

"Well, that's possible."

"What did the doctors say?" Luis asked.

"Well, they didn't know. One of them suggested, like Greg, that the first tests were wrong and I never really had it. But I did have PCP. Everybody agrees on that. Another doctor said maybe I developed a kind of antibody or something that *is* effective in fighting off the virus. He said he's seen one or two other cases that look like that. He was real excited. He wants me to come back so he can take samples of my blood to look for whatever did it. He said maybe they could clone it in the laboratory and give it to other people. Wouldn't that be great?

"Personally, I think I got a miracle. The *Course in Miracles* says 'Miracles are natural. When they do not occur something has gone wrong.' I just wanted to get well. That seemed perfectly natural to me. The *Course* also says miracles 'should not be under conscious control. Consciously selected miracles can be misguided.' I didn't have any way to plan how to get over this. Though Dr. Jampolsky got me visualizing my immune system working so it would protect me. That's what they have everybody do. Some doctor in Texas developed that idea for treating cancer."

"Carl Simonton," Jon interrupted. "I think he's in Southern California now."

"Yeah," Robyn continued. "I guess developing an antibody that kills the virus and protects me is perfectly natural. But since it doesn't seem to be working for other people, I guess it's kind of a miracle for me.

"Who knows? What I know is that I feel great now and that I want to share this with other people. I mean, I don't think I found some wonderful cure that nobody else knows about. Maybe this just worked on me. Maybe it wouldn't for other people. The Center doesn't make any claims at all for this kind of healing. What they say is that you can heal the attitudes you've got about your life and maybe that can allow physical healing, but what's really important is mental, you know, attitudinal healing. If you're gonna die, at least you ought to die happy and contented and loved."

"This sounds great," Chuck commented.

"I don't believe it," rejoined Greg. "It's just pie in the sky. It may — and I say *may* — have worked for this guy. But it ain't gonna work for me."

"Well, you're right," Robyn answered. "With that kind of attitude nothing's going to work."

"Robyn, this does sound real interesting," Jon said, ignoring Greg's cynicism. "Would you be willing to talk about this with us more?"

"Sure," Robyn answered enthusiastically.

"You know, we came together tonight outside our regular schedule because of the news about Pat. I think what Robyn's telling us is important. And, I think, tonight we ought to be looking at healing our hurt feelings about Pat's death — and the way he chose to do it. Maybe more than looking at healing our bodies."

"Well, Jon, they're not really so different," Robyn interjected. "How you all feel about your friend's death has a lot to do with how you feel about yourselves. And vice-versa."

"So how do I feel better about Pat's suicide?" challenged Greg.

"You have to forgive Pat for dying like that. And you have to forgive yourself for being hurt and angry at him."

"I'm not angry at him," Greg said, sounding astonished.

"I would be," came back Robyn's matter-of-fact reply.

"How come?" Luis said. "I don't feel angry. I feel terribly sad. I'll miss him."

"I think that's probably just why you might be angry with him: he deserted you."

"Robyn's probably right," Jon added. "Anger is a pretty common response to a death. Let me acknowledge that *I'm* angry at Pat. Not so much for dying as for the way he decided to do it. His jumping — or falling — off that ledge has sure created a headache for me. It's resulted in all sorts of headlines."

"Yeah, some people are already saying all the PWAs ought to kill themselves," Chuck said.

"I guess I have to admit I'm angry with him too," Greg said, calming down for the first time this evening. "Now I've got to think about whether or not I want to kill myself. You know, I was over there earlier in the evening. We were talking about suicide. Maybe I feel guilty." His voice faltered and he started to sob. "Pat had suggested we could all die together. Now he's left."

Jon realized he'd just heard one of the warning signals that demand an immediate response from anyone in the role of therapist. "Greg, are you feeling like hurting yourself?"

"Not exactly. But Pat had sort of convinced me that there might come a time when it would be the right thing. If death is okay, like Robyn says, then why shouldn't I?"

"When you heal yourself from fear then you could choose to die," Robyn answered. "Until then you probably can't and probably shouldn't."

"And, again I ask, how do I do that?"

"The same way," Robyn answered Greg. "You forgive."

"Who?"

"Everybody, everything, God, yourself — especially yourself."

"Forgive them for what?"

"I don't know that the kind of forgiveness I'm talking about has so much to do with the content as with the process of forgiveness. According to the *Course in Miracles*, forgiveness means recognizing that—" Robyn's voice changed so he sounded like he was quoting "—'the sin which I thought my brother committed against me never really happened at all.' And that means discovering that 'you are never upset for the reason you think; you are always upset because you see only the past.'"

"That's one of the basic principles of psychotherapy," Jon spoke up by way of affirming what he thought were ideas that might not be so readily accepted by the group because of Robyn's newness here and because of his youth. Jon was realizing how impressed he was with Robyn McCullough. *This young kid, barely an adult, is not only spouting important wisdom, but has apparently made it work in his own life.*

"A lot of therapy consists of helping people see that they are unconsciously associating people and events in the present with experiences in the past and then reacting to what happened in the past instead of to what's really going on in the present. Psychological healing comes from bringing those unconscious associations up into consciousness and seeing that they don't really apply."

"In attitudinal healing," Robyn continued, "forgiveness — that is, letting go of the past and the future — is the way of giving healing to others and accepting healing for yourself. One principle is that giving and receiving are the same. So when you forgive others, you get to receive forgiveness."

"And certainly one of the major problems people have, maybe gay people especially, is forgiving themselves," Jon said, affirming Robyn's comments again. "Most of us learned to feel guilty about being who we are, about feeling things like anger and desire. Many people who are sick feel guilty about that."

"That's especially true with AIDS," Chuck commented. "There are all these forces out there blaming us for it, telling us we brought this disease on ourselves and that we deserve to die on account of it."

"What you deserve is forgiveness," Robyn said. "All of us need forgiveness and we deserve it because we feel guilty about things that don't exist anymore. The past is dead and the future is imaginary. And in the present, everything is perfect."

"So how come I still feel so awful about Pat Stratford jumping out the window?" Greg retorted.

"Because it's real hard to live in the present and to leave the past behind," Jon answered.

"You mean I just have to forget my friend?"

"Not necessarily forget. And you can't escape having the feelings," Robyn said. "But you can go through them. You can experience them and love them for being your feelings and then you can let go. You don't have to drag Pat along with you. He'd decided he wanted out, after all."

"So what about me killing myself?" Greg said.

"Oh, you can do that," Robyn answered. "If you want to. Don't do it because of Pat. Do it because you love life. If you do everything out of love — instead of out of fear — then, well, then you're free."

•Three•

Thanksgiving

1

Jon sat quietly in what he guessed was probably called "the green room" out of theater tradition, though this one did not seem to contain a single item of green color. At the other end of the couch, poring over pages of notes, sat state senator Charles Wanamaker. Across the room at a small side table sat Paul Curtiss, the PWA whom Jon had met only a few minutes before. Wanamaker had conspicuously *not* shaken hands with Curtiss and let it be known by his body language that he expected Curtiss to stay on his own side of the room.

Having previously heard Wanamaker on TV news, Jon had felt real animosity toward the California lawmaker. Today, oddly enough he thought, he felt sorry for the man. He seemed so ill-at-ease and insecure. He also felt sorry for Paul Curtiss, not so much because he had AIDS — Jon had gotten used to being around people with the disease — but because he looked so nervous. He was practically quivering. *This is probably his first time on national TV,* Jon thought and realized that, though he'd been interviewed on San Francisco's local channels many times, it was *his* first time on national TV as well.

🙙

Jon had arrived in New York City two days ealier. This was to be the start of a two-week vacation for him. He was going to use it partly as a personal vacation and partly as a business trip.

Even before leaving San Francisco he'd called ahead and set up meetings with several AIDS educators and grassroots activists in the City. He'd known wnen he accepted the invitation to be on the Donahue show that he'd probably say some things that would anger some of his colleagues. He hoped to do some alliance-building before leaving New York.

Then, taking advantage of the opportunity the Donahue people offered him, he was going down to D.C. to spend Thanksgiving Day with old friends. Jon had made a tradition of spending Thanksgiving with Phil and Carol Sheehan when they lived in California; he'd missed the last few holidays because the family moved to Arlington, Virginia. This year he had an opportunity to revive the tradition.

Then he would fly out to LaCrosse to meet Mark, who was visiting his grandmother for the holiday, and spend the rest of the vacation in what he hoped was going to be a snowy mid-western winter — something he hadn't experienced in years. He was especially looking forward to the time with Mark. *High romance*, he joked to himself.

🔊

Earlier Jon had accepted a glass of orange juice from an assistant producer who'd welcomed him, explained a few basic rules, and introduced Jon to Mr. Donahue. Now as she entered the room, he downed the rest of the juice.

"Showtime, gentlemen," she announced spritely. "Senator Wanamaker, I'd like you to go first, then Mr. Curtiss, then Dr. Stiers. As I mentioned before, the tech will put your mike on you just before you walk out onto the set."

Jon stopped thinking about what he was going to say and let himself be guided through the technical procedures. A few minutes later, he was sitting on stage facing several hundred people and reminding himself to stay calm and speak slowly and clearly. The white-haired and imposing host was stalking back and forth across the front of the stage making jokes with the audience.

A moment of silence. The familiar theme music came up. The audience applauded in response to a signal from Donahue, then the host began to shout over the din.

"Last week the American public was shocked by the dramatic suicide of an AIDS victim in San Francisco. You may remember that this young man jumped out of his fourth-storey apartment window while a late-night crowd looked on. Let me get the reaction of this audience," Phil Donahue's voice boomed.

"AIDS is a fatal disease. Health care for its victims is costing the country billions of dollars a year. They're gonna die anyway. Why shouldn't they kill themselves?" Donahue's remark was met with only a spattering of half-hearted applause.

"Every American has a right to medical care — no matter what it costs." Another spattering of applause.

"Well, people," Donahue playfully scolded his audience from his place halfway between the studio audience and the guests on the stage platform, "got to get some reactions out of you. This is juicy stuff." He half-turned toward the guests spaced across the stage. "My first guest today is California state senator Charles Wanamaker. As you may know, the senator has recently submitted a proposal that would cut off public funds for medical treatment for people with AIDS after their second bout with a major opportunistic infection. Is that right, Senator?"

"Yes, sir, I believe—" Wanamaker started to launch into his statement.

"For the benefit of our viewers, I think you'd better explain what you mean by opportunistic infection," the host interrupted.

"I'm a legislator, not a doctor, Phil," Wanamaker answered, apparently shaken that he hadn't been allowed to complete his prepared statement. "But I'll try to answer that. As you know, AIDS doesn't actually cause death itself, but leaves its victims vulnerable to other infections. The Federal Centers for Disease Control have defined a set of so-called 'opportunistic infections' that signal the diagnosis of AIDS. Once that diagnosis is made, frankly, these people might as well be dead. There's nothing the doctors can do for them. And they're just creating an enormous expense for the taxpayer. My bill would limit the amount of money society would have to invest in these people's dying."

"Wait a minute," shouted Curtiss, "I've had three episodes of pneumocystis and I'm still alive."

"This is Paul Curtiss. You have AIDS, do you not?"

"Yes, Mr. Donahue, I do. And if the senator here had his way, I'd be dead today. But I'm not. And I'm pretty healthy." Curtiss' speech brought a round of applause.

"Let me ask you, Paul, if you ever considered suicide while you were sick?"

"Of course. That's a pretty common thought among people with supposedly fatal illnesses. But those thoughts passed when I got well. I'm glad *I* didn't jump out a window."

"How much has your medical treatment cost the American taxpayers?" Wanamaker asked accusingly.

"We're talking about my life. Not somebody's checkbook," Curtiss exploded back.

"That checkbook might be somebody else's life — somebody

who worked hard for that money for his family, who didn't run around and get some *sexually transmitted disease*," Wanamaker said the last words with obvious distaste.

"Are you implying I deserve to die?"

"Gentlemen, gentlemen. I'm the host on this show. I get to ask the questions," Donahue said facetiously and the audience roared with laughter.

"The recent case of. . ." Donahue looked down at his notes, "Pat Stratford involved a man who was pretty sick, I believe, and wasn't expected to live much longer. My third guest is Dr. Jonathan Stiers. I understand you work in an AIDS Education Program for the City of San Francisco. And you also conduct a support group for people with AIDS. This young man Pat Stratford was in your group. Is that right?"

Jon nodded affirmatively. The discussion had already gotten hotter than he'd expected. What was he going to say?

"Dr. Stiers, should people like your patient be free to kill themselves?"

Jon cleared his throat and started to answer Donahue's question. Jon's words were broadcast across the country to a wide variety of listeners.

2

Emily Hogdsdon was getting settled at her desk. She had a lot of work today: two reports were due next week on the nuclear weapons study the firm was doing and for a week now the computer had been churning out results on the teenage chastity project that somebody had to analyze. For a moment, Emily felt a wave of annoyance at Edward. *He spends too much time in that office reading those books of his and staring at that stuff in the closet.*

Her phone buzzed. "Liberty Bell Foundation, may I help you?"

"Emily, this is George Wilson."

"Well, good morning, George. I don't often hear your voice this time of the morning."

"No, Emily, you don't. Can I talk to Edward?"

"I'm sorry, he's on the other line. Can I give him a message?"

"Tell him there's a program on channel three this morning that I think he'd be interested in."

"When is that coming on?" Emily asked as she carefully noted the message on a pad on her desk.

"It's on right now," came the annoyed reply.

"Don't get testy with me, George."

"I'm sorry, Emily. It's just that I think Edward will find this important. You'll tell him, won't you?"

"Of course I'll tell him. Good day, George."

Well, should I interrupt his phone call for a TV show? Emily wondered. Then she noticed the second light on her phone blink out. Edward was off the line.

Emily walked into the office. "George Wilson just called to say there's a TV program he thought you'd want to see."

"What is it?" Buchanan asked.

"George said it was on right now on channel three. Shall I get out the TV?"

"Of course, of course. Let's see what it is."

Emily opened the ornate antique chest across from Buchanan's desk to reveal a modern television set. As she stepped aside, Buchanan switched on the set with the remote he had at his desk.

"Channel three you said?"

The sound came on immediately and then the picture formed. A slightly familiar face appeared.

"...enormous expense for the taxpayer. My bill would put a limit on the amount of money society would have to invest in these people's dying."

"That's Wanamaker from California, I believe," Edward announced, "Thank you, Emily. You can stay and watch if you want."

"Only for a minute or two, Edward, I have work to do." She perched herself on the edge of Buchanan's desk and let herself get interested in the program.

3

"I think this fellow Stiers comes off pretty well," Alice Graves remarked to Lydia, the secretary at the Visiting Nurse Association. "Though I don't know how I feel about people killing themselves."

"He's not really suggesting that, is he?" Lydia answered, only half paying attention. Alice, on the other hand, was captivated with the discussion on the little TV in the office. Alice was a news freak. She kept CNN continuous news on all day long — except for one hour when Lydia insisted on watching "All My Children" while she ate her lunch. Alice did her best to avoid getting interested in the story, but had to admit that recently she'd become almost as addicted to that "stupid ol' soap" as Lydia.

Now she was glad she'd switched over to Donahue while CNN did the sports news. Even though she'd already missed half the show, she was especially interested in this subject.

"Oh, I don't suppose so. . . ." Alice started to say as the familiar Donahue theme music came back on.

As the show started again, Phil Donahue was standing out in the audience. "Let's hear from a caller," he said.

"I'm a doctor here in Manhattan," the disembodied voice announced. "I'm a gay man. I am real concerned about what the politician is saying. I think this is just the tip of an iceberg."

"Would you explain that?" asked Donahue, staring up into space.

"I mean that ever since the Supreme Court decided that the basic rights of citizenship are not guaranteed to homosexuals, there've been more attacks on our rights. Now this man is suggesting that people who've gotten sick ought to be just left out to die."

"He wasn't singling out homosexuals."

"Indirectly he was. Society's become concerned about heterosexual spread of the disease, and that's a realistic concern. But the fact is that AIDS still shows up primarily among homosexual men. It's been used over and over as a supposedly logical justification for prejudice. And that prejudice is against homosexuals. Society is looking for a scapegoat, somebody to blame. Homosexuals are vulnerable to all sorts of oppression. I know it sounds alarmist, but I think American society is in about the same place German society was in the 1930s. And just like those people — who I'm sure were all nice people who never thought of themselves as monsters — all ended up supporting monstrous crimes perpetrated by Adolf Hitler, it seems like Americans are being talked into committing monstrous crimes against homosexuals."

"What kinds of crimes?" Donahue asked over the applause from some members of the audience.

"Gay men are losing their jobs and insurance coverage. They're getting beat up on the street. People are talking about quarantine. And all this is just being accepted by the public as part of controlling AIDS. When, in fact, it has nothing to do with AIDS. I'm sure your guests could tell you more stories."

Donahue looked over at Jon.

"The caller used the word vulnerable a moment ago. I think that's significant. So many homosexuals believe they have to keep their personal lives secret. That makes them vulnerable. I think it's particularly significant that AIDS is a condition of vulnerability: it takes away your ability to protect yourself from other diseases. Maybe it's not surprising something like that would show up among gay men or, for that matter, that it would show up at this time in history when we're *all* feeling so vulnerable because of things like toxic waste and pollution and, of course, nuclear war."

"Are you still there, caller?" Donahue looked up at the ceiling again. "You say you're a doctor?"

"I work in one of the big medical centers in the city. For obvious reasons, I'm not going to say more. We see lots of AIDS patients. We know this virus cannot be spread except by sexual or blood contact."

"Yes, the public has heard that message again and again. Why do you think it isn't accepted?"

"Why are people superstitious? Why do people believe absolute nonsense? Usually because some so-called authority is spouting it. The TV preachers have blamed sex and especially homosexuality for all the problems in society — problems that are really caused by modernization. But you can't scapegoat the whole modern world, so they blame gay people.

"It's very upsetting. We've got to turn to people like your audience and make them aware of the dreadful dangers homosexuals are facing in America. Your audience all believe they would have spoken out against Hitler—"

Donahue turned to the audience, "Would you have?"

There was a loud round of applause.

". . . well, now's the time to speak out against the same kind of thing happening here."

There were a few people applauding, then more and more. Soon the whole audience — and Jon and Paul on stage — was applauding.

"Thank you for the call," Donahue announced. "Senator, you didn't applaud. Do you disagree?"

"I think that is nonsense. The objections to homosexuality have nothing to do with popular prejudices. They are based on God's word."

"Now that just isn't true," Jon interrupted him.

"Now, now, let's not get into a battle about the Bible," Donahue said. "I've heard all these arguments too many times. None of you people ever seem willing to agree on what the Bible says."

"That's my point," Jon spoke up. "We live in a pluralistic society. Biblical believers can believe anything they want. But they have got to allow other people to believe other things."

"God doesn't allow you to believe lies," Wanamaker said.

"Okay, okay," Donahue tried once more to stop him.

🐾

"Well, I believe in the bible," Alice Graves remarked to Lydia, "but I don't like people who hit other people over the head with it."

4

It bothered George Wilson that idiots like Wanamaker spoke for the Bible. *They only end up making religion sound as stupid as they are*, he thought bitterly.

He realized he liked this Jon Stiers. He liked what he'd said about choosing to accept death when life got unbearable. *The man seems honestly concerned about individuals and about society. And he seems compassionate and kind. I can understand why he's a psychotherapist*, George thought and his mind wandered from the TV program as he recalled his own past experience with psychiatry...

🐾

"...all this talk about antibodies," a member of the audience was saying, "I thought antibodies were what protected us from getting diseases." George's attention went back to the program.

"That's right," Paul Curtiss spoke up, "the blood forms antibodies to identify foreign proteins and micro-organisms so the immune system can destroy them. But, unfortunately, these antibodies are not always effective. That's the case with the AIDS antibody. Its presence indicates you've been exposed, but it doesn't offer protection. HIV isn't the only virus, by the way, that the body doesn't produce the right kind of antibodies to destroy."

"You were a research biologist, were you not, Mr. Curtiss?" Donahue interrupted.

"I still am."

"Excuse me," answered Donahue. "Well then, is nobody immune to this disease?" he asked.

"That's why it's got to be stopped — at any cost," Wanamaker broke in. "Civil rights or no civil rights!"

"But that just doesn't seem to be true." Curtiss regained the floor. "A lot of people show positive for the antibody but aren't sick and maybe never will get sick. Maybe they're immune. But, even so, Wanamaker's argument is fallacious, because we know how to stop the spread of this disease without punishing the people who've got it. And, in fact, punishing them gives the wrong message about how the disease is spread."

"Paul raises an interesting point," Jon spoke up. "Apparently some people can develop an effective immune response to this virus, so they don't get it. And it even looks like a very few people have gotten over the disease altogether."

"Is this true?" Donahue asked.

"There's a young man in a group I facilitate who has apparently gotten over the disease. The tests show there is no virus in his blood anymore. Somehow he got over it."

"Lucky for him," Donahue remarked, wiping his forehead with the back of his hand. The audience laughed loudly.

"Well, maybe not just for him," Curtiss responded. "This is a relatively new disease, even a new kind of disease. I mean these retroviruses are something we didn't know about before. So we're seeing how the human race copes with what may be an altogether new phenomenon, I mean, a new evolutionary challenge."

"See, see," shouted Wanamaker. "There goes the secular humanist talking about evolution. God didn't say anything about evolutionary challenges in the Book of Genesis."

"Go on, Mr. Curtiss, I'm interested," said Donahue.

"There is an interesting new notion in biology about how evolution works. It's called the Theory of Formative Causation."

"Another theory," Wanamaker declared.

"Please, Senator, we know your opinion. Let Mr. Curtiss speak."

"A British biologist named Rupert Sheldrake has observed that certain forms of learning actually seem to happen on a species-wide level. One example he uses — that's really too complicated for me to explain here — was a study of rat behavior done, I think, at Harvard. Over several years the rats got better and better at swimming through a maze. The findings seemed to imply that learned or acquired traits could be inherited — and that's a major heresy in biology. So some other scientists in England set out to disprove the results. What they found was that their rats seemed to start off where the last experiment had ended. But these rats weren't genetically related, though they *were* of the same species. It looks like the learning happened in the whole species, not just the gene line at Harvard."

"That's remarkable," said Donahue softly.

"Well, not really. Don't we all see that things that used to seem difficult are now relatively easy? The obvious example is in sports. The four-minute mile used to be thought impossible. Now it's commonplace.

"Anyway, Sheldrake explains this phenomenon with what he

calls 'morphogenetic' or just 'morphic' fields. He says evolution really takes place on the level of these field interactions instead of on the level of individual organisms."

"Now, Mr. Curtiss, that's very interesting. Maybe we should get this fellow Sheldrake on this show. But what does that have to do with AIDS?"

"You were talking about the possibility of developing real immunity to HIV. The morphic field idea suggests that as enough people get exposed to this virus and develop neutralizing antibodies, so this information will change the morphic fields for human beings. After a while, maybe, most everybody will be able to form these antibodies. It's obviously that way for a lot of other diseases. When you look at history, you see that some people managed to survive every plague."

"I've got to break," Donahue interrupted as the theme music began to rise. "We're here in New York City discussing AIDS. And I hope you'll join us."

🐾

Hmmm, thought George Wilson as he poured himself another cup of coffee, only paying half-attention to the commercial for an alcohol treatment program, *maybe it's even simpler than that.*

5

Mark was working at his desk that afternoon. He'd accepted another architectural project. Though he still had a month before it was due, he'd already started work on it to give himself something to do. Jon had only been gone two days yet he was feeling restless and bereft. What had he done with his time before he met Jonathan Stiers?

The phone rang. Reaching around his draftsman's lamp, he groped for the handset. "Hi, Mark Hartman."

"Well, I really stirred up a hornet's nest," Jonathan's familiar voice began.

"Oh hi, did you? I thought the show went fine. I got it on videotape so you can see for yourself."

"Good, I want to see it. You know it looks like they got me to say that PWAs ought to commit suicide."

"I didn't hear you say that."

"I don't think it was as blatant as that, but that's how it got interpreted. I mean, I thought I was really very gentle. But now they've got me scheduled to be on the Today Show tomorrow morning. And reporters have been calling me all day long. Oh, Mark," Jon laughed, "I wish I were home."

"Well, so do I," Mark answered. "I've been lonely without you. But it'll only be a couple of days."

"Speaking of which, I saw on the weather tonight that there's been snow in Minnesota already. Maybe we'll get our White Thanksgiving after all."

"Look, seriously, are you okay? I mean, did you get yourself in more trouble than you expected?"

"Well, probably. I think I said the right things, but you know how things can get distorted by the media."

"I'll be watching the Today Show tomorrow."

"Hope I don't make a fool of myself."

"You couldn't."

"You're biased," Jon laughed affectionately. "Love you."

"Me too. Guess I'll let you go. My flight leaves tomorrow afternoon. I'll give you a call at the Sheehans' on Turkey Day."

"Bye, Mark."

"Goodbye, Jonathan," Mark said wistfully. As he switched off the phone, he wondered what he was getting himself into, having a boyfriend like this who was so obviously visible and so potentially a lightning rod of controversy. *Well, what difference does it make? That's what love's all about.* "Stand by your man" — the words of the old country-western song came to Mark's mind. And he laughed.

6

Billy DePalma had not seen the Donahue Show that morning, though he'd probably have been interested if he'd known what the subject was going to be. If he had seen it, he might have used Paul Curtiss's suggestion of the possibility of morphic field resonance to give immunity to the virus as an excuse to get out of the plan Lynn had talked him into. But he hadn't and tonight he found himself regretting that he'd ever gotten into this whole crazy thing.

Not only am I almost certain to be arrested for trespassing — how can I possibly manage to program the communications protocol into that computer in the seven minutes Lynn says I've got before the burglar alarm is activated — but, even if I succeed, I'm going to have to spend something like eight more hours cooped up in this locker. How did I let Lynn manipulate me into this? I must have been a fool. Maybe it'd be easier to just die of AIDS.

About ten minutes before closing time, Billy had arrived as planned at the front door of the Liberty Bell Foundation offices.

Lynn was waiting and quickly escorted him unseen into the employees' lounge. She'd already prepared the locker, by removing all her belongings and taking down the shelf. "There'll be lots of room for you — to stand," she promised. She even left some provisions: a thermos of coffee and a bag of sandwiches hanging from a coat hook in easy reach. As she'd discovered previously, by twisting a scarf through the latch mechanism she could prevent the lock from engaging.

"Can't you just manage to turn on the machine for a minute and enter a simple program?" he implored her when they cooked up this scheme and he realized what a dreadful job he was going to be assigned.

"Billy, I don't dare turn on the machine during the day. I've been watching for a chance all week. There just isn't any time I have alone in there."

"But what if I get caught?"

"You won't get caught," she said authoritatively. "Besides, I've already done my share hooking up that modem."

"There was nothing to that," Billy argued.

Now, as he thought about it, she probably did manage quite a display of prestidigitation. Following his instructions, Lynn had plugged a line into the back of Wilson's IBM and, under the guise of looking for an earring that had rolled underneath the desk, had run the line into a modem attached to a machine on the other side of the partition around Wilson's space.

But the job still required one more step: the communications protocol had to be read onto the IBM's hard disc and the program installed. It wouldn't take long, he'd assured her — and was now reassuring himself.

He'd stayed safely in the locker till after seven. He wasn't sure what all the sounds in the place were, but he was pretty sure the pattern of beeps he'd heard from down the hall at about five-thirty fit the description Lynn had given of the burglar alarm being activated. Then about an hour later — a very long hour for him — he'd heard the front door open and then another pattern of beeps that he assumed was Wilson disarming the system when he came to work.

Soon after that, Billy crept out of the locker and, in the partial darkness, crept down the hall toward the computer room and secretary's pool Lynn had described. Peeping up over the glass in the door, he could see the man he'd driven home just over a week before sitting in front of the green phosphor monitor. There were no other lights on in the room.

From where he was, he just could not quite see the screen. He still had no idea whether this whole adventure was necessary. What if there were nothing about AIDS in *that* computer either? For the first time it occurred to him that those pages Lynn found in the xerox room may not have come from Liberty Bell at all. Wilson — or somebody else — could have brought them in to copy and they might have nothing to do with the firm's research.

Lynn had described to Billy how he could hide in a storage room just across the hall from the computer room. From there, if he opened the door just a crack, he could watch Wilson and be ready to bolt into the room just as soon as Wilson activated the alarm and headed out the door. *Why did I let her talk me into this?* he asked himself again — for the thousandth time. The couple of hours in that closet while Wilson mulled over his computer literally brought suicidal thoughts to Billy's mind.

The easiest way, of course, was to forget this whole thing and just let himself die of the AIDS in a few years. He thought about what a relief it would be to stop worrying about the disease. For a little while he let himself cry very softly for Jeff, out of grief and out of regret. Then, in his anxiety-racked state, his mind was flooded with sexual thoughts. A few of them were of infecting Lynn as a way to get even for putting him through this. *But I've fallen in love with her. Fallen so much in love that I can't just do the easy and obvious thing and get out of here right now.*

Of course, he wasn't even sure he could get out. He was sure Wilson had locked the front doors behind him. There was no way out of this except to continue with the plan.

Almost in a dream-like half-delirium, Billy peeked through the crack in the door. The eerie green light that had been illuminating Wilson's face was gone. The room seemed to be empty. *Oh my God,* Billy thought, *what if I've fallen asleep and Wilson's already left? What if the alarm's on and I can't get out of this closet? What if I have to stay in here til morning and then somebody opens the door and finds me?*

Suddenly a bright white light stabbed through the crack in the door. Billy felt a wave of relief. Wilson must have just turned off the machine; he was heading out to the hall and had turned on the overhead lights. Billy let his eyes adjust a moment and peered out through the crack. To his dismay, he saw George Wilson walking directly toward the closet he was hiding in.

His heart started pounding. *Oh my God, this is it!* He tried to press himself back against the far wall, but nothing could hide him. The closet was full of reams of paper in paper-wrapped packages. There was no way to hide.

He had only a moment: the time it would take Wilson to walk the six feet to the closet. He tried to think what he could do, but his mind wouldn't function. He crouched low. Then realized how foolish that would look. He could try to overpower Wilson, knock him out, get his keys, get out of here...

That was it. Yes.

He pressed himself up against the wall next to the crack in the door. Maybe Wilson wouldn't see him when he first opened the door. Billy took a ream of paper in hand, held it up over his head and prepared to bring it crashing down when Wilson stepped in to get whatever he wanted from the closet. He peeped once more through the crack.

Oh God. Wilson's face was practically right up against his. Billy realized he wasn't breathing and tried to inhale very slowly and quietly, so at least he'd be ready to make a run. *What if Wilson has a gun?*

Suddenly his little closet was cast into total darkness. He heard a loud click, then silence.

All Wilson had done was push the door shut! Billy laughed to himself as his whole mind and body was flooded with relief. He struggled not to get hysterical as he thought about how close a call he'd had.

Billy waited a few minutes longer. He had definitely not heard the beeps from the alarm system, and he was sure he could hear shuffling noises from down the hall. He opened the door again and peered out. The overhead light was out now. *Thank God.* He could see a rectangle of light in the hall falling through the open door from the printer room. Wilson was in there!

Suddenly the hall filled with a buzzing racket. Billy's heart started pounding again, till reason and Lynn's voice in memory told him that that was the sound of the shredding machine. When that stopped, probably, Wilson would be on his way.

He crouched down again on his haunches and took several intentional deep breaths. He looked again at his wrist watch. He'd already set the digital countdown timer to six minutes, thirty seconds. He wasn't giving himself much time to get back to the locker. He hoped Lynn had been right that there was no alarm sensing device in the employee's lounge.

The racket from the shredder stopped. Silence. He pulled the door back, practically closing it. The light in the hall never came on. He could hear Wilson moving around. He peered out and saw a shadow disappear into one of the offices. He thought he could hear a clicking sound. It was very faint, but in the silence of the deserted office it seemed vaguely audible. A combination lock being turned. Wilson was locking something up.

Knowing how precious his time was, he made a snap decision and dashed quickly out the door of the closet, closing it gently but swiftly behind him, and then darted across the hall and through the doors into the computer room. He went straight for the IBM. In the faint light from the windows he could see surprisingly well.

The first hurdle was crossed when he ran his hand across the face of the C.P.U. and felt the key in the lock. Lynn had assured him that Wilson never took the key out of its switch. *Thank God.*

He heard an electronic beeping. Wilson was activating the alarm. Billy pushed the stem on his watch. It answered with a tiny beep of its own and Billy almost jumped out of his skin at the sound. He'd forgotten that was going to happen.

Listening carefully, he heard Wilson turn his key in the front door lock. That was the signal he needed. He reached around and switched on the IBM-AT console. Then, while the C.P.U. automatically checked its memory circuits, he stuck the floppy diskette with the communications program into the A: drive. In a moment, a prompt appeared on the screen in bright green letters: C>. He entered A:. The prompt changed to A>. The A: drive began to whir again and soon the screen blinked a couple of times, then filled with print.

The communications protocol program to connect the computer terminal to the mainframe modem was scrolling across the screen. In a moment it stopped and asked for a response. Huddling down low in hopes of being invisible just in case Wilson returned, Billy quickly punched the required keys to answer the program's questions about the configuration of the system. Billy could only hope it was standard and that the default values would all work for him.

He looked down at his watch. There were three minutes left of the six and a half he was allowing himself.

Now the hard disk in-use light was glowing as the memory accepted the programmed information. Then it stopped and the A> prompt appeared again. One last thing to do: he had to get back into DOS directory, rename the communications protocol, run it into a subdirectory that Wilson was liable never to call up and then create a path from the new subdirectory into DOS so the program could be accessed.

One minute.

It looked okay. There was no time to test it. *But, oh God, I couldn't bear having to do this again. It'll just have to work.*

He started toward the door, then realized he'd left the floppy diskette in the A: drive. He dashed back and, with his hands quivering, he flipped open the door of the drive and pulled out the diskette. He slipped it into the pocket of his windbreaker and ran through the door into the hall. It was dark, but the light through the front doors showed him a path back to the lounge. He was halfway down the length of the hall when his timer went off. Thirty seconds. He sprinted the rest of the way and made it into the lounge.

He was just closing the locker door when he heard a faint electronic beep from far away. The alarm was turning itself on, he told himself, and he sank down on his heels and let the fear and excitement overwhelm him.

He ate another of Lynn's sandwiches. He'd never tasted bologna so good before. He needed to pee, but, not knowing what would happen if he stepped out into the lounge, he suppressed the urge, and decided not to drink any more of the coffee.

In spite of his immense discomfort, in only a few long minutes, he fell fast asleep.

7

"Are you all right?" Lynn whispered, shaking Billy's shoulder.

"I think so," he murmured, waking up. "Can I get out of here now? *If* I can," he added struggling to straighten up. "I'm almost too stiff to move."

"Can you give me another thirty minutes? Somebody's liable to come in. Everybody's arriving just now."

"Oh, Lynn, I have got to pee so bad. I don't know."

Lynn's heart was pounding. She hated to cause Billy any more discomfort. She was a nervous wreck herself, just from worrying about him all night. She could only guess how stressed he was.

"Please. I'll be back as soon as I can."

🥢

Lynn busied herself as usual, straightening up first thing. She had the chance to make sure everything was in order around the IBM-AT by the window. She walked up and down the hall a few times under the pretext of emptying trash baskets.

She counted the office staff. It looked like everybody was there and at their desks. As usual, the reception area was empty. Mrs. Hodgsdon doubled as receptionist for the few people who walked into the suite. Her office, just beyond the lounge, was only a few feet from the front door.

Lynn slipped into the lounge and quickly opened the locker. "Hi," she said. "Coast is clear. I hope you'll be all right. You're a dear." She hated how inane she sounded. She really wanted Billy to understand how immensely moved she was by his willingness to carry out this plan with her. She hoped it would save them both. "There's a men's room just down the hall," she whispered.

"It's okay," Billy answered. His voice sounded far less pressured than before. He kissed her lightly on the lips as he came out of the locker and then managed to straighten up. "Lynn," he whispered with a smile in his voice, "just don't drink the coffee in the thermos."

A moment later, with a grin, he was out the door. Their plan had succeeded.

8

"Did you see Jon Stiers on TV this morning?" Blum asked.

"I thought that was yesterday," Robyn answered.

"That was on the Donahue Show. Apparently he made such an impression that he was offered a spot on the Today Show this morning. I was switching around and caught the tailend."

"How'd he do?"

"Oh, well, pretty good, I thought. I mean he looked good and seemed calm and self-assured. Bryant Gumbel asked him if he thought AIDS patients ought to kill themselves."

"Your friend Pat's suicide really got Stiers into a corner," Robyn observed.

"Jon answered that he didn't think every PWA ought to kill themselves just because they had AIDS, but that many of them would save themselves and their loved ones a lot of pain if they avoided so-called heroic measures or just stopped taking their medication. Gumbel asked him about the cost of treating AIDS. Gumbel observed that especially now with the new drugs keeping people alive longer, it was up to something like fourteen billion dollars a year now and rising."

"How'd he answer that?"

"Real diplomatically! Jon said the willingness to expend such money was indicative of the compassion and humanity of the American people. To some extent he blamed the medical industry for the enormous expense, pointing out that all that money is getting paid to somebody; it isn't just being destroyed. But then he added that perhaps some PWAs ought to recognize a responsibility to reduce those costs, at least they shouldn't drain the resources of the system just out of fear of the inevitable. I think that might have meant letting themselves die."

"Sounds pretty good to me. I mean for people who aren't doing anything to fight the disease and are just expecting the doctors to cure them. They might as well die. Leaving your life to doctors is no way to get well," Robyn answered.

"You know, all this suicide talk is bothering me. Not that I'm thinking about it. I'm healthy — at least I think so..."

"Of course you are, Blum," Robyn replied. "And you can keep yourself healthy. For that matter even people with the virus are likely to be healthy. The trick is to stay healthy, not to wait until you're diagnosed with AIDS and then demand some kind of cure."

"Well, I'm worried about the other PWAs in the group. Chuck said he was talking to Greg and Luis the other day about suicide and both of them seemed to think it might be a good idea sometime."

"Well, maybe it is for them."

"Yeah, but what if they pull off some kind of group suicide? I think Pat had suggested that the night he jumped."

"Would you like some more juice?" Robyn asked, changing the subject. He'd invited Blum over for lunch and really didn't want to spend the whole time talking about serious matters. Robyn was getting to like Blum and even hoping for a little romance. After all, most people who met him, once he'd told them his story of — apparently — having gotten over AIDS, treated him just as gingerly as if he still had the disease but didn't show him the compassion they would have if he were an invalid. Blum Blumgarten, on the other hand, didn't seem at all freaked and, in fact, seemed to admire Robyn for his succesful victory.

For lunch Robyn had fixed sandwiches of tofu and sprouts on dark seven-grain bread, which he served with carrot juice.

"You're on a real health kick," Blum answered, sidestepping the question of more carrot juice.

"Well, if you'd been through what I have, you probably would be too."

"Yeah, I guess so. Well I hope you'll eat at least a little of the turkey I got for dinner tomorrow afternoon." Blum held up his empty glass, "Hey, got any iced tea?"

"Herbal tea." Robyn grinned.

9

Just after nine p.m., Billy arrived to drive Lynn to the airport. He hadn't come by earlier because he was busy at his computer.

"I've got good news," he said as he rushed past her into the apartment. "B-r-r-r, it's gotten cold." He stood over the radiator. "Well, I'm pretty sure I got the memory from Wilson's disk drive to copy to mine. At least, something's taking up a lot of memory space on my disk. For all I know it could be blank space. I haven't figured out how to get into the files yet.

"But I have gotten into that file you found in the Xerox machine. It wasn't hidden behind a password. And that seems to confirm that that machine's got data about the AIDS studies."

"Yea-a!" exclaimed Lynn as she wrapped her arms around Billy.

"And, I've discovered that 'Vir. Anti.' stands for 'Viral Antidote.' I think that means it isn't just a statistical sum or a control group. Unfortunately, the file didn't give any information about where this viral antidote is being studied. But the words 'viral antidote' certainly suggest a cure.

"Now I've got to figure out what kind of password or code this guy Wilson has on those files. That's gonna take a while. I mean, if I can manage it at all."

"Oh, Billy, I'm just sure you're gonna find the key and inside find out how to get this antidote," Lynn answered.

🕊

"I wish you were coming with me," Lynn said as she finished her packing. She was catching the red-eye flight to Milwaukee and then making connections to LaCrosse. With the time change she expected to be home by two a.m.

"Me too, I guess. Tell your parents I said hello. I'll be okay. I suppose I'm not quite ready to meet the family. Besides I've got work to do," Billy answered.

Lynn hated leaving him. But she had to admit deep down that she too was glad he'd decided not to come with her. *I don't dare tell them he's got the virus,* she thought, and she tried to suppress the pang of guilt that went with that thought.

"What're you doing on Thanksgiving?" she asked.

"I told you. I'll go find a turkey dinner around here. I've got work to do on the computer." Lynn felt a twinge of excitement. If Billy was successful in finding the apparent cure for the AIDS virus that Liberty Bell Foundation was monitoring, her whole future was going to be different.

Lynn had been bustling around the apartment, with Billy following along trying to carry on a conversation, as she got more and more anxious about going home for her first time since setting out on her own. "Lee Ann, you ready?"

"Give me a few more minutes," her roommate answered from the bathroom.

"Don't take too long," Lynn shouted. "Our plane's leaving in less than two hours. And the airport's gonna be crowded."

"Lynn," Billy asked, sounding very serious as she came into the front room and dropped her suitcase and sat down on the new sofa. "You know, I could only get in to copy those files when Wilson had them open. I think I did that without him knowing . . . but I don't know."

"You mean, Mr. Wilson — or Mr. Buchanan — could know what we did?" Lynn exclaimed. Billy had never indicated there was any way Liberty Bell could know they were spying.

"I don't think so. But—"

"Oh, you don't think they could trace it to us, do you? I'd hate to lose that job." Even as she said it, she realized how it sounded; if they found a way to cure the virus Billy was carrying, what difference would that job make?

"It'll be okay," Billy responded. He sat down next to her, put his arm around her shoulder and pulled her against him. "Lynn Graves, I love you," he said. "And when you get home, I bet I'll have great news for both of us."

10

Just before one a.m. Lynn called her mother. "Hi, Mom, I'm sorry. We got put on stand-by in Milwaukee because the flight was overbooked and then there wasn't room for us. So we're waiting for the next flight, which doesn't leave here till six a.m. I'll call you when we get in."

At eight-thirty she called again. "Hi, we're here. We'll be waiting outside the baggage claim," Lynn said, "so you can just drive right through."

“Welcome home,” her mother said as Lynn climbed in the front and unlocked the back door for Lee Ann.

“Is that all your luggage?” Alice asked, seeing that each of them only had a small bag.

“Yup,” Lynn announced. “We're traveling light. Let's get out of here. I am so tired.” She leaned over and kissed her mother on the cheek.

“Hi, Mrs. Graves,” Lee Ann spoke up. “Thanks for picking us up.”

As Alice maneuvered the car out of the airport traffic, Lee Ann started describing her job and then Lynn interrupted with a story about their apartment and the new sofa they'd just bought. Then she interrupted herself. “Oh Mom, you'd mentioned you were treating an AIDS patient. How is he?”

“Oh Lynn, he died last week, didn't I tell you?”

“That's too bad, Mom. You know, I was going to tell you that at this place I work I've found out about a new treatment for AIDS that seems to be a hundred percent effective.”

“Not really,” Alice exclaimed. “How come I haven't heard of that?”

“Well, I guess it's some sort of experimental drug that's still pretty hush-hush. I don't know. I'm still seeing if I can find out some more.”

“It's just wonderful what doctors are coming up with these days,” Alice answered, then changed the subject. “Lee Ann, I'll take you right home if that's okay, then I need to stop by the DeGutis place out by the new mall for just a minute.”

“Aww, Mom,” Lynn said, obviously disappointed that she wasn't getting to go home right away.

“Is that old place still there?” Lee Ann asked. “I thought they were gonna tear it down for a parking lot.”

“They are. But now they're waiting for Alma — Mrs. DeGutis — to die. And she's getting pretty close.”

“You know her?” Lee Ann inquired interested.

“I've been doing private duty nursing for her lately. She's a nice old lady. I'm going to drop in and take her that fruit basket back there for Thanksgiving. I want to make it a good one for her — it'll probably be her last. Her grandson's supposed to be here for the holiday.

“I remember the grandson,” Lynn spoke up. “He was a couple of years ahead of us in high school. Cute kid. Nice, but kinda shy.”

“He was a sissy,” Lee Ann spoke up from the back seat.

"Now, Lee Ann, don't be judgmental," Alice chided, as she turned off the main highway and headed into the residential neighborhood where Lee Ann's family lived. "Tell your parents Happy Thanksgiving for me." Alice pulled up in front of the house. "Maybe you all would like to stop over this afternoon. We're having our usual open house."

"Thanks, I'll tell 'em," Lee Ann answered as she got out of the car. "I'm so sleepy, I think I'll spend the whole holiday in bed. Bye, Lynn. I'll talk to you soon."

"Do we really have to go by the DeGutis's?" Lynn complained, as Alice drove away.

"Now, Lynn, we'll only be a minute. This'll be your last chance to see the old house. They're gonna tear it down, you know."

"Some treat. I'm so sleepy."

"I promise I won't be long."

                        🔊

On the way over Alice talked to a half-asleep Lynn about her concerns for Alma DeGutis. "I've been worrying about Alma lately. She's been getting more and more rambunctious and argumentative ever since her daughter was killed in that awful accident a couple of years ago. She's got a psychologist who says it's hysteria and a psychiatrist who says it's senility. Personally, I think she's got Alzheimer's Disease. After all, Alzheimer's is characterized by restlessness and periods of irritability and truculence," she said, obviously quoting medical literature. "And if there is anybody around here, at least as far as the city council is concerned, who's being truly truculent," Alice laughed, "it's Alma DeGutis."

"What about the city council?" Lynn asked sleepily.

"Well, you know, way back when the plans for the shopping mall were announced, Alma tried to get the city to make the house a museum. There was some interest on the council, but the developers didn't agree. They said the house wasn't suitable for renovation into retail space and they just didn't think the novelty attractive enough to bring shoppers to the mall. Besides, the house was located in what was planned to be the parking lot. The developers said the DeGutises were going to be making enough money off the land. They didn't need to be bribed into agreeing with some sort of plan to save that crazy old house."

Alice obviously enjoyed telling the story. Even though Lynn had been living in LaCrosse during all this history, she didn't say anything. She was too tired.

"Well, Alma wouldn't sell the house or the yard. She's an old lady; I guess the developers and the council decided they could wait her out. So the plans for the mall went on. In actual fact, the value of Alma's house increased. I wonder if she isn't being shrewd. She obviously loves her grandson. Maybe she just wants to make sure he gets the biggest inheritance possible. I am glad that boy had the courtesy to come visit for Thanksgiving."

The DeGutis mansion was one of the wonders of the county. Old Abner DeGutis had made his money from the city's biggest papermill. After his beautiful bride died young, leaving him only one daughter — Alma — Abner began to build what was to have been a fabulous house. But with no young wife to insist on the niceties, Abner didn't design the house to be beautiful. He built it to be strange. Having heard about the Winchester House in San Jose and being fascinated with sleight of hand and stage magic, Abner created a house full of stairways that went nowhere, trick mirrors and optical illusions, and rooms that could only be entered through secret passages and concealed doorways.

"When I first started working for Alma, I loved roaming around the house," Alice remarked. "One time I got myself trapped in a garret room up on the third floor. I managed to get out only by screaming my head off out one of the tiny porthole windows till Ellie, the maid, heard me.

"'Oh, Miz Graves, that was one of ol' Mr. DeGutis's favorite tricks,'" Alice gleefully mimicked the elderly black maid. "'There ain't no way outta that room, less'n you put somethin' to stop the door from closin' or somebody come up and get you out.' After that I decided to stick to the bottom floor where Alma lived.

"Well, I worried that Alma was going to wander up there and get locked in. So, just in case, I recently broke the spring latch off one of the exits from that room."

Lynn was only barely listening.

              💕

As they approached the half-built mall, Alice turned off the main road onto a side street that appeared to be torn up from the big machines that were about the only vehicles that used it anymore. After all, the road didn't go anywhere — except to the old DeGutis mansion.

Alice drove on to what was supposed to be the back corner of the extensive parking lot. There, instead of the open paved field, stood the tall stand of stately firs that local legend said Abner DeGutis had planted before starting to build his dreamhouse over a century ago.

"It's really a shame to destroy those trees," Alice remarked as she pulled up in front of the rusty old iron gate. "Though I guess they're probably no older than the rest of the trees in these woods that got cut down for the mall."

As she pulled up in front of the house, Alice insisted that Lynn come in with her. "Just for a minute. If you're with me, I'll have a good excuse to just drop off the basket and leave."

"Ah, all right, Mom. But please, make it snappy."

Alice rang the doorbell and was fumbling for her keys when the door opened. A young man with curly hair and blue eyes was standing in the open portal. "Happy Thanksgiving," he announced.

"You must be Alma's grandson. I'm Alice Graves, your grand-mother's nurse. This is my daughter Lynn. We came by to bring Alma..."

"I know," the young man said, "Grandmother's expecting you."

"I remember you from school," Lynn piped up. "I was a couple of years behind you."

"Well, come in," he said.

"You don't live around here now?" Alice asked.

"No, you know, my parents died a couple of years ago and I, uh, wanted to get away. I moved to San Francisco."

"I hear that's a beautiful place."

"Oh it is."

"I just moved to Washington, D.C.," Lynn spoke up. "That's a real pretty city too."

"Don't leave me in here while you do your socializing," the old lady shouted from her room down the hall.

🐾

Alice made some small talk with Alma while the two young people stood watching. She gave Alma the fruit basket, then asked about her health and if there were anything she needed.

"It's your day off," the old lady said grumpily. "Not your time to wait on me."

"Now, Alma, you know I help you because I like you, not just because it's a job."

"I don't know about that. And if that's true, I think you must be crazy."

Everybody laughed except Alma.

"How come you put up with old people like me, people who oughta be dead?"

"Not all my patients are old. And none of them ought to be dead," Alice answered in her best bedside manner.

"Well, I think I oughta be dead. I'm tired. Who else ya got for patients if not old people?" she asked rather perkily.

"Sick people," Alice answered matter of factly.

"What kind of sick people?"

"Young ones, old ones, people in between," Alice was intentionally being as noncommital as possible. There was no reason Alma DeGutis should know about her other patients.

"Got any patients with this here A-I-D-S?" she asked inquisitively.

"Why do you ask?"

"Sonny here was just telling me about his friend out in 'Frisco who helps people like that. Thought maybe you could give him some hints."

"I'm sure they know all about the disease. There're many more cases of it out there than here in LaCrosse."

"You never know," Alma said. "Can't trust nobody out there on either coast. The heartland. That's the place. Middle of America," Alma started on what sounded like it was going to be a new subject.

"You know someone who works with AIDS patients?" Lynn asked.

"Yes, I do."

"I just heard about a new treatment for the virus," she said proudly.

"Oh, really?"

"I work for a company that does government research. They're investigating some new treatment that's supposed to be one hundred percent effective."

"Really?" he answered dramatically. "I bet my friend would like to know about that. *I'd* sure like to know about it."

"Look, you kids, I need to get home to fix dinner. And Lynn you need to get some sleep..."

"Yes, I guess I need to start getting Grandmother ready. We're going out to the Country Club for dinner," Mark rejoined.

"That sounds real nice. Good to get her out."

"I'll say," Alma remarked. "Haven't played golf in years."

"Grandmother, we're going for dinner, not golf. It's too cold. There's snow on the ground."

"I usta ski," Alma answered.

"We're gonna say goodbye," Alice interrupted before Alma went off on another track. "Well, both of you are welcome to come by our house after four this afternoon. We have a little open house every year."

"Maybe we will. Or maybe if Grandmother's tired I will. I'd like to hear more about this AIDS treatment."

"I'll tell you all I know," Lynn spoke up. "I think it's real good news."

🐾

As Alice was driving out of the property along the torn up road, she remarked that Alma's grandson seemed very nice.

"He's cute," Lynn responded. "But, you know, he's gay."

"How do you know?"

"Oh, mom. Whadda you mean how do I know? It's obvious, isn't it? I mean he lives in San Francisco."

"Well, that's nothing to hold against him."

"I wasn't holding it against him," Lynn answered. "I just, well, I just..."

"You must be tired, dear," Alice said in response to Lynn's obvious fluster.

11

"There is something wrong with the computer you assigned me."

"What is that, George?" Edward Buchanan answered into the phone.

"Several times last night it acted up. Once it spontaneously dropped out of the program into the operating system. That cost me about an hour's work—"

"Well, you should have saved your work. You should have saved. You know that."

"Of course, I should have saved, Edward. Don't patronize me. The point is, I didn't. And the computer acted totally out of the ordinary. Twice it displayed its directory without my having asked and it announced it was copying files. I think it needs repair."

"But that's practically a brand new machine."

"All the more reason to get it fixed."

"Are you sure you know how to use it?"

"Of course, I know how to use it," George answered irritably. "Are you sure nobody around that office is fooling with it during the day? Maybe I should start locking it."

"No one's using it during the day. And, George, if there is something wrong with it, we'll get it fixed," Buchanan said with a tone of exasperation. "Look, it's the start of the holidays. If you're still having trouble with it next week, we'll get the serviceman in."

"Thank you, Edward. I'm sorry I snapped at you. I'm just feeling edgy these days. I went to church the other day—" George stopped himself in mid-sentence. "You know, this project and all."

"Nonsense, nonsense," Buchanan replied. "Everything's going just as planned."

"No. It is not, Edward. Wake up. Nothing's worked the way we planned. Don't you read the papers?" George was almost screaming into the phone.

"Now, now. Well, perhaps you're right. Perhaps it's time we call the Board together and discuss this."

"Call the Board together! Edward, stop the project now. Before this thing really blows up."

"Well, George. Tell me. What plans have you got for Thanksgiving dinner?"

"Edward, don't change the subject on me."

"I'm not going to discuss this over the phone. Look, I'd be happy to have you over for dinner this afternoon. We could talk afterwards. Joanne would love to see you..."

"Oh, come off it. You and I both know Joanne and I don't get along."

"Well, then, I'll come by your place. Say tomorrow afternoon. We can talk."

"Okay, that sounds good. Edward, thanks for the invitation to dinner. I'm just not up for visiting these days. I'll see you tomorrow afternoon. I'll be here."

After he hung up, George resumed his vigil by the front window. *What if we're being spied on?* he wondered, thinking about the mysterious behavior of the computer. But he couldn't even get himself motivated to worry about that. It was all just part of what was depressing him. *I wish there were somebody I could talk to.*

Outside, brittle gold and yellow leaves swirled around the base of trees as the autumn winds came blowing winter in. The view out the window was spectacular. *Too bad I don't have the energy or mood to appreciate it. I've been really depressed — ever since that priest refused to give me absolution.*

12

"Hi, Jon, this is Mark. Happy Thanksgiving."

"Well, hello. I'm glad you called. How're things in Wisconsin?"

"It's beautiful. Just beautiful. The sun's been out most of the day, but it's been real cold. There was a little snow last night and today a lot of the trees have icicles in them from where the snow melted in the sun. It'll be beautiful for your arrival."

"I just confirmed the reservations. I'm supposed to leave here tomorrow evening at six. How's your holiday going?"

"Grandmother and I had a great dinner this afternoon. She's a little hard to take for too long. Her mind keeps wandering and she occasionally gets temperamental. But she's still a lot of fun. Right now I'm at an open house at her nurse's. I heard something interesting I thought you'd like to know about. Maybe check into while you're in D.C."

"What's that?"

"Lynn, the nurse's daughter, lives in D.C. and works for a consulting firm that sounds like it's auditing anti-AIDS drug research. Lynn's found a report on something called Viral Antidote that's supposed to be a hundred percent effective in killing HIV."

"Wow. I never heard of such a thing."

"I thought you'd like to look into it. Lynn says she doesn't know where the study's being done. She really didn't want to tell me very much. It seems she wasn't supposed to have seen the report at all."

"Did you get a name for the consulting firm?"

"I promised we wouldn't say anything about her. Just call as though we knew about the audit. Think you can do that?"

"Tell me who to call."

"George Wilson. Liberty Bell Foundation. 922-4500. You'll probably get an answering service, but maybe they can connect you. The other name you should have is Billy DePalma. He's Lynn's boyfriend. She said he'd help. Maybe you should start with him. The number's 545-4647."

"Well, thank you. Maybe I can find something out tomorrow before I leave. It's worth a try anyway."

"How's your day been?" Mark asked.

"I ate too much for dinner. We're all going out for a walk now along the Potomac — they're starting out the door. I'll see you tomorrow evening. Maybe I'll have some interesting news about this research. Love you."

"I love you too," Mark answered.

Jon put the phone down and hurried toward the front hall. *I'll call this consulting firm first thing in the morning. Maybe somebody'll be in the office,* he thought. *Guess I should try the boyfriend tonight when I get back from the walk.*

13

The phone in the dark apartment rang a couple of times. When no one answered it, the electronic circuit cut in, "Billy's unable to come to the phone now. After the beep you can leave a message and he'll call you back. Thanks."

After the machine produced its electronic beep, a voice boomed out in the empty room: "This is Jon Stiers. I'm visiting from San Francisco. Your girlfriend Lynn gave me your number and suggested I call you. I'll call back in the morning. Or you can try me tonight, till about midnight, at 774-7144. (click)." The answering device switched off and the red light on its face began to blink to announce that there was a message in the memory.

Meanwhile, Billy DePalma was leaning against the bar at a popular night spot called Jocko's in downtown D.C. He was feeling both a little excited and a little despondent.

Earlier in the evening it had occurred to him that with Lynn off on holiday he was free to do whatever he wanted with the evening — even something sexual. The thought of that scared him, but also aroused him.

It's getting almost like Lynn and I are married, he thought to himself. *I'm not sure I'm ready to be married.* In the back of his mind a little voice said very quietly, "I'm not sure I'm ready to be straight." That thought scared him enough to justify his decision to go out to the singles' bar to test his sexuality.

But now that he was here, he felt uncomfortable and out of place. He wasn't sure what he wanted out of this escapade: To see if he was attracted to women? To pick up some girl and go home for sex? To pretend this awful AIDS nightmare never happened? To prove his manhood? To establish his independence? All of the above?

Billy stood around for a couple of hours. Occasionally he noticed women he found attractive, but he was too shy to approach any of them. He did discover that he wasn't particularly attracted sexually to the men in Jocko's and that was a great relief to him.

He was vaguely horny. His sex with Lynn had become very strictly curtailed by the concerns of safe sex. Understanding that that was now just a fact of life, he didn't exactly mind that with her, but still ... something was missing.

Billy had never gone cruising for sex like this before. Some of the time he felt positively excited. Some of the time he felt desperate. By one a.m., he felt guilty.

What am I doing in a place like this? I have a wonderful woman who loves me and is willing to stick with me through the ordeal of this disease. Why expose myself to more people and, maybe even, more diseases?

But once back home, Billy found himself nervous and unable to sleep. He found a couple of messages on his answering machine. One was from a stranger named Stiers. It was too late to call back.

He sat down in front of his computer to spend a little more time trying to break into George Wilson's files. He determined that, indeed, he had the contents of Wilson's files now transferred to his own fixed disk memory, but he still hadn't ascertained how to get in. All he'd managed to see so far was the additional write-up on the Viral Antidote, describing its effectiveness. He called that file up again:

VIRAL ANTIDOTE

The antidote to the antigen's primate retroviral vector stimulates a response that suppresses the vector within a matter of days.

Preliminary studies indicate that after immune cell proliferation caused by the vector virus has begun fulminant infection of the tagged antigen will resist the effects of the antidote in over 90% of the cases. This allows for complete manifestation of disease process in spite of administration of antidote. Upon replication of viral vector in target immune cells, the development becomes self-sustaining and protects itself from the neutralizing effects of the competing antidote.

Prior to proliferation, however, the antidote directly exchanges viral RNA with complementing immune cells and instructs them to produce enzymes that inactivate the viral vector. While the inactivated virus may continue to carry tagged antigen, without proper host the antigen will likely remain underdeveloped.

Billy read that over again. He still wasn't sure what it meant. It was written in medical jargon that effectively made it nonsense. What did phrases like "viral vector," "fulminant infection," and "tagged antigen" mean? What was it tagged with?

Well, if he interpreted correctly, it seemed to say that whatever this viral antidote was, if it was given before the AIDS virus began to grow, it would instruct the immune system in how to fight it off.

That's good news for me, Billy thought. *Not very good for people who've already got ARC or AIDS. But at least this would stop the spread of the virus. But I need to get this stuff soon. Every day I wait I might be getting closer to "fulminant infection," whatever that is, and then it'll be too late. And where do I find it?*

The answer to that was obviously somewhere in Wilson's files. But he had tried so many different passwords: address, initials, dates, abbreviations, key-words, military terms — and none of them worked. *Damn!*

Then suddenly a vision came up for Billy, a visual memory of his trip to Wilson's house. *Of course, why didn't I think of that? The antidote kills the virus. The virus is the dragon.*

Quickly Billy typed in the commands to get back to the proper subdirectory and then, when the cursor began to blink at the center of the blank screen — where Billy assumed it was asking for the password because the program always froze up at that point — he began entering the letters: S-T-G-E-O-R-G-E.

A moment later the screen filled with characters. "Whoopee!" Billy exclaimed aloud laughing.

"Casualty Approximations," he read. The title was followed by a list of the familiar AIDS high-risk groups, showing numbers of cases both in these groups and outside. Billy was a little taken aback by the odd terminology of these two columns of numbers. One was labeled "Peripheral Casualties." The other was "Target Casualties."

What a strange use of the word target, he thought. Of course, he knew that in consultantese "target" meant something like "subject-in-question." *But still—*

He paged through the report, looking for references to the Viral Antidote. He found projected timetables for "Dispersal of Antidote" and another, rather similar, description of the mechanism of the antidote. But still no identification of the company or research facility where it was being developed or tested. In fact, the only reference he could find to a research facility at all was Ilebo Station. *Where's that?* he wondered.

He pulled out an old atlas, but couldn't find any reference to Ilebo. Under Cities, U.S.A. he found nothing. He was paging through the maps absent-mindedly, thinking about how late it had gotten, when his eye caught the map of Africa.

AIDS is an African disease, he reminded himself. He looked at country names. Zaire sounded familiar. *That's where most of the African cases are.* And there it was: Ilebo, a tiny dot on the Kasai River.

"Fuck," he shouted aloud. "What good is this going to do us? The research is going on in Africa."

A little angry and a little despondent, Billy switched off the computer. There was lots more to look through in George Wilson's files. But now it was time for sleep.

14

A little after nine a.m., Jon called the number Mark had given him for Billy DePalma. He was concerned about calling early on a holiday. Perhaps this guy Billy was sleeping in. The phone rang three times and Jon was just about to hang up when the answering machine came on. Jon hung up. He'd left one message already; he'd try again later.

Then he punched in the other number Mark had given him. The phone rang a couple of times and then was answered. "Liberty Bell Foundation. This is the answering service."

"I'm calling for Mr. George Wilson," Jon announced.

"Sir, this is the answering service," the voice repeated. "The office is closed."

"Oh, I see. May I leave a message for Mr. Wilson?"

"Certainly, though he may not get it till Monday."

"Any chance of getting to talk with somebody at the firm today? I'm leaving town before Monday."

"The secretary may call in to get messages. She sometimes does on holidays."

"My name is Dr. Jon Stiers. I'm with the City of San Francisco Department of Health. Right now I'm at 774-7144. I'm anxious to talk with Mr. Wilson, but I'm not sure I'll be at this number very long. Could you ask him to leave a number with you where I could reach him?"

"I can't guarantee he'll get the message," the operator repeated.

"I understand that."

"Thank you, sir. Good day."

🐾

"Well, Jon, you're up early," Carol Sheehan said as she wandered sleepily into the kitchen where Jon was calling from.

"I've already made coffee," Jon answered as he turned to pour a cup for Carol and refill his own. "Phil coming down soon?"

"He rolled over and went back to sleep," Carol answered. "Let's not fix his yet." Her voice was beginning to sound more alert.

"I missed most of what you were saying yesterday about your appearance on the Donahue Show. Wanna repeat it?"

"Did you see the show?"

"Had to work. Sorry."

"Well, I really made some enemies, I'm afraid, with the AIDS groups in New York. I didn't think what I said was so bad, but they all exaggerated my message about suicide. And now I think I'm really in hot water."

"What did you say?"

Jon started to repeat his version of the show. *I've told this story so often*, he thought to himself, *I can almost do it without paying any attention.* As he talked, his mind was on Mark's excited news that there was an antidote to the AIDS virus. *Antidote*, he thought to himself. *Isn't that a strange word for a medical treatment?*

15

"That's my friend Jon," Mark pointed out to his Grandmother as they sat in the spacious living room of the DeGutis mansion in front of the TV and videotape player Mark had rented.

"A good-looking young man," Alma commented. "What else is on?"

"No, Grandmother, this is a tape I brought all the way from California to show you. I want to watch this program. And I would like you to watch it with me." He spoke to her as though she were a child.

"Oh, yes, Mark. I forgot. You said you were going to be on TV?" she asked quizzically.

"Not me, Grandmother, my friend Jon. There," he pointed. Mark was a little taken aback at how far gone his Grandmother was. Some of the time she was quite lucid, but often she seemed spaced out with virtually no memory. Mark thought about all the talks he'd had with Jon about AIDS patients choosing to die when their mind was going, and he wondered about his Grandmother. She didn't seem especially unhappy. Maybe there was no reason for her to die. But still, she wasn't herself anymore; she wasn't the wise and dynamic woman he remembered.

The Donahue Show was starting. Wanamaker was giving his opening statement.

"That your friend?" Alma asked. "He sounds crazy to me."

"No, not him. Jon's on the opposite side, against this guy Wanamaker. Let's listen."

Mark turned up the volume.

"Of course, I believe people with AIDS have a right to decide that they've been through enough suffering and choose to die," Jon was answering Donahue's question. "I don't think society should force them to die by denying medical treatment. That's obviously inhumane."

"What about the extreme costs Senator Wanamaker spoke about?"

"In the long run," Jon answered, "I think we have to value life more than money. Otherwise we're setting a bad precedent for our society. I mean, when are we going to decide that somebody's too old to keep alive? Will the Senator's next bill propose a maximum number of years an elderly person can receive medical treatment?"

"That's a totally different issue," Wanamaker objected. "Old age is natural. AIDS is unnatural. And most of the people who get it are unnatural."

"Now, Senator," Donahue chided, then looked out at the camera and added, "you may be talking about my viewing audience."

"Well, how about people with heart disease or liver problems or cancer from smoking or drinking alcohol? Are those any more natural? Would you deny medical services to them?" Jon got the attention back. "But I wanted to say that in the short run, I think the senator has a good point. I've seen an awful lot of my friends and clients get sick and linger for a very long time with this disease. Some of them get well, like Paul here, others don't. There are a lot of doctors who seem committed to keeping their patients alive as long as possible regardless of the quality of their life. That resistance to allowing death to be a natural part of life, it seems to me, causes an enormous amount of individual suffering and costs society an excessive amount of resources."

"So what are you suggesting?"

"Perhaps people with fatal illnesses — not just AIDS — ought to be helped to make their peace with themselves and then allowed to decide when they want to stop medical treatment and die."

"I agree totally," Mark's grandmother blurted out during the spattering of applause that followed Jon's statement.

"Paul, are you willing to stop medical treatment?" Donahue continued.

"I'm not receiving any medical treatment, Phil. But I disagree with Jon. If you'd asked me six months ago if I wanted to make my peace and die, I'd probably have said yes—"

"You were in the hospital at that time?" Donahue clarified.

"Most of that time I was at home, but was flat in bed and getting I.V. treatments every day from a visiting nurse. My buddy from the AIDS Project came over and fed me."

"Did that cost you or the public anything?" Donahue quizzed, turning the topic back to Wanamaker's issue of finances.

"The nurse and medication cost something and Medicare picked that up. The AIDS Project paid for my food. And the buddy didn't cost anything."

"I think the buddy did cost something," Jon spoke up. "Not in money, but in emotional resources. The AIDS crisis has really brought out some admirable qualities in people. The buddies around the country are doing great work. And the disease has brought out wonderful qualities in the patients as well. I mean, many of them have been real heroes. But all that has emotionally drained everyone — especially the gay community. The long drawn-out deaths, the obvious suffering, the fear of the disease, the backlash from people like Lyndon LaRouche and Senator Wanamaker here — these have really exhausted people. It seems to me a lot of that cost just comes from our fear of death, I mean, instead of our love of life."

"Well, I don't want to die," answered Curtiss. "I want to live as long as I can. And I'll fight for that last breath. And neither you nor this (beep) politician is going to change my mind."

"I think your courage and conviction is admirable, Paul. I only mean to say that it shouldn't have to come from fear."

"Well, there are lots of us who fear this disease," Wanamaker spoke up. "It'd probably reduce the spread of the disease if the patients died sooner."

"Senator, that seems to me a mistaken notion of how this disease spreads," Donahue objected. "We've had lots of experts on this show. And they've assured us that the virus is not being spread so much by the people with symptoms, but by all those people who've been infected and don't know it. I want to go back to Dr. Stiers's patient. Did Pat Stratford make the right decision in jumping out of that window?" Donahue turned to Jon.

"I don't like how he did it. That was pretty messy—"

"The street sweepers refused to clean up the blood," Donahue interrupted.

"Yes," Jon acknowledged. "It was violent and angry. Pat had just been denied entry into an experimental drug program because he didn't fit the requirements."

"Would that have saved his life?"

"Probably not. But who knows? Pat must've decided he'd suffered long enough. He really was past the point of no return. I think he probably made the right decision."

"What kind of therapist are you?" Curtiss asked angrily.

"A compassionate one, I hope," Jon replied softly.

"Should other AIDS patients make that same decision?" Donahue asked.

"I guess each of them has to decide for themselves and with as much information as they can from their doctors when they've reached that point of no return. But maybe when they have, it would be a good thing for them to choose to accept death."

"Senator?" Donahue asked.

"I'm surprised to hear this fellow agreeing with me—"

"I didn't think I was," Jon shot back. "I think I'm speaking about compassion, not money. And I'm speaking about reducing the overall amount of suffering in society, maybe especially gay society, because I think it just drains us of our appreciation of life."

"That's the spirit. Tell him off," Alma DeGutis shouted at the TV set.

Mark laughed. He was pleased to see she'd gotten interested in the subject.

16

"C'mon in. I'm Billy DePalma."

"I'm Jon Stiers. As I mentioned on the phone your friend Lynn gave us your name."

"Hey, I'm sorry about the phone," Billy said. "I was out pretty late last night and missed your call and musta slept through the first call this morning."

"Oh, that's okay. Lynn told my friend Mark that you'd discovered some information about a treatment for the AIDS virus. As I said on the phone, I work in an AIDS program in San Francisco, so naturally I was interested."

"Well, to be honest, I'm not sure what I've found. Maybe Lynn told you why she and I got involved with looking for this."

"I didn't talk to Lynn directly. All I know is that she told my friend that her company, the Liberty Bell Foundation, was auditing some sort of AIDS research."

"Well, I guess that's true. Here, sit down, I'll explain what we know."

A little while later, Jon was reading over Billy's shoulder as he scrolled through the STGEORGE file he'd broken into the previous night.

"Do you know what to make of that?" Billy asked.

"Strange, isn't it? It looks like a model for the spread of the disease that's linked with a schedule for releasing this so-called 'antidote.' It's almost like these people have a treatment, but are holding off announcing it."

"Well, not a treatment," Billy corrected, "a way of neutralizing the virus in people who haven't gotten sick yet."

"But then why haven't they released it?"

"Maybe they're still studying it?" Billy suggested.

"I work with a lot of doctors who are studying treatments and such. None of them are keeping their work secret. And they wouldn't, especially if it had results like that list suggests this 'antidote' does. And why is it called an 'antidote'? Doesn't that sound kind of sinister?"

"So what do you think?" Billy asked.

"I think I'd like to talk with the Liberty Bell Foundation. I called this morning, but there was nobody in."

"No, the place is closed for the holiday. But I've got a phone number and address of this guy Wilson who seems to be in charge of this project."

"Really? Great. Maybe I can make an appointment to see him."

17

"Have you got a will?" Alma DeGutis asked Mark as the credits for the Donahue Show were running across the screen. "My lawyers tell me every day about the importance of a will."

"Grandmother, I'm only twenty-four."

"Mark, you should have a will. I'm going to die soon. I know that. And you're going to inherit a lot of money. You shouldn't wait. Why, you could get hit by a truck on the way to my funeral," she laughed. "You wouldn't want all that money to go to the government, would you?"

"No, of course not."

"I know about government," Alma started in again. "Why when I was your age, the government came in here and wanted to take Daddy's house away because . . . No, I think that wasn't when I was your age. That was. . . ."

"That was more recently," Mark finished the sentence for her. "Exactly."

"Maybe you're right, I *should* have a will. Who should I leave the money to?"

"I like your young man on the TV. Why don't you leave it to him?" Alma put her fist down on the arm of her chair, looking smugly proud of herself. "Use the money for something good."

"I'm glad to hear you say that," Mark answered. "I guess I've always thought you wouldn't want me to give the money away."

"Wouldn't want you to give it to strangers, like those people out there in the yard watching me . . ."

"Who is that?" Mark asked, not sure if he should take this seriously.

"Those developers," she announced. "I know they're out there, just waiting for me to die. Well, it'd serve 'em right. Let's put all that money into some good cause."

"Can I buy a house for myself with it?" Mark asked playfully. He thought about his three-storey Victorian on States Street.

"Write this down. Write this all down," Alma commanded. "Got to have it on paper."

18

This morning George Wilson was sitting in his living room, drinking coffee and occasionally looking at the book he had open in his lap. He didn't feel like reading. His mind was filled with things he wanted to say to Edward Buchanan.

The telephone rang.

"Hello, George."

"Well hello, Edward. I suspected it was you. We're still going to meet this afternoon?"

"That's not why I was calling, George. That's not why I was calling. Emily just called me and said she'd spoken with the answering service this morning. There is a message for you."

"Well, thank you, Edward. Shall I call them or did you take the message?"

"I'm not calling to tell you about the message," Edward blustered.

"Then why are you calling, Edward?"

"I'm calling to warn you. This message was from a Dr. Jon Stiers."

"Who's that?"

"I didn't recognize his name at first either. But Emily reminded me that he was the homosexual activist on the Donahue Show last Tuesday. You remember — you called and told us to watch."

"Oh, yes, I remember. Why would this fellow be calling me?"

"I don't know. But I don't like it. George—" Buchanan's voice shifted into military command mode "— don't you tell him anything if he finds you. Don't tell him anything at all."

"I'm not a fool, Edward," George snapped. "Look, you said you were coming over this afternoon so we could talk about the project. Are we still on?"

"What good is talking going to do, George?"

"Well, I think we have things to talk about. Especially now. What if this fellow you mentioned knows something? Now is the time to stop the project."

"This is not the time to do anything rash."

"Rash? Rash? You think this whole plan of yours wasn't rash?"

"Look, George, calm down. I didn't mean to dismiss your concerns. It's just, well, Joanne's sister and brother-in-law are here and it's going to be awkward getting out."

"Well, I'm feeling pretty awkward sitting here, Edward. We need to talk. You come over this afternoon. I mean it."

"At least I'll call you back later," Buchanan said, hanging up.

George listened to the dial tone for a moment, feeling simultaneously angered and depressed. Buchanan just was not paying any attention to his concerns. It was as though he didn't believe him.

George Wilson had fretted over the call from Edward Buchanan for only a few moments when the phone rang again. Perhaps it was Edward calling back to apologize.

"Edward?" he answered.

"May I speak with Mr. George Wilson?" an unfamiliar voice asked.

"This is George Wilson."

"Mr. Wilson, my name is Dr. Jon Stiers. I work for the City of San Francisco Health Department."

"What can I do for you?" George asked nervously.

"Well, sir, I'm sorry to call you at home, but I'm here in the District just for the holiday. I'm working on a study of AIDS treatment programs and I understand your firm, the Liberty Bell Foundation, is doing a similar study. I hoped we might be able to exchange information."

"I don't know what you're talking about," George said hastily.

He wondered how he could avoid dealing with this man. And how did Stiers know about the project?

"I understand your work may be classified. And I certainly wouldn't ask you to divulge anything that's protected by confidentiality or official security. And, sir, I have here in my possession a report comparing the effectiveness of various anti-viral treatments against something called 'Viral Antidote.'"

"How do you know about that?" George snapped, his heart starting to pound.

"I'm really not so much interested in the audit or whatever it is your firm is doing. I am very interested in knowing what laboratory is researching this Viral Antidote."

"I can't give you any information."

"Mr. Wilson, if the report I have here is correct—"

"Where did you get that?"

"If this is correct, well, it could save many lives. Don't you think there's an overriding moral concern more important than patent infringement or something like that?"

"It's nothing like that," George snapped. "I shouldn't be talking to you at all. You have no idea—"

"In fact, Mr. Wilson, I'm concerned looking at this that you may know something about the AIDS virus that the public should know. I don't exactly mean to pressure you. But I think there's information here that the media would be very interested in."

"Look, you've got to promise you won't go to the media."

"Mr. Wilson, I'm really concerned that your company might have a cure for this disease and is holding it back till you think you can make more money on it. That's totally indefensible."

"Yes, yes, I suppose you're right," George answered.

"Then you'll talk to me, sir?"

"I can't talk about any of this."

"Look, Mr. Wilson, all I really want to know is what laboratory is doing the research on Viral Antidote. You don't have to give me any other information."

"You don't understand."

"Maybe it isn't important that I understand, sir. I'm really only interested in saving lives. Let me come over and talk with you in person."

"No, no. You mustn't do that. Look, there isn't any laboratory. There's nothing I can tell you."

"But you must know how I can find out."

"Leave me alone," George shouted and hung up the phone.

A moment later it rang again.

"Look, Mr. Wilson, I need this information. I don't understand why you're being so evasive. If you don't at least explain that, I'm going to have to go to the media."

"Oh God," George groaned. *What do I do now?* "Okay, Dr., uh, what did you say your name was? Maybe we should talk. I can meet you somewhere."

"Stiers, my name is Stiers. I'll come over to your house. It's not far."

"How do you know where I live?" George asked anxiously.

"We could certainly have more privacy at your home, if that's a concern to you."

After a prolonged silence, George answered, "Okay. Maybe that's a good idea. You come over here. I'll be waiting for you."

"I'll be there in fifteen minutes."

George hung up the phone. He stood still for a few minutes, then said aloud to himself, dismayed, "Stiers didn't even ask my address. He knows where I live."

George trembled. He walked slowly out of the living room into the entry hall. Above him his prized window of St. George glowed brightly with winter sunlight. He stared up at the window and uttered a prayer to his patron, "St. George, pray for me. Help me . . ." he hesitated, "help me to be heroic."

George Wilson went back into the living room to his safe hidden in the side of the fireplace. There, along with a full report on the project, he had a strange souvenir, something he'd kept from his military days. Once, just once, he'd been privy to a secret about nuclear weapons that could have changed the balance of power in the world. He'd asked for something he'd seen in spy movies: an artificial tooth. It contained a small dose of cyanide.

He opened the safe and peered in. *A micro version of Edward's collection.* He smiled morbidly to himself. He withdrew both the report and the waxy tooth-shaped pellet. The report he placed carefully in the center of his desk; the "tooth" he kept in his hand. He walked slowly into the entry hall once again. Aloud, once more, he said with intense seriousness, "St. George, pray for me."

19

Jon had borrowed Carol Sheehan's car, but Billy offered to drive him. "I know the way," he said rather convincingly. "Though I want to stay hidden. I don't want Lynn to get into trouble, and the less they know about us, the better."

"Well, thanks, Billy. I *am* glad to have company. I pushed him pretty hard on the phone for this meeting, but the truth is now I'm scared of what I'm walking into. Wilson sounded like a nervous wreck."

"Maybe he is. High-power business and all, you know. Could be on coke for all we know."

"I thought you said these people were real right-wing."

"You think the right-wing doesn't use drugs?" Billy laughed. "I think they just want to keep it all for themselves."

"You may be right. This whole thing does sound like a paranoid delusion. Anyway, thanks for driving," Jon said as they were entering the Georgetown area.

"Look, Jon, Wilson might be watching out the window. So I'll let you off at the end of the block. Okay?" From the corner Billy pointed out the house, identifying it by the large stained-glass window. "I'll park here. I'm gonna run get a cup of coffee at that café over there," he said pointing across the street. "I'll be watching for you."

"Thanks, Billy." Jon shook his hand, then got out of the car. He walked back toward the house, already anxious about what he might encounter. This had started as an effort to find out about a new treatment for AIDS; now it had taken on trappings of a spy thriller.

Walking up the front steps, Jon could make out the figure of St. George on horseback. An appropriate image. On several occasions, he'd suggested just that image of the conquering warrior for a visualization exercise of the immune system fighting off the invading virus. *Before I always thought St. George was on my side. Maybe it's going to be different now.*

No sooner had he rung the bell than the heavy wooden door swung open. Standing there, slightly shadowed by the door frame, was an aging and tired man dressed in a tweed jacket. Behind him on the floor and far wall, Jon could see brilliantly colored patches of light cast by the window of St. George. "George Wilson?"

"Come in, Dr. Stiers. I recognize you from your TV appearance last week."

"Oh, then you know who I am?" Jon answered. "That makes you one up on me."

"How is that, sir?" Wilson politely extended his hand to usher Jon into the living room. When he closed the door, Jon heard the distinct sound of the deadbolt being turned.

"I mean I know very little about you, Mr. Wilson," Jon answered, then thought he'd better start at the beginning with this man. "I'm told you're a weapons specialist now working for a private consulting firm. And, as I mentioned on the phone, I've also been led to believe you or your company has been auditing AIDS research."

"Perhaps," Wilson answered, gesturing for Jon to sit down.

"I gather you want — or need — to maintain a low profile on that. And I'm quite willing to cooperate with that. I'm not interested in your audit. I'm only interested in learning about this so-called 'viral antidote.'"

"As I told you, Dr. Stiers, I'm not at liberty to discuss these matters," Wilson responded, then changed the subject. "Would you care for coffee or tea? You must be cold. It's very brisk out today."

"I don't want to take up your time, sir. I'd be happy just to get a reference for the research program and be on my way."

"But surely a cup of coffee—"

"Mr. Wilson, let me be very frank. From our telephone conversation, I thought it clear you felt we were adversaries for some reason. I'm quite willing to work at changing that. I don't like adversarial relationships. *And* I'm only after a very small bit of information from you. From some of what I've been told about your research, I'm concerned that you or your company is purposely delaying announcement of a cure for AIDS—"

"Dr. Stiers, you came alone, didn't you?" Wilson asked, not responding to Jon's challenge. Jon didn't like that question. What did that matter? "I didn't see your car," Wilson added. "Perhaps you've left someone waiting out in the cold?"

"I missed the turn and parked around the corner," Jon answered. No need to mention Billy.

"I too do not like adversarial relationships. I am a religious man. I do not believe in making enemies. Do you think that odd in a weapons expert?"

"I don't know. I've never met a weapons expert before. I've been told you are very sensible."

"Well, then, let us be sensible. Here, I insist you join me in a cup of hot coffee. Then I'll explain my work to you."

"Thank you," Jon answered, suddenly feeling the barrier between them dissolve.

"I'll only be a moment. There's a report on the desk there you might be interested in," Wilson said, excusing himself as he walked out of the room.

Jon got up from his place on the settee to look at the report Wilson mentioned. He sat down at the desk and paged through the document. The first thing he noticed was that it was printed, apparently in sections, on vivid multi-colored paper. The title page, printed on dark magenta that made the print hard to focus on, bore the name: "Strategic Applications Of African Viruses, submitted to Edward Buchanan by George Wilson." The word "CONFIDENTIAL" was stamped on the page several times. Jon noted the date: May 21, 1983."

The second page bore a table of contents. Jon's eye ran down the chapter titles: "Historical Survey of Genetic Engineering of Animal Viruses; Cross-linking Possibilities for Weapons Development; Ilebo Station Research Project," (Jon remembered that Billy had said the only research program he could find in the files was this Ilebo Station in Central Africa), "Failure of Rabies Research; Description of Viral Vector; Ilebo Station Accident and Possible Consequences in African Animals and Humans; Appendix: The Problems at Home in America; Proposal for Benefitting from Project Failure; Identifiable Targets and Susceptibility to Epidemic; Vectors for Antigen: Limitations of Sexual Transmission; Dispersal of Antidote; Cost Analysis," and finally — Jon read with mounting apprehension of what he seemed to be seeing — "Moral Imperative vs. Social Dismay: Need for Absolute Secrecy."

Jon felt stunned. Of course, he wasn't yet sure what this thing was about. Maybe it had nothing to do with AIDS at all. It did seem to be a report on the failure of some biological weapons research program along with an appendix suggesting applications for the weapon here in America. This looked like evidence of the paranoid fantasy most homosexuals in this country had entertained at one time or another.

20

"More coffee?" the waitress asked.

Billy put his hand over his cup and shook his head. Three cups of that stuff was all he could handle.

Billy had expected Jon Stiers's meeting with George Wilson to last about ten minutes. But it had been over twenty minutes now. *Maybe he came around the corner while I wasn't watching and turned the wrong direction. But no, that doesn't make sense. He certainly wouldn't have gone far. What if something happened to him? What if Wilson drugged and kidnapped him?*

Billy realized his imagination was likely getting the best of him. Probably Jon and Wilson were simply enjoying friendly conversation.

Still feeling antsy, Billy decided to call Lynn. He missed her, especially now that this adventure was underway. She'd really started this whole thing. Surely she'd want to know what was going on. And surely it would be reassuring for him to hear her voice. She was always so positive.

The pay phone was right inside the door. Billy could keep his vigil while he talked with her.

He dialed his access code, then entered his authorization number and then, checking in his wallet for Lynn's parents' address, he entered the area code and phone number. After several rings, the phone was answered.

"Oh, hi, Billy," Lynn exclaimed. "I'm so glad to hear from you. But I really can't talk now. One of Mom's patients just had a heart attack and has been rushed to the hospital. Mom's left already. I'm supposed to call the doctor now. You okay?"

"Yeah, sure. I'm with your friend Jon Stiers."

"Who?"

"Dr. Jon Stiers. You know, the guy you told to call me. You did tell this guy to call me, didn't you?" Billy asked hesitantly, suddenly realizing for the first time that he'd never confirmed the story with Lynn and maybe this whole thing was some kind of scam to set him up for breaking into the computer. His mind raced quickly through how Liberty Bell could possibly have traced the modem transmission to him.

"Oh, yeah, Mark's friend. About the HIV? Well, did you find out any news?" she asked excitedly.

"He's talking to Wilson right now. I'm waiting for him in a café."

"Wow, sounds like espionage stuff."

"I guess so. I've been killing time." *Getting nervous*, he thought to himself, but didn't say that aloud to Lynn. He felt a little silly. "Maybe in a minute I'll walk over there and see if I can tell what's up. Lynn, you know, I don't like any of this stuff. What we found in the computer memory sounds like something fishy's going on."

"Oh, Billy, I can't talk now. But, uh, look, tell me what you're talking about, but talk fast, please."

"Oh, well, it looks like they're keeping this antidote a secret so they can fix the price or something after a large enough population gets infected. I mean, what we found were charts predicting the spread of the virus graphed against various schedules for releasing the antidote. Pretty eerie."

"Oh God," Lynn answered. "Could you be misreading the charts?"

"Well, of course. I mean, I don't know what that stuff is about. It's mainly just charts and graphs and computer programs for calculating different parameters. Not enough info to make sense of."

"Call me later. Maybe this friend of Mark's will have some good news. Oh, you know, I guess I should get you to tell him that it was Mark's grandmother who got taken to the hospital. Maybe he should call Mark."

"I'll let him know. I love you, Lynn."

"Love you too," she answered as he hung up the phone. *Well, this sounds like a traumatic day*, he thought. *I hope Jon's all right. I think I'll go look.*

21

The die is cast, George Wilson thought to himself as he stood in the kitchen watching the last of the hot water filter through the coffee grounds into the bottom chamber of the Chemex. He carefully extracted the conical filter full of the black gummy grounds and tossed it in the basket under the sink; he wanted to give Stiers time to look over that report. *That might make all this easier. At least, showing him the report will keep me from changing my mind.*

As he poured the coffee into the thermos he realized his hands were shaking. *This is going to be harder to do than I thought. But I don't see any alternative. Edward's not going to help me. I've got to take responsibility for this myself. This is the only way. Oh God, help me in my hour of need. Forgive me my sins. Hold not my offenses against me.*

Another unforgivable sin, he thought to himself, remembering the reaction of the old priest he'd tried to confess to. *Well, sometimes what seems like a sin is the only way to accomplish a greater good.* He put out the sugar bowl and filled the creamer from the refrigerator. He reached in his pocket and took out the cyanide-filled wax tooth.

✺

"I hope this isn't cold," George said as he walked into the living room with the tray. "My thermos here wouldn't hold the whole pot so I've poured the first two cups. Cream or sugar?"

"What is this?" Stiers said, pointing to the report and ignoring the question about how he took his coffee. "Is this what I think it is?"

"I imagine you must find that surprising," George said,

reminding himself to remain calm. He concentrated on pouring cream into his coffee. "Come, come sit down, I'll explain that in a moment. You must have your coffee first."

"Wait a minute," Stiers said, practically shouting. "How can you calmly sit there and offer me a cup of coffee after you've just shown me this report?"

"I thought perhaps you were cold from being outside," George answered.

"I don't care about being cold. I want to know what this is." Jon remained seated at George's desk.

"Wouldn't you like me to sweeten this? It's strong. It may be bitter."

"You can do anything you want with the damn coffee," Jon snapped. "Maybe a little sugar."

George placed the cup he'd prepared for Jon Stiers on the desk and then went back to the settee and sat down. He stirred his coffee and then took a sip. "When I saw you on the Phil Donahue Show the other day, Dr. Stiers, I was impressed by what you said. As I told you, I am a religious man — in spite of my career. I sensed that you too — I suppose perhaps in spite of, uh, who you are — are a religious man."

"Are you going to answer my question about this report?"

Ignoring Stier's outburst, George continued slowly. "I understand that you are a psychologist. I saw a psychiatrist for a while when I was much younger. I can't say I got what I wanted from him, but I did enjoy talking with him. He was a very good listener. I imagine you can be a good listener, too."

"Are you going to answer my question about this report?" Stiers repeated.

"Please, just listen for a few minutes. I'll tell you more than you want to know."

"Okay," Jon said softly, leaning back in his chair.

"Your coffee's going to get cold."

"That's okay. Let me hear what you have to say."

"There's so much to tell, much more than I can even remember. I'm not sure where to begin. But let me tell you something I've never told anyone else but that psychiatrist. About my mother.

"She was a very beautiful woman, very sweet, very kind. I loved her. I guess all children love their mother. I thought I was more dependent on her than my friends were on theirs. I mean, they said mean things about their mothers. I never said anything against Mama. Not at all. Then when I was about ten or eleven, she changed. She became very erratic. Her moods changed dramatically from moment to moment. Sometimes she'd be very kind and loving to me and then within only a few minutes she'd suddenly start screaming at me.

"That's when I started staying away from the house," George continued, his voice soft and quiet, his mind relaxed and almost dreamy. "That's when I turned religious. I used to go to church. I didn't know where else to go when she was acting like that. I sometimes went over to friends' houses, but the easiest place was church. I didn't have to make up any excuses. I'd sit in the silence and admire the light pouring through the stained glass and smell the stale incense. And I'd beg God to make my mother like she'd been before.

"One day she suddenly hit me with a leather belt, I guess one of my dad's. Oh, I didn't mention my father, did I? He was a salesman, worked for many different companies over the years. He was seldom around the house. He'd come home for weekends and then be gone. He never seemed to like me anyway. At first I think he thought I was a mama's boy, and then later, when she changed, that I was to blame. After she died, he arranged for me to go to military academy. Then he disappeared. I used to get small checks from him now and then, but never saw him again till after I'd entered the military during college.

"Anyway, my mother hit me with this belt over and over and I went to church to cry. I knelt under a window that depicted Jesus being whipped and crowned with thorns. And I begged Jesus to change my mother or to take her back to him. I thought about how those Roman guards had sinned against him when they whipped him. And, I guess, rather megalomanically, I thought she was sinning like them by hitting me with the belt. And I prayed that God not allow her to sin anymore."

Wilson fell silent. "Go on," Stiers whispered softly, almost affectionately.

"When I came home, I found her lying on the floor in the living room. She was unconscious. I didn't know what to do. I thought at first that God had struck her down. I could tell she was still alive. Her chest moved now and then. I sat for a long time waiting for her to get up. Then I decided I'd better call for help. I called the family doctor and he came over right away. The next day or two is still a blur. But then, I remember I was at the hospital and the doctor came and took me into a private office. I remember that he fixed me a cup of coffee with cream. I liked that taste. It made me feel grown up — drinking coffee with a doctor.

"He told me that my mother had a very serious and unusual

illness, that she had an infection in her brain, and that it had caused an abcess. That's why her behavior had changed," George explained, altering his tone of voice.

"I asked him the name of the disease. At first he didn't want to tell me. But I assured him I was old enough and would understand." George added an aside, "I don't think I *was* old enough to understand. He told me she had syphilis, probably in the secondary stage.

"Well, I knew what syphilis was. The nuns had told us it was a punishment God sent to people for committing sins of impurity. I didn't see how my mother could have been like that. Not then, anyway. After I became an adult it made much more sense.

"I think I thought I had caused her disease by my prayers — though, of course, the fact was that those prayers only started after her behavior had been affected. Anyway, she died while she was still in the hospital. Had a stroke.

"I felt very mixed up. On the one hand, I felt that God must have loved me very much to answer my prayers. And on the other, I felt very guilty and sad about killing my own mother."

"I understand how that must have been very confusing for a young boy," Jon observed.

"Maybe you know enough about Freud and all that to figure that that whole thing really screwed up my ideas about sex."

"Yes, I can imagine."

"I've never really allowed myself to be sexual. I mean, I've fallen sometimes, of course. But I worked very hard to suppress those urges. They'd killed my beautiful mother. I didn't want to give in to them. I was pretty successful. You know, there's lots of talk about sex in the military: all those young men talking about girls. But it was pretty easy to just be above all that.

"Then back in the 1960s, things started changing. People started talking about sex all the time. It was on television. There were articles about the "sexual revolution." And, well, I started feeling very troubled. But, look, you don't want to know about all this..."

"It's okay," Jon answered. "I'm a therapist. I'm used to hearing people's stories."

George suddenly felt very ashamed. *Why have I told him all this? Well, it won't matter.*

The ringing of the phone interrupted them. George picked it up. "Hello. Oh, Edward." George's heart started pounding. Suddenly he felt really caught. Here he was, his soul open and vulnerable, and he was caught between these two forces, each of them demanding something very different of him. "Just a minute, Edward, I'm talking with someone."

He put his hand over the mouthpiece and spoke to Jon. "Excuse me. I'll only be a moment."

"That's okay," Jon replied.

"Your coffee," he reminded Jon, before removing his hand from the mouthpiece and returning his attention to Edward Buchanan.

22

The ringing telephone scared Billy. He thought perhaps he'd set off a burglar alarm as he carefully and slowly pushed open the casement window of George Wilson's living room.

After speaking with Lynn, Billy walked over to Wilson's house. Avoiding the lasers he'd seen the time before, he crept around to the side. There, spying Jon and George Wilson sitting across from one another, he tried exerting upward pressure on the window. It began to move. He hoped to be able to hear what they were talking about.

He pulled away from the window and ducked down behind the bushes outside the living room when the phone rang. Then, recognizing the sound, he resumed his effort. As the casement moved up an inch or two, the first thing he noticed was that he could hear Wilson's voice pretty clearly.

"Yes. Well, well, I'm busy right now. But maybe a little later . . . Yes, yes, I know I said I wanted to talk to you . . . Okay I'll see you in a little while."

The second thing Billy noticed was that the rich aroma of coffee, wafting through the open window as Wilson poured himself a cup from the carafe on the table in front of him, smelled warm and good now that he was cold. He envied Jon.

"Coffee is so good on a cold day like this," Wilson remarked, further tantalizing Billy. "Don't you want to drink yours?"

Billy could barely hear Jon, who was facing away from him. He appeared to bring the cup to his lips, then put it down again. He said something. Half out of common sense, Billy figured out the gist of his comment: ". . . gotten cold . . . pour out?" He watched Jon get up and walk toward the kitchen.

Wilson, left alone for a moment, withdrew something from his pocket. He held a small brownish-yellow pellet about the size of a lump of sugar between his fingers for a moment, then quickly and stealthily secreted it in the sugar bowl on the tray in front of him.

A moment later Jon walked back into the room. "Go on with your story," he said as he extended the cup toward Wilson, who refilled it from the carafe. Once again the rich, warm aroma tickled Billy's nose. But now he was suspicious. What had Wilson put in the sugar bowl? He sighed with relief when Jon answered, "No, black's fine this time," to Wilson's gesture toward the silver tray.

As Jon started to sit back down behind the desk, Wilson said, "No, please come sit over here." He motioned toward the chair adjacent to the uncomfortable-looking antique couch he was perched on. "I'm not sure what to say next," he added as Jon accepted his invitation.

"Tell me about that report." Jon pointed toward the desk. Billy was pleased Jon had moved; now he could hear the full conversation.

"The details you can read for yourself. Listen, Dr. Stiers, I didn't ask you here to recount that history. It's all written down. I asked you here because I need to talk about the state of my soul."

"And you want me to play psychotherapist to you," Jon asked, "in spite of what I think that document says?"

"Ironically, you're probably the only person I can tell. And I've got to use this last opportunity to get this off my chest."

"Okay, I'll listen. But what about this person you just talked to on the phone? You said he was coming over here."

"We have time to talk before he gets here." It seemed to Billy that Wilson's voice was breaking. He wondered what was going on. It obviously involved something on the desk.

"I didn't want what happened to my mother to ever happen again. I mean, I wanted to stop all the suffering that was caused by sexual sins. Oh, don't you see?" Wilson continued, now beginning to weep openly. "But we didn't understand. We misinterpreted what would happen. We've just caused more suffering."

"I don't understand, sir," Jon responded gently.

"Whoever would have thought homosexuals donated blood? That's such a generous and community-spirited thing to do. We never thought homosexuals were married to women. Oh, we talked about these issues," Wilson's voice had grown strident and choked, "but Edward said the only real problem was the young boys the homosexuals would rape or seduce, but that it was too late for them anyway, they'd already have been recruited and had to be sacrificed."

"Are you saying that you consciously planned out how AIDS would spread?" Jon asked.

Oh my God, Billy thought, *what in the hell have we stumbled on?*

"I *tracked* the spread, if that's what you mean, after it was clear that a new disease was showing up among homosexuals and I began to suspect that this might be related to the Ilebo Station project."

"Ilebo Station project?"

"Read the report. Buchanan and I discovered the damn stuff in Africa. The project had been a failure, a colossal waste of money and lives."

"Are you suggesting they created HIV?"

"Who knows? The reports we'd found said they developed a virus that targeted immune cells and was concentrated primarily in blood and semen — it was designed to attack males. It was aimed at soldiers, after all. We researched other blood-borne viruses, like Hepatitis-B," Wilson calmed down a little as he struggled to explain himself. "We saw that the risk groups were homosexuals, drug-abusers, and hospital workers. We really worried about the doctors and nurses. We didn't want to hurt them. But the African research had shown one of the advantages of this particular weapon was that, since it required large inoculations, it wasn't likely to get out of control: accidental needle-sticks didn't seem to carry enough of the virus to transmit it. But it did get out of control." Wilson's voice broke. "That was supposed to be my job: to determine when to release the antidote."

"Then there is an antidote?"

"We never told the Pentagon or Arlington Military Consultants, the firm we did the original audit with, what we'd found in Africa. But we brought back a sample with us."

"The disease or the antidote?"

"Why, both."

"Why didn't you release the antidote when you first saw people getting sick and dying?"

"Oh, we were expecting the homosexuals. And, of course, I knew there would be some innocent casualties..."

Billy could not believe what he was hearing. He wanted to scream bloody murder. He thought about how much he alone had had his life disrupted. And he was only one of maybe a couple of million people.

"Innocent?" Jon sounded incredulous. "But you didn't tell anybody?"

"It wasn't time."

"I don't understand. What were you up to?" Jon asked.

"Edward had sort of a revelation. He's got this, uh, hobby. And, well, he thought he'd seen God — or maybe hell. Anyway, he became very religious, Fundamentalist in a way that bothered me, you know, because Fundamentalists are so anti-Catholic."

"Okay," Jon replied.

"But Edward is my friend. I wanted . . . I wanted to show him that I, uh, believed in him." Wilson sounded like a little boy struggling to get his excuse right. "I wanted him to, uh, believe in me," he hesitated nervously. "Edward said we had an obligation to stop the spread of sexual perversion. Even though it turned out that the virus wasn't specific enough to do that, it looked like the social backlash would. By that time we'd delayed announcing what we had so long already, we decided to wait for public pressure to restore morality."

Jon jumped to his feet. He staggered backward away from Wilson, as though he had to distance himself. He bumped into a chair, pushing it back so it partially blocked Billy's view of the room. "You haven't understood anything of what you've done," Jon said angrily, obviously belying whatever sort of therapeutic role he'd been playing. Billy felt relieved that at last Jon had stopped being so understanding. This man didn't deserve sympathy. "You've caused immense suffering and a huge drain on the economy and a wave of persecution against people who are no more guilty of choosing perversion than left-handed people are of choosing to be sinister."

Wilson stood and walked over to the desk. He picked up the thick document. "Ironic, isn't it? Emily Hodgsdon just loves colored paper. She made this thing look like a rainbow. It could be the Doomsday Book for the whole world." Wilson struggled to tear the thick report in two. When he couldn't tear it, he began pulling pages off the front and back.

"Stop it," Jon shouted.

"What good is any of this now?" Wilson screamed.

"Sit down," Jon commanded authoritatively. "Mr. Wilson, sir, why are you telling all this to me?"

"Because it doesn't matter anymore. Because I've got to tell somebody before I go crazy. Because I saw you on television and thought I, uh, I liked you. Because this all has to stop."

"Yes, it has to stop. You have to release the antidote and give this information to the public."

"No," Wilson announced. "The public can't know this. It

would destroy their faith in morality. The good people can't be made to look like the villains. And only Edward can release the antidote. No, all I want is peace of mind. And to keep the secret."

"But you haven't kept the secret. You've told me."

"Who'd believe you anyway?"

"You'll testify. You'll explain all this."

"It's over, Dr. Stiers. Here, sit down," Wilson seemed to be struggling to control himself, as though at any moment he might begin to scream or break down in tears. Billy worried about Jon. He began to suspect he ought to either climb through the window or go around to the front door and force his way in. "It's almost time for you to go. Won't you have another cup of coffee?" Wilson returned to his place on the settee.

Jon sat down near Wilson. He was obviously wary of the man. Wilson was about to break. Trembling, Wilson poured coffee from the carafe into his cup and then into Jon's cup.

Billy could not quite see what was happening; the chair Jon had moved was blocking his view of the silver tray with the creamer and sugar bowl. He thought about what Wilson put in the sugar bowl. Billy began scrambling to push the window up higher. It wouldn't budge anymore.

He saw Wilson raise the cup to his lips. "Goodbye, Dr. Stiers."

"Jon, don't drink the coffee," Billy shouted through the crack in the window and then ran around to the front of the house. He rang the doorbell fiercely.

After too long an interval, the door opened. "Billy, come on in. What's happened?" Jon said. "Where were you? What did you shout about the coffee? What happened to Wilson?"

As he was asking these questions, Jon led Billy back into the living room. Wilson was lying on the floor in front of the couch. "He suddenly seemed to convulse and then fell over."

"Oh my God, Jon. I thought he was trying to kill you."

"Is he dead?"

"I don't know."

"What are you talking about, Billy?"

"I was watching through the window. He had put something in the sugar bowl earlier. Whatever it was he must have taken it himself."

Jon crouched down and felt Wilson's neck for a pulse. "Nothing."

"Let's get out of here, Jon."

"Let me get this report," Jon said as he gathered up the pieces of paper Wilson had strewn about. Billy ran on toward the front door. "Shouldn't we call the police?" Jon asked as he picked up the last of the torn pages.

"There's a Mercedes pulling into the driveway right now," Billy announced as he closed the front door and turned the dead-bolt. "Jon, let's try to get that window open and get out that way."

Billy hurried to the window where he'd been listening; he pushed and pulled on the bottom edge. It wouldn't budge.

"Maybe there's a back way," Jon said. Just then the doorbell rang.

Billy stepped back and looked hard at the window. "There it is," he proclaimed. He reached up and flipped two small toggles out of the channel in the window frame that blocked the casement from being raised any higher, then he flung the window open. "C'mon. I know what we're doing this way."

With Billy in the lead, they both climbed out the open window. As Jon clambered out, a sheet of dark magenta paper slipped out of his grip and sailed gently back into the center of the room. Jon started to go back, but Billy pulled him out of the window.

Outside Billy pulled the window down, just as they both heard the deadbolt in the door snap open. *Whoever it is must have a key*, Billy realized as he gestured for Jon to keep quiet and follow. He ducked around a couple of bushes, then they were out on the street, walking as fast as they could toward the corner.

•Four•

The End of November

1

"It was a peaceful death, wasn't it?"

"It's good you were here," Alice Graves replied.

"Oh," Mark answered, "I think Grandmother would have been okay anyway. I doubt she really needed me around to die well. But I sure benefited. We had a wonderful last day together."

"Wasn't she kinda spaced out?" Lynn spoke up. She'd been sitting quietly in the back of the booth in the hospital cafeteria listening to her mother and Mark Hartman discuss Alma DeGutis's death.

"Now, Lynn, that isn't a nice thing to say," her mother chided her.

"Oh, but it's true," Mark seemed to jump to Lynn's defense. "Grandmother was like a baby. Some of the time she barely knew what was going on. And she was pretty ornery and irritable. But we had a really loving time yesterday. And we talked about death, it was so appropriate. She insisted on me making plans for my own death. I guess that was her way of getting ready for hers. We watched the TV show that my friend Jon was on."

"TV show?" Lynn asked.

"He was on Phil Donahue last Tuesday. I brought a videotape with me."

"Maybe I saw that show," Alice interjected. "About the boy that jumped out the window?"

"Yes, that was it."

"Your friend was the nice man who said maybe people who are dying ought to let themselves go peacefully?"

"That was Jon."

"I'd like to see that," Lynn spoke up. "This is almost like knowing a celebrity . . . especially now since Billy knows him."

Mark grinned. "Sure," he said. "I'll bring the tape over."

"Who's Billy?" Alice asked innocently.

"Oh, uh, this friend of mine in Washington," Lynn answered just a trifle too fast. "I told Mark to tell Jon that this friend of mine could maybe tell him more about this AIDS treatment."

"Oh. . ."

"Grandmother really liked Jon," Mark continued, suspecting he was rescuing Lynn from something she didn't want to talk about. "She said she wanted some of her money to go to fight AIDS. I doubt she really understood what that was all about, but I was glad to hear her say it. You know, I guess I'm going to end up with a lot of money from her estate. I want to use that money right."

"Maybe Jon will have found out something that'll solve this whole problem," Lynn said. She was still excited and perplexed by the phone call from Billy this morning.

"Oh, that reminds me Jon's arriving tonight. What a time for him to come. Maybe good. You know he works around death all the time."

"But this is different," Alice spoke up. "This was an appropriate death. Your grandmother was ready to go, even looking forward to it. Not like that young man I had die last week. He was too young. That's why something like this discovery Lynn's been talking about would be so important."

2

"Breast of chicken or salisbury steak?" the flight attendant asked.

Jon looked up from his reading. He'd been so engrossed in the almost unbelievable document, he hadn't been paying attention to the details of the flight. "What was that?"

"Breast of chicken or salisbury steak?"

"Chicken, thanks," Jon answered and carefully tucked the ragged report under his leg and brought down the tray-table.

"Must be pretty interesting reading you got there," said the man in the seat next to Jon. He was a big red-faced middle-aged man whom Jon had pegged as a salesman.

"I guess I was pretty wrapped up in it."

"Couldn't help noticing what you were reading," the man continued. (*Oh God*, thought Jon.) "I'm a veterinarian myself. Bet I know about as much as anybody about rabies. I was wondering what that was there you were reading about rabies infections."

Funny, Jon thought, *with all this crazy stuff in here, what this guy noticed was the part of the project that failed. Guess it can't hurt to tell him what that was about.*

"This is classified information, sir. I shouldn't be reading it here in public, I suppose. But since you asked about it, I'll tell you a small part of this report that does, indeed, deal with rabies."

"You're not giving away spy secrets are you?"

"Not really. This concerns a study that was done in Africa over a decade ago. I guess that makes it pretty outdated now. Nothing a spy would want," Jon fibbed just a little. "But this is kind of shocking, I think. It seems that a private research lab was working on a biological weapon for the Army. They were trying to develop a strain of rabies that could be sprayed from the air into an enemy army."

"The soldiers would go crazy and kill each other," the veterinarian answered with an expression of delighted insight. "But couldn't the disease spread all over the place?"

"The thrust of the research was to combine the rabies genome with a harmless virus that could be neutralized by another virus. After the initial inoculation the antidote virus could be sprayed over the army and stop the spread of the rabies."

"Neat trick. Whatever happened to it?"

Here's where I need to be cagey, Jon thought. "The primate virus they were studying turned virulent all by itself and infected everybody in the lab. When the personnel were sick and weak, somehow the rabid animals broke out and attacked them."

"Gee. Makes you glad you're not in research. 'Specially not over in the jungle. Seems like there're a lot of pretty nasty viruses over there. You know, they say this AIDS virus started in Africa. Think that had anything to do with that study of yours?"

Bingo, thought Jon. "You never know," he answered noncommitally. "Would you like my cake? I'm on a diet and I noticed you really scarfed yours down."

The veterinarian laughed. "My contribution to keeping food from being wasted. Thanks," he answered as he accepted the dry-looking slice of white cake Jon offered.

"Look, you won't say anything about this, will you?" Jon said conspiratorially. He thought about how surprised this guy was going to be in a couple of days when he heard on the evening news that that primate virus Jon had mentioned did turn out to be the cause of AIDS. "Alert me if they come by with coffee," Jon asked the vet, partly by way of letting him know he wanted to resume his reading.

"Thanks for telling me the story. You were right."

"Huh?"

"I mean it is sort of shocking to think of the government doing something like that."

That's just the half of it, Jon thought as he turned back to the report. He was now reading a section printed on sunny yellow paper called "The Problems in America." He cringed mentally as he read the argument that the relaxation of sexual morality during the late 1960s, combined with communistic influences in the civil rights and the peace movements, were responsible for the breakdown of the family and the rest of the problems that faced modern American society.

Curiously, at the very heart of the discussion was the notion that pinko-leaning homosexuals were undermining American morality. Jon wondered what was supposed to be so capitalistic about heterosexuality or why communism was supposed to be anti-family. As far as he knew, they still had families in Russia. *In fact,* he thought humorously to himself, *the only society in the modern world which has experimented with institutional alternatives to the family is Israel. And the usual bigot's notion of Jews is that they're capitalistic in the extreme.*

Somehow the people who wrote this report — Jon corrected himself: George Wilson — thought that wiping out the homosexual population in America would end homosexuality and restore pre-modern stability.

What was most ironic, Jon thought, was just how close to being right he was. Not that killing homosexuals would solve anything, but that this disease — along with other elements of "future shock," of course — was truly scaring people into such an attitude of blaming and selfishness that most of the progressive reforms of the mid-twentieth century were being overturned.

And at what tremendous cost! For a moment his mind flashed back to Ted's funeral, just a week before he left San Francisco. He thought about Pat Stratford. He thought about the PWAs who might have heard him on the Donahue Show just the other day. *My God, I was telling them to have pity on America and let themselves die rather than exhaust the national treasury. That's not the answer at all, not in the light of what I know now. They should rise up and destroy the bastards that did this to them.*

Jon felt an enormous surge of indignant rage roll through him.

"Here comes the coffee," the veterinarian said, tugging at Jon's arm.

3

"Hi, Robyn, I'm glad you're home. I need to talk to you."

"Oh, hi, Blum. Yeah, I'm home. Sorry I took so long to answer. I was doing my meditation and didn't realize the phone was ringing. What's up?"

"I just talked to Greg Bens, you know, from the PWA group."

"I know."

"Greg's lover just moved out of town without telling him. It really upset him. He's been talking to Chuck and Luis. They're all still upset about Pat's death and maybe about what Jon said on the TV."

"Oh?"

"And, I think, maybe they're planning ... well, to do something..."

"You mean the group suicide Pat talked about?"

"I think so. Greg was real evasive. But he said I didn't need to know about this."

"Well, maybe they're doing the right thing?"

"You think so? How about the *Course in Miracles* and meditation and healing and all that?"

"Blum, look, it worked for me. And I'm real glad. Maybe it'd work for them, maybe not. I mean, at least right now they're all so angry..."

"Yeah, at Jon."

"That hardly seems fair. It's like they're blaming him for being on their side. One of the single most important notions in attitudinal healing is not blaming other people for your problems. You've got to own your own problems, take responsibility for your own life."

"Easier said than done."

"Well, yeah. One of the ways you do that is by looking out for other people, I mean, taking responsibility even for the people you can't do anything about. Remember: 'To give and to receive are one.'"

"So, that's why I'm calling you. I thought maybe you'd talk to them. Maybe you could convince them, well, to hang on a little longer and try the meditation."

"That's a big order. They haven't seemed all that interested in what I had to say. Jon's the only one who's paid any attention."

"I wish I could talk to Jon. Maybe he could get some sense into them, but I don't know where he is."

"Isn't he in Wisconsin with his boyfriend Mark?"

"How would I call him?"

"Did you try calling Mark's number? Maybe there's a referral message."

"Well, Robyn, okay, maybe I'll try that. But will you call Greg and the others? Please?"

"Okay, on one condition. Come over tonight. It was so great sleeping with you last night after that wonderful dinner you fixed. After I try talking to these guys, I know I'm gonna need a hug."

"Hey, yeah, no problem. Anytime, Robyn. I really mean that."

"Oh, so do I," Robyn chuckled, "I don't mean sex — though that's not such a bad idea either — but a good hug. That's an important part of healing yourself and keeping yourself well."

"I'll be over in a little while."

"Oh, Blum, wait a minute. Gimme the phone numbers..."

4

Jon wandered around O'Hare Airport. He had an hour and a half before his commuter flight to LaCrosse. Staring out the window at the planes taxiing along the runway, he thought about what a mad dash he and Billy DePalma had made to return the Sheehans' car, get his things, and then get to the airport — all the while trying to avoid thinking specifically about what had just happened to them and about George Wilson's sudden death. Billy had said he trusted Jon with the information in that report — and he was clearly afraid to have the report in his own possession. Billy seemed practically scared to death of Edward Buchanan and the Liberty Bell Foundation.

Even now, as he turned away from the window to scan the faces of people sitting in the waiting area, Jon wondered if Buchanan could have found out who he was and where he was going and have sent his henchmen after him. He was sure he'd left a trail. Until the moment George Wilson keeled over, Jon hadn't realized how important secrecy might be.

Now, as he reminded himself of that, he regretted even the superficial conversation with the veterinarian on his previous flight. *Though I'll be damned*, he thought, *if I'll let myself start getting paranoid about everybody I talk to.*

He checked the time on the big clock. His flight to LaCrosse was probably ready to board. He hurried down the corridor to the gate.

There were a number of empty seats on the plane: LaCrosse apparently wasn't that popular a destination. *Well, I'll be glad for the seclusion for a couple of days. Give me time to think this thing through.*

When the flight attendant announced departure and started her short talk about seatbelts and oxygen masks, Jon thought he recognized the back of the head of a man on the other side of the aisle a few rows forward. He'd just dismissed the suspicion when the man turned around slightly, as if to check out the other passengers, and then continued turning till he was looking Jon right in the eye. He smiled amiably. Jon felt his heart sink.

It was the veterinarian.

5

Mark was waiting at the gate as the passengers came off the plane. He was looking forward to seeing Jon and was anxious to hear news about the HIV antidote. He was also feeling high-strung just on account of the mix of emotions that followed his grandmother's death and the media attention which that drew.

As the passengers came through the gate, Mark searched the faces. *There he is.* As Mark stepped forward and opened his arms, Jon hurried his pace a little. They embraced one another warmly.

"I'm sorry to hear about your grandmother," Jon said after a moment.

"Oh, that's okay. I'm sort of happy for her, in fact. Her mind was going, you know. She was ready to die. Really it's kinda good news. Wait till I tell you. But let's get out of here before another reporter sees me."

"Reporter?" Jon asked, as they started away from the gate.

Just then a big, heavy-set man clasped Jon by the shoulder and jovially extended his other hand. "Well, hello there." A surprised look passed over Jon's face.

Jon warily took his hand.

"Learn any more about that rabies?" the man asked.

"What's this?" Mark asked.

"Your friend and I sat next to one another on the flight out to Chicago," the man said to Mark, then turned back to Jon. "Well, it was nice talking to you. Maybe we'll meet again." He set off down the corridor.

As they hustled toward the baggage claim, Jon acknowledged, "I was scared shitless for a moment there. I think maybe that man is following me."

"Why would somebody be following you?"

Jon answered with a nervous laugh and a sigh. "You won't believe."

"Well, that guy looked pretty harmless to me. Too fat to be dangerous."

"Oh?" Jon answered quizzically. They walked on a little ways further. "What's this about reporters following you?" he asked anxiously.

"You know, my grandmother was a bigwig around here. I told you about this house she's got . . . she had," Mark corrected himself, "right in the middle of the parking lot for the new mall. Everybody in town practically has been waiting for her to die. Her death is really getting publicity. You wouldn't believe the number of reporters I talked to today."

"Oh, you scared me for a minute. I thought maybe the reporters had something to do with AIDS."

"Well," Mark answered hesitantly, "they do. A little."

"Huh?"

"That's part of my good news. Grandmother and I watched the tape of you on the Donahue Show yesterday. I thought you did wonderful. So did she. And she instructed me — in writing no less — to give a portion of her estate to AIDS research."

"That's wonderful."

"That's not all, though. I told a couple of reporters this afternoon, and they wanted to know where I was going to donate the money. And so, well, so I told them that I knew about this new treatment for HIV and I wanted to fund that research."

"Oh God," Jon said, half under his breath. He started laughing nervously. "I'm not sure those people should get any money. But let's get out of here and I'll explain." Even as he was saying that, his suitcase came bouncing along the conveyor.

※

A light spattering of snow was falling as Mark drove Jon the long way home. The night was surprisingly bright. Reflection from the snow, Mark explained. He took Jon up to the top of the Mississippi bluffs to show him the town and "The River." Even in the semi-dark, Jon easily understood why no other river in the area could possibly compete for that title. At the same time that Jon was enjoying the sights in this part of the world, he was also recounting to Mark the events described in the multi-colored report that lay in his lap.

"The idea apparently was to use this monkey virus like an off/on switch for the rabies. It had to get into some kind of cell where it could replace the cell's DNA with the rabies genes and turn the cell into a factory for rabies virus. They may have intentionally designed it to attack the T-helper cells so the immune system couldn't even get started fighting it off. I mean, it looks like, at least by the time they were finished with it, the same carrier virus intended to turn on the rabies production could also turn off the immune response.

"What's really eerie is that the virus turned out to be pretty male specific. Maybe they even engineered it to be in semen. Oh, no, I don't know. Maybe that doesn't make any sense," Jon stopped himself, commenting on his own conjecture about the research.

"Doesn't the report explain all that?" Mark asked.

"Well, this is not the report of the research team. This was written by one of the consultants who went over to audit the project — I suppose to determine its efficiency and cost-effectiveness and stuff. But they found everybody dead. They also found the viruses that killed them and, apparently, an antidote — a virus that would come along and turn off the rabies production."

"What happened to the rabies?"

"From what I understand, the project never entirely succeeded at getting the rabies genome into the monkey virus. They were still mucking around with redesigning this virus so it could be spread through aerosol spray.

"So what happened?"

"My guess is that the virus got out, maybe in rabid monkeys. The report explains that the animal cages were all broken open. That could have spread the virus all over the place.

"Wilson explains in here how long he spent studying the characteristics of the virus before it dawned on him that since it was in semen but had to get into blood, it was likely to target male homosexuals. From hepatitis-B parallels, he realized it could spread to junkies, which, he then decided, was okay."

"What about hemophiliacs and Haitians?"

"I think he was just medically naive enough to fail to consider hemophiliacs. I can't say I blame him. After all, when AIDS first appeared I sure didn't understand how the hemophiliacs fit into the epidemiology. As for the Haitians, I don't know. Chance, I guess.

"Jon, do you really believe all this?" Mark asked, for the first time seeming skeptical. "I mean I know we've all talked about the idea that AIDS was a CIA conspiracy or something. But whoever really believed that? I'm thinking about that book you bought me. It sounds like we've woke up from somebody's paranoid nightmare. Don't you think this could all be made up?"

"Do I really believe it?" Jon repeated the question. "Frankly, no. I don't want to believe it; it's almost too horrible. But when you look at how AIDS has been treated by the government and a lot of the American public, this is not so surprising. People really didn't get concerned about AIDS prevention till they realized it could spread to heterosexuals. And the big push has always been to find a vaccine that could protect heterosexuals, not a treatment that would eliminate HIV in the people already exposed — because, of course, those people were the homosexuals and the junkies."

"But just letting this spread—" Mark objected.

"Look what they've done to homosexuals over the years. How many have been thrown in prison or mental hospitals? How many were burned by the Church as heretics and witches? How many were killed at Dachau and Auschwitz? My God, when the Allies liberated the camps they transferred the homosexuals to new prisons. A while back when the pope was condemning the Nazi horrors, he totally ignored the homosexual victims."

"He probably thought the final solution was 'understandable' for homosexuals," Mark interjected. "I remember when the Vatican declared that homosexuals brought AIDS on themselves and that anti-gay violence was understandable."

"So maybe we shouldn't even be surprised if it turned out Wilson and Buchanan were actually spreading the virus. It'd be perfectly consistent with history."

"Yeah, but does the idea of an antidote virus make sense?"

"That's a good question. I remember reading about some plan to treat AIDS by biologically engineering a new virus that could go in and destroy HIV. I also remember reading about a study in Senegal that discovered that a large number of prostitutes were positive for the HIV antibody but none of them were getting AIDS. What was special about Senegal was high incidence of another virus — the article called it HTLV-IV. It looked like HTLV-IV exposure prevented AIDS."

"You think the antidote got released in Senegal?"

"I don't know what to think," Jon answered. "I don't know what to believe. But I have evidence of something right here in front of me."

"What if that's just somebody's fantasy?"

"Well, it still deserves to be checked out, doesn't it?"

"Are you going to release the information to the press?"

"If it would force them to release the antidote virus, then I would — I mean, if there really is one. But, you know, I don't know that that'd work. Everybody might just laugh at me. This Buchanan guy could just deny the whole story. He'd say Wilson was crazy — he killed himself, you know. And then they'd probably kill me soon after."

"Oh no, they wouldn't dare."

"Mark, if this is true, these people have already allowed nearly fifty thousand people to die. One more isn't going to matter."

"Jon, I wish you could just go back to sleep and undream this one." Mark turned onto a road alongside the half-constructed mall. "Here's the house," he said a few moments later as he pulled into the driveway.

At the end of a long tree-lined drive, the house stood eerie and handsome in the snow-lit darkness. The light falling of snow glistened in halos around two big lamp fixtures on either side of the front door. The sparkling of fresh snow lay over a series of roofs of various levels outlining a panoply of gingerbread adornment of the old Victorian mansion. To the right of the front porch a tower with circular rooms on each floor rose up into the darkness higher even than the peak of the steep shingled roof of the house itself.

"Wow, neat looking place. Haunted?"

"Wait till you see," Mark laughed. Then he turned serious, "Jon, does this Buchanan guy know you have that report and where you are?"

"I don't know. Maybe."

Mark felt a chill run through him. "Were you followed?"

"I thought by the Fat Man," Jon said with an effort at a Peter Lorre accent.

"No, I mean, seriously."

"I don't know. I hope not. Mark," he added, "that's why I was a little worried when you said you'd told the media about the antidote. What if that story gets all the way back to D.C.? But why did you ask?"

"Because there's a car coming down the road behind—"

6

"Edward, would you like another cup of coffee?" Joanne Buchanan asked, fussing over her husband's breakfast.

Edward was engrossed in his thoughts and in the newspaper. He didn't answer.

"More coffee? Edward?"

"I'm sorry, dear. I just read something here that's, well, caught my attention. No, no. No thank you. No time for more coffee now. I've got to make a phone call and then get down to the office." He got up from the table, kissed his wife perfunctorily, and headed into his study.

Edward was upset. He hadn't slept well last night. He kept remembering his friend and protege's body lying sprawled in the living room. *And where did that report go? If indeed he had had a full copy of the report. Damn him, damn him. He knew better than to keep that thing where somebody could find it.*

Now the morning paper had a curious item:

AIDS CURE RUMORED

LaCrosse, Wisc. Mark Hartman announced intentions to donate a substantial portion of the estate of his late grandmother, Alma DeGutis, heiress of the NorthCountry Paper Company fortune, to AIDS research. Hartman told reporters that he knew of secret research on an antidote to the AIDS-producing virus, called HIV. He vowed to use his grandmother's money to make this antidote available to the public.

Edward felt uneasy — especially because of the word "antidote." He picked up the phone and punched a number.

7

Lynn was blissfully dreaming of an idyllic life with Billy — with no fears of disease and lots of kids — as she drove down the bumpy road toward the tall grove of fir that surrounded the old estate. She began paying attention to her driving as she realized the car was sliding a little on patches of frozen snow. The snow had already melted on major streets, but here the absence of asphalt left the roadbed colder and more susceptible to icing.

After their talk at the hospital yesterday, Mark had invited Lynn over to the DeGutis mansion for Saturday brunch. He had been very sincere in wanting her to meet his friend Jon, and he knew she was anxious to hear what news Jon and Billy had found about the viral antidote. At the time, Mark hadn't realized how really anxious she'd be.

Billy had called last night, sounding very mysterious, telling her he didn't want to talk on the phone, but that "a friend" would be in town soon to explain. That had really gotten her emotions running high.

She turned into the property and drove up toward the house. Her eye was caught by what looked like a man running across the front of the driveway and disappearing into the scraggly bushes near the garage to the left of the house. She drove into the circular drive and pulled up right in front of the main entrance. Quickly she jumped out of the car and ran up the steps and banged on the door.

"You're right on time," Mark announced as he opened the door.

"Oh, Mark, I just saw a prowler."

"Oh?" Mark answered, "Where?"

"It looked like a man in a black jacket. He was in the front yard."

"Could have been one of the construction workers from next door. My grandmother said they occasionally come over here, sometimes just to get a look at the place. She used to run them off. Maybe they heard she'd died. Anyway I don't think it's anything to worry about."

"I do," Jon said, stepping up behind Mark.

"Oh, Jon, don't you think you're being alarmist?" Mark asked. "Well, anyway, Lynn, this is Jon Stiers. Jon, Lynn Graves."

"Billy sends his love," Jon said as he took Lynn's hand.

"Come in, come in. It's cold," Mark ushered her through the doorway.

"I know you think I'm being suspicious," Jon remarked to Mark as the younger man led the threesome back toward the kitchen. "But last night after we drove in here we saw that other car drive past the entrance. Somebody could've been following us. It was your idea."

"Yes, that's true. Your story was just giving me the willies. There's lots of traffic around here."

"The road doesn't go anywhere."

"Yeah, but in the dark of night people don't know that. They think they're turning onto a major street that runs alongside the mall. It's my grandmother's fault the road doesn't go anywhere."

"Do you think somebody would be following you?" Lynn asked.

"When you hear what happened to Billy and me yesterday, you'll agree. Did he call you last night?"

"He did. Said he didn't want to talk about it on the phone and I should ask you."

"Good," Jon commented. "He's a sensible young man. Real nice looking too." He smiled at Lynn.

"Come on back to the kitchen. We were just starting on breakfast," Mark said. Before they could go, the phone rang. A moment later Mark called from the little alcove off the entrance hall where Jon was helping Lynn with her coat. "It's for you. Blum Blumgarten."

8

"So I think they've been waiting to release the antidote till enough political pressure develops against gay people." Jon completed his summary of what he'd learned.

"Oh my God, I just can't believe it. I mean, I mean," Lynn blustered apparently out of confusion and hurt, "that's so cruel. How could anybody do that?"

"How could the Nazis have sent the Jews to the gas chambers?" Mark spoke up.

"Yeah, but that's different. I mean these people were endangering innocent bystanders," Lynn answered.

"They're all innocent bystanders," Jon answered. "But, Lynn, I know what you mean. There's something especially repugnant about the idea of just allowing this stuff to run wild through the environment."

"Yeah, that's what I meant," Lynn said, clearly embarrassed. Jon felt sorry for her. She seemed so naive and innocent, such a small town girl from middle America. "Mr. Buchanan is a real manifestation of pure evil," Lynn added.

"I doubt that," Mark answered. "I bet the Liberty Bell people thought they were motivated by virtue. They were probably outraged that other people weren't like them and so they were going to do something about them — for their own good."

"It's a great example," Jon rejoined, "of how good intentions, especially when they come out of somebody who is convinced they're right and that they've got God on their side, can turn out to be the source of horrible evil."

All of a sudden, Lynn sat up and put one hand on her hip and said to Jon, "Are you telling me the truth? Aren't you really just making up a story?"

"No, Lynn. I'm telling you what's in the report I got from your Mr. Wilson. Now maybe it isn't true. But I can't believe Wilson was so committed to covering up some innocuous statistical research that he'd kill himself. But still, maybe he was insane and made up this whole thing and his suicide was just part of his insanity."

"Well, I hope it is real," declared Mark.

"What do you mean?" Lynn sounded surprised.

"I mean it's repugnant that these people intentionally let this virus spread," Mark answered. "But it means there's a solution. What if we blackmail them now? Let them know we know? And that we'll keep their secret if and only if they release the antidote?"

"You mean you're willing to let them get away with this?" Lynn sounded incredulous.

"Right now I'm interested in getting the antidote," Jon answered. "We don't know where it is or what to do with it, so we have to get Buchanan to cooperate. I'll threaten him with exposure, of course, to force his cooperation. But if we just turn the information over to the press — even assuming they'd believe it — Buchanan might destroy the antidote to protect himself. We can't risk that. Besides, I don't know if the public would believe this whole thing anyway. I'm not sure I would have. I'm still not sure I believe it now," he emphasized. "And if we turn this over to the police, the antidote will probably never be released. How can we trust the government? I mean, wouldn't some bureaucrats claim it and then spend months, if not years, testing it — and maybe never approve it?"

"What if it doesn't work? Or is toxic itself?" Mark asked. "*Shouldn't* there be some sort of research?"

"Well, maybe that's a possibility. We don't know what kind of research was done. Maybe—"

"No," Lynn spoke up. "It ought to be made available right now — at least to all the people who are HIV positive."

"Billy's positive, isn't he?" Jon asked softly.

Lynn nodded affirmatively as she started to cry.

"He didn't tell me, but it made sense."

"If you blackmail them into giving out the antidote virus, how would they do that?" she asked, brushing away her tears.

"Well, ideally they'd turn it over to a medical team. But who knows? Wouldn't that expose who they are? I think it was designed to be sprayed in the air."

"Sprayed in the air?"

"Maybe from an airplane over the big cities: New York, Houston, Chicago, L.A., San Francisco. It'd probably spread from there on its own. But we don't know how much of it Buchanan's got."

"Even if you blackmail Mr. Buchanan into doing that, isn't he liable to kill you?" Lynn changed the subject.

"I guess that's a possibility. Maybe that wouldn't be so bad: one life to save tens of thousands. I have to admit I've always had a sort of martyr complex," Jon laughed.

"I don't want you to die," Mark said.

"Well, neither do I," Jon answered. "But I think about all those guys dying of AIDS — my God, all those guys I said on TV ought to let themselves die. And the guys in the support group planning to kill themselves—"

"What's that?" Mark spoke up surprised.

"Oh, I didn't tell you about that call from Blumgarten. You'd already started telling Lynn about the report. Well, Blum said Greg and Chuck and Luis are planning a group suicide — sort of in honor of Pat. Robyn tried talking to them, but I think that just upset them more. So Blum wanted me to do something."

"What can you do?" Mark asked.

"Oh, I think that was easy. I told Blum to tell them I'd discovered something so surprising they wouldn't want to die at least until they'd heard the dish." Jon laughed. "I don't mean to stereotype them as hysterical queens, but at least for the time being, I think, the best intervention is to arouse their curiosity."

Mark grinned.

"What are you guys talking about?" Lynn interjected. "I don't think any of this is a laughing matter."

"Gotta keep a sense of humor," Jon replied in a clownish voice. "Besides, if I'm going to walk right into the lion's den, I'd rather be laughing than crying."

"Let me do it," Mark said, suddenly changing the tone of the conversation. "I can go see Buchanan instead of you."

"Oh, baby," Jon smiled warmly, "that's so sweet. But you're still young. You don't have to be sacrificed." No one laughed at his attempt at humor.

"The fact is we'll all be sacrificed," Lynn said solemnly. "Don't you think they'll find out about all of us?"

"That's why secrecy is still important," Jon answered. "Let's not get any more people involved for the time being. Though let's make sure the information will get out even if all of us *do* mysteriously disappear."

"Oh, Jon, you're giving me the willies again," Mark laughed. "Can't we all just wake up and discover the crazy dream's over?"

"Please, let's do something soon. I'm so worried about that virus in Billy."

"Lynn, you're right. We've got to act quickly."

"So, what? We go back to D.C.?" Mark asked.

"*I* go to D.C.," Jon answered firmly. He could tell by the look in his eyes that Mark was disappointed, but seemed to accept Jon's leadership.

"Well, then, how about another cup of coffee?" Mark said, getting up from the dining room table and moving toward the kitchen.

🕭

Mark was only gone a moment when he dashed back into the room. "Come here, you two," he whispered loudly.

Jon followed Mark into the kitchen with Lynn trailing behind. "What is it?"

"Lynn thought she saw a prowler in the yard earlier. Remember? I just looked out the window. And I'll swear I see something — or somebody — out there in the bushes." Mark motioned them all down into a crouch. "Now, stay down, but see if you don't see a kind of dark lump right in the middle of the hedge out there."

Jon peered up over the bottom of the window. At first, all he could see was the wall of firs surrounding the house, and some leafless bushes near the wall of the garage. "I don't see anything."

Mark peeked up again. "He's still there."

Lynn was now at their side. She rose up and peeked out the window. "I think I see what you mean. Maybe a man crouching?"

"Right."

Jon tried again. "Are you sure you're not just seeing a pile of leaves or something? I think I see what you mean, but it doesn't look like a man to me . . . uh-oh, it just moved." Jon's heart started beating like crazy. "I guess you're right. That *is* somebody. He just stood up."

All three peered up through the bottom of the window. It was obvious now that they were seeing a man, apparently hiding in the bushes.

"Should I call the police?" Mark asked.

"Yeah, call the police," Lynn responded immediately.

"No, not yet," Jon said. "If that's somebody from Buchanan, we don't want him arrested. I mean, I don't want my hand forced yet."

"What if he's trying to kill us?"

"Well, then we get him first. Can we do that?"

"Hey, hey," Mark answered, starting to laugh. "You know, this house is full of traps. Of all the places in the world, where could we better capture somebody?"

"Hmm, but you're the only one who knows them," Jon answered.

"Right. Well, then I'm in charge. Okay?"

Jon and Lynn nodded. Jon was a little reluctant, but what choice did he have, he asked himself.

"How are we going to get him to come inside?" Lynn asked.

"Why not invite him?" Mark answered.

"What if he's got a gun?" Jon objected.

"There are three of us. And my grandmother's got enough guns in this house for an army. You know she was a real N.R.A. supporter." All three of them laughed nervously.

9

Lynn didn't especially like guns. She told Mark her aim couldn't be very good, so he equipped her with a repeat-action shotgun. "You don't have to aim with this," he joked to her. "Just blow 'em away."

She kept remembering those words — and the sense of power behind them — as she accompanied Jon out the front door. Her instructions were to stay at least ten feet or more to the outside of him, so she'd have time to fire just in case Jon were hit. Mark, she knew, was coming up from behind the garage. Between the three of them, they had the prowler surrounded.

"Put your hands in the air and drop your gun," she heard Mark shout, followed by a blast from his rifle.

"I don't have a gun," an unfamiliar voice responded. Lynn saw a man stand up.

As the man stepped out into the open space in front of the garage, Mark shouted, "Who are you? And what are you doing on this property?"

"I just wanted to see the house," the man said innocently. "I heard they were gonna tear it down."

"Well, then come in. We'll show you the place," Mark

answered but kept his rifle leveled at the man's chest. Lynn wondered if Mark really believed him.

She followed at a distance as Mark and Jon escorted the stranger into the house. Once inside the front door, Mark instructed the man to take off his heavy jacket and hang it on the coat rack on the wall. At Mark's instruction, Jon frisked him for weapons. Nothing. Mark then asked for identification. The man, looking appropriately frightened, handed him his wallet.

"John Houston," Mark read aloud, "from Camden, N.J. What's a New Jerseyite doing out here looking at old houses?"

"I'm working over here on the mall," he answered.

"Mr. Houston, you picked a bad time to come snooping around here. We just got some other bad news and we're kinda jumpy. And my grandmother's sleeping upstairs."

"Sorry, wouldn't want to wake up your grandmother," Houston said. "Didn't mean to offend. Just wanted a look. Maybe I should leave."

"Well, sir," Mark said, lowering his gun, "you said you wanted to see the house. Let me show you the upstairs."

"Mark, are you sure it's okay?" Jon asked. Lynn felt relieved.

"I'm sure," he replied. Then he added to Houston, "The best view's up from the third floor. You want to go on up?"

"You're not gonna carry that gun, are you?" Houston said.

"I'll leave mine right here," Mark said laying the rifle on a side table. "Jon, you keep yours handy though, just in case."

"Look here, mister, I don't want any trouble," Houston said.

"Us neither," Mark answered smiling. "Let's go on up." Bounding ahead of the man, he leaped up several steps at a time. Houston, seeming a little reluctant, followed. Jon and Lynn trailed along behind.

At the top of the stairs, Mark was standing holding open a door into a room in one of the turrets. "Jon, hold the door," Mark instructed as he walked over to the small oval window in the opposite wall. "Great view from here."

Houston followed him over and looked out the little window. In a flash Mark was back with Jon by the door. Just as quickly, he closed the door behind him, leaving Houston in the garret. "The trick about that room is that once you get in, you can't get out until somebody opens the door from outside. I used to get trapped in there as a kid."

"How come you locked him in?" Lynn asked.

"Remember when I said my grandmother was asleep? Anybody who'd worked around here would know she just died."

"I don't think that's so convincing," Jon answered. "I think your secret room's a great idea, but I'm not sure your evidence really proves we've got somebody worth locking up."

Houston began to knock on the door, "Hey, I can't find the handle."

"Just sit down for a little bit, Mr. Houston. We need to talk about this."

"Hey, you can't lock me in here."

"I think we already have," Mark answered.

🥀

"Look, Lynn," Mark answered her worried objections after the three of them had returned to the dining room to discuss what to do next, "all we have to say is that this Mr. Houston came by to see the house and happened into that room. It's not entirely my fault that my grandfather built such a trap," Mark grinned. Then he added, "Hey, I was going to make some fresh coffee when all this started. Still want some?"

Jon nodded affirmatively. "Well, I think Mark's right that we've got some justification for leaving that guy up there for a while, till we can determine whether he really is just a curious passerby or an agent or something from the Liberty Bell Foundation."

"Look in his coat," Mark shouted from the kitchen where he was running water into the carafe to fill the coffeemaker.

Jon picked up the coat from the rack and, feeling in the pockets as he walked, carried it back into the dining room. Lynn and Jon arrived to find Mark sitting at the table with Houston's open wallet in his hands. Jon spoke up. "Nothing in the pockets, but I can feel something hard and flat inside the lining here."

"Maybe there's a secret pocket," Lynn suggested.

"Hey, look at this." Jon reached through a torn seam and pulled out a flat metal container, a gadget that looked like a remote control of some sort, and a blackjack.

"What's in the box?" Lynn asked.

Jon held the metal box open for them to see. "It looks like a burglar's tool kit. Look, here are picks to open a lock, this thing is a switchblade knife. And this, I think, is some sort of miniature gun."

"Well, that man's hardly an innocent passerby," Mark observed. He was searching through the wallet. "There's hardly anything in here except some money and this I.D., which is probably fake, and a Visa card in John Houston's name. And this," he held up a thin piece of plastic the size of a credit card. It had numbers embossed on it but no printing of any sort. "There's a magnetic tape on the back."

"Maybe it's a key, you know, to open electronic doors," Lynn offered.

"I think you're probably right. But how are we going to find out?" Mark asked. "We can't very well call in the F.B.I., can we?"

"What about just asking him who he is? I mean, now that we have this stuff, he might be more willing to explain himself," Jon suggested.

"How could we trust him?"

"Well, I don't know that we can. But he can't get out of that room till we're satisfied. Look, let me go up and talk to him through the door," Jon said.

"We're coming along," Lynn announced.

🐾

"Mr. Houston, I'd like to ask you a few questions," Jon announced loudly as he rapped at the door. There was no reply. "Mr. Houston?" Still no reply.

"Maybe this is a trap to get us to open the door so he can get out," Lynn offered.

"There's a spy hole from another room," Mark said, leading them around to a short blind corridor.

"Where does this go?" Jon asked.

"Nowhere really. But there's another entrance into that room through a panel in the woodwork here — I guess so you could suddenly appear in that room and surprise whoever you'd locked in. Though you'd still need a third person to open the door from the outside." Mark led them into the corridor and then peered through a brass fixture, like the eyepiece of an old-fashioned telescope. "I don't see him," he said nervously.

"Is there any place he could be hiding?"

"You look," Mark answered Jon. "I don't see where, except maybe right under the wall here, but he'd have to know this lens was here."

"Even if he did, it wouldn't matter," Jon answered as he put his eye to the lens opening. "The mirror on the opposite wall reflects this side of the room."

"Gee, I never noticed that," Mark answered, then suddenly became quite sober. "Then where is our prisoner?" Even as he spoke he jiggled the spring latch that held the secret door. It was loose. "Uh, oh, this lock has been broken."

"Could Houston have done that?" Lynn asked.

"No, but somebody else could have any time in the last few years. And if Houston pressed against the panels on the inside he'd have popped this open. That means he's loose in the house."

Lynn felt a chill. "You know, I think I remember my mom saying something about undoing some lock . . . Let's get the guns," she said as she turned to run back to the stairs.

"Remember, we've got to keep him upstairs. And we need to stay together. This place is full of traps and doors and stairs that lead nowhere. He's bound to get lost again," Mark answered as he carefully followed behind her.

"He could kill us all in the meantime," Jon observed ominously as he followed behind. "Look, just in case something happens, if one of us manages to get away, be sure and get that report. It's lying on the desk in the living room." He whispered the last sentence.

10

Mark led the way down the stairs and back to the dining room. The first thing he noticed was that the steel case they'd found in the secret pocket of Houston's coat was gone from the table where Jon had left it. "He must have already come down here," Mark deduced. "Be careful now. He could be almost anywhere and he could be armed. Get your guns and c'mon." He led them back into the kitchen and through a doorway hidden inside the pantry, then up a steep spiral staircase. "Lock that door behind you," he instructed Jon. After only about half a flight, the steps opened into a small octagonal room with benches built into the walls all around.

"This is the secret room," Mark whispered grinning.

"What are we gonna do?" Jon whispered. "I think we should decide some plan of action."

"I'm in favor of shooting him," Lynn spoke up. "That'd get it over with."

"What if he's an F.B.I. agent or something? Besides we need to find out what he knows," Jon objected.

"Right," said Mark. "I think we'd better try to trap him again. There's another way. And I know he can't get out of this one. But I'm gonna need you to lure him into it," Mark said to Jon.

"I don't think that'd be safe. Maybe he'll just shoot you," Lynn exclaimed.

"Shhh," Mark held a finger to his lips. "Did you hear that? That creak, I mean? He's up on the second floor. Just where we want him. I need to go up first and unlock a door."

"Will you be safe?" Jon asked.

"Hope so," Mark answered. He scurried up the stairs a little

further and then crawled into a small chamber that opened into the
linen closet on the second floor.

Mark took a deep breath and then pushed through the trap
door into the linen closet. He listened at the door for a moment,
then opened it a crack and peered through. No sign of Houston in
the corridor. Swiftly he let himself into the hall and rushed down to
a door at the end of the hall. A tattered sign in red letters an-
nouned: WARNING. Quickly Mark pulled the sign down, tearing
it off the tacks that affixed it, and unlocked the deadbolt, then he
ran back to the linen closet and shut the door behind him.

A moment later he had crawled back into the secret room with
Jon and Lynn. "Now we have to get him to walk through that
door."

"What's there?" Lynn asked.

"Nothing," Mark replied cryptically. "Lynn, you stay here.
Jon, I need your help."

They climbed the stairs halfway, then crawled into another
narrow tunnel running the opposite way from the linen closet.
Mark led the way into another closet. "We'll come out in the bedroom behind the shaft. You wait here a minute. I'm gonna lock the
door so he can't get into this room."

And a moment later Mark was back with Jon. "I need you to
stand over here." Mark led him out into the room and showed him
a faded spot painted on the floor. "See the mirror there? That
reflects into another mirror over here," he whispered as he unlocked and opened another door with a warning sign tacked to it.
This time he didn't bother to remove the sign. "Now, when
Houston opens that door out there, it'll look like you're standing
right across from him. You raise your rifle and look like you're aim-
ing at him. Now give me another count of ten, and then call out
Houston's name. Let's see if he'll come."

Mark hurried back into the closet and through the passage
behind the walls. By the time he'd counted to eight, he was back in
the linen closet on the other side of the trap. *Now if only Houston will
fall for it*, he thought.

"Hey, Houston, come here. Houston," he heard Jon shout. By
listening very carefully he could hear shuffling sounds in the hallway. He figured Houston was softly slipping down the hall along
the wall. *Probably afraid of an ambush.*

Mark felt the door to the linen closet move slightly as Houston
leaned on it in the process of traversing the length of the hall.

"Hey, Houston, I'm waiting," he heard Jon call out again. It sounded like Houston was trying the doors at the end of the corridor. Mark knew that most of them simply didn't open at all.

Mark quietly started to ease open the door he was hiding behind. He was going to have to make a dash in a moment. He heard a loud click as Houston turned a doorknob that worked. That had to be the door Mark wanted him to open. There wouldn't be much time now.

Even as Mark heard the telltale creak of the door moving, he heard Jon exclaim in surprise and heard a gunshot and then a shower of breaking glass. He threw open the closet door and dashed down the hall the ten feet to where Houston was standing, legs spread, knees bent slightly, his midget pistol aimed at what he had just discovered was a shattered mirror.

Mark threw himself right into Houston, pushing the man over the threshold through the open doorway. As he struck, Mark pulled himself back so that he wouldn't follow Houston's fall.

⊻

"This was going to be an elevator," Mark explained to Lynn and Jon as they stood a few feet from the open shaft. "It never got installed. But my great-granddad set up this arrangement with the mirrors, so he could stand in the bedroom and appear to float in space above the elevator shaft. Grandmother hated it. Thought it was too dangerous and kept the doors sealed all the time."

"Let me out of here," they could hear Houston shouting. "I'm hurt. I think my leg's broken."

"He's still got the pistol. Don't go near the opening to the shaft," Mark warned. "But maybe we'd better get the police, now, or at least a doctor. You don't think he'd shoot a doctor, do you?"

"Let's call the police," Lynn urged.

"Well, I'd like to get out of here before the police show up," Jon said. "I have business with Buchanan and don't want to get arrested here for assaulting an F.B.I. or C.I.A. agent."

"That's okay," Mark answered. "I'll call the police. In the meantime, Lynn can drive you over to her house and then we can make arrangements for what to do next. Okay?"

"Okay."

The three of them headed downstairs toward the phone, as the mysterious John Houston shouted imprecations from the bottom of the ten-foot shaft.

Immediately upon picking up the telephone receiver, Mark said, "Uh-oh. No dial tone. He must've cut the wires after you talked to Blum earlier. Hey, that guy was really serious."

11

"Look, I don't think we can just leave him down there," Jon said.

"I'd better go get the police or a doctor or something. Lynn can take you over to her place."

"I can't drive," Lynn said, apparently only half-joking.

"You'll be okay. C'mon." Mark started toward the front door.

"What if there's somebody with him?" Jon suddenly asked. "What happened to that electronic gadget he had? Maybe that was some sort of signaling device."

"Whatever it was, he's probably got it," Mark answered. "It wasn't on the table. The only thing of his I got was the wallet with this I.D. Hey, Jon, you take this. Maybe that card'll let you through some door in D.C. or something."

"Good idea. But let's go before his friends come after him."

Mark walked around into the living room, pounded on a panel in the wall, and shouted, "Mr. Houston, we've gone to get you a doctor. You just calm down in there and don't try anything funny." Then he beckoned Lynn and Jon to follow him.

"Jon, be sure and take this." Mark handed him the multi-colored document from the desk. "Will I see you before you leave?" he asked, suddenly realizing that once the police were involved, he might not get a chance to be with Jon again before he left for Washington.

"Who knows? Give me a hug."

They held each other warmly. Then Lynn snuggled up to them and squeezed her way into the hug. They all laughed with a sense of great relief, then headed out to their cars.

🐾

"You go on ahead," Jon instructed, "so in case somebody's watching they won't see us leave together."

"Right." Mark jumped into his car. He had a little trouble starting it because of the cold. He almost flooded it. Jon could smell the acrid-sweet gasoline fumes. But then it started. Mark let it warm up just a minute, then headed out the driveway.

"Are you okay?" Jon turned his attention to Lynn. She seemed to be trembling.

"Oh, I guess I'm just pretty shook up."

Mark's horn tooted twice in an affectionate farewell as the car rolled down the long driveway. Jon looked up fondly to watch, thinking about how brave his young lover had been. He felt proud of him.

Then, without warning, Mark's car began to skid. It shot wildly off toward the side of the road, then there was a loud explosion and a ball of fire blossomed out from the car.

Only at that moment did Jon realize that electronic gadget Houston had wasn't exactly a signaling device.

12

Mark had been feeling proud of himself as he drove off, leaving Jon in what he hoped would be Lynn's good care. He'd gotten to like her in the past three days, and he was feeling very protective of Jon. He was glad he could shield Jon from whatever investigation was going to follow.

Mark laughed to himself as he recalled how easily he'd knocked Houston into the shaft. He'd been scared up till the moment he started barreling down that hall; then he'd known it was going to be okay.

This whole thing is going to be okay, he thought to himself. *I think we're really going to change history.* He thought again of Jon, and tooted the horn by way of final farewell as he drove out the long driveway.

Suddenly he felt the car shoot forward. It seemed to skid and slide off the road.

Oh my God, he thought. *I'm gonna crash.*

A part of Mark's mind was paralyzed with fear and surprise. Another part watched calmly as the accident proceeded in slow motion; he even remembered, as it took place, a previous auto accident in which the same time distortion had occurred. That observer self reminded Mark that this could be "the big one." As one part of Mark's mind screamed in fear of that possibility, the other suggested it was time to pray.

The car came to an abrupt stop as it plowed off the road into an embankment. Mark felt himself thrown forward. He noticed that the floorboards were suddenly hot, as though the engine had been overworking. The warmth felt strangely good on this cold November day. But it continued to grow in temperature. Mark wondered if the car would be okay getting this hot.

He looked down and saw the floor actually beginning to glow red; then he noticed little jets of flame breaking through the rubber mat. Then the whole interior seemed to fill with bright red and yellow gas. *It's almost like jello*, the observer self commented, and the rest of his mind screamed in horror of the flames that seemed to engulf him.

🕱

That was a really serious accident, he thought to himself. And he realized, a bit surprised, that it seemed to be over already. He wondered what had happened. *Maybe it was a bad dream*, he thought, and wondered where he was.

Maybe I'm in a hospital. Oh God, don't let me be burned. I think I'd rather die than be burned into a monster.

He couldn't exactly feel his body, though he sensed that he was still the same person he'd always been. He looked about him. It seemed to be very dark. He wasn't sure if he was standing up or sitting down. He tried to move, but discovered he couldn't tell if he was successful or not. He was surprisingly without fear or emotion.

He peered out into the comfortable darkness. A light appeared in the distance. With a start, Mark realized where he was and what had happened.

"I am not going to be afraid," he said aloud and seemed to hear echoes rebounding back to him. He remembered himself saying so recently that love is the key to changing universes. And he remembered Avalo-be-walla-walla and smiled. He had an odd inkling that he'd done this many times before and that he was waking up to his real identity.

He willed himself toward the light, and suddenly was rushing into it. The searing blue-white brilliance surrounded him, accelerating him forward. He had the thought that he could stop this forward motion and return, that maybe he could even stop death and go back into his body. He remembered Jon and for a moment a pang of longing burned in his heart. He'd loved Jon so much. But he knew he was not going back; that was not the thing to do. And he felt his heart filling up with excitement and joy. He knew Jon wouldn't want him to turn back now. And he felt that part of him that had been observing so detachedly begin to melt away . . . until there seemed to be only the light and the joy and the rush of forward movement.

13

"You goddamn bastard. You *killed* him. You killed him for nothing," Jon pounded on the panel in the living room. "You can rot in there till hell freezes over for all I care."

"Jon, come on, calm down," Lynn urged. All of a sudden the roles had reversed and she was the strong together one. "Let's get out of here. I'll get my mom to call the police later. He doesn't matter anymore. Let's just get away from here."

Jon was sobbing. To Lynn it seemed like he must be burning with pain and rage. She herself felt abysmally empty. *Why hadn't it dawned on us what that detonator was? I've seen enough movies to know.*

"Come on, Jon. Come on. Let's go home."

14

Jon spent the rest of Saturday in shock. At first, he wandered aimlessly around the DeGutis mansion as Lynn repeatedly urged him to come home with her. He stood in Mark's room for a long time, looking at his things, gently touching his luggage, holding an old shirt to his face to catch the smell of Mark's presence. He sat on the bed for a while and cried, as Lynn looked on helplessly. He picked a book out of Mark's green canvas totebag, searched through it a minute, read a passage over to himself, then stood up and announced to Lynn, "Let's get going."

Jon gathered up his own belongings; he didn't expect to come back to this house. They agreed that "Mr. Houston" could stay in the elevator shaft for a couple of days, at least till Jon had confronted Edward Buchanan. Jon was reluctant to call in the police at this point; he was sure he'd never get to Buchanan then. Besides, he doubted the police would believe his story — especially if that man in the elevator shaft turned out to be a government security agent. It would be Jon's word against his.

Before they left the house, just to make sure Houston didn't die from shock or starvation, they tossed a couple of blankets and a pillow down to him. They also dropped some food over the edge of the shaft — a loaf of bread, some lunch meat they found in the refrigerator, and a six-pack of Coke. Believing him armed, they were cautious not to come in his line of sight. Then Jon locked the doors into the elevator shaft.

Lynn was concerned about how incriminating it looked for the two of them to run off and leave Mark's body in the wrecked and burned car.

"We should be more concerned about forcing the release of the antidote than about protecting ourselves," Jon answered stoically.

Since Jon didn't seem to care about such practical matters,

Lynn devised a plan. "I'll get my mother to call the police tomorrow afternoon and say she's worried about Mark Hartman: he's apparently disappeared; could the police go out and check on him? They'll find the burned wreck. Then I'll call them from Washington on Monday with an anonymous tip that Mark's murderer is locked in the elevator shaft," she plotted. "By then the police will certainly be looking for clues; they'll find Houston and the electronic detonator on him."

"At any rate," Jon answered, "let's worry about making sense of the whole story once we've taken care of the business in Washington."

They flew back to Washington Sunday morning. Lynn and Lee Ann already had plane reservations. Lynn managed to convince Lee Ann it was more important that Jon get to Washington quickly than that she be on time for work Monday morning. It took a bit of doing, but Lee Ann finally gave Jon her ticket and agreed to take a later flight.

Lynn called Billy and asked him to pick them up at the airport but she didn't discuss what had happened in LaCrosse. She'd caught Jon's paranoia. She began to worry that Billy's phone was tapped. In fact, she got herself so scared that when Jon offered to show her — or even just explain in detail — the report he got from George Wilson, Lynn demurred in no uncertain terms.

"Look, Jon, I'll help any way I can. But I don't want to know any more about this. At least not right now. What if they torture me or something?"

"Lynn, that's not going to happen," Jon answered. Later he realized he had no justification for such assurance. Maybe she would be safer in the dark.

In the air, Jon fiddled with the report — now sealed in an overstuffed business envelope — turning it over again and again in his hands. Finally Lynn snatched it away from him and stuck it in her purse. "Calm down," she ordered. Jon smiled and then relaxed a little.

Once they were on the leg of the flight from Milwaukee to Washington, Jon pulled two small books out of his pocket. One was a yellowed copy of *The Lazy Man's Guide to Enlightenment* by Thaddeus Golas, the book Jeff Kettner had recommended. He quickly scanned through it. The other was the book he'd retrieved from Mark's luggage, the book he'd bought Mark that morning only a few weeks ago when they'd talked to Kettner. Over and over he read the inscription he'd written:

Mark,
> that all your dreams
>> (especially with me in them)
>>> come true.
>> Love,
>>> Jon

His eyes burned and blurred till finally he couldn't see the page anymore. *Oh, Mark, wherever you are, please be dreaming that I can accomplish the next step of this nightmare.*

He turned to the passage that had snapped him out of his state of shock the day before: "He never spoke any bitterness at all, no matter how awful the things he said. Are there really people without resentment, without hate ... People who never go cross-grained to the universe? Who recognize evil, and resist evil, and yet are utterly unaffected by it?"

Immersed in the symbolism of LeGuin's novel, Jon intended that his confrontation with Edward Buchanan be effective and bring about a new world: a world in which AIDS disappeared. *Oh God, please,* he prayed, *let Mark's dream of that world come true.*

He wished it could be a world in which Mark Hartman had not died. But he knew such miracles were possible only in fiction, and not even LeGuin's character had had the power to resurrect the dead. He began to cry again softly as he realized that he would never see Mark again and that the love he'd been so pleased to find was lost once more. Could he ever find it again?

Mark was gone. *But maybe others can live.* Jon was becoming more and more convinced that his suspicions about the plot to spread AIDS — or at least to delay ending the plague — were true. Mark's murder seemed like proof that the Liberty Bell Foundation was as sinister as Jon had feared. And, Jon knew, this was not just a political battle or a criminal case. This was a real battle of good against evil. Jon knew he would have to steel himself with virtue. *Buchanan will see he has to release the antidote. I will make him see.* Jon's quiet grief and resigned hope alternated with surges of rage. *I'll threaten Buchanan with exposure. I'll unveil the hypocrisy. I'll bring down the whole edifice of Fundamentalist bigotry.*

The more he mulled over the conspiracy, the more vicious it all seemed to him and the more concerned he became about his approaching confrontation with Buchanan. *What if they inject me with the virus?* That, of course, was the fear that had lurked in his life nearly the last eight years: the fear that he'd get AIDS. Everything he's done to fight the disease, it occurred to him, had been a kind of bargaining with the universe: *if I do this, I won't get AIDS.*

Now, he realized, he was perhaps going to expose himself to the disease in a very different way than he'd ever imagined. *The issue now isn't safe sex — I've learned that safe sex is just a fact of life — the issue is intentional contamination by bigoted monsters who've caused — or, at least, by their silence orchestrated — the whole tragedy.*

He remembered the advice he'd read to his PWA group about accepting disease as just another reality. *That's the way I have to think about my confrontation with Buchanan: it's just the next thing on my agenda. Fear has no place in my heart, It's okay if they give me AIDS* — he shuddered — *it's okay,* IF *I force them to release the antidote. What they do to me doesn't matter. In fact, I'd be willing to get the disease if that would be what it took to get the antidote released.*

Oh God, what a crazy muddle of thoughts, he told himself, trying to relax. *Things just are the way they are*, he reminded himself. Oddly, he found that a consoling thought. And, after a while, he fell asleep.

15

Billy was waiting at the gate.

"God, it's good to see you," Lynn exclaimed, hugging Billy. "You won't believe what we've been through."

"Hi, Jon." Billy shook hands. "I wasn't expecting you back so soon.

"We'll explain on the way home. Let's get out of here now as quick as we can." Jon was still in a grief-stricken daze.

Just as the three of them were walking away from the gate area, they were approached by a young man in an airline uniform. "Please come over here." The attendant smiled amiably, looking down at what Jon slowly realized was a photograph he held in his hand. He led them toward a door marked "Authorized Personnel Only."

Uh-oh, this isn't right, Jon thought. As the young man opened the door, Jon started to grab Lynn and pull her away. But then he realized another man was standing right behind him, pushing him through the door.

That door led into an industrial-looking stairwell. Standing in the landing was a big man in a blocky-looking black suit. "Lynn Graves?" he asked.

"Who are you?" Lynn answered.

"Are you Lynn Graves?"

"And what if I am?"

"You must be Jonathan Stiers," the man said directly to Jon.

"Hey, are you a policeman or something? Do you have a badge?" Billy said angrily. "If not, we'll just be on our way."

"Calm down, buddy," the first man said to Billy.

"You can't arrest us just like this," Jon objected.

"Dr. Stiers, you'll be coming with me," announced the man standing behind Jon. "Don't worry, your friends will be safe." The man started to pull Jon away.

"Wait a minute, Charlie," said the first man. "We're supposed to look for something. Ms. Graves," he said, "your purse, please."

As Lynn shouted, "What do you think you're doing?" the man calmly pulled her purse away from her and, setting it down on the railing at the top of the stairs, began looking through it.

"Maybe this is it," he said, pulling a thick envelope from the purse.

Jon's heart sunk. That had been his insurance: the report George Wilson had given him. If they confiscated that, he had no evidence at all of the plot he suspected the Liberty Bell Foundation of — and no way to threaten Buchanan with exposure.

He wished now that he hadn't been so stupid as to bring it with them and that Lynn and Billy hadn't been so squeamish about reading the report. At least then he wouldn't have been the only one to know what this was all about. *Well, there're still the files Billy copied into his computer,* Jon consoled himself, only then realizing they might not live long enough to use the information.

The agent tore open the end of the envelope and peered in. "Yup, multi-colored paper. This is it." Without looking at the document any further he handed the envelope to the man he'd called Charlie. "Ms. Graves, will you and your friend here please come with us? We have a few questions to ask you."

"No, wait a minute," Lynn quarreled.

"I'm sorry, you have no choice," the agent replied. "Let's just go quietly. If you don't, we'll have to get uniformed officers and that'll just embarrass everybody."

Jon felt "Charlie" grab his arm tight around the bicep and begin pushing him down the stairs. He started to resist, then realized it was hopeless. *Well, I was planning to walk right in on Buchanan,* he thought. *I guess I'll be getting an escort.*

Charlie said very little as he sat next to Jon in the back seat of

the car that had been waiting outside the baggage claim. "We'll take
care of your luggage," was all he'd said when Jon objected to being
hustled away from the airport so fast. His only other comment had
been about the weather. Jon hadn't responded. He was going over
in his mind what he wanted to say to Edward Buchanan — if that's
where they were taking him.

16

"Look, lady. I don't think we have any quarrel with you and your
friend here. We were simply asked to meet you at the airport and
escort this Dr. Stiers you were with to an interview."

"An interview?" Lynn burst out. "With who?"

"I think that's Dr. Stiers' business, not yours. But just in case
you want to keep asking, let me tell you I don't know."

"And just who are you?" Billy asked. He was driving his own
car. The agent was in the front seat; Lynn was in back.

"Let's just say I work for the government," the man said.

"Aren't you supposed to show us your badge and explain our
rights to us?"

"You're not under arrest. Besides, I'm not a cop."

"Well, then why should we obey you?" Lynn spoke up.

"Because it would just be easier on you," the man said, press-
ing his right hand against his chest as if to remind them that he was
armed. "Now, get off at the next exit."

A few minutes later the agent instructed them to pull up in
front of a large office building.

"But there's nowhere to park around here," Billy objected.
"What if I get a ticket?"

"Oh my God, Billy," Lynn moaned. "They're going to kill us
and you're worrying about a parking ticket."

"Calm down, lady," the agent said. "Park along here in this
emergency zone. It'll be safe. I promise."

Billy did as he was told.

17

Jon and his taciturn escort arrived at the Liberty Bell Foundation
office. He was glad to see they'd brought him here and not killed
him on the way. He'd been feeling brave, but now, as they entered

the office suite, a wave of terror of what was about to happen washed over him. There was nobody in the reception room. Charlie pushed him toward the first open door.

A pasty-faced older woman was typing in the office. "Oh, hello," she said looking a little startled.

"Mr. Buchanan, please," Charlie said.

"Mr. Buchanan is a busy man. He only sees people by appointment. Do you have an appointment?"

"I believe Buchanan is expecting us," answered Charlie.

"Well, perhaps he could fit you in," she replied looking right at Jon and cocking her head slightly in a way that unnerved him. "Just a moment."

The lady, whom Jon knew from Lynn's briefing was Emily Hodgsdon, got up quickly and walked into the adjoining office, pulling the door closed behind her. Jon had a feeling that halfway through her initial brush-off she'd understood the situation or recognized him. He'd discovered Phil Donahue had made him something of a celebrity.

A moment later Ms. Hodgsdon came back out. "Mr. Buchanan will see you now, Dr. Stiers."

Jon noted she had never asked his name.

"Goodbye, Dr. Stiers," Charlie said ominously, as he stepped back to allow Jon to enter Buchanan's office. Jon felt a chill as he walked though the open doorway.

Across the large room, sitting behind an oversized mahogany desk with virtually nothing on its expansive, shiny surface, sat an equally large and commanding figure. "Well, sir, what can I do for you?" the man asked without getting up.

"Edward Buchanan?" Jon asked tentatively. Then, seeing his silence, he continued, "I'm Dr. Jonathan Stiers." He extended his hand. Still seated, Buchanan gestured toward one of the cushioned chairs on Jon's side of the desk, obviously declining to shake Jon's hand.

"I think I should ask you that question," Jon replied. "I have been brought here against my will."

"I believe you spoke with my associate George Wilson last week," Buchanan said sternly.

"Then you know what my business is about?"

"I know that you talked with George last Friday. I suspect you took a document from George's safe. And I know that George Wilson is dead." He paused. "That does not surprise you?" he asked. "No, well, perhaps not."

"No, it does not surprise me. I was with Wilson when he died.

And what Wilson told me about himself — and about you, sir — certainly leads me to understand why he took his life."

"Are you saying George killed himself?"

"Are you suggesting I killed him?" Jon replied, suddenly realizing that Buchanan had put all the facts together in a very different way.

"Well, that is certainly what it looked like to me when I arrived."

"I didn't. I went to see Wilson because I'd heard he might know about research on a cure for the AIDS virus. He showed me a document which implied that you and he knew something very unusual about the origin of the virus and that you have an antidote. Then he told me a very long and personal story about his own life. He got rather hysterical at that point, tried to tear up the document, and then after calming down, drank a cup of coffee and suddenly died. I'm sorry he died but, right now I want to know about what was in that document..."

"Which you stole."

"Which I took with me, as I understood Wilson intended me to," Jon corrected, "because I think he wanted me to correct the wrong he'd committed."

"Where is it now?"

"I believe your agent, Charlie, has it. But I warn you," Jon said, fudging the truth a little, "I've made a copy which my associates will reveal to the press if anything happens to me."

"Why would George kill himself?" Buchanan ignored Jon's threat.

"Out of guilt."

"Guilt? George Wilson was an upstanding and religious man."

"George Wilson, in his own estimation, was a mass murderer. And according to him, so are you, Mr. Buchanan. You've let thousands die horribly. And yesterday I watched my lover burn to death in a fire bomb which I think you helped cause." Jon felt rage surge through him.

"I know nothing about that," Buchanan answered. "I didn't ask that anybody be killed, only that you be followed ... because I believed you killed George ... and because I feared you'd do something foolish with that report. I'm genuinely sorry about your friend. Apparently we have both just lost friends." He looked down at his desk. "I was quite prepared to make you out to be the villain, Dr. Stiers. But I believe that you did not kill George." Buchanan heaved a great sigh and then looked at Jon straight in the eye. "George Wilson was a very bold and creative man in his day. He dared to think things other men would be frightened of. Do you know he was one of the architects of our modern nuclear policy? But lately, well, the pressures had been getting to him. He was prone to exaggeration and, shall I say, imagination."

"What do you mean?" Jon shot back.

"I mean that not everything George talked about was exactly real. And I suspect that both you — and he — have fallen victim to his imagination."

"You mean there is no antidote to AIDS?"

"I mean that an unusual virus George and I discovered ten years ago while auditing a research project in Africa may — or may not — have something to do with AIDS. And the treatment for that virus may — or may not — be effective on the disease in America. What evidence do you have for your allegations?"

"Wilson told me you planned to allow tens of thousands of gay men to die before releasing this antidote!"

"I told you George had a fertile imagination."

"Are you saying it isn't true?"

"To be frank with you, sir, when George presented the idea to me I thought that that would be a noble goal . . ."

"Murder?" Jon interrupted.

"The elimination of homosexuality. But I recognize it isn't as easy as that."

"But what about the virus? And what about the antidote?"

"Perhaps you should tell me what you think you know," Buchanan replied.

18

Thirty minutes later Jon Stiers and Edward Buchanan were still talking.

"I know you think I'm a monster," Buchanan was saying. "In the past I probably thought you were, I mean being a homosexual and all. But I think I've changed. I know better about you. You may not believe this, Dr. Stiers, but when I saw you on television last week, I . . . well, I admired you. I see you and your kind are not monsters. I hope to make you see I am not either."

"Well, thank you, but . . ."

"But I also have to say that I felt angry with you. You may be a fine man, Jon — may I call you Jon? — but what you are doing is wrong."

"I could say the same thing to you."

"Of course you could. Maybe you'd be right. Do you think I haven't worried about that myself, young man? But there's too much at stake."

"You mean your plot to wipe out the homosexuals?"

"There was no plot, Stiers. But you probably can't believe that because you've become so committed to your deviant lifestyle. That is what I mean is at stake: the whole moral fiber of society. I mean that if you took that document to the *New York Times*, they would misunderstand it. They would use it to make all the good, moral, self-disciplined, religious people in this country look like Nazis."

"And that would be true, wouldn't it?" Jon felt his rage again and struggled to calm himself.

"No, it would not be true. Good people were not the cause of this. You still don't understand. We have to do something to save the world from sin and from God's wrath."

"But *you* don't understand ... What you call sin is just people being honest with themselves—"

"I don't believe that honesty is as important as God's law."

"Do you want to debate Scripture?"

"No, Dr. Stiers, I do not. We're not getting anywhere with this conversation as it is. I want to tell you something about myself. And then I want to show you something, something you may not care to see.

"You said George Wilson — he was my best friend, you should know — George told you about his life. I don't know what he told you, but I believe it should have made you respect him as a, uh, a holy man."

"Perhaps. But perhaps misguided."

"Perhaps we're all always misguided. Only God can judge that, Jon," Buchanan answered thoughtfully. He paused for a moment and then continued. "For almost twenty-five years now I have been one of the men who determined how wars would be fought in this world. That has been an awesome responsibility. When I started in the weapons field, I suppose I enjoyed it. There was power in those bombs and rockets, especially in the nuclear weapons.

"Have you ever witnessed a nuclear explosion, Jon?" Buchanan looked off into space. "It is as close to seeing God and his wrath as ... Well, over the years I became more and more conscious of the terrible danger the world is in. We could accidentally destroy God's creation. I devoted my life to stopping that."

"By becoming a consultant to the Pentagon?" Jon asked cynically.

"Where else?" Buchanan answered simply. "George and I developed a partnership. We found out the truth about the weapons the world was building. And we advised the people who had their fingers on the triggers how they could remain strong without having to pull those triggers. We were very good at what we did. And it cost us our lives.

"A long time ago we discovered that if he was meek and friendly and if I was boorish and demanding, we could intimidate and manipulate the truth out of people who didn't want to give it to us. Do you know, Jon, do you know?" Buchanan smiled, "I purposely developed this foolish habit of repeating myself for the sake of that role.

"And George. Do you think I don't know he was a terribly unhappy repressed homosexual? But he controlled himself. He wasn't 'honest with his feelings,' as you say. He was dedicated to a higher cause."

"But you were wrong. Didn't Wilson tell you that?"

"George got frightened at the end. And, yes, things didn't go the way we expected."

"Didn't go the way you expected!? Look, Buchanan, you committed a heinous crime against humanity. There's been countless suffering — that you could have stopped at any time, but haven't."

"You don't know that, Dr. Stiers. You still don't know what you're talking about."

"Because you still haven't told me the truth. Is there an antidote? And will you release it?"

"You misjudge us. You misjudge us. Obviously we have a different set of values from you. But let me assure you we are not common murderers. We are not without great, I repeat, great regret for the suffering of those with this disease. But most every victim has brought it on himself. Isn't that proof that something has gone terribly wrong with the world?"

"What's gone wrong is you."

"No sir, no sir. It isn't me. And, I have to admit, it probably isn't you. But its a moral cancer that is eating away everything good and holy in man, that's turning us all away from the Truth. It's the devil himself that's eating away at the souls of all of us."

"You're the devil, Buchanan," Jon said bitingly.

"Maybe I am. Maybe I am. God knows, I've thought about that myself. And I've seen that indeed the devil's cancer is in me too."

"So you've known you were wrong and you still did nothing about it."

"I've known that something had to be done to clean up the filth that was taking over the souls of men. Now, look, I'm not saying any of the so-called plot you think George told you about is true. I'm not saying it's true. Just that you still don't — won't — understand. But let's suppose it were true. I mean that God gave me an instrument by which I could end this homosexual plague. Wouldn't it be logical to wait till this godawful 'sexual revolution' had been squelched for good before revealing it? I mean, wouldn't that stop other plagues like this from starting in the future?"

"But you've misunderstood the sexual revolution. It was much less about being promiscuous than about seeing that sex can be healthy and natural, that human nature is good, not sinful. The major aim was education and willingness to talk about our bodies without guilt or embarrassment. Ironically AIDS has forced that education and frank talk—"

"Well, perhaps so."

"But, Buchanan, you've punished the wrong people. Homosexuals aren't responsible for the world's problems."

"Frankly, Jon," Buchanan suddenly said almost intimately, "I'm sorry this thing worked the way it did. I guess you're right that homosexuals are not nearly the problem the pimps and prostitutes and the adulterers are and the teenagers having babies and the abortionists profiteering from it all."

"Who are you to judge *anybody*?"

"Probably nobody," Buchanan said softly, shaking his head. "But somebody had to do something."

"Do something. . .? Why?" Jon shot back at him. "Is there an antidote? Answer me!"

"Enough of this," Buchanan silenced Jon. "The only way you'll understand is to see a little of what I've seen." Buchanan stood up. "Come over here," he beckoned to Jon as he opened a set of double doors in the wall behind his desk.

With some reluctance, Jon obeyed. He stepped around the desk and then followed Buchanan into a deep, well-lighted closet lined on one wall with bookshelves and on the other with cabinets.

"Over the years I've collected souvenirs — I guess you might call them — of the work and research I've done. Here are hundreds of photographs of the horrors of the human heart. Look here," he said, pulling down a large folio-sized book and laying it out on an inclined shelf. "Sit down, sit down," he added as he slid a stool out from under the reading shelf for Jon and then pulled another beside it for himself.

He opened the huge book near the middle. On both pages

were black-and-white enlargements of photos Jon found familiar: emaciated bodies strewn atop piles of rubble which, when you looked closer, turned out to be composed not of broken bricks or concrete but of more bodies.

"I've seen photographs of the Holocaust," Jon said simply.

"Of course you have. Of course you have," Buchanan answered excitedly. "Here, look at this," he pulled down another book, a dime-store photo album. He looked through it a moment and then set it in front of Jon. One page showed a color photo of a soldier — American, Jon assessed — stretched spread-eagle between two posts. Blood poured in sheets down the body from what appeared to be scores of inch-long gashes across the chest and torso. The man's face was contorted in a cry of anguish. Beside the tortured soldier stood an Oriental man in military uniform throwing something grainy at his bloody chest.

"Rock salt," Buchanan explained. "He's throwing rock salt into the wounds."

Jon was repulsed by the photo though, as he'd experienced before looking at such graphic depictions of violence, he was also slightly fascinated. He looked at the close-up photo on the other side. At first he couldn't make out what he was seeing. Then, with a start, he realized the bloody mass was the tortured soldier's crotch. His penis had been sliced open and then pulled back to either side and pinned, it appeared, to his thighs with thorns or needles.

"God, Buchanan, this is gross," Jon exclaimed.

"This is human nature." Buchanan paged through the album further to find a photo of what seemed to be a woman pulling at a ragdoll. "That woman is wringing her own baby's neck," Buchanan explained. "Actually tore the head off." He paged on further. Here was a woman, her dress ripped to shreds, laid across a table with the neck of a broken liquor bottle protruding from her vagina. Around her a circle of men seemed to be laughing.

"What's all this supposed to prove?" Jon asked reproachfully.

"Jon, you've barely looked at the collection," Buchanan answered. "Here, look at these," he paged through the book holding each page just long enough for the revulsion it elicted to show on Jon's face.

Following the scenes of torture of human beings were detailed photographs of animal experiments — rabbits with acid-inflamed eyes, pigs burned to char with flame-throwers, cats and monkeys strapped into harnesses to keep them from scratching at electrodes implanted into their exposed brains. Next came faded images of the disaster at Hiroshima (Jon recognized the skeletal skyline), with close-ups of the burned and torn bodies of the survivors.

Then Buchanan pulled down another book which contained sketches, descriptions, and specifications of various kinds of weapons including anti-personnel land mines, booby traps of all sorts, and incendiary bombs — weapons from small scale nuclear arms to knives with specially serrated edges for slitting throats. "Here's how the human race spends most of its resources," he announced solemnly.

"Look over here," Buchanan said, setting aside the book and pulling a key out of his pocket and unlocking one of the cabinets in the opposite wall. In the cabinet were both actual weapons and scale models of large weapons. "Under here," Buchanan said, opening another cabinet that sat directly on the floor, "are the chemical agents." In the cabinet were metal cannisters of various sizes. Jon was amazed by the possibility that Buchanan had actually managed to bring home weapons like these as souvenirs.

"Jon," Buchanan instructed, "get down that red book up there with the silver lettering on the spine."

Cooperatively, Jon stood up and reached for the volume Buchanan was pointing toward. When he opened it he saw it contained photos, in the front, of World War I gas victims and, toward the back, of napalm and nerve gas casualties, he surmised, of Vietnam and Afganistan.

"These are samples of biological weapons," Buchanan said, opening another bottom cabinet. "Maybe what you want is in this stack, eh?" he teased.

Jon wondered if the original AIDS virus — and its antidote — could really be in one of those innocent looking tanks stacked haphazardly in that cabinet. *It doesn't make any sense. And yet* . . . "Look, Buchanan, I don't understand what all this is about. What am I supposed to see? Tell me about the antidote."

"You don't know what you're supposed to see? My God, Stiers, what you're supposed to see is that your beloved human beings with all their precious 'honest' feelings are cruel, rapacious brutes who'll kill and maim just for the fun of it and who spend billions of dollars developing ever more heinous weapons while their neighbors starve. Here, look at this," he shouted as he pulled out yet another photo album, this one full of aborted fetuses and mutilated babies. "In China, I hear, they smash the brains of girl babies against the wall in the name of population control."

"As repulsive as all this stuff is, it's no surprise to me. And it shouldn't be to you, Buchanan. You're the weapons expert, the warmonger..."

"Warmonger! It's because of a few people like me that the world hasn't killed itself — just for fun. We're the ones who have dared to use the force and power it takes to control 'human nature.' Don't you see, Stiers, that's why somebody had to do something about all this sex that was going on everywhere? Sex, sex, sex — raw human nature at its ugliest and cruelest, human sinners copulating like animals, my God, worse than animals, doing things even dogs wouldn't do, like your own disgusting sex."

Buchanan's voice had grown very loud; his face was red. Jon was beginning to get frightened again. *This man is losing control.*

"You want your precious antidote to save the homosexuals — you and your worries about them. That's the real reason the plague got out of control. You and your kind warned each other how to avoid it," Buchanan's voice was getting more and more strained. "You told each other all that sinful nonsense about safe sex. 'Unnatural sex' is more like it. You stopped each other spreading the virus where it was supposed to go and you let it get out into the population. But, goddammit, even if you escaped the plague, you didn't escape the sin..."

"Shut up, Buchanan, shut up," Jon shouted. "You don't know what you're talking about. The real sin isn't sex; it's being power-hungry and selfish and wanting to be right. But what about the antidote virus? What are you going to do about the antidote?"

Buchanan sat down hard on his stool. "You still believe in the antidote, don't you?" he sighed. "What if that's all just wishful thinking?"

"Well?" demanded Jon.

"What's the use of telling you? You know too much already without me giving you the pleasure of more knowledge. Besides I'll be forced to ... But, look, Stiers, I'll make a deal with you. You've just seen the evidence for my assertion that human beings are intrinsically sinful and evil. Answer that."

"Answer?"

"Yes, tell me what all this means, if you can. Tell me I'm wrong if you can. Tell me why sinful nature shouldn't be beaten down and punished and suppressed and frightened with threats of plague and hellfire. If you can answer me, I solemnly promise you — if, and I say if, there is an antidote, I will release it. If you can't, well, I guess the world will go on coping."

"Buchanan, that's not fair. Too many lives are at stake to make this into some kind of game with me as the player."

"Oh, Jon, you're wrong," Buchanan answered as he walked back into his office and sat down at his desk. "I'm not making up the rules for this game. That's the way it always is. I mean, don't you know that every choice you make affects somebody's life? You're always at the center of the game."

"So what do I do in the 'center' of this game of yours?"

"You win or you lose."

"And if I lose . . . ?"

"So many have already died. What's one more?"

Jon felt a wave of terror. *Is he serious? Isn't this all a bad dream?* He remembered Mark's burning car. "You say I'm supposed to answer your riddle." Jon followed him out of the closet of horrors and, after considering whether he ought to try to just bolt out of the office, resumed his seat on the far side of the desk. *This is all an elaborate game of wits, isn't it?* "But how are you going to know if I'm right? I mean, how do you know if *you* won your turn at the game, Buchanan?" he asked accusingly.

"I don't, Jon," Buchanan answered solemnly and sadly. "I'll have to be thinking about that. I'll tell you what I think is a sign from God: Jesus Christ on the cross. Look what human evil did to Him. I think I have a responsibility to Him — to my Lord and Savior — to stop the offense against Him, to stop sin, to punish the sinners. But I don't know.

"That's why I give you my word that if you can answer the evidence of evil I've shown you I'll release the antidote — I mean, if there is one," he stuttered. "I'm not an evil man, Jon, maybe just a weak one who took on more than he could handle. Thank you for bringing it all to an end. I'm grateful for that." There was an air of finality in Buchanan's voice. He sounded tired. Leaning forward slightly, Buchanan reached under his desk.

"What are you talking about?" Jon asked as he felt suddenly very afraid. *What's happening to the game of wits?* But before he could even begin to stand up, there was a commotion at the door behind him and he felt himself grappled by strong arms and held down in his chair. He wondered for a moment if it was Charlie that held him. He felt a pad pressed against his nose and recognized the pungent odor of ethyl ether.

"I have an engagement this evening, Jon. Dinner with the Joint Chiefs," Jon heard Buchanan through the daze that was sweeping over him. I'll be back later for your answer."

Suddenly Buchanan's heavy face loomed in Jon's vision. Jon tried to pull away. Charlie — or whoever — held his head. To Jon's dismay, Buchanan bent forward and kissed him lightly on the lips.

Jon felt his body go limp out of his control and his mind suddenly flew up to the ceiling in a rush of pleasure that was turning quickly to stupor. As he was losing consciousness altogether it occurred to him that Jesus's passion began with the gentle kiss of Judas.

•Five•

Beyond Time and Space

1

Jon gradually regained consciousness. The first thing he was aware of was a terrible chemical taste in his mouth. His head was pounding like crazy and the headache hurt deep into his eyes. He didn't want to open them. But finally did. He was startled to discover he couldn't see anything, even with his eyes wide open. *Oh my God, they've blinded me. Was that ether or nerve gas they knocked me out with?*

The truth quickly dawned on him as he thrashed his arms about and found himself in a very narrow space. *I'm locked in a closet or something.* He managed to smile at the irony of ending up in a closet.

He slowly got to his feet and felt the space around him. One side felt rough like woodgrain. *The door.* The handle turned but didn't release the latch. There was no light coming under the crack. *It must be dark outside as well.* The other side seemed to be full of something wrapped with paper. Jon reached around trying to see if he could get a grip on something he could use as a weapon or, at least, help him understand where he was. *These are reams of paper, aren't they? I must be in a storage closet for the office. How am I going to ever get out of here?*

What's going to happen to me if I don't get out? he thought morosely and leaned his back against the door and slowly let himself slide down into a crouching position. His head was still pounding. For a moment he thought about Mark and was comforted by the thought that if he were killed as Buchanan threatened maybe he would

225

reunite with Mark. But the comfort quickly evaporated into fear of dying and gnawing doubts about the reality of afterlife.

His thoughts of Mark brought up for him the grief he'd been holding at bay with his anger. He struck with both fists at the wood of the door he was leaning against. "No," he shouted. The blow made a great noise that sent reverberations through his spine, but all it did was hurt the heels of his hands. Suddenly from down inside him a torrent of tears and grief welled up. He couldn't get out of his mind the thought — the gruesome thought — of Mark burning to death.

The image that haunted him, he realized, was right out of Edward Buchanan's collection of horrors. And with a start he remembered he was going to have to answer Buchanan's question about the nature of evil. *Oh my God, what time is it?* He struggled to press the stud on his watch to turn on the backlight. "9:34" the display read. *Still early.* He didn't want to release the stud and turn off the light. It was one piece of his past he could cling to. That he could still perceive anything at all was a lifeline. But as he watched the seconds slip slowly by on the watch display, he realized he shouldn't be wasting what time he had left.

Jon focused his thoughts on the material Buchanan had showed him. *Maybe there was a clue in what he showed me. Maybe this is a word game, a riddle.* He remembered the story of Oedipus and the Riddle of the Sphinx. *Is that what this is about? What if I answer 'Man'? Does that make any sense? Man is the measure. No, Buchanan would only answer man is the source of evil.* He discarded that thought. *What about the order of the things he showed me? The Holocaust, war atrocities, animal mutilation, nuclear weapons, anti-personnel devices, chemical and biological weapons, abortions — it seems random.*

He tried to recall individual photos. *Maybe there was a clue in one of them.* As the images came back to him, he felt more and more revulsion: emaciated bodies, torn flesh, blood and gore, flames, explosions — horror after horror. *No wonder Buchanan drove himself crazy with a hobby like that,* he managed to crack a joke to himself.

And then suddenly, uncontrollably, he began to cry. He cried for the suffering of humanity. He cried for all the victims. He cried for Mark, for Pat Stratford, for Ted. He cried for himself. He began to shake violently as his mind, now getting out of his control, reeled the scenes of suffering across his visual field — but now *he* was the victim. It was his flesh that was torn, his body that was riddled with bullets or ripped apart by explosions or subjected to atrocities.

"You are going to die," a voice spoke inside his head.

"Buchanan is going to kill you . . . and probably gruesomely." *No, no,* Jon tried to answer the voice, trying to push away the unacceptable reality his internal voice was announcing. "Don't you think Charlie will love gouging out your eyes and crushing your balls in his fist. . ." *Stop it.* ". . . maybe he'll burn your cock off with his BIC lighter. Sure. He'll flick your bic," the voice joked sardonically.

"Or maybe they'll tie your arms and legs to different cars and pull you apart out in the parking lot." Jon remembered a medieval woodprint in Buchanan's collection of a heretic being drawn and quartered.

"Maybe they'll shoot you up with AIDS," the voice suggested almost gleefully. "How'd you like that? Wouldn't that be ironic?" Jon shuddered at the awful suggestion that kept coming back to haunt him. "Probably got a fast-acting version right there in one of those steel cannisters. Maybe they've got the rabies version. Lock you in the closet here and leave you to beat yourself to death against a wall. Maybe they've already injected you with the virus. . ."

Jon realized how possible that was. He clutched at his arms to see if he could feel any tenderness that might have remained from an injection. The voice laughed, "Don't you think he'd shoot it up your ass?" *Shut up, shut up.* But even as he tried to stop the crazy thoughts he felt his body quivering. He couldn't help feeling infected, dirty, as though something hideous were growing inside him.

He was getting more and more hysterical. His heart was racing. He was hyperventilating; his fingers were starting to tingle. His head was spinning, his recollections and emotions running away with him. He began to fear he'd been drugged — or poisoned, that his mind was being stolen from him. He remembered the psychiatrist's machine in *The Lathe of Heaven*, the dream augmentor. Maybe he'd been hooked up to something like that. Terrified, he grabbed at his scalp, trying to pull away the electrodes that were feeding him this nightmare. But there was nothing attached to his head. *This whole thing, being in this closet and everything — it could all be an hallucination.*

He tried to calm himself, to slow his breathing, to remember to be without resentment, without hate, to remain utterly unaffected by evil, to follow the way that cannot be followed. . .

He realized there was yet another self in him, separate from his ego and separate from the hysterical voice that had been taunting him. There came over him a calm, almost serene consciousness — "the Witness," he remembered a term from Hindu meditation for the abstracting self that is able to view human life from a detached, almost divine viewpoint.

"Remember your study of religion," the Witness self offered peaceably. "This is, after all, a religious question you're supposed to be considering."

And again Jon remembered abruptly that he was going to have to answer Buchanan's riddle. In his fear he'd forgotten to think about that.

Now isn't the time for riddles. No matter what I say I'm going to die.

"Then die," the Witness answered matter-of-factly.

But I don't want to die.

"That's okay too," the Witness replied as though it didn't see what difference that made.

Fuck you! he hurled the epithet at the abstracting self. *What good is all that crazy spiritual thinking now? I need help.*

"You're feeling hatred. Balance it with love."

Love — the word burned through Jon's consciousness. "Love is letting go of fear," he remembered the name of Jerry Jampolsky's book. But he felt so bereft, lonely, lost. He felt himself swept with memories of pleading for love and finding none. His heart ached. He couldn't manage to remember the good times, the times when Ted and Mark and countless others held him and told him how they loved him. Those memories seemed to linger at the edge of consciousness but he could not grasp them. He could only recall the pain and emptiness.

"You've been a stupid shit," the taunting voice resurfaced, "a worthless homosexual, a pervert. Of course nobody loved you. You're ugly. You're abnormal. You're a freak." Recollections poured into him of his childhood, of the kids in school teasing him with shouts of "sissy" and "queer." He felt all over again the pain of longing for love but feeling it unnatural, feeling himself dirty and unlovable, scorned even by other queers. His whole life seemed like a torment of homophobia.

"God is life, God is love," the Witness rejoined. "To love God means to love life." Jon struggled to find such love in his heart. He tried to love his life, but right now his life seemed anything but lovable. It had all just been too much. *I just can't take anymore*, he complained bitterly. *Where is God?* He was swept with emptiness and hopelessness.

"Jon, remember," the abstracting voice called out to him. "What did you think it *was* that needed to be loved?"

He thought about that epigrammatic question, then about the little book he'd tried to read on the airplane, about the conversation over breakfast with Jeff Kettner, about the advice he'd given so many of his clients. *What does need to be loved?* he asked himself.

The answer was obvious: *This.*

Again he remembered the ironic suggestion of the taunting self. He was going to be infected with AIDS. Images rushed through his mind of friends and lovers, clients and patients — all of them dead. A phantom memory suddenly assaulted him, a dread event that had never happened but that, in spite of reason, he'd kept waiting for: the discovery of KS lesions on his legs. He cringed in abject terror. Now it seemed as though the unthinkable had happened. He clawed at his ankles and calves trying to feel the sores he feared were forming. *I am going to die.*

Well, death is an escape. Better to die than to suffer the agony of this disease.

But it is not a disease I'd be escaping, he reminded himself, *but the responsibility for confronting and beating Buchanan's plague. No, I don't choose death, not now, not while I can still fight. I've got to come up with the answer to his riddle.*

In his delirium Jon felt AIDS wasting his body, draining his life force away as he'd seen it drain so many. He remembered what he'd told the guys in the group: to accept reality, just as it is, with equanimity.

The philosophical attitude burned in his mind, bitter like vinegar, no consolation at all. But he urged himself to fight the temptation to anger and despair and to go on, to grieve for what was being lost, but not to resist its inevitable passing, to "love it the way it is."

"Jon, the possibility of final enlightenment stands open to you at this very moment," the abstracting self announced peremptorily. "Don't fail now."

What do I do? the vestige of Jon pleaded.

"Remember who you are. Remember to feel compassion."

Jon remembered his Catholic upbringing, the teaching to live like Jesus, to become one with Christ, "so that no longer I, but Christ lives in me." The Pauline quotation then merged with a recollection of Jesus's prediction of the Judgment: "Whatsoever you did to the least of these, that you did to Me."

Suddenly he was racked with pain and guilt. He was ravenously hungry and burning with thirst. "When I was hungry, you did not feed me. When I was thirsty, you did not give me to drink." He heard the definitive words of Jesus proclaiming damnation.

Have I failed to recognize You? Am I being damned? He writhed with fear of hell. In his imagination flames burned at his soul. And then he realized the hell that had tormented him and his kind had not been imposed by God, but by other men, by homophobic bigots. The epithets of "queer" and "faggot," the rejection by parents, the beatings by fag-bashing teenagers, the persecution by police, the loss of jobs and homes, the indignities of secret, guilt-ridden sex, and AIDS, overriding everything, the unconscionable way that people with AIDS were being treated — all these were the hell that the self-righteous had imposed on "the least of these."

Who I really am is Christ, Jon realized dramatically.

The symbolic flames of that hell unexpectedly brought back to Jon the real flames of the fiery crash that killed Mark Hartman. And the memory seemed to pull him up out of the hellfire. He thought lovingly of Mark and of the young man's innocence and insight. Then, just as he was starting to grieve, his gentle joke with Mark — "Avalo-be-walla-walla" — came back to him, and he thought of the bodhisattva who discovered that the world's suffering was the greatest treasure of all. He recalled the story Jeff Kettner had told at the Jung Institute. *What does this mean?* he thought and reluctantly imagined in his own hand the treasure-seekers' fourth quill.

"The treasure of the ages," the Witness announced excitedly.

Jon was perplexed, then felt a pang of realization. *Recognizing suffering as treasure turns upside down all the self-serving desires that inadvertently become intentions for other people's misfortune,* he answered his own question, and felt the quill drop from his fingers.

Okay, okay. I embrace the whole of human experience, Jon shouted to himself, *to share the burden of the sins of the world with Jesus and with Avalokitesvara.*

Jon felt himself part of the ocean of consciousness, ". . . a drop of water in an endless sea," he observed blissfully, once again letting the Witness self absorb his awareness.

"Jon," the Witness spoke intimately, "you've seen the path through suffering."

"When you learn to love hell, you will be in heaven," Jon remembered the words of *The Lazy Man's Guide.*

Suddenly God was all around him. A little voice in Jon's consciousness asked quizzically, "What's happening? Something's really strange. This is the most wonderful experience of my whole life." A feeling of wordless joy permeated his being.

In his mind's eye, he looked up to see dawn upon him the glowing light of what he knew could only be the Beatific Vision of God's face. He wasn't sure if his eyes were open or closed. Indeed the brilliant light seemed to shine right into the depths of his soul.

He had the odd sense that this spiritual light was actually illuminating the closet. Though his vision was dazzled by the streaming brilliance, out of the corner of his eye he thought he could see reams of paper piled neatly on shelves. For a moment he thought about peripheral vision hallucinations and remembered they were often a side effect of psychoactive drugs. He wondered again what Buchanan might have done to his brain.

"It is said no man can look upon the Face of God and live," a voice announced — the taunting voice, Jon surmised.

"Do you mean I'm dying right now?" Jon asked with equanimity.

"The Face of Glory and the Face of Anguish are one and the same." A Voice spoke in stentorian tones from out of the light burning before him. "To live on you must let go, Jonathan Stiers. You must let go.

"Unless a man die, he shall not have life in him," the abstracting voice added, providing a proper Scriptural footnote to the revelation.

"Have I been judged and found victorious?" Jon asked, feeling more strength and self-confidence now. "Was Buchanan wrong?"

"I know no right and wrong," the Voice spoke. "Edward Buchanan was no more wrong than right."

"How can you say that?" Jon objected, daring to challenge God. "He allowed thousands to die because of his bigotry and error."

"If you judge him and make him wrong, you only repeat the error you accuse him of," the Voice spoke, now sounding almost like the previous voice Jon had recognized as his own abstracting self.

"You mean I must forgive him for what he's done?"

"You *may* forgive," the Voice said matter-of-factly.

"Maybe this is the answer to the riddle," said an eager voice in Jon's consciousness. "He wants you to let him off."

"How can I forgive genocide?" Jon bellowed in rage, "Forgive that bastard for killing my people and risking the extermination of all human life?"

"This outrage is just your self-importance, Jon," the Voice spoke. "I have forgiven the universe without end because I have never known sin." Jon recognized those last words as something he'd read by modern American mystic Thomas Merton. He remembered Robyn McCullough saying, "Forgiveness means realizing the sin I thought my brother committed against me *never really happened at all.*"

Jon began to weep. "But I must tell the story. I must reveal Buchanan and the Liberty Bell Foundation. I must expose them. How else can I save my people?"

"Would you believe your forgiveness might be the source of the antidote? It might be the means to change the universe," Jon said to himself, beginning to lose the distinction between the Voice of God, that of the Witness Self, and that of himself.

"How can I believe that?" he begged, and realized that once again suffering surrounded him. This was perhaps the greatest pain of all, he realized: to forgive your enemies.

"Oh God, oh God," he wailed. "How can I do this?"

"Evil arises from ill-wishing. Good people will evil into existence when they measure their own good by judging it against what they perceive as others' evil," the Voice explained. "You end the evil by forgiveness."

"You mean the disease will disappear if I forgive Buchanan?"

"Edward Buchanan promised to release the antidote if you answered correctly."

"He never really admitted there was an antidote," Jon objected.

"Does that matter? What matters right now is healing your attitude."

"Do you mean that 'answering correctly' means absolving him?"

"You must make that choice yourself, Jon Stiers," the Voice said. "The ultimate human suffering is, after all, the freedom to make choices."

"What difference will it make anyway?" Jon objected. "Buchanan's still going to kill me to keep his secret. Forgiving him isn't going to change anything."

"All minds are joined," the Voice answered. "You are not alone in experiencing the effects of your seeing."

Jon recognized that idea as one of the principles of the *Course in Miracles* Robyn talked about.

"You mean my thoughts now can affect Buchanan?" he quizzed the Voice, but there was no answer. "Well, if my death can affect Buchanan's plan, of course, I'd die willingly." He shuddered as he made his declaration. "But how can I believe that?"

Spiritual anguish burned in Jon as he had never known it before. "How can I forgive the suffering he's caused? How about Ted?" he begged pitifully. "How can I forgive Mark's death? How can I bear that humiliation?"

"Love as much as you can from wherever you are," the Witness reminded.

"Will I remember what I've done?" Jon asked the question as an aside, almost as though inquiring of a parliamentarian a point of procedure.

"Who cares?"

"I fear I cannot live with that memory. I fear I cannot live without the memory. How can I keep Buchanan's plot a secret?"

"Your announcement would just change the villain from one to another. But the treachery of wrong-making and ill-wishing would go on."

"But people must know the truth. They can't live in illusions."

"No one is ever free of illusion. Not God even," the Voice answered.

"I'd rather Buchanan were the villain and not me and not the people with AIDS."

"Then nothing changes. If you give up self-importance and forgive — it will be as though none of this has happened," the Voice said kindly.

"You mean AIDS will have disappeared?" Jon asked excitedly.

"I do not promise that. The Face of Glory and the Face of Anguish are one and the same," the Voice thundered, flashing again with blinding Light. "You cannot have one without the other. That's the way it is and you must take things the way they are."

"Then it is You I must forgive, isn't it?" Jon asked humbly but courageously.

"You have answered correctly, Jon Stiers. Now you need only say the words."

"'I forgive you' and it's over?" Jon asked quizzically.

"And forgive yourself," the Voice said gently.

Is this going to satisfy Buchanan? He looked at his watch. One-thirty. *My God, he could be here any minute.* Jon felt the press of time — the last of the human sufferings, he realized.

And how easy to forgive. How easy. "Oh God, I forgive you, yes, I forgive you."

Jon felt very, very tired. His fear was gone. It didn't matter what Buchanan would do anymore. He slumped back against the door and let himself relax. He slept.

2

Lynn Graves and Billy DePalma had also slept. Without intending to, they'd both fallen asleep in the small interview room in the federal office building they'd been taken to. They'd been asked a few superficial questions and then been left alone. For hours. Ten minutes ago one of the agents abruptly woke them, told them it was morning, and that they were free to go.

"We've got to look for Jon, don't we?"

"Oh, I wish this would all just go away," Lynn sobbed as Billy hustled her out the front door of the building.

"Well, it won't if we don't do something. Right now!"

"Okay." Lynn composed herself. "Look, let's just get away from here."

"There's the car." Billy pointed to the emergency only zone. "No ticket," he observed. "Let's get over to the Liberty Bell Foundation fast."

"Oh, no, Billy, not there. They've had hours to take him somewhere else — if they ever took him there in the first place."

"Well, I don't know where else to suggest looking," Billy shouted in exasperation as he opened the door for Lynn.

3

Jon's eyes hurt from the bright light. For a moment he wondered if he was hallucinating again, seeing that Light of the Beatific Vision. His mouth still tasted of ether; he felt dizzy and his head ached.

Then realizing he was somehow lying on his back, he slowly opened his eyes. He was on the floor in the main corridor of the Liberty Bell Foundation. *They must've opened the door and I fell out,* he managed to explain to himself.

"Good morning, Dr. Stiers, good morning," boomed Edward Buchanan's voice from above him. Here, let me help you up," the big man reached out to take Jon's hand. "Come into my office. We have a little while before the office staff arrives. I've just made some coffee."

Jon felt confused. He'd been expecting a dramatic confrontation, after which he was fully expecting to be killed. Now instead Buchanan seemed to be concerned about having a chat before they were disturbed by secretaries. He let Buchanan help him up and then followed him obediently to his big office.

Jon took a seat. He watched Buchanan's movements, but said nothing. He couldn't quite shake the daze he was in.

Buchanan poured two cups of coffee, inquiring if Jon wanted cream or sugar. Jon nodded no.

Buchanan waited a moment for Jon to take a few sips of his coffee, then very businesslike asked, "I wonder if you had time to consider our conversation last evening." Buchanan was fussing with the coffee pot.

Jon looked at him incredulously. *Am I dreaming? Doesn't this man realize he scared me to death last night?* "Look Buchanan, I don't know what you're up to. . ." Just then the events of the dark night in the closet came flooding back to Jon. He'd learned a lesson. Now was the time to put it into practice.

"I'm not up to anything. I only asked you if you'd given any thought to the question I posed to you." He carried his cup over and sat down next to Jon in the other side chair.

"Mr. Buchanan, you've just put me through quite an experience. I'm still reeling from that. I wasn't expecting you to serve me coffee and treat me like a business associate this morning. I guess I was expecting you to come for me in the middle of the night and, well—"

"It got very late last night. I had some thinking to do myself. So I didn't come back here after the dinner party," Buchanan explained.

"But yes, I have an answer for you," Jon gestured toward the doors behind the big desk. (A strange and fleeting thought, like a dream trace, insinuated itself in Jon's consciousness: *The treasure of the ages.*) "It's okay. I mean, whatever you do to me. It's okay."

"That's your answer?" Buchanan cocked his head as though he was not understanding.

"Yesterday you mentioned Jesus on the cross. I don't know if there is any answer to the cross. How can you expect me to solve a problem that's troubled the best minds of the human race? But I remembered Jesus. I remembered what He said."

Buchanan looked at Jon closely, expectantly. *I wish my mind were clearer. Maybe we're back to the game of wits.*

"'Forgive them, Father, for they know not what they do,'" Jon said. "I forgive you, Buchanan. I forgive you for whatever you're gonna do to me." Again he pointed toward the closet. "I forgive all that. Why try to answer it?"

Buchanan shuddered noticeably. He drank his coffee in a long draft. "More coffee?" he asked Jon as he got up to refill his cup.

Just then Jon remembered George Wilson's offer of coffee. He looked down at his half full cup, wondering. *Maybe that'd be an easy way out.*

"Is that your answer?" Buchanan repeated his earlier question.

Jon shook his head. He felt surprisingly enlightened even though his head was still aching and his muscles were sore from sleeping in a cramped position. He smiled, "Buchanan, I even forgive you for asking the question."

Extending the steaming cup to Jon, Buchanan returned the smile. He looked a little sad behind the effort to appear cordial. "I didn't sleep very well last night. I was trying to solve the problem you raised: how would I know how to evaluate your answer? I was very troubled. I kept thinking of all the suffering I've witnessed and collected." He looked over toward the closet. "I kept thinking of all the people who might be disillusioned and lose faith if you took your story to the newpapers." He paused, staring into the coffee he was compulsively stirring. "Then sometime in the middle of the night — I remember looking at the clock by the bed and seeing it was nearly one-thirty — I felt, well, something come over me. I knew what I was going to have to do. I don't know, Jon," he shook his head. "I slept after that."

Buchanan seemed nervous. He got up and started pacing. That made Jon even more nervous. *Maybe he's still up to something. I've got to stay calm. Now isn't the time to screw up on my commitment from last night.* Jon still didn't know what Buchanan had in mind. *Maybe what calmed him was the realization that I can be so easily done away with.*

"You're sure that's your answer?" Buchanan asked from somewhere in the room behind Jon's back. His voice was soft but strained.

Without turning around, Jon replied, quoting Jesus, " 'Love your enemies. Do good to those who hate you.' Was that an answer? I don't know whether there's an answer to your question or not. It's all I know to say. I'm not going to judge you or the human race or what's going to happen next. And I'll accept the consequences."

"Yes, Jon. That's an answer." Buchanan sounded almost frightened.

"Okay, Buchanan, what about the antidote?" Jon asked, just as he realized he was smelling an unpleasantly familiar chemical odor again. He managed to set the hot coffee down before Buchanan's hand clasped him tightly on the shoulder, holding him down in the chair.

He started to struggle, then relaxed as he felt a cotton handkerchief pressed against his face. He looked up resignedly at Buchanan's face towering above him. "Thank you, Stiers, for ending all this," he thought he heard Buchanan say. And Jon let himself inhale the ether.

4

"Why don't you park in the alley?" Lynn suggested as they approached the building. "It's almost time for people to be coming to work. I don't want anybody to see me."

As Billy turned into the driveway alongside the building, Lynn saw Edward Buchanan outside the front doors. He was struggling to put something in the trunk of his car.

"Damn," she said. "There's Buchanan. What's he got?"

"I don't know. Looks heavy. It could be a body," Billy observed ominously. "Get the license plate number. We'd better call the police. Tell them anything. Just get them over here." Billy swung the car around, then pulled into a tight spot beside a dumpster.

"Okay, come on," Lynn answered, as she ran ahead of Billy along the side of the building toward the front entrance where she knew she could find a pay phone in the lobby. Buchanan's car was just pulling out into the stream of traffic.

5

"Jon, Jon," Billy's voice seemed to be shouting at him from high above as though he were down a well. "Hey, wake up. Come on, Jon. Are you okay? What happened?"

A feeling of terror roared through Jon's mind. *What if the ordeal isn't over?* He realized he was expecting to be dead.

"Jon, please, wake up," he heard the young man imploring. "Are you paralyzed? Can you just open your eyes?"

Oh, God, no, please don't let me be paralyzed, Jon thought as he was impaled by Billy's suggestion. Again the ominous specter of nerve gas haunted him. He struggled to open his eyes.

Quite suddenly, the powerlessness of sleep dissipated. Bright light from the fluorescent tubes overhead filled Jon's vision. His eyes were dazzled for a moment and then focused on Billy's face looking down at him with concern. He saw that Billy suddenly smiled.

"Thank God, you're alive. Can you move?"

"I don't know," he stammered.

"What happened? Did they drug you?"

"I think so," Jon said as he slowly pulled himself up into sitting position. He realized he was lying on a bench in the hall by the elevators outside the Liberty Bell Foundation.

"What happened with Buchanan? The antidote? Did he take it?"

Jon felt baffled. He felt like he must have forgotten something important. But he just couldn't remember what he was talking about. "How long have I been out?"

"I don't know. Hours maybe."

"Look, pal, is this the guy you said was in danger?" Jon realized a policeman was standing behind Billy. "He looks drunk to me. Hey, buddy, you okay?" he shouted at Jon, word by word, like an American tourist in a foreign country, as though volume equaled intelligibility.

"Think so," Jon answered. "Just got a headache. I think."

"Where is everybody?" Billy asked again.

Jon looked around and saw the plate-glass doors to the Liberty Bell Foundation office were closed and the lights off inside.

"Closed," he answered rather concretely from his daze.

"It's still early in the morning."

Billy walked over to the glass doors and peered in. "Oh God," he exclaimed, turning back to Jon. "What if they've done something to your brain!"

Jon searched his mind to understand Billy's alarm. He felt dizzy and still a little groggy — as though he'd slept too long. But, in fact, he was beginning to feel pretty good. *If I could just wake up a little more.* He remembered he'd had a dream. He thought it was a good dream. He wished for a moment that Billy and the policeman would just go away and let him return to the dream — or at least remember it. Billy's sense of urgency upset him.

"Can you stand up?" the policeman asked.

"Oh, I guess so." Jon obeyed.

"That's fine," he said. "Now, can you tell me what's going on here?"

"Yeah," added Billy. "What happened? What about Buchanan? What about the antidote?"

"Antidote?" the policeman asked. "Do you think your friend's been poisoned?"

"Oh, no. This is something else," Billy answered abruptly, now apparently annoyed with the policeman. "Jon, look, Lynn's down in the lobby with the other policeman. Let's go downstairs."

"Hey, buddy, you been hurt or something? Do you want to report a crime?"

"No, officer," Jon answered groggily. "I think I'm okay. Just give me a minute."

"Well, let's not take all day. I asked if a crime has been committed."

"No, no, I guess not. I think it was all a misunderstanding."

"What?" exclaimed Billy.

Jon sat back down on the bench a moment and tried to clear his head. "Buchanan didn't know Wilson had killed himself. That's what he wanted to see me about..."

"Yeah, but the virus and the antidote?"

"What are you talking about, pal?" the police officer interrupted.

"I think that was all a misunderstanding too, Billy," Jon said. "Looks like George Wilson had, uh, gone off the deep end and was imagining things."

"Jon, you're gonna have to explain this to Lynn. What about what I—" Billy looked at the policeman nervously "—uh, *found* in the computer?"

"Hey, fellow, c'mon now. Like your friend said. Let's go downstairs."

🕮

"Thanks, officers," Billy said. "Sorry we got you out on a wild goose chase."

"Well, we're glad it wasn't serious," the officer who'd been waiting downstairs with Lynn replied.

"You make sure your friend there gets, you know, some help," the other policeman said, making the familiar corkscrew gesture beside his head.

"Oh, sure," Lynn answered as the policemen climbed into their car.

Jon was very quiet. He knew he didn't understand all that had happened, but he felt so peaceful and unafraid.

"We're parked around back. C'mon," Billy said.

"It's okay," Jon remarked. "Everything's going to be just fine."

The car was parked in back of the building right where they'd left it.

"Hey, there's the garbage bin," Lynn observed. "I got an idea."

"Be my guest," Billy joked, bowing slightly and extending his right arm toward the steel garbage container beside the car.

Opening the lid and sticking her head in, Lynn shouted,

"Maybe they brought the trash down. What if there's a clue in here..." She started riffling through the contents of the bin.

Jon slowly walked over beside her and peered in. Silently, he pulled out a tangle of paper streamers.

"What's that?" Billy asked disdainfully.

"The output of the shredding machine," Lynn answered.

Jon cradled the web of paper shreds thoughtfully in both hands as though it were some kind of treasure.

"...oh, that stuff's useless," Billy muttered. "There ain't no way of ever putting any of that back together again. Look's like they were making confetti," he joked, "...with all that colored paper."

•Epilog•

Five Years Later

1

Jonathan Stiers let himself into the refurbished Victorian on States Street. There didn't seem to be anybody home. He noticed in passing that the outside entrance to the ground floor apartment where Blum and Robyn were living had finally been completed — the renovation of the house appeared to be coming along well. He mounted the steps to the second floor entry hall.

Jon walked down to the kitchen. Nobody there. Coming back to the front, he went up the stairs to the upper floor of the two-storey flat. "Lynn," he called out. "Billy? . . . Anybody home?"

No answer. "I guess not," he said aloud to himself. *Some reception this is*, he griped mockingly to himself. *I should have told them what time I was getting in. Can't blame them for not being here to meet me.*

Jon walked on down the hall to the room he'd lived in for the last four years before his move at the beginning of the past summer. He dropped his suitcase on the floor, walked over to the windows, and threw open the curtains. There, just as he remembered it, was that marvelous view of Twin Peaks. For a moment his heart fluttered with memory.

A little timidly, he walked into the adjoining room, the glassed sun porch. It was still almost the way Mark originally had it arranged. The drawing table still stood in one corner — with the art supplies tucked neatly into the pigeon-holes of a Coca-Cola case. The bed was gone, replaced with a brightly upholstered settee. *Well, it's not so crowded in here now*, Jon thought, realizing sadly that

242 PLAGUE

he missed the bed. That he still missed Mark. He was surprised that that pain was still alive in him. It all seemed so long ago.

"Jon . . . Jon," he heard Lynn DePalma call his name. The sound of her voice grew louder as she clattered quickly along the hardwood floor of the hall. Jon headed toward the door to greet ner.

She flew into his arms. "How wonderful to see you."

"The house looks beautiful," Jon exclaimed.

"You've only been away four or five months. We haven't done that much to it."

"Well, I see you finished the entrance to the first floor apartments. And you moved Mark's bed out."

"Oh, yeah," Lynn replied, her voice softening, as if in accord with the halting tones of Jon's last sentence. "We moved it to the downstairs bedroom. That's gonna be the nursery."

"Nursery, hmm?" Jon asked perkily.

"Well, not just yet. But we're working on it. Billy was tested again last month. His blood is still clear of the virus. It's a miracle. It's just like —"

"Well, son of a gun," Billy exclaimed from the door, interrupting Lynn, "If it isn't Jon Stiers back from the woods."

As Jon stepped toward him, Billy took Jon's hand, then threw his arm around his shoulder and pulled him close and slapped him repeatedly on the back.

"Oh, you two, come on downstairs. Let's have a glass of wine to celebrate and to toast Jon's return," Lynn urged.

"Well, there's so much to tell," Jon answered Lynn's question. "It's like I've started a new life."

"We've all got new lives. Thanks to you," Lynn said from the kitchen as she closed the refrigerator, "and Mark," she added softly, almost reverently. She uncorked a bottle of Liebfraumilch and decanted the chilled white wine into stemmed glasses. "Here we are in San Francisco, living in a dream house, managing the Center. . ."

"Tell us about this 'monastery,'" Billy asked Jon. They were sitting in the sunny breakfast nook behind the kitchen.

"It's not a formal monastery. The place has been a meditation and retreat center for the past few years run by some friends I used to know in the city. We all used to talk about retiring to the woods one day, living in community — like monastic life — but without the crazy ideas the Church imposed on monasticism. . ."

"Crazy ideas?" Billy asked.

"Oh, you know, the anti-sex, anti-world, anti-human stuff we're so used to hearing from Church authority — oh, thanks, Lynn," Jon said as he took one of the three glasses from the silver tray Lynn held out.

"To Jonathan's return," Billy toasted as he took another of the glasses.

"Wait for me," Lynn implored jokingly, as she put the tray down on the side table and picked up her glass. "It's like having our family back together again," she said.

"How long are you staying with us, Jon?" Billy asked.

Jon ceremonially clinked his glass against both Billy's and Lynn's, then sipped the wine. "Well, really not long. That's part of the news. I think—" he continued hushing his voice dramatically to a stage whisper "—I've fallen in love."

"Congratulations!" Lynn exclaimed. "Who is it?"

"His name is Rif Koestenbaum."

"That's a mouthful," Billy joked.

"He's a beautiful redhead, with gorgeous green eyes."

"Where did you meet him?" Lynn asked seriously.

"At the meditation center. He'd come for a prolonged retreat last spring, kinda looking to find the meaning of life or something like that."

"And he swept you off your feet?" Lynn waxed romantic.

"No, I was really very cautious. I certainly wasn't expecting to meet a boyfriend. You know, I'd gone there half-planning to disappear into eremitical obscurity. I guess I was still getting over Mark. But Rif was real gentle, real attentive. We got to be good friends and then, well, one thing led to another..."

"We know," piped in Billy and Lynn almost in unison, which caused all three of them to burst out laughing.

"The relationship fills a big hole in my life," Jon smiled wistfully. Then, "It sure is good to see you," he said, breaking the emotion of the moment.

"Well, tell us more about the meditation center," Billy said.

"Look, my friend Father David Omar — he's in charge of things around there — flew back to the City with me. I hope you don't mind: I invited him to dinner."

"Oh, that's wonderful," Lynn answered.

"He can explain better than me the plans for developing what we're calling a 'freelance monastery.' And," Jon said hesitantly, "I've got another agenda for this visit. I've been talking with David a lot. And I realize it's time for me to tell the truth to him and to you two."

"The truth?" Lynn asked quizzically.

"About what happened at the Liberty Bell Foundation. The fact is that what went on with Edward Buchanan was a lot more involved than just me explaining to him that I didn't murder George Wilson and him acknowledging to me that Wilson had gone off the deep end with all that stuff about AIDS and then me taking a nap after he went home..."

"I never really did believe that story," Lynn interjected. "Especially after Buchanan disappeared and the firm closed down. But why didn't you tell us the truth?"

"I'd agreed I'd keep the secret."

"That's why you erased my disk? and told us we'd imagined the whole thing?" Billy asked with an undertone of anger and resentment. "To keep an agreement with Buchanan?"

"Oh, the agreement wasn't with Buchanan. It was more, well, more like with, uh, God," Jon blushed.

"What's God got to do with it?" Billy rejoined sharply.

"Billy, don't scold," Lynn chided. "I'm sure there was a good reason. And look at all Jon did for us anyway," Lynn leaned over and kissed Jon on the cheek. "Even if he did lie to us ... through the teeth," she added in mock derision.

"I hope you'll understand," Jon replied. "It was very important then. But that was a long time ago. Now I think you have a right to know. And, I guess, I think I have a right to tell — at least to talk about what I think happened." Jon put both hands to the sides of his head and, in imitation of a pounding headache, said, "Besides, the secret's burning to come out ... and there's just nobody else I dare tell about this."

2

"...so with the money from Mark's estate that Jon was executor for we came back here and set up the Center." Lynn finished her part of the story.

"The center?" Father Omar inquired. David Omar was a big man with grey hair cut to a burr and deep blue eyes. Over dinner Lynn and Billy had come to like him a lot.

"The Twin Peaks Center for Attitudinal Healing," Billy answered. "Jon wanted to get back to his work with people with AIDS. After all that happened in D.C., he invited us to come back to San Francisco with him. It seemed like a good idea. Lynn's job was gone and I wanted to work with other people who were antibody-positive — you know, to find ways to keep the disease from developing, like attitudinal healing.

"Robyn McCullough convinced us that attitudinal healing and Jon's ideas about 'suicide' fit together. The name Twin Peaks was Blum's idea. He said the two peaks symbolized the two possible results of stopping major medical treatment and choosing to confront death with a spiritual perspective: either you allow yourself to die with dignity *or*, as happened for Robyn and lots of others, you get better on your own."

"What about the other people in Jon's original group?" David asked.

"Of the original group," Lynn answered, "Chuck and Luis died peacefully at the Center. Chuck's death was particularly moving. He became such an enlightened man towards the end. Even as he was dying, he was joking about what a shit he'd been before he got sick. He was actually able to be grateful to the disease for transforming his life—" Lynn's eyes misted with sentiment.

Billy spoke up to complete the answer to David's question, "Buz Kramer killed himself when complications from an experimental drug he was on started causing hallucinations. Greg Bens, on the other hand, got well completely."

"From attitudinal healing?" David asked.

"Well, yes," she answered, "but not magically. I mean, maybe changing attitude worked because people were developing effective immune defenses to the virus, you know, like that guy who was on the Donahue Show with Jon predicted — morphogenetic fields and all that."

"That's what seems to have happened to me," Billy said. "I changed my attitude, learned to love my past and forgive myself and my body killed off the virus."

"What about this retraclone we've heard so much about?" Omar asked, "what they're calling the vaccine?"

"That's probably how I fought off the virus," Billy responded. "It's not really a vaccine, of course. That's sort of what Lynn was talking about. Retraclone is an immune enzyme called Reverse-Transcriptase Receptor Antagonist which prevents retroviruses, like HIV and some of these cancer viruses they've discovered, from replicating. The cells that make it can be cloned from the blood of people who've got over HIV. It provides most people who don't have it naturally with the ability to mount an effective defense against the virus."

"It helps a lot of people who are in the ARC stage," Lynn added. "And it's worked for a few full-blown AIDS cases, though not for most of the people who were really sick. The damage was already done."

"But thanks to safe sex and nation-wide education about sex and the research that discovered RTRA, the epidemic's under control," Billy concluded.

"Well, this is the most interesting part of all," Jon spoke up. He'd been silent since he finished recounting his side of the story. "Retraclone was discovered when the test for the virus itself came into widespread use and it was noticed that a surprising number of people, especially in New York, were positive for the antibody, but not for the virus. They seemed to have a natural immunity or to have gotten over the virus."

"Morphogenetic fields?" Lynn offered.

"Well, maybe. But just maybe because of Buchanan's 'viral antidote.'"

"You mean there *was* an antidote?" Billy exclaimed.

"That report I got from Wilson said the 'off-switch' for the rabies weapon they were working on in Africa would cause the body to neutralize the vehicle for the rabies genome. Buchanan and Wilson, at least, believed that vehicle was what got out of the lab and showed up in America as AIDS. I think the antidote was another virus that had engineered into its DNA the information for producing this RTRA."

"You're suggesting that Buchanan's antidote worked?" David asked.

"Well, I think some people were probably already producing RTRA. Some studies in San Francisco back in 1986 had shown that certain T-suppressor cells produced a substance that inactivated HIV. Now maybe that substance was RTRA. And, of course, maybe it was just a matter of time before this got identified and synthesized on its own.

"But maybe Buchanan did indeed spread that antidote virus of his around New York City, so all of a sudden a lot of New Yorkers showed up with what seemed like naturally-occurring retraclone and, maybe even, whatever information his antidote carried was what's made it so easy to start cloning RTRA-producing cells. Maybe."

"Wow," Billy remarked softly.

"Do you know what did happen to Buchanan?" David asked.

"He just disappeared," Lynn answered. "That was the end of the Liberty Bell Foundation .. and my job."

"Jon?" David turned to his friend.

"Well, there was more to it than that. The summer after my,

uh, ordeal, I heard on CNN that a Lear Jet had crashed on the beach out on Fire Island. The sole occupant was identified as Edward Buchanan.

"I didn't tell you guys this," Jon said sheepishly to Lynn and Billy. "I contacted the Fire Island Park Ranger's office saying I had an uncle by that name and thought I might be a relative. The ranger was pretty helpful. He said he'd had no luck tracing this Buchanan, and so he was happy to hear from me.

"The ranger said they couldn't find any trace of who this Edward Buchanan was. The guy seemed to be rich, at least from the looks of him and the plane — but very mysterious. His Social Security number, the New York driver's licence, the plane registration — all of them proved to be phony. And there was just no explanation for why the plane would've flown straight down right into the beach. The ranger's explanation, a pretty good one I suppose, was that Buchanan was some kind of a spy or secret agent for our side or theirs. But he didn't have any idea why he crashed. He thought maybe he'd been spying on Brookhaven National Labs nearby. So he called in the FBI. But they said they weren't interested. I think that's why he was willing to talk to me. He felt snubbed.

"The ranger said — and here's the clincher — the plane had been equipped with something he thought was a rich man's idea of a crop spraying device. The apparatus had an empty cannister in it that he sent to the police lab. They couldn't identify the contents, but said it seemed like a harmless protein."

"The antidote?" David asked.

"Your guess is as good as mine," Jon replied. "But, yeah, it sure sounds like it. The RTRA in the New York cohort was identified just six months after Buchanan's crash."

"What else do you know that we don't?" Billy asked, resentment still echoing in his voice.

"How about George Wilson?" David spoke up.

"I went to the Coroner's Office. The death certificate showed he'd died of a heart attack at home. The date was the same as the day I met with him. But the cause of death sure sounded different. There was no suggestion of foul play or suicide. Somebody must have fixed it. Maybe to avoid an investigation?"

"So what about Wilson's files in Billy's computer?" Father Omar asked, getting right to the heart of the matter.

"Jon erased them 'by accident,'" Billy answered sternly. "That was the end of that."

Jon grinned sheepishly.

"What about Mark's death?" Omar continued his queries. "I thought you believed he'd been killed in an attempt to get you."

"Well, that's why we were willing to believe Jon when he said we'd imagined the whole thing. It turned out we'd totally mis-perceived Mark's death," Lynn answered. "Oh, the police were happy to get that guy we trapped. He was a wanted man — but for ripping off banks' automatic teller machines. That magnetic card he had — and, the police think, the electronic device — were used to trick the machines into dispensing money. But he didn't have a gun — what we thought was a miniature pistol turned out to be, oh God," she laughed, "a cigarette lighter. The mirror shattered from pressure on the wood when Houston forced open that sealed door. And the investigation didn't show any bomb in the car. The police said it was just a fluke accident that killed Mark. Skidded on the ice, you know. Gas fumes exploded."

"How about the phone line being cut?"

"Unlucky coincidence," Jon answered. "They were installing phone lines for the mall. Probably thought the house was deserted since Mark's grandmother had died. Didn't bother to reconnect that line while they rewired the pole.

"Looking back, I realize I'd gotten pretty paranoid," Jon con-tinued. "Fear causes you to imagine a lot of things and see threats even where there aren't any. I still don't know how much of what happened was real and how much was my imagination playing off of what maybe was George Wilson's imagination. Or, on the other hand, how much we might really have changed history. This is all pretty crazy, isn't it?"

"Yeah," replied Lynn, "but also pretty believable. I think you ought to go to the media with this. Jon, you could be a hero."

"Oh no. I wouldn't do that."

"How come? If you really believe it, why don't you want to acknowledge the role we — you especially — played in all this?"

"Because it doesn't really matter. There's no evidence. But, besides, what good would it do to give them somebody to blame? Blaming and disapproving is what caused the whole problem in the first place. That's what creates homophobia and fear. Regardless of the truth or falsity of Wilson and Buchanan's plot, that's what delayed intervention and allowed AIDS to spread. That's been the *real* plague all along."

"Is that what you learned from your night in the closet?" David asked.

"Maybe so. Something changed: about me, about the world,' Jon continued. "You know, it was several days after that experience before I recovered from the daze. And it was really several months before I was able to recall most of it — and even then it was more like a dream or a drug experience than real. For all I know that's really all it was.

"But I still sometimes wake up at night with a feeling I've been dreaming that experience over again. There's always an undercurrent of pain and fear, but also of transcendence. I wake up feeling everything's going to be okay now, that I don't have to worry. And I'm overwhelmed with a sense of forgiveness. I mean it's like I'm not holding anything against anybody anymore. Everything's perfect."

"That's what we teach at the Center: forgiveness is the key to changing things. The source of healing is recognizing the world's innocence — and one's own," Lynn said, "taking things the way they are without judging them."

"To never speak any bitterness at all . . . and never go cross-grained to the universe," Jon interjected softly, "to see evil, and resist evil, and yet be utterly unaffected by it."

Jon turned to Father Omar, "David, I think I wanted you to hear this because it suggests to me that reality's more mystical than we normally think. And you've got the kind of spiritual mind to comprehend that."

"What do you mean 'more mystical'?" David questioned.

"Well, maybe there are different realities — oh, you know, like the 'many worlds hypothesis' in physics. And maybe what decides which world is real is the kind of intentions people put out. In a world full of blaming and hatred, bad things happen. When you forgive, things change. . ."

"I don't think you need a mystical explanation for that," David responded.

"Well, in my world, something really changed." Billy said, the tone of resentment now gone from his voice. "I used to be positive for HIV and now I'm negative. And I'm not alone. And, I guess, it *really* is as though we shifted over into another world." He paused, then added, "But does that also mean there are other realities in which AIDS wasn't caused by genetic research gone wrong and in which there is no antidote and no happy ending. . .?"

"I don't know," answered Jon. "I'm not sure it makes any difference. Maybe the speculation is meaningless."

"Maybe you're right," David answered, "The important thing is that forgiveness and love can heal individual lives. You all have changed yourselves, haven't you? It sounds like each of you has found a better life than you were expecting."

"Indeed, we have," Billy agreed.

Jon smiled. He still didn't know if his acts of heroism had really made any difference in the world. But he knew they had somehow changed his attitudes. He wasn't afraid anymore. Not of death. Not of life. Not at all.

The Author:

Edwin Clark (Toby) Johnson, Ph.D., is author of two autobiographies, *The Myth of the Great Secret: A Search for Spiritual Meaning in the Face of Emptiness* (Morrow, 1982) and *In Search of God in the Sexual Underworld: A Mystical Journey* (Morrow, 1983). Both present psychologically sophisticated, modern-day understandings of religion and myth applied to such real-life topics as the quest for truth, future shock, and contemporary sexual-social problems.

He collaborated with gay scholar (and namesake) Toby Marotta on the production of *The Politics of Homosexuality* and *Sons of Harvard*.

Johnson lived in San Francisco through the 1970s. Recently he has been a psychotherapist in San Antonio, working in the struggle to deal with AIDS, both assisting individuals to cope with the disease and educating the gay and non-gay public about prevention.